SEAN DORMAN, as a boy at an Irish public school, was awarded a prize and the English master regularly read his essays to the Form. He became editor of the school magazine and winner of an essay competition open to all public schools in Great Britain and Ireland. After a short career in London as a freelance journalist in his early twenties, he contributed to some twenty British and Irish periodicals. He also ghosted half a dozen non-fiction books for a publisher. He had a burlesque of Chekhov staged by the Dublin Gate Theatre, a radio play broadcast by Radio Eireann, and he published a few short stories, one being broadcast by the BBC. For five and a half years in Dublin he published a literary, theatre and art magazine, *Commentary*. In England, from 1957 until a few years ago, he ran the Sean Dorman Manuscript Society for mutual criticism, a Society still run by others under the same name and listed in *The Writers' and Artists' Year Book*. His magazine *Writing*, also listed during its career in 'The Year Book', was founded in 1959, and sold after twenty-six years. While his family was growing up, he had to seek a more regular income, and taught secondary school French and junior German for some twenty-five years. To make up for lost time, between 1983 and 1993 he wrote and published, under the imprint of his Raffeen Press, eleven books. They embraced novels, autobiography, essays, a three-act play, theatre criticism, short-stories and a solitary poem. Many of the books were re-writes or extensions, now allowed to go out of print, so the present tally is six. Five of these have been included in his three-volume hardback, *The Selected Works of Sean Dorman*, now gradually finding its way into national and university libraries throughout the world.

COVER GIRL
Once again my Irish compatriot,
FIONA (with myself).

Also by Sean Dorman

BRIGID AND THE MOUNTAIN
a novel

PORTRAIT OF MY YOUTH
an autobiography

RED ROSES FOR JENNY
a novel

THE STRONG MAN
a play

PHYSICIANS, PRIESTS & PHYSICISTS
essays

and published by The Raffeen Press

Under Composition
SEX AND THE REVEREND STRONG – a novel

Further copies of
THE MADONNA
may be obtained through
WH Smith, Waterstones and other good bookshops.
Also from The Raffeen Press
Union Place, Fowey, Cornwall PL23 1BY.

THE MADONNA

Sean Dorman

THE RAFFEEN PRESS

Cover montage: MADELEINE DORMAN
Photograph: Jim Matthews
Painting: Madeleine Dorman

THE MADONNA
A RAFFEEN PRESS BOOK 0 9518119 6 7

PRINTING HISTORY
In paperback: *The Madonna* 1991, *Madonna Again* 1992
Reissued as one book, under the title *The Madonna*,
and thus included in three-volume hardback
The Selected Works of Sean Dorman 1993
Raffeen Press reissued in paperback 1996

Copyright © Sean Dorman 1995

All rights reserved. No part of this publication may be reproduced, stored in a retrieval system or transmitted, in any form or by any means electronic, mechanical, photocopying, recording or otherwise, without prior permission of the copyright owner.

Conditions of Sale
This book is sold subject to the condition that it shall not, by way of trade, or otherwise, be lent, re-sold, hired out or otherwise circulated without the publisher's prior consent in any form of binding or cover other than that in which it is published and without a similar condition including this condition being imposed on the subsequent purchaser.

Printed and bound in Great Britain by Short Run Press Ltd, Exeter.

THE MADONNA

Chapter One

Judy Summers, arrested by the sound of men's voices, paused on her way to visit the Madonna. Her cheap gay cotton dress fluttered about her shapely legs in the autumn breeze. Judy Summers liked men. She liked them very much. Also, it had become imperative that she should acquire a husband.

She listened intently, her dainty features lifted to the September afternoon sun. Her mouth, vividly lipsticked as one might expect in the nineteen fifties, half opened to show two rows of small white teeth. The men's voices were shouting, and occasionally there were cheers. A football match of some sort? Then the men would be big and husky. Judy Summers liked big husky men. She liked them very much. Although not more than five feet herself when not wearing her shoes, very high-heeled to compensate for her lack of stature, she could manage them perfectly. She had only to raise her plucked and pencilled eyebrows and flutter those vivid blue eyes of hers, and she had wound them round her little finger.

How to find the football field? That wouldn't be difficult, of course, but it was approaching three o'clock, the match might soon be over, and she must find it quickly.

To her right, rising above the lane-side brambles, was a small slated roof. She picked a blackberry and popped it into her mouth, the purple juice slightly staining her scarlet lips. She sucked her finger, then poked with it at her brief perkily 'permanently waved' light brown hair. However short of money, she could always find enough for a 'perm'. It was essential to be bright and perky in the nineteen fifties. The grey years of the Second World War in Europe were six years past and King George VI, though delicate it was said, still sat firmly on his throne.

She saw a wooden gate, its bottom hinge adrift, bearing metal lettering reading, *The Brambles*. As she clip-clopped towards it with quick short steps, the expanding view through the gate disclosed a vegetable patch. The patch included a washing-line bearing a pair of pink 'bloomers' fluttering in the warm breeze. Two women were pegging further garments on to the line. Their hands were large and strong from house and garden work.

Judy glanced down with satisfaction at her own elegant hands. *She* would never suffer their humdrum fate. She was born for romance, for being 'stood' cigarettes and drinks, ultimately for a fine home and a servant or two. She had no doubt of it. She had an intuition about such things.

She paused with her hands resting on the top of the small gate, fastened shut with string. She scrutinised the women (it was almost as if she divined the fateful part that they were to play in her life), their drab clothes, the frumpish bloomers on the line. 'Could you tell me where the football is, please?'

'Oh, that would be the rugby match.' It was the elder woman, the mother, the religious one, the one with the grey scarf tied severely round her hair, in short, Mrs Finch, who had replied.

'I *love* rugby football. I want to watch.'

Mrs Finch surveyed Judy with the suspicious expression common to women married to drunkards. 'Continue on up the lane. You'll see a big grey building with what-d'you-m'-call-'ems-'

'Castellations,' put in her nineteen year old daughter Rose Finch, she of the soft face and hands and buxom body.

'That's it. Castellations and turrets and a Union Jack flying from the flagpole. You'll see a board at the gate with "Worcester Hall Preparatory School" written on it.'

'Oh, I know,' exclaimed Judy Summers. 'I've seen it before.'

Mrs Finch's expression remained suspicious. More than twenty years of marriage to 'Sergeant' Finch, he of the pinched red nose and dubious military title, had rendered it permanently so. 'You turn right before you reach it. There's a Roman Catholic shrine on the corner with a little statue of a Madonna and Child.'

'I know that too. I discovered it last week. I was walking up to look at it again.'

The grey scarf tied uncompromisingly round Mrs Finch's scant hair turned a slightly darker shade of grey. Perhaps it was just the effect of a fleecy cloud crossing the face of the sun. 'Are you a Roman Catholic?'

Her daughter Rose's gentle face ('Rose' she was by name, and an English rose she seemed in her wholesome country prettiness) showed concern.

'No,' said Judy, 'I'm nothing really. Well, thank you very much' — and she was on her way.

The Grey Scarf seemed uncertain how to react. *Nothing!* Was being nothing better than being a Roman Catholic? Perhaps it was; it still left room for hope. The Grey Scarf itself was a member of the Plymouth Brethren, and its ambition was one day to set up a 'Christian' guest-house, that is, a guest-house where alcohol was neither sold nor served. But it was difficult to save the money, what with Sergeant Finch's daily thirst for beer and his formidable powers to propagate further little Finch's when so fuelled. Mrs Finch had nine to date, of whom Rose was the eldest.

Mrs Finch watched the tall twinkling heels of Judy Summers as she tapped her way up the lane and vanished round the corner. 'She'll come to no good, that one. Too flighty by half. Too up in the air. It's not rugby she's interested in. It's men.'

' 'Tis only natural, Mother.' Secretly, Rose herself liked big husky men. In fact, for quite some time she had had her eye on one, a master at Worcester Hall Preparatory School where she and her mother worked as part-time domestic staff. Not that *he* would ever notice her, what with his fine stone built cottage and Oxford degree.

'Yes, maybe, but . . . That one's too interested in them. I see in her evil and destruction.' Mrs Finch had second sight. Everyone said so, including Mrs Finch. She added after thought, 'But there's one great good in her too. One *great* good.'

'What's that, then?'

But her mother's thin lips had compressed themselves, as they always did when people tried to push her too far. She turned towards the clothes line. Beside the pink bloomers (Rose's) fluttering in the breeze, she pegged up an equally voluminous white pair of her own.

Judy Summers, hardly pausing at the Madonna, turned as instructed down a lane to the right. Entering the rugby field by a gate just behind the nearer goalposts, she was at once confronted by a curly headed mud plastered Samson, his mighty shoulders clawed at by the hands of opponents as they sought to bring him down. But he continued to drive his way onwards towards the goal-line, in his great hands an oval leather ball. Hurling his body over the line he fell upon the ball, thus touching down for a 'try'.

Ten minutes later the referee blew a long blast on his whistle. The sprinkling of spectators left the field. The players trooped towards a wooden pavilion at the far side, doubtless for a shower and to change. Judy withdrew to the hedge, ostensibly ferrying black berries to red lips.

After half an hour, large men re-crossed the pitch in one's, two's and three's. Judy drifted ever closer to the gate. A distant curly head filled the corner of her eye. He was the last — and he was alone! Her heart fluttered. But, though highly strung, she was also single-minded in getting what she wanted. In childhood, she had always led the other orphans in their play.

He approached the gate, football togs and towel over his left arm, football boots carried in his right hand. Her blue eyes looked him boldly in the face. 'Hello!' Though her small face was raised cockily to his, her heels jiggled nervously.

George Brown, his thick red hair plastered down with the water gleaned from the shower, had of course noticed the slim figure by the gate. Half way across the pitch, he had decided that she was pretty. Two thirds of the way across, he had decided that she was exceedingly pretty. She would not be waiting for *him*, of course. For one thing, he didn't know her. For another, no girl, especially one as gay and sophisticated as she obviously was, would want to meet a stodgy settled bachelor approaching middle-age. What was it? Thirty-five. She'd be only twenty-five or twenty-six, he shouldn't wonder. Probably, since the field was now deserted, she was wanting to ask him the time, or the way to somewhere. 'Hello! Can I help you?'

'I just wanted to say, what a marvellous try it was you scored!'

Still she was looking him full in the face, holding herself very close to him. The mixture in her of nervousness and boldness emerged to him through those blue eyes as a vibrancy that quickened his pulses. 'Thank you. You follow rugby?'

'I love it, but I don't know much about it.'

'D'you come down here often?'

'As a matter of fact, I was only out for a stroll. I came across the match purely by chance.' Judy never allowed herself to be circumscribed by so humdrum a trifle as the truth. 'Just as you were scoring!'

'That was good management!' Evidently she didn't want to know the way or the time. If she had, she would have asked one of the other fellows as they passed her. She must be interested enough in the game really to want to express her appreciation. That was very friendly of her! 'Well, I must be sauntering home. Got to get myself some tea.' And he made to pass on and dismiss her from his mind — as he had dismissed so many other girls. In the past, some of them had shown an interest in him. But, when it came to dances, he had no ear for music and felt himself, at six foot one and fourteen stone, to be large and clumsy. Other parties seemed to exist for the sake of drinking, and he had no taste for drink. Merely made him unfit for rugby. Schoolmastering was not well paid; he had little to offer a girl when he took her out. Even less in matrimony. The years flowed by. When he found himself past the thirty mark, he took for granted that bachelordom was for him.

Judy had been thinking. 'Got to get myself some tea,' he had said. Looked as if he wasn't married! She clip-clopped rapidly to keep up with his vast stride. 'Have you played for other teams?'

He slowed down to accommodate her. 'I played for my school. Then for my college first team. All the Oxford colleges maintain several teams. Finally I reached the dizzy heights of The Greyhounds. There I stuck.' She was determinedly keeping pace with him! Prolonging the conversation! Yet it couldn't be that she wanted a man friend. If she had, she would have sought the acquaintance of one of the younger chaps.

She wrinkled up her forehead. 'The Greyhounds?' So he had been at Oxford! He must be rich, rich!

'The Oxford University second team. I never got a Blue. Perhaps I would have made it if I'd been a bit bigger.'

Judy looked up at him from her five feet. 'But you're *huge*! Look at your shoulders, look at your hands! You could crush me in one of them!'

He was not unpleased. 'Not all that big for a prop forward, a front row forward. At international level they're quite likely to be sixteen stone, though not too tall. Six foot or six foot one, perhaps. The chaps in the centre of the second row of the scrum, the 'engine-room' or 'boiler-house' as we call it, are quite commonly seventeen or eighteen stone, and anything from six foot five to six foot eight. Of course, at fourteen stone, I would have been big enough at university level if I'd been outstanding, but I was never outstanding. I needed everything on my side physically, including height for the line-out.'

'How tall are you?'

'Only six foot one.'

Judy fluttered her eyelashes at him in admiration. Hers was not a subtle sensibility. On the other hand there was no cynicism in her playacting. She totally believed in her theatricalities as they occurred. 'I think that's enormous. And I think it's wonderful that you got into The Greyhounds. That's something not everybody could do. I expect you've got a degree as well.'

'A not very brilliant M.A. I'm a born in-between-er; not very good and not very bad. I wouldn't have got a job at the school without a degree.'

'You teach?'

'Geography. Over there.' He nodded at the grey castellations and turrets (quite bogus; it was a modern grey plastered building) of Worcester Hall Preparatory School.

So he had a secure and well paid job at what was obviously a very high class prep school! Look at the size of the building, and there were others behind! Look at the coat-of-arms on the gate notice board! He had to have an Oxford M.A. to work there! Security. Blessed security. Security such as she, brought up in an orphanage after both her parents had been killed in the same car accident, had never known, with no family behind her should she ever fall ill or lose her job. She *must* get married at once. She couldn't go on another day as she was or, at least, another week or, at the most, another month. (Patience was not a virtue that had ever lodged in Judy's breast.) 'My name's Judy Summers.'

'Pleased to make your acquaintance, Miss Summers. I'm George Brown.'

They had reached the wayside shrine. The little Madonna gazed down with rapt painted eyes upon her painted Baby. Judy paused before it. He paused too.

'It was put up by an Irish couple, Miss Summers. They had my cottage before me. There are quite a number of these wayside shrines in Ireland, I believe. Rather garish, isn't it?'

'Oh, I *love* it. All the love of a mother for her baby is there.' For a moment she had forgotten to flirt.

His brown eyes regarded her, surprised. 'Yes,' he said in measured Church of England tones (the 'low' side of the Church, of course), 'but to elevate the Virgin Mary to a semi-divine status! A bit thick, wouldn't you say?'

'Oh, I think it's rather nice. I think being a mother is the supreme thing for a woman. I think motherhood is the greatest thing in the world.'

Suddenly he looked concerned. 'I'm sorry. Are you a Rom — Are you a Catholic, Miss Summers?'

'No.'

'High Anglican?'

'No. I'm nothing, really.' She fluttered her lashes again. 'Do call me Judy.'

'You're full of surprises — Judy.' He had to wrestle briefly to overcome his bachelor reserve.

'How's that, George?'

He started at her uninvited familiarity. But the shock was not unpleasant. 'I'd put you down as the cocktail party smokes and drinks type.'

'Oh no, George, I'm really *most* domesticated. I *love* cooking. I know how to shop; I can save *pounds* that way. I'm a country girl; I *adore* the countryside. I'm always going for *huge* walks. I *hate* drinking and smoking.' Judy was nothing if not vehement and sweeping. She dealt exclusively in blacks and whites; half tones were unknown to her.

She sounded just his cup of tea! Full of surprises indeed she was!

Soberness returned to her as she stared at the painted Child with the golden halo behind his head. 'I love little boys. They're so *dirty*.'

George Brown laughed. 'Well, you'll find plenty of those at Worcester Hall, Miss Summers.'

'Judy!'

'Er — Judy.'

They moved on down the lane.

'What's that small house, with the bigger one beside it?' She pointed to the right side of the lane.

'They both belong to Mr and Mrs Hare. The Reverend Charles Hare, to give him his full title. "Charlie" to his friends. He's a master at the school. Teaches Scripture, as you might expect. He and his wife live in the small house. They let out the big one in the form of two flats.'

'And that lovely cottage just beyond?'

'Lucky for you that you called it "lovely"!' He grinned. 'Because it's mine.'

'But it's *charming*, George. Those roses!'

'Don't ask me about gardening! That's all I can grow — roses.'

The other two houses were merely modern and brick-built, but the cottage was old and built of stone. Stone! And quite large! Yes, he must be very comfortably off. 'George, *do* invite me in to see it.' She stood close to him. Her blue eyes looked up. Her red lips smiled enticingly. Again his pulses quickened.

He hesitated. 'You'll be disappointed. It's clean, but that's about all that can be said for it. I'm only a crusty old bachelor, you know.'

'You are *not*, George. You're a very attractive man. I find younger men boring. Let me whip round the house. I can set things to rights in minutes.'

'I can't impose on you like that. But I can offer you a cup of tea.'

'That would be lovely.'

She pronounced the interior gorgeous but — it needed a woman's touch. Why didn't he let her re-decorate it; she loved interior decoration? She inspected the bookcase, and threw up her hands in horror. Manuals on rugby, manuals on cricket, paper-backs of detective fiction. She could go to auctions for him and get, for next to nothing, leather-bound volumes for looks and good authors for reading. She herself was a tremendous reader.

George was not at all offended but, on the contrary, delighted. His life was among the boys at the school, and he knew that he had treated his home as little more than a shelter from the weather. He was infected by her enthusiasm. And everything done by her so economically! He crossed the room past the telephone and the bowl of coins, added to whenever he made a call. He put his ancient rugby shorts, which had sustained a tear, by his bag of mending materials.

'Where d'you have your tea?' she asked.

'We have a staff evening dinner at the school. At least, from tomorrow onwards. Term starts tomorrow.'

'Why don't you stand me a little supper in the town? I know a sweet little restaurant.' She was about to add: not at all expensive — but where was the point with someone as well off as he?

George, who happened to have his back to her as she spoke, surreptitiously slipped his wallet out of the inner pocket of his Oxford blazer and consulted its contents. Yes, with somebody as considerate and economical as she evidently was, there was enough. It was the last day of his holidays. He had done precious little with them. Why shouldn't he lash out on a modest scale just for once?

They made their way down the lane. A couple of Kentish oast-houses for drying hops raised their strange crooked chimneys against the ruby sunset. As they passed the string-fastened gate of *The Brambles*, Judy noticed the girl with the soft work-strong hands and country prettiness watching them. She was taking down the washing from the line. Judy waved gaily to her. The other replied with a small restrained motion.

'Somebody you know?' asked George.

'Just a girl who told me how to get to the rugby field. At least, her mother did.'

His bushy eyebrows lifted. 'I — I thought you said you came across it by chance.'

'Oh, did I?' She laughed. Judy was for ever being caught out in her fibs. 'I suppose in a way I did find it by accident.'

His brown eyes were on her. But he said nothing.

They made their way along the High Street of Kingsbridge with its many half timbered houses. The small town was situated only a mile or two from fabled Tunbridge Wells, the paving stones of whose Pantiles once were trodden by the feet of Fashion, and around which still lingered the hauteurs of gateaux and delicate afternoon tea. They passed a building whose enormous sign yelled in multi-coloured letters, *The Rainbow Inn*. George averted his eyes. He drew Judy's attention away from the display case of scantily clad young ladies with chests by no means ill developed, by pointing to a restaurant

on the other side of the street. 'Is that the place you had in mind?'
The Rainbow Inn was not the type of hostelry to which a gentleman took a lady. Mr Featherstonhaugh, the headmaster of Worcester Hall Preparatory School, when obliged on one occasion to refer to it at a Staff Meeting, had given a small cough and visibly reddened. A ripple of embarrassed laughter had passed over the Staff Room. People had avoided looking at one another.

'Yes,' said Judy. 'You'll *love* it. It's *Continental*. The cooking's miraculous. Cooking is an art, I always say.'

George Brown's fourteen stone quivered as the Rainbow Inn without warning, in the gathering dusk, suddenly blazed out in a myriad electric bulbs. He seized Judy's arm. 'Let's cross.' Pleading traffic, he hustled her over.

She ordered fastidiously. She could see that she was impressing him by the anxious look in his eyes as he studied the menu over her shoulder; obviously he was keen to learn. It was a trifle disappointing therefore when he himself chose so *very* frugally.

When the waiter brought the wine list, George waved it away.

'Oh, *do* let's have a little wine,' cried Judy.

'I thought you didn't drink!'

'Virtually never. But this is a *special* occasion.'

Displaying an unbounded knowledge, she helped him to order it.

'Wine,' she pronounced after the waiter had gone, 'is civilised. I'm only a very light drinker; scarcely a drinker at all. I never get drunk. I think it's disgusting getting drunk. My father before his death taught me *never* to drink spirits.'

He learnt that she was a governess in the household of a wealthy company director. He asked her where the house was. Her reply was vague, and he was too much of a gentleman to press her.

At one point she put her knee against his. Its rounded feminine softness quickened his pulses. There was a magic for George the bachelor in that secret communication, the intimacy of that hidden gesture under the table-cloth, which not all his friendships with the men of the Kingsbridge Rugby Club, nor his friendship with the Reverend Charlie Hare, could equal. In that moment the conviction came to him that there was no comradeship like the comradeship between a man and a woman. A woman completed a man as could nothing else.

He paid the bill, which was large. He added as a tip an exact ten per cent, calculated to the last penny.

On their way out through the foyer they passed a bar.

'What d'you say we have a nightcap?'

He was about to protest.

'One last little drinkie,' she wheedled, holding up her finger and thumb only a trifle apart to indicate the minuteness of the proposed drink.

He surveyed her small ear-ringed ears, her head set so pertly on her soft rounded neck, her chic light brown hair, her pretty legs in their smart shoes and sheer silk stockings. How could he refuse her?

She asked for a sherry.

'I thought,' he ventured, 'that you never drank spirits. Sherry's a fortified wine, you know.'

She swept this aside. 'Oh no, it's just a Spanish wine. Wine is civilised.'

'It's got brandy in it.'

She laughed lightly. 'Has it? I didn't know. Oh, but it's essentially a wine.'

He ordered it and, for himself, a small glass of beer.

As they stepped out into the street, she collided slightly with the doorpost. For a moment she clung to the wall. As he took her arm, the look of surprise was again on his face.

She caught the look. 'You're right, there must be spirits in sherry.' She laughed. 'Shows you how little I drink! I just can't take it at all!'

Of course, of course, that was the explanation. 'Look, you must let me see you home.'

'I'll be all right now. My employers are very nice, but they're a bit old fashioned. I'll see myself home. It's only just down the road. You know how it is.'

'Yes,' he said — but he wasn't at all sure that he did.

'Ask me out again, won't you?' She was looking up at him, holding her mouth as close to his as she could manage. 'Tomorrow?'

'No chance! First day of term. All will be chaos. And it's my turn on the roster to be master-on-duty. What about Friday? My half-day.' His breath came short. It was so long since he had kissed a girl . . . Could he burst through the barrier that the years had built up and accept the invitation on her lips?

'Under the clock in the station forecourt.' Her hands on his vast blue-blazered shoulders, she was up on her toes.

He felt the softness of her lips on his. Then, just for a second, the tip of her tongue slipped into his mouth and was out again. She was gone, tapping her way along the pavement.

He too turned away. Euphoria filled him. The childlike openness of her! Such an eagerness, all the more marvellous for being inexplicable, to get to know him! If she had led him into extravagance it was, as she had pointed out, a special occasion. Very special indeed! Plainly she was normally a good manager. For all her outward sophistication, she was a simple country-loving girl. He strode towards his cottage with empty wallet and full heart.

Back in the High Street of Kingsbridge, Judy Summers had paused before a shop window feigning to examine the dresses on the dummies. Out of the corner of her eye she watched the broad back and head of thick red curly hair retreating until they vanished. She returned on her tracks. Reaching the Rainbow Inn, she paused a moment to glance up and down the street. Then, slipping up an alley, she entered the building by a side door.

Chapter Two

George Brown strolled across the playground of Worcester Hall Preparatory School in the company of the Reverend Charles Hare, known to his friends as 'Charlie'. Though memories of his outing with Judy Summers occupied much of George's head, he had room in it to spare for what the Reverend Charlie was telling him.

'There they go!' Charlie was scrutinising, through the monocle attached to his person by a black ribbon, Mr Featherstonhaugh the headmaster and his housekeeper cum matron, Miss Lewis. 'Strolling up and down, up and down, gravely conversing, Socrates and Plato, sure that they know it all. To watch them, you'd never imagine that *I* was the Senior Master, supposedly Featherstonhaugh's right hand man. There they go, he in his dapper grey suit, his dapper little smile under his dapper moustache; she with her arse rolling like a ship in a storm. There they go, he King-Emperor, she Toady and Spy.'

The burly George glanced at the almost equally tall but slightly bowed figure beside him. Charlie's grey hair was cut in a bob on his neck, as though a bowl had been placed towards the back of his head and his hair had been chopped off round its brim. This gave him the appearance of an eminent barrister or, rather, of an actor playing the role of eminent barrister. He wore his clerical garb only when actually functioning as a clergyman. Then the appearance was that of an eminent dean or, rather, of an actor playing the role of an eminent dean. But all the carefully built up effect of his upper parts was ruined by a childish looking pair of round toed sandles, made necessary because of bad feet.

'You're a wonderful man, Charlie! You can be fired as easily as I. One term's notice will do it. Yet you never mince your words. I'm a terribly cautious chap.'

Charlie's large mobile features, which he boasted that he could control closely (he fancied himself as an actor), produced a smile over a spotted bow-tie and a freshly laundered white shirt. 'No, no. If you're given your notice to quit and have to look for a job elsewhere, you lose your home. Even if you didn't sell your cottage, you'd have to let it. But I! I've got Miss Lewis, toady and spy, as my ground-floor tenant. One false move, and she leaves. She's my insurance.'

'Toady and spy? I suppose so.' George, a tiger on the rugby field, a gentle giant off it, regarded Miss Lewis. Leaning slightly forward she made her way along, her legs encased in supporting irons. Each forearm also was clamped in a cage which at its extremity altered into a metal walking-stick held by its T-shaped top, its foot capped with a rubber stub. She wore a vivid blue beflowered dress that emphasised her ample buttocks, made the more prominent by the attitude in which she was obliged to progress. 'Perhaps it all arises out of frustration; the need to feel power in some direction. She's been denied physical strength. No doubt also the possibility of marriage and children.'

'It's you that are the wonderful man, George. I believe that you'd find excuses for Satan himself.'

'Hardly! I can't pretend that I like her either. But I sometimes get a conscience about her.'

'D'you get a conscience about Featherstonhaugh?'

'Well . . . As headmaster, he's got a lot of responsibility.'

'He's certainly a very *devout* headmaster. He believes in the Holy Trinity, you know.'

'Holy Trinity?'

'God, Shakespeare and Cricket, in that *ascending* order.'

George prodded Charlie in the ribs. 'I have the faintest possible suspicion that you're not deeply fond of him either. Have you ever thought of going into the Church full time?'

'No. I much prefer teaching.'

'What made you enter into Holy Orders then?'

'My grandfather left money for me to go to Cambridge, provided that I read Theology. So it was a case of losing my inheritance or agreeing. I've never regretted entering into Holy Orders. It's made me a lot of money. When I stand in for these parsons who are ill or away on holiday, I don't just get paid a fee, you know. I'm also reimbursed for the petrol I use in driving over. Oh yes, it's proved a very profitable sideline.'

George fairly exploded into laughter. The Reverend Charles Hare's light grey eyes, for once forgetting to act, had been set on him in an expression of intense earnestness, totally innocent of any reflection that work for the Church might be regarded by some as a dedication rather than a money spinner. But George knew also that when Charlie went home after a hard day at the school, it was to turn to, cheerfully, and clean the house. His wife was 'delicate', no one knew why, and no one ever liked to ask. The Reverend Charles Hare prayed his deepest prayers in the pushing of a vacuum cleaner, and preached his most eloquent sermons in the rattling of crockery at the sink.

'Why are you laughing?'

'Oh, just a thought that came into my head.' A luxurious Daimler was making its way cautiously round the angle of the main school building on to the tarmac-surfaced playground situated behind it. The car bore a father, a mother, a boy, a tuck-box and a trunk. 'Here comes the beginning of the deluge.' Over the next hour similar cars similarly laden were to draw in with similar caution, no parent wishing inadvertently to run down the offspring of another parent.

'Sergeant' Finch (it was now 1951, he had been demobilised as a private some five years before, and had spent the interval quietly promoting himself), he of the pinched red nose broken in a pub brawl, appeared with a trolly. Collecting the trunk and the tuck-box, he swept them away and deposited them by the wall of the building just below the luggage hoist. Later, with the assistance of some senior boys working under his direction, he would cause each trunk and tuck-box, with the aid of block, tackle and a large net bag, to be drawn skyward and swung in through wide open doors at third storey level. There they would await unpacking.

George became increasingly involved in ticking off the names of some seventy-five boys listed in a ledger as they reported in to him. He also accepted from them cash for their pocket-money fund, duly noted down in the same ledger.

'I'll leave you to it.' Charlie departed to prepare his wife's supper.

George perceived the dapper medium height figure of Mr Featherstonhaugh approaching, accompanied by a father, a mother and a boy.

'Oh Mr Brown,' said Mr Featherstonhaugh in his most suave in-the-presence-of-parents voice, 'would you see Mrs Carruthers and Tommy up to the Pink Dormitory. Mr Carruthers and I have a few details to discuss. Tommy is a New Boy.' Mr Featherstonhaugh half bent his knees so as to lower himself nearer to Tommy's height. 'But he's a very bright young man and I'm sure he is going to settle in with us very happily.'

Tommy, his face a mask of misery, made no comment.

'Certainly, Headmaster.'

Upstairs, George ushered in before him Mrs Carruthers and her son. 'Tommy's the first to arrive in the Pink Dormitory. He can choose any bed he likes.' He hung back by the door to leave mother and son alone.

'Which one would you like, darling?'

Tommy's small finger pointed wordlessly at a bed in a corner. Thus, on two sides, the walls would enclose and shelter him from this terrifying strange world into which he was being pitched, out of the warm cosiness of his familiar home. On a third side he was partly protected by the small locker, a screen about it, beside the top of the bed. In this locker his possessions would eventually be stored.

Mrs Carruthers sat down on the bed. 'Look at the lovely pink roses on the wallpaper!' She put her arm around him.

But Tommy buried his face in her lap. 'I want to go home. I want to go home.'

His sobs wrung the heart of George, who responded by retreating clean out of the Pink Dormitory into the neighbouring Brown Dormitory, its wallpaper covered with chocolate-coloured gnomes. From long range he observed Mrs Carruthers's grey eyes and gentle distressed face.

She bowed over the small head. 'I *know* you're going to be happy, darling.'

The break had to be made. She rose, the little boy clinging to her, his protection, his hope, his guardian angel.

George advanced quickly. 'I'll keep an eye on him, Mrs Carruthers.' He went down on his knees before Tommy. He took a small hand in his vast palm. 'I'll straight away get a nice big boy to look after you. He'll show you what you have to do and where you have to go. He'll take you to your table at tea time. You'll get lots of jam and cake. All the boys who have jam or cake take them to the new boys. And I'll be there all the time watching to see that you're all right.'

Tommy, staring at the big man with the red curly hair and kind brown eyes, didn't pull away his hand. Besides, cake was cake and jam was jam. George felt on his shoulder a quick touch from the finger tips of Mrs Carruthers, and then she had slipped from the room.

Later, in the dining-hall, with its long polished wooden tables, polished wooden chairs, and polished parquet flooring, the mantlepiece over the great fireplace crowded with silver trophies, Mr Featherstonhaugh stood at the head of one of the tables. Half of this was occupied by the more senior boys of School House, of which Mr Featherstonhaugh was himself housemaster. The 'houses' were mythical; all lived for the most part in the same building. The lower half of the table was occupied by the more senior boys of Fenwick House, so called after a previous long-serving master, with George their housemaster presiding.

There were two other houses similarly seated at the other long table by the opposite wall. At its head, as senior master, was the Reverend Charles Hare, returned from his home. Commander Robinson presided at its foot. Commander Robinson, a retired naval officer, was feared and respected by the boys as a stern but scrupulously just disciplinarian. If a boy sinned, he not only never escaped, but knew exactly what his punishment was to be. For a minor sin, he wrote out an imposition of twenty appropriate lines. For a more substantial sin, he wrote out fifty times, 'I must not be late for roll-call'; or, 'I must not be out of bounds'. For a Deadly Sin, such as bullying a boy, he got six of the best on his backside from Commander Robinson's slipper. To add a stern naval dimension to the occasion, the punishment was always carried out in the gymnasium, with the culprit bent over and made to hold the lowest rung of the wall bars. This almost precluded the shedding of part of the force of the blow by squirming. Seldom was it that one of these chastisements took place, but when a boy was perceived preceding Commander Robinson's stocky figure and jutting jaw in the direction of the gymnasium, a hush would descend over the playground.

In the centre of the hall, and at right-angles to the two long tables, were three shorter ones. Miss Lewis, encased in her irons, ruled over that which seated the new boys. The Assistant Matron (Miss Lewis was helped by an Assistant Matron and an Assistant Housekeeper) controlled the second table of slightly older boys. The third table, of boys older yet, was monitored by a junior master, a Mr Snipe, notable for a long sharp severe nose, a mouth perpetually half open with anxious moral concern (he was a loyal imitator of Mr Featherstonhaugh in all matters), and a heavy crop of pimples. The rest of the staff consisted of part time teachers who came in as required.

'At the beginning of every new school year,' said Mr Featherstonhaugh, smiling and stroking his moustache, 'we have many new boys to welcome and to make feel at home among us. You have all been allowed to go to your tuck-boxes and to get out what you want. Many I see have brought back cakes and jam. We encourage unselfishness at Worcester Hall; a little gentleman is always unselfish. As you older boys know, you are permitted to leave your places and offer your jam and cakes where you will. I ask you especially to think back to the first day of your own first term. I ask you especially to remember the new boys. And now we shall say grace.' All heads were bowed. 'For what we are about to receive, may the Lord make us truly thankful.'

From his position at the foot of Mr Featherstonhaugh's table, George observed with satisfaction that young Carruthers was thankfully receiving everything that he could lay his hands on. Soon the edge of his plate was ringed with little pools of jam and slivers of cake. Starting with bread and butter and the jams, he worked his way steadily up from gooseberry jam, through plum jam and strawberry jam, to Golden Syrup and, finally, to the dizzy pinnacle of honey. Then came seed cake (which he didn't like very much), sponge cake, fruit cake, coffee cake, right up to chocolate cake itself. The only weakness in this otherwise admirable policy was that, by the time he reached the super goodies, he was so sated that he was scarcely in any condition to enjoy them. Indeed, not to put too fine a point on it, when everyone was called upon by Mr

Featherstonhaugh to stand up for the concluding grace, young Carruthers was scarcely able to rise from his seat.

George, as master on duty, positioned himself by the exit from the hall, overseeing the boys as they filed past on their way down to the Big Schoolroom for prayers. Carruthers stumped along slowly, bent slightly forward, his stomach distended.

'A greedy little boy,' murmured Miss Lewis, who was standing beside George. During tea, as though mesmerised, she had watched Carruthers's fantastic feat in packing away into his diminutive person such an array of foodstuffs. 'He'll make himself sick.'

'Not at all. A small boy is like a boa constrictor. You wonder how on earth he's going to wrap himself round his prey, the next moment he's absorbed the lot, and then, after a brief period of lethargy, he's as frisky as ever.'

'A very greedy little boy,' repeated Miss Lewis firmly. 'He'll need watching.'

'No,' said George with a touch of uncharacteristic asperity. 'Just a small boy forgetting his heartache for a moment.'

'I sometimes think that you're much too soft with the boys, Mr Brown.'

'Cheer up, Miss Lewis!' He was smiling, but his bull neck had reddened. 'You've no need to worry. Any contentment he may be feeling will be purely temporary. Soon he will be back in his misery, until he cries himself to sleep tonight.'

Abruptly she made her departure in the direction of Mr Featherstonhaugh, a beflowered, rolling, malevolent bum.

There, thought George, goes another black mark against my name.

At prayers, Mr Featherstonhaugh took his place on the dais behind the high desk. In the attempt to make himself taller, he stood on the outer edges of his shoes with the inner edges propped at an angle against one another. Behind him were ranged the staff on chairs. Before him, the boys sat two by two at double desks in which back-rest, tip-up seat and the two desks formed a single unit. The lids of the desks were deeply scored with the carvings of many generations. The junior boys occupied the front rows, and those more senior the back.

'The first thing you new boys will have to learn is our school motto. What is our school motto, Juniper Major?'

Juniper Major, his face shining with soap and Clean Living, rose at the back of the room. 'Mens sana in corpore sano, sir.'

'Mens sana in corpore sano.' Mr Featherstonhaugh slowly mouthed the words of the stale Latin tag as though he were savouring a plum. 'And what, Juniper Major, does that mean?'

'A healthy mind in a healthy body, sir.'

'A healthy mind in a healthy body.' Mr Featherstonhaugh again savoured the plum. 'I want you new boys to turn round in your seats and look at Juniper Major. He is Head Boy, and a prefect. There are other prefects. When a prefect gives you an order you must obey it, just as if he were a member of the staff.'

Carruthers was staring open-mouthed at Juniper Major. He didn't know the word 'prefect', and thought that Mr Featherstonhaugh had said that Juniper Major was a *perfect*. Never before had Carruthers seen a perfect boy.

'Now face your front again.' Small heads revolved. Juniper Major resumed his seat. 'A healthy mind in a healthy body. That means never doing anything dishonest or mean — being straight. We have a phrase for a shabby act. We say of it, "It isn't cricket." It isn't quite straight. You must learn to play life with a straight bat. What happens, Juniper Major, when you don't play the ball with a straight bat, but hit across its flight?'

Juniper Major rose from his seat. 'You get out, sir.' He sank down again.

'Exactly. You get out. So, even as in Cricket you must play the ball with a Straight Bat, so you must play Life with a Straight Bat. Sometimes you are tempted to tell yourself that what you are doing is all right, but in your heart of hearts you know that it isn't. You are then playing Life with a Bat that isn't *quite* Straight. It sometimes happens that the ball is bowled at your leg stump; that it is coming directly at your legs. You are tempted to get your legs out of the way by stepping back to square leg. But what should you do, Juniper Major?'

Juniper Major arose, as though activated by springs. 'Stand your ground and glance or sweep the ball to leg, sir. Or hit it to square leg.' He subsided.

'Stand your ground. Don't step back towards square leg. And neither, when you are playing the Ball of Life, must you Step Back to Square Leg. What, Juniper Major, do we call a Boy who Steps Back to Square Leg?'

Juniper Major shot up and down. 'A funk, sir.'

'A Funk. A little gentleman is not a Funk. And that is what we try to teach you to be at Worcester Hall — a Little Gentleman. We shall now sing hymn one hundred and twenty-two, *Glory Be to Jesus*.'

The hymn every evening would be *Glory Be to Jesus*, played by Juniper Minor, the musician of the family, squarely and expressionlessly and with an extremely straight musical bat (no stepping back to square leg), until such time as he had completed those immediate studies which would render him capable of offering also, *Soldiers of Christ, Arise*. Mr Featherstonhaugh's religion was nothing if not military; the Church, in fact, Militant. Sergeant Finch was required at frequent intervals to conduct much marching and countermarching in platoons on the playground. The boys opened gates for, and saluted, staff and parents. In the mornings, though they didn't make their own beds, they were required to leave pillows and under sheets immaculately smoothed, and blankets and top sheets turned down neatly to the foot of the beds so as to form a fold eighteen inches in width. It was difficult to see how a boy, who did not have the fold of his blankets and top sheet eighteen inches in width, could have a healthy mind in a healthy body.

Indeed the very next morning at General Assembly the Blue Dormitory, the one with the blue unicorns all over its wallpaper, was in trouble on this score. No less than two beds had not been up to scratch. 'Thoroughly sloppy!' Mr Featherstonhaugh glowered. 'Get yourselves organised. And Huntington and Godfrey-Travers in the Red Dormitory were being thoroughly silly. I've already given them The Slipper.'

It being an article of faith with Mr Featherstonhaugh that no upper middle class boy (about the Lower Orders, he wasn't so sure) could be evil, the most dreadful and ultimate thing that might be said of him was that he was being silly. Miss Lewis, in her role of Head Matron, had walked into the Red Dormitory, the most senior that fell within her sphere, to find Huntington and Godfrey-Travers scrutinising one another's private parts. A lady, naturally, does not comment upon or even permit herself to observe so disgraceful an episode, so she departed again with averted gaze and made her report through a well understood code of hints and elaborate circumlocutions.

As Friday, George's half day, approached, so rose also his excitement at the prospect of meeting Judy under the station clock at two. Suppose she had changed her mind! No, of course she would be there. She had proposed it herself, and she was so transparently sincere, reliable and truthful.

Friday morning saw George putting on his best lemon coloured shirt and yellow tie before proceeding from his cottage to Worcester Hall. During lunch, the conversation buzzed with the terrible event that had polluted the eleven o'clock break. Mr Featherstonhaugh was clearly under strain. Although the sweet had been suet pudding with a spoonful of golden syrup poured over each slice as it was served, favourite of boy and master alike and universally known as 'stodge', Mr Featherstonhaugh had been observed to have only one helping. No one present could recall a previous occasion when Mr Featherstonhaugh had not had a second helping of stodge. The concluding Grace, instead of being pronounced by him on the stroke of a quarter to two, was concluded over five minutes earlier.

George was naturally not displeased. But the next moment he froze at the words that followed. 'I should be most grateful if the *whole*' (Mr Featherstonhaugh was looking directly at him) 'of the teaching staff would assemble immediately in the staff room for a short meeting.' Short or long, it would make him late for his rendez-vous. And he could not get in touch with Judy. After such an apparent snub, would she ever consent to see him again, even if he could find her?

The staff meeting was held behind drawn curtains and with only one light on. The facts were as few as they were terrible. Very young Juniper Minimus of all people, his elder brother the Head Boy already accepted for Eton, his younger brother the pianist reliably tipped to become a prefect in the near future, his father an Anglo-Irish gentleman farmer in the County Carlow and a colonel retired after a distinguished career in the army (the *British* army of course), had shouted out in the playground, shaking his fists above his head, and in the full view and hearing of everybody, 'To hell with the bloody Union Jack.' Very young Juniper Minimus, having inherited his father's bluff outspokenness and fearless dash, had very naturally elected to rebel against everything that his family held sacred. His politics motivated by cussedness rather than conviction, he had picked up the phrase from a minor member of Sinn Fein whom he had overheard addressing a small crowd on the outskirts of Carlow. Before this blasphemy, uttered in such ungentlemanly language, the activities of the whole playground had shuddered to a halt.

'What, asked Mr Featherstonhaugh of the staff, was to be done? As he pointed out, the school's penal code carried no punishment adequate to deal with this un-thought-of, nay, impossible, crime. It was like spitting on an altar, or urinating against one of the walls of Buckingham Palace, or calling down curses upon the Almighty, or even saying, 'Cricket is boring.' Mr Featherstonhaugh for the first (and only) time in his life was nonplussed. After much low voiced debate it was decided to do nothing. It was all too — too awful.

Later a white lipped Mr Featherstonhaugh, reversing the decision of the meeting, secreted Juniper Minimus, as one might secret a leper, into the sanatorium, fortunately at this grave juncture unoccupied. There he was made to write out one hundred times, in his best script, I MUST NOT BE SILLY.

George hurried away from the school, his heart in his boots and his eye on his watch. It was already a quarter past two. Superbly fit, he broke into a run which he intended to maintain right up to the station entrance, even if the resulting perspiration ruined the appearance of his freshly laundered lemon shirt. But he hadn't taken twenty strides when he perceived Judy in the lane.

'Hello!' Her vivid blue eyes looked up at him, and she jiggled on her tall heels so that her ear-rings jiggled also. 'I've been cutting some dried plants to decorate your cottage.' In one hand she held up secateurs, and in the other a small collection of ferns, autumn-dried grasses, wild flowers, and twigs of interesting shapes. 'I always take my secateurs when I go for a walk. So much cheaper than buying flowers, which cost the *earth*.'

With her usual impatience, Judy had arrived under the station clock twenty minutes too early. She browsed at the book and magazine stall for ten minutes, but that was as much as she could stand. There was only one possible route that George could take; she would go and meet him. When, five minutes later, she still hadn't made contact with him, panic seized her. She would lose face with the girls at the Rainbow Inn. She had been boasting to them of her schoolmaster 'man-friend'. She had repulsed their attempts to refer to him as a 'boyfriend'. He was a *mature* man, in fact, *Senior* Master. She had even considered describing him as headmaster, but had decided that there were too many inherant hazards. For one thing, there was Mr Featherstonhaugh's name on the board at the school gate.

George apologised for his lateness and explained its cause. 'Let's make up for lost time. How about starting by getting your cuttings into vases?'

Just at that moment Mrs Finch emerged with her daughter Rose through the school gate, the washing up of the lunch things having been concluded. As they passed, George nodded, and Judy smiled, at them.

'I know them by sight,' said Judy. 'But who are they?'

'Oh, that's Mrs Finch, wife of our stalward Sergeant Finch, who drills the boys — when he's sober enough. The girl is their daughter, I imagine. I've heard Miss Lewis, our head housekeeper and matron, calling her "Rose". I see them from time to time serving at the food hatch or laying the tables. Why d'you ask?'

'It was they who told me the way to — They told me the way once.'

Just before Rose's buxom figure turned the corner in the lane, she glanced back surreptitiously.

Her mother had caught the glance. 'Didn't take her long to find one, did it?' But, as she observed the depression in her daughter's gentle eyes as they dwelt on the massive George, then shifted to the slender form of Judy standing so close to him, the expression of severity softened to one of thoughtfulness, then to concern.

At the cottage, Judy completed her plant arrangements. It *must* become her cottage. It *was* her cottage. Once again she surveyed in dismay the contents of George's bookcase. 'We can pick up a few volumes cheaply at a secondhand bookshop in Tunbridge Wells.'

'I've no car, you know.'

She looked shocked. 'Oh, you *ought* to get a car.'

They went by bus. They made their purchases in the narrow passage way leading to the Church of King Charles I, Martyr: novels by Walter Scott, Jane Austen, Dickens, Thackeray, Bulwer Lytton, George Eliot, the Bronte sisters, Mrs Gaskell, Anthony Trollope. There were twenty volumes in all, strung together in two bundles of ten, which George carried one in either hand.

Afterwards he gave her tea in the Pantiles. She asked him, as she sipped her second cup, why he had never married.

'The years overtook me and caught me out. Too old now. Thirty-five.'

'Oh, I think a man is absolutely at his best at thirty-five.'

He looked at her closely. 'Do you really?'

Back again at Kingsbridge, they parted at the station. They would meet under the clock a week hence on his next half day. This time it was he who volunteered to kiss her, aiming at her cheek. But at the last moment she turned her head and the kiss fell full upon her lips.

Chapter Three

Two days later George found himself unexpectedly free during his last class period of the afternoon. The senior French master had taken the Sixth Form to see a French film at a matinee performance for schools, in Tunbridge Wells.

George made his way into Kingsbridge. Finding his favourite cafe closed for redecoration, he looked about him. His eye was caught or, rather, assaulted by the Rainbow Inn. He surveyed its rows of multi-coloured bulbs, not yet switched on; its garish sign; its showcase of girls, their comely bosoms half spilling out of lacy containers. His rugged face pursed up in distaste; he liked quietness and decorum. If he had his way, the place would be closed down. It stood out like a sore thumb in the old High Street with its half-timbered houses. Most decidedly it was not the sort of place a gentleman cared to patronise.

But — a gentleman requires a cup of tea, particularly after taking a class of small boys in Geography. The Rainbow Inn advertised, among the other basic British needs which it satisfied, that for a cup of tea. He glanced at his watch. Nearly five o'clock. If he searched Kingsbridge for an alternative, it might be only to find that teas were 'off'. Nearby was a newsagent's. He bought two picture postcards of Kingsbridge. One of them he would send to his parents in Cornwall, the other to his sister in Guildford. He was a compulsive writer of picture postcards over tea in restaurants.

He entered the Rainbow Inn. Its interior lived up to the threat of its exterior, being in the same Candyfloss school of architecture carried out mainly in stucco. He sat down and passed a large palm over his eyes, as though something were hurting them. While awaiting service, he selected a pen from the row of pens and pencils clipped to the edge of the breast pocket of his ancient dark blue blazer, with its badge of three golden crowns and an open book bearing the motto of Oxford University, *Dominus Illuminatio Mea*. He wrote steadily.

As he was addressing the postcards, he became aware of a waitress approaching. His eye fixed on the menu, he said, 'A pot of tea, please. Toasted scones and some cakes.' He reached into an inner pocket for his wallet to extract stamps. At the same time he glanced up at the girl writing down his order on a pad. 'Judy! What are you doing here?' Despite himself, the genteel George was shocked. Judy, menially waiting on a table!

Evidently she too found it infra dig. As always when caught out, she met the situation with an extra dash. She hadn't been able to escape it. At this fag end of tea time, and before the initiation of the evening routine, she was the only one on duty.

She laughed gaily. 'They asked me if I'd just flick round the tables.'

'What about your employers? The — the company director?'

'A friend of mine is manageress here. She's been begging me to give her a hand. So — here I am!'

'It seems rather a big sacrifice to have made. What did your parents say?'

'No parents.' She kept her manner chirpy. 'Both killed in the same car crash.'

'Oh, I say! Do forgive me.'

'Not to worry. Long time ago. Here comes the manageress. Mrs Betty Coombes.'

He looked over his shoulder. Betty Coombes had just appeared out of the wall. That is, she had pushed back a sliding panel to reveal a bar, herself standing behind it. She was tall, raven haired, full breasted, voluptuous, somewhat overweight, her red lips parted in a sexy smile that revealed two rows of pearly teeth, both of which he suspected were false. Curled up purring beside her on the counter lay a huge ginger tomcat.

'I must,' said Judy, 'get your order in quickly before teas are off.'

She hurried away, as much he thought to recover from an embarrassing encounter as to secure his meal.

Mrs Betty Coombes half closed her eyelids and looked at Judy through her long false lashes. 'That's a good-looking hunk of man you've got over there! He wouldn't be . . . He wouldn't by any chance be . . .'

Judy hesitated before confirming that he was. She liked Betty Coombes immensely, but she had to keep a wary eye on her. Betty Coombes had an insatiable yet romantic appetite for large men. She never had mere affairs; she always insisted on marriage. Thereby she presented herself with the most appalling difficulties and expense as, closeted with solicitors, she struggled with the courts to release her from the last romance in order that she might embroil herself in the next. Learning nothing from the past, she was totally persuaded that the next enormous idol was the true and final one. She never treated the discarded husband negligently. Having persuaded him that the parting was best for them both, she then spent further hours in fixing him up with someone else. At all times she sang his praises to anyone who would listen.

'My, my!' She cast her dark eyes over George's bull neck and broad shoulders. 'You've done well there.' She lifted up the ginger tom and gazed into his face. Shorn of a part of his tom-hood by having been 'doctored', he had thereby grown to his present vast and placid bulk. 'Jeepers, creepers,' she smiled as she sang, 'where did you get those peepers? Jeepers, creepers, where did you get those eyes?' She kissed him on the nose.

Judy intervened quickly. 'How's your divorce going?'

'My husband's a Catholic, you know. We were married only in a registry office. The Catholic Church doesn't recognise the marriage, so we've the priest on our side. I've fixed up a Catholic girl for my husband. He was too big for me. That was our trouble. He's got thighs like this.' She indicated dimensions suggestive of the trunk of a tree. Yet apparently she was hell bent on acquiring something even larger. 'The man I want is a sergeant in the army. He's six foot ten tall and weighs eighteen stone.' The thighs required to support such a frame could surely be no saplings.

Having been served, George lifted the cup to his lips and unobtrusively watched Judy over its rim. As she continued to move daintily about the rococo splendours of the large room clearing the tables of their tea things, he became aware of a gradual invasion of it by bosomy girls in low cut gowns. They complemented Judy's work by re-laying each table with evening-dinner and wine menus, wine glasses, and cruets of salt, mustard, pepper and vinegar.

Presently they were joined by two large men with hardbitten features. One of them was a giant of six foot five. Probably, George thought, they were 'bouncers', throwers-out of drunks if the need arose. He surveyed their ample proportions with the appreciative eye of a rugby man. The shorter of the two wouldn't make a bad prop forward. He wore a bright yellow shirt with a red tie, and was a six-footer of about his own size and weight. The giant, in a black polo-necked pullover, with pock-marked features, he estimated at seventeen stone. He could see him packing down nicely in the middle of the second row. They rolled up a portion of the carpeting in the centre of the room, revealing a dance floor. The carpeting they bore away with them.

He became aware of Judy at his side. 'Don't be too long. They have to lay your table for supper.'

'Don't worry!' He smiled in acknowledgment of her gay manner, but he felt certain that she was uneasy. Now why? 'I'll be finished in five minutes.'

'I'm sorry for hurrying you like this.'

'My own fault. I left things late. Got a bit of unexpected time off from the school.'

'How nice for you!' She preserved her brightness.

'Who are the girls in the evening dresses?'

'They,' she said with a grand inflexion, 'are hostesses. Well, I must go and collect the wherewithal for dinner.'

On her way to the kitchen hatch, Judy was intercepted by the proprietor, 'Captain' Archie Simpson. Like Sergeant Finch, he had been busy promoting himself since leaving the army. Retiring as a corporal, he had, in the intervening two years, discovered in himself military capabilities which the army authorities had failed to discern. And he was still young. A field marshal's baton one day . . . ? Hardly. But with someone as audacious and self-pleased as Captain Archie Simpson, nothing could be ruled out.

For Judy, he had no more than some routine instructions. But no matter what the subject of a conversation with a pretty girl, he always contrived to turn it into a flirtation.

'You won't forget, Judy, to lay on the cruets?' He drooped his eyelids sexily.

'Oh no, of course not.'

'Check the cutlery carefully.' He stroked his little toothbrush moustache.

'I won't forget.'

'Can't have the customers complaining, what, what?' With the back of his manicured hand he smoothed an invisible piece of fluff off his flashy freshly pressed suit.

'That would never do, Captain Simpson.'

'Call me Archie.' His smile was dazzling.

'Archie.'

He leant forward and whispered in her ear, 'Do we need a fresh tablecloth?'

'Oh no, I think that one will do, Archie.'

'Are you right-handed or left-handed?' His voice was a velvet murmur.

She knew what was coming. 'Right-handed.'

'Oh,' he purred, 'I'm left-handed, you know.'

'Really!' It was the twentieth time he had so informed her.

'I was an officer in the Household Cavalry, the Horse Guards, you know. I had to carry my sword in my right hand. When I rode in a Sovereign's Escort, had anyone made an attack on His Majesty, I should have had to change my sword over before I could have cut him down.'

'How awkward!'

'Our uniform, what with those plumed helmets and breast-plates and riding-boots, cost a hundred and fifty pounds. You could hardly breathe in them. We had to be laced into our back- and breast-plates on the instalment system. I joined the army at fifteen and was on active service at seventeen. I retired from the army on a pension after twenty-two years' service. I'm still only thirty-nine. Put my slippers on, you might say.'

She escaped and collected the things for George's table.

'Who's the flashy gentleman?' he enquired.

'*Captain* Archie Simpson. Retired from the *Household Cavalry*.'

'Household Cavalry! Captain!' He regarded the firm unlined face and strong growing cropped sandy hair. 'Seems a bit of a vulgarian.'

The indignation in her face gave way to delight. 'Are you jealous?'

'It's just that I don't like the look of him. I should watch your step there.'

She glanced at the serving hatch. 'I must get going. They don't like us talking to the customers too long.'

He rose. 'I'm on my way. See you under the clock on Friday.'

He took her punting on the river. She lay back on the cushions of the bow seat in her light cotton dress, her fingers trailing in the warm early autumn water. He stood on the stern decking looking down at her and steadily poling them along. Now and again, when his pole caught in the mud or became entangled in the reeds, he half turned to free it with a sharp twist of his wrists. A kingfisher, hugging the bank, flashed by them skimming the surface.

They drew into the bank. He lay down beside her, in his nostrils the smell of the punt's fresh varnish warmed by the sun. The drooping willows were a curtain between them and the passing punts. Her slim passionate body clung to him, arousing in turn not only his passion but also that tenderness that he had for all small things. He touched her breast. Sharply she pushed his hand away. He pulled back and lay nonplussed, chilled by the snub. When it came down to it, had she discovered that he was indeed too old for her? But she had seemed to be enticing him on! She drew closer. He made no response. She fairly put herself against him. He encircled her with his arm and so remained passive, the movement of the milky air over his brow quieting his unease.

She began to speak, injecting into her voice all the friendliness that she could. 'I do all the flower arrangements at the restaurant. Sometimes I help the chef with the cooking. I'm a very good cook.'

'Are you a — hostess?'

'No. I haven't a big enough . . . Their evening gowns don't suit me.'

'I think you'd look nice in anything.'

'Do you? How sweet of you to say so! I — haven't a big enough bust.'

So that was it! She was sensitive about her small breasts. Well, it didn't matter to him. He wasn't a breast man. He was a leg man. And there was nothing wrong with Judy's legs.

'I'm glad,' she said, 'that I haven't big breasts. They can become so dreadful in later life.'

'You have very nice breasts,' he said, and snuggled his cheek down on her blouse. George, the apparently confirmed bachelor, was finding that, given the stimulus, it was as easy to break through his mental block as it had once been to allow it to form.

Presently, in what seemed the most natural progression in the world, he opened her blouse and snuggled closer. He manoeuvred aside her bra and began to suck one of her breasts, finding therein an immense peace that seemed to stretch clear back to his babyhood. She didn't reject him. Presently she began to run her fingers through his hair.

The astonishing idea suddenly flashed into his mind to ask her to marry him. Ridiculous! Though she might like him as an occasional companion, marriage was another and much larger matter. She would surely consider him too old. They had only just met. She would think him insane, and he would lose her even as a companion. Yet everything she said or did seemed to be prompting him to ask her; to be reassuring him that he would not meet with a snub. After an inward review of his limited financial resources followed by an outward and apologetic reference to them, it was with something like astonishment that he heard his voice proposing.

Judy (a gentleman plays down his wealth) accepted with alacrity. They would, she declared, live on potatoes. She would give up smoking entirely. She opened her bag, extracted a packet of cigarettes, and pushed it into his hands. In this matter, she would place herself entirely in his care.

Back in the town's main post office, under his nose and with the utmost display possible, by telephone and by notes penned on pink flower-bordered notepaper just bought, she elaborately set about putting off 'dates', real and imaginary, to impress upon him the magnitude of the prize he had won. Her cherry lips parted in a laugh. 'I'm a most popular young lady.' In the same thought with which he noted her lack of subtlety and breeding, he was also charmed by her childlike quality and the huge importance that she attached to her engagement to him.

Instead, she reflected, of being a waitress flicking round tables, she was about to become Mrs M A. Surrounded by grubby little boys! Her advice eagerly sought by parents on the future of their sons! Eventually a grubby little boy of her own! Bliss! Bliss! That future, which had always glowed in the distance, was now breaking about her in red and orange flames.

'We must celebrate,' said George. 'What about supper at the Windsor Hotel, followed by the play at the Civic Theatre? It's a West End farce. Should be good for a laugh.'

'How *can* an educated man like yourself go to such rubbish! Let's go to the Arts Theatre. It used to be a barn of some sort, but it's been very well converted. They're doing Jane Austen's *Pride and Prejudice* made into a play. I *adore* Jane Austen. And all the costumes! I *adore* historical costumes. I *adore* history.'

When she had chided him about his books and so enthusiastically set about the reform of his library, he had accepted it in good part. Indeed, he had enjoyed being taken in hand by a gay and immensely pretty girl. But this time, somehow, he felt deflated. Perhaps because it was like having his invitation turned down. By the time the evening came, she had even succeeded in getting him to eschew the solid English cooking of the *Windsor* in favour of an Italian restaurant.

The wine at the *Ristorante Garibaldi*; and later, at the Arts Theatre, the charm of Judy's childlike absorption in the play, so total as to cause it to have for her the force of immediate reality, raised his spirits. In the first interval he observed that one of the miniature spotlights, with which the small foyer was dramatically illuminated, was focused on a grey head. The hair was cut in a bob on the neck, as though a bowl had been positioned not exactly on the top of the head, but at an angle towards the back, and the hair trimmed off round its edge. Charlie was seated on one of the high stools by the coffee bar, drooping interestingly in his venerable-barrister-pondering-a-point-of-law pose (had it been Sunday and he in his canonicals, it would have been his venerable-dean-pondering-a-point-of-theology pose).

George, his arm about Judy's slender waist, piloted her over. 'Judy, this is my best friend Charlie. The Reverend Charles Hare, to give him his full title, and Senior Master at Worcester Hall. Charlie, Judy Summers, my fiancee.'

The monocle dropped from Charlie's eye to the full length of its black ribbon. 'Oh — er — congratulations.' She didn't look at all the right type for old George, or the school. 'It is — it is indeed quite a surprise.' He recovered his composure, his affected voice, and his monocle, screwing the last back into his eye. 'We all thought, Miss Summers, that George was the most settled of bachelors. You must have worked some special magic on him.'

'She did indeed. And how's Mrs Hare?'

'Poorly, I'm afraid, poorly. She's delicate, you know. My daughter's staying with us at the moment, so I took the chance to catch what has become these days a rare whiff of the stage.' He assumed his intellectual voice. 'If you can call this the stage. These modern actors! Talk with their mouths closed. Still, I suppose it's better than the French theatre. The most certain place to acquire a headache is in the French theatre, where the actors never think that they are acting unless they are yelling. And the most certain place to cure it is in the British theatre, where the actors are totally inaudible. About my wife, of course I enjoy looking after her. But so does my daughter. She's very like me in that. I always say the bough doesn't fall far from the tree. She even takes cold baths in the winter, just as I used to do. Daren't now. My heart, you know. I may be wrong.' He slipped off his stool. 'You must excuse me, Miss Summers. The toilet calls.' His monocle twinkled. 'The wise man goeth when he can; the fool goeth when he must.'

Emerging at the end of the show, they bumped into him again. George felt obliged to invite him to join them. Indeed, he wished further to show off his brand new fiancee. Charles walked beside George but half a pace ahead, his shoulders (he was conscious of Judy's eyes on him) arranged in a droop, a scholarly man in pensive mood.

Feeling herself outgunned by all this weight of scholarship and gentlemanly breeding, Judy responded with her usual nervous dash. 'It seemed too lovely an evening to take a taxi.' (They never had had the smallest intention of taking one.) 'We preferred to walk.'

Charlie turned his head and shone his teeth at her. 'I used to be one of the finest walkers in the south east of England. My daughter's going for a long sponsored walk this weekend to raise money for the hospital. The bough doesn't fall far from the tree. I would have accompanied her myself but — my feet, you know. I may be wrong.'

'With the agreement of the Headmaster,' said George, 'I've persuaded every boy in the sixth form to take part in the walk, except of course Billington. It's a shame, the amount of class time he misses through these asthma attacks. He's such a clever boy.'

Charlie jumped in. '*All* asthmatics are clever. I myself am exceptionally asthmatic.'

George paused at the alley leading to the side door of the Rainbow Inn. 'This is where Judy and I say goodnight.'

He noted with satisfaction Charlie's jaw drop. He was enjoying his role of tearaway Bohemian. He enhanced this further by kissing Judy possessively on the lips.

She jiggled on her heels, her ear-rings twinkling. 'I must hurry. They want me to do some flower arrangements for tomorrow morning.'

Charlie regained the use of his tongue only by the time that they had reached the lane leading to the school. 'How much d'you know about this girl?' His pale eye, forgetting to act, was round with concern. 'Don't take offence but, speaking as a plain man in the street and not to beat about the bush — I may be wrong — I believe that place has not a very savoury reputation.'

George laughed. 'Don't be such an old fuddy-duddy! Oh, I know I used to think the same as you. It's vulgar, it's brash, but it's not as bad as it paints itself. I had a late tea there the other afternoon. Things were being got ready for the evening, but I saw no signs of anything particularly dreadful. The girls were improperly dressed, but they were no more than dance partners.'

'Are you sure of that?'

'Sure as eggs are eggs. Charlie, you can't conceive how marvellous it is to know that one is going to be helped out by an economical wife. She talked about our living on potatoes. She speaks of decorating the cottage herself. She's giving up smoking. D'you know, she drinks so little that, the other evening, she was made quite tipsy by just a little wine over a meal! Poor dear, she was so embarrassed. She has a great regard for my job. She's quite fanatical about little boys.'

The dubious expression on Charlie's mobile features only deepened. But he felt helpless before his friend's euphoria. Well, perhaps she might pass if she kept in the background; didn't nourish any ambitions to involve herself in George's work and enter into the life of the school.

Next day George suggested to Judy, as she perched on his lap with her arm about his neck, that they should have a full scale wedding down at his parents' home in Cornwall. 'The ceremony could be held in the parish church in St Austell. I'm sure that my family and my family's friends could make the church reasonably full.'

Through his enthusiasm he gradually became aware that she was unusually quiet, her blue eyes wandering vaguely from his bookcase to the rugby trophies on his mantlepiece, then on to the public school and university photographs on the wall. Of course! How stupid of him! She had no family to enable her to hold her end up. He became filled with tenderness towards her.

He kissed her cheek. 'No, I'm being silly. My parents and sister must come up here. We can have a quiet ceremony in the Kingsbridge parish church. Perhaps the manageress of the Rainbow Inn, that Mrs Betty . . .'

'Betty Coombes.'

'Betty Coombes and one or two other of your special friends would come. The vicar might even allow Charlie Hare to share in conducting the service. I don't know if that's possible.'

At once she brightened up. 'Betty Coombes would help me with my dress. She's a marvellous dressmaker. We have a whole wardrobe department at the Inn. I'm sure that Captain Archie Simpson would make me a wedding present of the material.'

George's tough rugbyman's features registered a momentary distaste at the sound of the 'Captain's' name. But all he said was, 'A good idea!'

The following afternoon the Reverend Charles Hare, it being his half day, was doing the shopping for his household. As he emerged with a packet of rubber rings (the roller-brush of the vacuum cleaner had been playing him up), he observed Judy Summers issuing from the *George and Dragon*. She staggered and put her hand on the doorpost. He took a step forward to help her. He paused, then pulled back into the shop entrance. A medium height man in loud checks had also issued from the *George and Dragon*.

He caught her arm. 'Steady, old gel.' He hiccuped. With

an immaculately laundered handkerchief he wiped his toothbrush moustache.

She pushed him away. 'Leave me alone, Archie.' Her voice became a slurred mumble. 'I know what I'm doing. I know what I'm doing. I'll be all — all right.'

Her very tall heel caught in the iron shoe-scraper set into the stone step, and Captain Archie Simpson caught her only just in time. He laughed. 'I wonder what that toffee-nosed schoolmaster of yours would say if he saw you now!'

She pushed him away again. 'Leave me alone. I know jus' — jus' what I'm doing. He's not toff — toff — nosed. He's worth ten of you.'

'Ten of me, eh!' They were now approaching the Reverend Charles Hare, who pulled right back into the shop. 'Come on, old gel, admit it. He's not for you. He's a bit of a wet, isn't he?'

'Nussing of the kind. He's worth ten — ten — ten of you.' She swayed alarmingly. 'He's an *Oxford M A.*'

'Well, Mr Oxford M A doesn't seem to be able to afford to show you a good time. When it's smokes and drinks, you still seem to have to come to old Archie.'

'That — that's only because he doesn't smoke and drink. He's a *brilliant* rugby player. He's an *Oxford Blue.* He's got *plenty* of money.'

'They don't pay teachers all that much, do they?'

'He's from an important county fam'ly. He's got stocks and shares.'

'Stocks and shares, eh! Oh, my my! Well, I've got stockings and chéries, and I think there's more money in that.'

Captain Archie Simpson was still roaring at his own joke as they passed out of earshot.

Chapter Four

The fat boy advanced like Goliath into the Pink Dormitory to do battle as the champion of the hosts of the Brown Dormitory. It was going-to-bed time for the youngest boys. 'The Brown Dormitory can lick the Pink Dormitory. The Pink Dormitory are cissies.'

Who would be the David from the Pink Dormitory to oppose and expel the Fat Boy, half a head taller than any of them and the heaviest boy around. The Pink Dormitory was garrisoned only by new boys aged from seven to eight, whereas the Brown Dormitory was manned by seasoned second year warriors of eight to nine.

The diminutive Carruthers, his lips pale, advanced a pace or two from the bed in the far sheltering corner that, on his first arrival, he had timidly chosen under the gentle grey eyes of his mother. He was conscious now of other eyes upon him; those of the members of the Pink Dormitory. They watched to see whether he would fulfil his duty as dormitory captain and deliver them out of their peril. Mr Featherstonhaugh had so appointed him on the very first day of term, because he had a particularly gentlemanly voice free of any common local accent. After all, that was a prime prerequisite for a Little Gentleman. A Straight Bat could be added later after due practice next summer in the nets. (It was devoutly to be hoped that one would not detect any inclination to step back to square leg.)

Carruthers forced himself forward another couple of paces. 'It's against school rules for a boy to go into another dormitory,' he piped.

To his horror, he perceived that the awesome words 'school rules' held no terrors for the Fat Boy. Plainly he had an unhealthy mind in an unhealthy body.

'Yah, you're a funk, Carruthers.' The Fat Boy advanced upon him.

'I'll report you to the Matron.' Carruthers' pipe had become a little shrill as he took a step back.

'Yah, the Matron doesn't like you. She says you're greedy. So yah!'

Indeed Miss Lewis had been whittling away at Carruthers' reputation with the headmaster ever since that first teatime.

'I'll report you to the master on duty,' shrieked Carruthers as the Fat Boy rushed at him.

The latter raised his fists above his head and began to rain down blows. Carruthers bent forward and so stood appalled, listening to the drumming on his back. Gradually it dawned upon him that he was suffering no pain at all. Emboldened, he struck out under the flailing arms and his fist connected with the Fat Boy's nose. Instantly it spouted blood. The Fat Boy yelled and fled back to the Brown Dormitory, on his way passing George who had arrived in time to witness the fracas.

It was George's turn to be on evening dormitory duty. The morning duty Mr Featherstonhaugh reserved for himself. The most senior boys slept in two dormitories in a separate block that included the gymnasium and the rooms of Mr Snipe, the eighteen year old Junior Master. At unexpected moments Mr Snipe, that devout disciple of Mr Featherstonhaugh, would thrust his pimples and his sharp nose, his mouth half open with anxious moral concern, into one or other dormitory to assure himself that no boy was playing Life with a Bat that wasn't entirely straight.

'Tunney!' George's rugged countenance wore its most severe expression. 'What d'you think you're doing, going into another dormitory?'

The Fat Boy maintained his headlong dash towards the row of basins. As he reached them, Miss Lewis emerged from the Blue Dormitory, reserved for third year boys. The Blue Dormitory opened into the other end of the long-shaped Brown Dormitory. Her buttocks rolling agitatedly, she made her metallic way to the basins. Dipping a sponge into cold water, she fought to stem the red flow.

Presently she left the Fat Boy to minister to himself. Ignoring George, still standing at the entrance to the Pink Dormitory, she called past him furiously, 'Carruthers, you've cut his nose. You've half killed the boy. I'll report you to the Headmaster.'

George spoke quietly, but loud enough for Carruthers to hear. It was unthinkable of course for two members of the staff to quarrel in front of the boys. 'I know, Matron, that you will also be reporting that Tunney entered the Pink Dormitory; that when Carruthers did his duty as dormitory captain and told him to leave, Tunney, much the bigger boy, attacked him; and that Carruthers hit him solely in self defence.'

Miss Lewis retreated in silence to her patient. But her decision was firm. She, Miss Lewis, had been reprimanded and she, Miss Lewis, would make those who had, directly or indirectly, contributed towards her humbling, feel the weight of her power. They would be made to learn that they were dealing with no negligible cripple, but with the Head Matron and the Head Housekeeper of Worcester Hall. Carruthers no longer was to her, if indeed he ever had been, just a little seven year old boy. He was a pawn in a power struggle that had to be won, for defeat was the extinction of Miss Lewis. The whittling away at Carruthers' reputation with Mr Fetherstonhaugh would be intensified. The reputation of Mr George Brown would also not be neglected.

'Carry on, Carruthers,' said George, smiling at him.

He departed to oversee the Red Dormitory, the one with red dragons all over its wallpaper, into which the fourth year boys were beginning to arrive.

Next day, during the Milk Break (with tea of course for the staff), he stood by the staff room window sipping from his cup. The rest of his colleagues were still in the dining hall. His brown eyes were on the Penal Drill squad hopping on one leg round and round in a circle. The Penal Drill boys would have to have their milk later with their lunch. Presently Huntington, he of the Red Dormitory who had been slippered by the Headmaster for being silly and inspecting the private parts of Godfrey-Travers, lowered his non-hopping leg in exhaustion.

Sergeant Finch's pinched red nose, broken in a pub brawl, reddened further. 'Keep them legs up, keep them legs up,' he bawled, after a sly glance up at the staff room window. He couldn't see through the window because of the reflection off the panes, but was conscious that one or more of the staff might be standing behind it — even possibly the Headmaster himself.

Huntington made a weak effort to obey, then lowered his leg again.

'Fall out, that boy there!' The tones of a sergeant of the Brigade of Guards could not have been more stentorian. 'Approach me! Pick up them feet! Left, right, left, right, left, right!'

Huntington, paying not the smallest attention, sauntered up. 'Please, Sergeant, may I be excused?' He put his hand in his trousers pocket.

George moved sharply to one side of the window to alter his angle of vision. Yes, as he had recently begun to suspect, a coin had changed hands. That boy Huntington had far too much pocket money. This, married to Sergeant Finch's thirst for beer, was not a healthy combination. Huntington departed to the toilet block, from which he would not emerge until the sounding of the bell for the third lesson period. Sergeant Finch's commands took on an increased ferocity, but the drill proceeded as languidly as before.

Suddenly George stiffened. There was the rattle of a cup in a saucer as he banged them down on the table. In two strides he was over at the notice board. One of the slips of paper drawing-pinned to the green baize was headed, *Penal Drill*. He read the words, 'Fighting in dormitory.' He strode down a corridor and knocked on a door.

'Come in.'

'Headmaster, I've just noticed that Carruthers is on Penal Drill. I wish to protest in the strongest possible terms.'

He gave the full story.

Mr Featherstonhaugh arranged a dapper little smile under his dapper little moustache. 'I cannot, Mr Brown, interfere with Matron's decision. After all, you did not report the matter yourself.'

'I naturally assumed that Matron would deal fairly. It is absolutely outrageous that Carruthers should be out there.'

Mr Featherstonhaugh's smile became a trifle less dapper. 'It will do him no harm.'

George's bull neck reddened. 'It will do him no good either. He has his name up there on the board, earning him a bad mark. This bad mark will be placed against his name on his House chart, cancelling one of the stars he had won. This loses a star to his House in its competition with the other Houses. His House captain and vice-captain will have him up on the mat about it. Indeed other members of his House will have it in for him.'

'Mr Brown, every day one boy or another is receiving a bad mark and so losing a star. They survive. I realise, of course, that Carruthers is in *your* House . . .

It was on the tip of George's tongue to retort, 'And Tunney is in yours.' He halted the words. He drew in several deep breaths. If he lost his job, he would, in one degree or another, also lose his cottage, and so Judy her new home before she had even had time to take up residence in it. He turned on his heel. In the doorway he paused. 'We teach the boys to play life with a straight bat. How straight is this bat?' He closed the door behind him.

The bell was sounding for the third period. During the ensuing Geography lesson, George snapped at one boy for saying that Manchester was on the River Avon, and at another for saying that Snowdon was the highest peak in the Alps. He set a stiff 'prep' for that evening, forgot that he had, and five minutes later set one even stiffer.

On his return to the staff room he consulted the afternoon's games lists. Ah, he had been put in charge of the senior rugby squad's training session. He gave a cursory glance at the Penal Drill list, then turned towards his locker to get out the books, including a pile of corrected exercise books, required for his next lesson. He halted. He swung round. He strode back to the notice board. A series of red ink lines, Mr Featherstonhaugh's hallmark, had scrawled out the name so that it could no longer be seen. Almost, that is. But for someone with prior knowledge, not quite. Yes, there beneath the red lines was the letter 'C'. Anyway, that was the position at which Carruthers' name had occurred. Certainly it was no longer on the list.

George sauntered into his classroom. He smiled indulgently when Godfrey-Travers asserted that Cairo was the capital of the Congo, and laughed genially as he returned Huntington's exercise book, in which the latter had constructed from memory a strangely shaped map of Africa placing Capetown squarely in the middle of the Sahara Desert.

*   *   *

George and Judy, in the presence of his parents and the Reverend Charles Hare, were married towards the end of January.

Not that all had gone smoothly. Before travelling up from Cornwall, his father had written him a letter. 'She is neither your social nor intellectual equal.' George had replied, 'Father, you were much concerned at having no grandchildren to carry on the family name. I was settling down ever more deeply into bachelorhood. I never was a very adventurous sort of chap, except on the rugby field. It took Judy to prise me out. She has brought me alive. Without her, I know I'd just sink back again.'

On their arrival, they were installed in the spare bedroom of the cottage. Judy had spent much paint and many hours on its redecoration. After being introduced, she had fulfilled the conventions by leaving to spend the night with Betty Coombes. George had seen her to the Rainbow Inn.

'Your parents don't approve of me.'

'Good heavens, darling, wherever did you get that idea from!'

She had caught the lack of conviction in his voice. 'I could feel it. They think I'm not in your class. I've got no family. I haven't had your education.'

'Love, there never were yet parents who didn't think that nobody was good enough for their wonderful children. Now don't you worry your head about it. *You're* marrying me, not them.' He had kissed her. 'I have told them that it was only after meeting you that I came alive.'

Her face was alight. 'You told them that!'

'I did. And it's true. See you in church tomorrow!'

Captain Archie Simpson, wearing a vast rose in his buttonhole and a cynical smile; and Betty Coombes, elegant in black, trimmed with white lace, supported Judy, as they had done also prior to the ceremony. Captain Archie Simpson, not incapable of good nature, had supplied materials from the cutting room of the Rainbow Inn. Betty's skilful scissors and sewing-machine had turned them into a set of wedding and going-away clothes. George and Judy had departed on their one week honeymoon.

George had been all for the Isle of Wight. 'Either Sandown or Ventnor seem to head the ultra-violet and sunshine tables in Britain.'

'Oh, George, that's so bourgeois! It will be seedy hotels full of commercial travellers.'

'We can go on to the beach even at this time of the year. There'll be a sun lounge in the hotel. We'll be able to go to — go to —'

'Paris!'

'What! We couldn't afford —'

'We'll live on potatoes when we come back. Once, when I lost my purse, I lived on potatoes for a whole fortnight. I saved *pounds*.' She had perched herself on his lap. 'G-e-o-r-g- e! I've never been abroad. I've always *dreamed* of going to Paris.'

They stayed at a *pension* close by the Gare du Nord. It was the cheapest on a list of hotels and pensions close to the station. But to Judy it might have been the Hotel Ritz near the Champs Élysées. She enthused over the bottle of *vin ordinaire* served as routine with the meal. Wine was civilised, and French wine was the quintessence of civilisation. As for the salad of slim slices of cold potato in olive oil, that sent her into raptures. 'English cooking is so *coarse*. Look what the French can do with the simplest ingredients!'

They sat at a pavement cafe in the boulevard des Italiens, its outside tables sheltering in a glass enclosed space heated by charcoal braziers. As they sipped hot chocolate and nibbled at gateaux, she alternately enthused over the coiffeurs and clothes of the women passers-by, and admired the new Oxford blazer she had nagged him into buying. She wanted, she said, to show off her new husband at his most distinguished. She had comforted him for the loss of his beloved old blazer by pointing out that he could still wear it when tending his roses, and even while teaching and refereeing games.

The pension was not good on sanitary arrangements. She merely found this 'Continental' and 'romantic'. George, wanting a hot bath, prevailed upon Madame la Patronne to heat, on her coal- fired range, large iron pots of water. He ferried them up under the watchful eyes of Judy. Standing naked at the head of the bath, he placed a hand on either edge and swung himself in.

Judy, controlling the cold tap at the other end, exclaimed, 'What a huge fellow you are!'

He lay back, soaking. She dipped in the sponge, held it aloft, squeezed it, and sent its contents cascading on to his genital organs. 'Why don't we ever do anything sexually unusual? We're so unadventurous!' Seeing his slight look of distaste she said, 'Oh, you're an old stick-in-the-mud!'

She made him sit up in the bath while she soaped the hard muscular expanse of his back. Stick-in-the-mud or not, she had enjoyed having the breath half crushed out of her in his powerful arms, the weight of his body when he lay upon her, his breath hot on her cheek. Once he had felt her running her hands over his back and she had cried out passionately, 'I like to feel how strong you are.'

Home again, she gave herself one day of leisure before unleashing herself upon her master plan. This leisure included spending much of the time in the company of Angus. She unpacked him carefully. He had been left to her by her mother.

'Angus is in good voice this morning,' she exclaimed, as the last tinkling notes of *The Bluebells of Scotland* died away. She closed the mother-of-pearl lid of the little music-box.

She crossed to a wall shelf. 'Why have you put this vase of dried grasses in front of your mother's photograph?' She moved the vase to one side. 'It's a shame to obscure it. Your mother looks beautiful there.'

He glanced across the room at the studio portrait. His mother's patrician features, the white fur wrap about her neck and shoulders, gazed back at him. Rather large features, and steady grey eyes . . . Certainly she wasn't pretty. But handsome — yes. And all love.

'It's very generous of you, darling, to say so, after the way she had rather — doubted you.'

'Oh no. I'm sure that I'll think that no girl is good enough for *my* son.'

She moved into the scullery. His great form spread over an armchair and bliss shining from his rugged countenance, he watched her through the open archway. Standing at the old stone sink, she duly peeled the promised potatoes, depositing the curly mud-brown skins onto the wooden draining-board. After three days, to his mild surprise, small pieces of bacon began to appear among the potatoes. On the fifth day, to his astonishment, there was more bacon than potato. On the seventh, all pretence of a potato regime was abandoned.

To his expostulation she replied, 'I didn't mean it *literally*.'

In consternation he retired to a small side table and his accounts. By the time that he rose from his seat, he had written letters cancelling his subscriptions to the Oxford Union, his college society and a number of others. Overwhelmed with a sense of loss, he slipped away quietly while she was upstairs.

On his return, he saw a small form standing daintily in the trellised porch. 'Where have you been?'

'Just to the post-box.'

'But only this morning you were thanking heaven that you were up to date with your correspondence.'

He hesitated. He had been brought up never to tell a lie. 'Just cancelling a few of my Oxford subscriptions.'

'Because of the bacon?'

'The subscriptions were quite unnecessary. Just a luxury. I can't afford to go up to Oxford anyway.'

'Oh yes. You've got your degree, after all.' The spriteliness of her tone was belied by the touch of uneasiness in the blue eyes raised to his.

He nodded and, heavily, ascended the stairs into the bedroom.

She followed quickly. 'There's no need to buy that double bed. We can go on managing with the two divans put together and made up as one.'

He sat down on the edge of the makeshift bed, the mattress sagging under his massive form. He unlaced his outdoor shoes, pulled them off, and replaced them with leather slippers. 'That would help.'

She perched herself on his lap. Fluttering her lashes she said, 'I've cut down my smoking from twelve cigarettes a day to ten. Next it will be eight.'

'Not bad.'

'I'm feeling much better for it. The sore throats and the heart palpitations are a thing of the past.'

'Good.'

She put her arms round his neck and curled herself up like a kitten. 'Tell me I'm a clever girl.'

He emerged from his torpor. He looked at the blue sparkle of the ear-rings in her dainty ears, picking up the vivid blue of her eyes. He looked at the brief blue cape that he loved so well. Suddenly he

was moved by her littleness to an intense tenderness. He kissed her.
'You're a clever girl.'

She put her mouth close to his ear and began to sing in a small voice, 'Tiptoe, to the window, by the window, that's where I'll be — Come tiptoe, through the tulips, with me . . .'

Chapter Five

At first she was in paradise, sweeping and polishing her new home, and cooking for her new husband. She wanted none of the servants of her pre-marriage daydreams. He would come home from the school to find the furniture rearranged again and again. Though continuing to aver that wine was civilised, she excluded it to sustain her role of one who scarcely touched it. The number of novels by good authors grew in his bookcase until his manuals on rugby and cricket were quite overwhelmed. She even bought and put on display a large work-basket filled with reels of white or black cotton, cards of darning wool, and packets of needles large and small.

'No more sewing and darning for you! Put your torn rugby clothes there. Or any socks or sports stockings with holes in them.'

'Thank you, darling.'

He put them there. Then he put more there. And that was where they remained — there. One day he began to remove them quietly, one by one, and returned to mending them himself. He reminded himself of how much time she spent on decorating their home: painting the walls, staining the floors, arranging flowers.

When, only three weeks after their marriage, she showed no signs of being pregnant, she became a little uneasy; after three and a half weeks she grew alarmed, and after four weeks declared herself to be barren.

'I might as well return to smoking and drinking.'

George's brow, under its thick hedge of red curls, crinkled. 'Return to drinking! I didn't know you drank, except once in a way.'

'I didn't mean it *literally*.'

'Oh. Look here, aren't you assuming rather too soon —'

'My mother was barren.'

'What!'

'Well, almost. My aunt once told me so, the only time she visited me at the orphanage. I'll have to throw myself into working at the school. Make the boys my children.'

'Yes, why not. They've got a full staff, but sometimes teachers are away ill. Being able to keep order is something that has to be learnt over the years. But you'll be all right with the juniors. With the juniors, they won't expect a university degree of course. You're a tremendous reader; you could take English. Yes, Featherstonhaugh might be very glad to know that he has a stand-in so close at hand. Especially the wife of a member of the staff. The parents would accept that. Of course he'd have to pay you. Not a regular salary; just for each occasion. How much, I don't know. Part time teachers often earn relatively more than regular teachers, hour for hour. I'll speak to the Headmaster.'

Mr Featherstonhaugh interviewed her in his study. Though, like the Reverend Charles Hare, thinking her hardly the right type for the school, nevertheless he was not entirely impervious to the smile of small white teeth between lips vividly lipsticked, ear-rings twinkling at dainty ears, and a head, smartly coiffeured, set pertly on a soft rounded neck. Graciousness itself, he pencilled in her name (it would be inked in only if she proved a success) on a short list of standby teachers.

Judy emerged on to the playground. No longer was she Miss Judy Summers, waitress, flicking round tables. She was Mrs Brown, nay, Mrs M A, a qualified and salaried teacher. On the far side of the playground was a figure in a bright blue flower-patterned dress. Judy recognised the leaning forward posture, each forearm clamped into a metal cage which at its extremity altered into a metal stick or crutch grasped by its T-shaped top, the legs encased in supporting irons. Miss Lewis was talking to a gracious looking lady with grey eyes and a gentle face. At the lady's elbow stood the diminutive Carruthers. Judy, in her very high heeled shoes, clip-clopped over the tarmac to them. As a member of the staff and the wife of a housemaster, she would be able to help in any problem.

'... and he is a little apt to wolf his food,' Miss Lewis was saying as Judy drew within earshot.

Mrs Carruthers' cheekbones reddened. 'He's thin, isn't he? Doesn't he need to eat up, perhaps?'

'Well — within reason. And I'm afraid the other day in dormitory he delivered a rather vicious attack on another boy. Made his nose bleed.'

'Oh no,' cried Judy.

Miss Lewis started, and half turned.

'It wasn't like that at *all*, Mrs Carruthers. I heard about the whole affair from my husband. He's a *Housemaster*. I myself am a part time member of the staff.'

'Really, Mrs Brown!' Miss Lewis's hands were trembling. 'It is I, as Head Matron, that Mrs Carruthers is consulting. I must ask you —'

'Do go on with what you were saying, Mrs Brown.' The gentle Mrs Carruthers, driven by a desperate concern for her son, had half turned her back on the Matron.

As Judy presented the facts, Miss Lewis clanked her way across the playground in the direction of the Headmaster's study. She had been told in advance about the possibility of Judy's joining the pool of reserve teachers. Despite doubts, she had been willing to give her a chance and not hold her responsible for her husband. But not now. Now, the reputation of Mrs Brown would receive the same treatment as the reputations of Mr Brown and Carruthers. They would be taught, all three of them, with whom it was that they were dealing.

Judy's first lesson took place a few days later in the Art Block. This stood on the opposite side of the playground to the main building. Each boy had been set work in advance. Judy was required only to invigilate. For a while she watched the nine year olds busy at their drawing and colouring, or at their modelling with plasticine.

'Grimshaw's always drawing girls,' piped the treble of one of the artists.

'Do you know why he's always drawing girls?' enquired his companion.

'Because he says it's the only thing he can draw.'

'He's not likely to be able to draw anything else, if he keeps on drawing girls all the time.'

'The reason he draws girls is because they're the easiest thing to draw.'

Judy's delight in their conversation was halted by a single voice that had arisen among the modellers. 'I have,' said a rather larger boy with a sly grin, 'a little warm mouse nestling beside me in bed.' He held up a limp piece of plasticine.

Judy watched, both intrigued and surprised.

Another boy looked up.

Sly-grin repeated, 'I have a little warm mouse nestling beside me in bed.' He held up the plasticine higher and displayed it around.

The boy who had looked up giggled. This caused others to pay attention.

Judy became uneasy. She was there to keep order. She herself championed sex and was particularly intrigued to observe its manifestations in the male. But how should Mrs M A feel? How should Mrs M A react?

'In the morning, the little warm mouse wouldn't be so little. It would be like this.' Sly-grin parted his hands as he stretched out the plasticine.

This time there were half a dozen giggles. One boy was so amused that apparently he knocked himself against the pinewood wall of the smart modern 'prefab', with its slightly tilted felt-lined roof.

Judy stared. The boys were only nine years of age! Only *nine*! Well, one of the girls at the Rainbow Inn possessed a son of six, and she had told Judy that sometimes he had an erection.

'Then,' said Sly-grin, 'I would do this if I had the strength.' The elongated plasticine was jerked up and down.

This was absurd! She had read that the age of puberty in boys and girls was getting earlier, but nine!

Again there was the knock against the wall, but this time it was followed by the clank of metal. With impeccable timing, Miss Lewis was making her way down the path running along the back of the prefab, observing the scene through the row of windows as she passed. For how long had she been listening?

Judy rose to walk over to Sly-grin. But there was no need to assert herself. Sly-grin, frozen by a single glance from the Head Matron, had lowered the plasticine and was hastily turning it into a locomotive. His audience had already buried themselves in their work.

Judy swung round to glance out through the window behind her, in the opposite wall of the classroom. Miss Lewis had rounded the end of the block. An ample pair of beflowered malevolent buttocks were rolling their way across the playground towards the grey castellated main building. There lay the Headmaster's study . . .

Plainly, ruminated Miss Lewis as she clanked along, a lady couldn't speak of such matters. Indeed, a lady couldn't even permit herself to understand such matters. How then should she report them to Mr Featherstonhaugh? Would even her circumlocutions prove equal to the task?

As it turned out, Miss Lewis's circumlocutions were shown to be equal to any task. Had she been obliged to report a scene of drug taking accompanied by sexual obscenities, by the time that she had processed the material it would have sounded like a cup being accidentally spilt during afternoon tea on the vicarage lawn. But Mr Featherstonhaugh's sensitive antennae could be trusted to pick up and retranslate back to the original even the most delicate of the nuances. This retranslation would inform him that here was a little gentleman practising in the Nets of Life with a bat that was quite appallingly crooked. Such an action simply laid one wide open to having one's bails scattered by a googly from the Devil.

Later, Sly-grin came to learn of the strength that resided in Mr Featherstonhaugh's right arm, and of the solid construction of his leather slipper.

Later still Judy came to learn from the Headmaster, smiling under his dapper moustache, that *perhaps* she wasn't *quite* up to it. Dealing with boys could be — difficult. Now a position on the *domestic* staff . . . The salary wasn't so high, but there would be more occasions when her help would be welcome. Was she interested? She was? Ah, good, good.

'How could I have prevented it?' she exclaimed to George that evening. 'It all happened so suddenly.'

'Don't worry. Boys will try on anything with a new teacher. Keeping order is an art that has to be learnt. More teachers lose their jobs from an inability to keep order than from any other cause.'

'I had to make sure, first, what he was up to. After all, they are only nine.'

'An experienced man teacher would have stamped it out at the first move. An experienced woman teacher would have done the same, but in a different way. For a new teacher, man or woman, it was difficult. A new teacher needs a first and a second and a third chance. You didn't get them. I think we can thank a certain Head Matron for that. I think the same Head Matron wouldn't be sorry to see me too come a cropper.'

'It was, after all, only sex. Sex is a natural thing.'

'Good heavens, you can't expect the Headmaster to allow sex into Worcester Hall. It's not — not cricket.'

Unfortunately Judy's drive to take over, as she had taken over George, was not to be curbed. Within a few days of her appointment to the domestic staff, she had succeeded in antagonising the Assistant Housekeeper by, without first seeking her agreement, decorating the dining-hall tables with arrangements of twigs, dried plants, and anything else that her secateurs could cull from a winter countryside. The Assistant Housekeeper complained to Miss Lewis in her capacity as Head Housekeeper. The delighted Miss Lewis jogged the elbow of the Headmaster. Mr Featherstonhaugh, wearing a delicate smile under his impeccably scissored moustache, suggested Judy out of her post so smoothly that it was half an hour later before she fully comprehended that she had lost it.

But, within the brief time vouchsafed to her, she had succeeded in capturing the friendship of both her immediate workmates. Mrs Finch's was extended only cautiously. A girl who had announced that, where religion was concerned, she wasn't 'anything really'! One couldn't be sure where one stood. Mrs Finch had unknotted her grey headscarf then reknotted it more securely into place, as though seeking within its circle shelter from an uncertain universe. As to her daughter Rose, she gave her friendship freely — Rose, too gentle to feel hostility or, when she saw George and Judy together, to escape pain.

When George returned home that evening from the school, Judy gave him the news of her dismissal. 'Now what have I got to live for?'

He looked at her small form standing framed in the scullery doorway, a knife in one hand, a half peeled potato in the other. No flutter of the vivid blue eyes now. They were filled with tears. No chic, no perkiness. Just a distressed child, or so in her neat smallness she seemed to him. He strode across the flagged kitchen-dining-room and swept her into his arms.

But it was no child, but a grown woman, that shook herself free of him. 'You never take me anywhere. We've never been to the theatre again. We never even have a party here. All I ever hear from you is that there's no money for this, and no money for that. I'm fed up with it.'

Chilled, he stared at the small features, pink with resentment, as at those of a stranger. 'I'd no idea —'

'You don't treat me as a woman at all. You treat me as a child.'

'I'll — I'll have to take on some coaching in the evenings. Private pupils. Just twice a week or so. It would mean that you'd have to do your knitting or reading in the bedroom.' He added hastily, 'I'd turn over all the money to you. You'd do the deciding as to how it was to be spent. You manage these things better than I.'

She returned to the sink. But a moment later she was back in the doorway. She regarded the worried lines beneath the hedge of red curly hair. 'Just a *small* party.' Her voice had softened. 'Only two or three people. Here at home. It needn't cost much. I'd make scones and cakes.' Perhaps he hadn't quite so much money as she had supposed. But of course *basically* there was plenty there. Of course, of course.

She acquired a fresh perm and a bottle of sherry to accompany the candles, joss-sticks and box of crackers.

The Reverend Charles Hare was the first to arrive. He wore a plum coloured smoking jacket and, above his gleaming white shirt, a bow-tie to match. George found himself glancing from the magnificent upper parts to the childish looking pair of round toed sandals.

Charlie had caught the look. To recover his dignity, he spoke in his most affected voice. 'Suffer from my feet. Arthritis, you know. I may be wrong.'

George's embarrassment at having had his thoughts read, was covered by Judy's bursting out into an indignant complaint to Charlie about her treatment at the hands of Mr Featherstonhaugh. Despite Charlie's previous doubts about her, his sympathy was instantly engaged. It enabled him to enter upon one of his favourite themes.

'If he had done that to me, I can tell you I would have thrown the Old Vic at him.'

He spoke frequently of throwing the Old Vic at so and so, by which he meant giving them a piece of his mind. This, and his frequent references to Shakespeare (he always, notwithstanding that the examination papers he set were supposed to be confined to Religious Knowledge, ended the choice of essay subjects allowed to candidates with the single word, 'Shakespeare'), built up the impression that he had been a Shakespearean actor at the Old Vic Theatre in London. But George discovered one day that he hadn't acted since he left school!

Judy was looking at Charlie in delight. 'Would you really have told him off?'

'I once had the same kind of trouble from a previous headmaster. He came into my room and started to throw his weight about. I stood up and looked at him. I said to him, "I've got a very nice door. Please use it." And he went!'

George smiled to himself. All of these stories ended with the triumphant dismissal of an employer from the presence of the Reverend Charles Hare.

'Here's your sherry, Mr Hare. I shall call you Charlie.' She shepherded him over towards the range. 'Sit down here and warm yourself.'

'So kind.'

There was a knock on the front door. Mr Snipe, the junior master, diffidently thrust in his long sharp severe nose, his mouth perpetually half open with anxious moral concern, and his heavy crop of pimples. 'You said I was to walk straight in.'

'Come in, come in!' Judy instantly took the eighteen-year-old under her wing. 'Have a sherry.'

Charlie, bowed forward over his drink like a reflective crane, quipped, 'I can vouch for its being *sherry* nice.'

Mr Snipe tittered. If he was a disciple of Mr Featherstonhaugh, imitating him in all things, he was also considerably impressed by the Reverend Charles Hare. He therefore laughed at his joke. Indeed he laughed at all his jokes, however feeble.

Charlie picked up one of George's exercise books. When reading, he was obliged to surrender his monocle and thus a part of his distinction, and don a humdrum pair of spectacles. 'Humf! Godfrey-Travers. I see that he writes the same kind of tripe for you as he does for me. I had to throw the Old Vic at him this morning. Bone idle, that lad. Needs the slipper —'

He was interrupted by an explosion into the room. It was Betty Coombes arriving. She billowed across to them arrayed in a short tight-fitting low-cut dress, pearly false teeth, long dark false eyelashes, and a generously padded bra, showing all that she had and much that she had not.

Charlie hastily removed his spectacles and resumed his monocle. Putting down the exercise book, he rose from his seat.

To Judy's mingled amusement and alarm, Betty Coombes began to flutter those eyelashes at George. He however, armoured by his devotion to his wife, remained impervious and offered his guest a glass of sherry.

Charlie, becoming aware that Betty had noted his scandalised eye on her plunging neckline, felt the need to re-establish himself as a man of the world. Above his bow-tie and natty shirt, his teeth gleamed in sheer delight at himself. 'I was reckoned to be one of the handsomest men at Cambridge in my day. We knew how to handle women then, I can tell you. It was a case of throwing *girls* before swine.'

Mr Snipe, whose pimples had reddened at the sight of Betty's dress (what would Mr Featherstonhaugh have thought of it?), duly tittered.

Betty laughed. 'I made it myself. I design all the dresses for the girls at the Rainbow Inn. They tell me my designs are a bit bosomy.' She regarded George archly. 'You were at the Rainbow for tea. I expect you noticed.'

'I noticed.' He couldn't be too disapproving. Whatever her faults, he was discovering Betty Coombes to be jolly and unaffected.

Charlie evidently still felt the need to display broadmindedness. 'In my student days at Cambridge, some of us went on a package tour to Paris. The tour included a visit to the Casino de Paris. The girls paraded on the stage without — er — without — that is, bare breasted.'

Betty Coombes exploded. 'I think that's absolutely dreadful. I think that's absolutely dreadful. They're sexual organs. *Sexual organs!*'

Charlie's monocle plunged from its lodgement in his eye to the full length of its black ribbon. He took a hasty step back.

George gazed at her. The Cabaret Queen wedded as securely to the conventions as she was to the institution of matrimony!

To restore calm, he praised her Rainbow costumes.

At once she recovered her customary cheerfulness. She smiled mischievously. 'Do they make you want to push your hand down the girls' fronts?'

He considered. 'Yes. Yes, I suppose they do.'

Abruptly Judy rose from her chair. Her slight form quivered. Earrings jingling, she clip-clopped out of the room and the house.

He stared after her. 'What brought that on?'

Betty looked at him. 'Don't you know?'

Jealousy? The craggy prop-forward brow furrowed. Once, when they were at the cinema in Tunbridge Wells, he had admired an actress in the film. Judy had expressed her annoyance. 'What!' he had exclaimed. 'Just photographs? Shadows on a screen?' 'Even so I mind.' If she were going to be as jealous as that, life with her might become a stifling affair.

'Don't you know?' repeated Betty. She smiled significantly. 'She herself is — flat chested.'

George cast a look of distaste over Betty's full blown body. He was damned if he was going to become involved in a behind-her-back discussion of his wife.

Charlie approached. He put a hand on George's arm. 'She'll come round. Give her a few minutes.'

'Excuse me, Charlie.' He rushed out.

He paused in the lane. There was a moon behind the clouds. Right towards the town, or left towards the school? Suddenly he knew. He turned left.

She stood before the Madonna and Child. He put his arm about her small shoulders.

'My father,' she said, 'taught me not to believe in religion. He said that the only two times he had been diddled, it was by a clergyman. But . . .' She remained staring at the painted eyes of the little Virgin Mother bent down in adoration upon her painted Baby. 'That's what breasts are for.'

The half gloom was pierced by a flicker of light. George looked back over his shoulder to see that the sickle moon, after spilling a beam through a rent in a cloud, was concealing itself again. But all that Judy noticed was an effulgence from the twin haloes of the Mother and Child — a golden gleam that came, and then was gone.

On the first day of March, she was sick at the breakfast table. Her face shining, she left for the doctor's. George held his breath. Had he indeed fathered a child?

When she returned, she threw her arms about his neck. 'It was the Madonna. I *know* it was the Madonna.'

Chapter Six

A large man with a mass of red curly hair and wide-flung shoulders stood at a front upstairs window staring out. A back copy of a newspaper drooped from his half open hand. It displayed a broad black border framing the contents of its front page. King George VI, it said, had died in his sleep during that night of February fifth/sixth 1952. Princess Elizabeth had received the news while staying with her husband at *Tree-tops*, the African 'hide' for watching the animals as they made their way down to a watering-place. For the first time in the history of the world, it proclaimed dramatically, a young girl had climbed into a tree one day a princess, and the next day a queen.

Outside the upstairs window, in the March sunshine, the thaw was proceeding faster on the surface of the lane than on the grass in the garden between the rose bushes, at present no more than pruned back bunches of stalks. George believed in hard pruning. But even in the lane the snow lingered in all the shadows. There were three inches of it by the foot of the blackberry hedge. White streaks jutted out along the shadows cast by the taller parts of the hedge. As the shadows moved, the streaks melted. A horse, ridden by one of the girl grooms from the stables down in Kingsbridge, clip-clopped past, snorting through distended nostrils, lifting its feet in little bucking motions, rolling its eyes, and generally regarding life with a considerable alarm.

Another and lighter clip-clopping sounded along the passage leading to the bedroom. The door opened. George turned from the window to see Judy. With short high heeled steps she approached him — but no little blue cape any more. For long he had adored it and for long, to please him, she had worn it. Then, one day, she had not. When he remonstrated, she had turned on him with a sharpness that shook him. 'I'm not going to be imprisoned in it for ever. I'm not a doll!'

Now, she began playfully to rearrange the row of pens and pencils in the breast pocket of his shabby Oxford blazer (the splendid new one hung in the wardrobe, reserved for high occasions).

He held up the newspaper. 'D'you want to keep this old copy? Historical interest.'

'Yes. I *love* history. But never mind about that now. No more smoking for me!' She poked a half full packet of cigarettes into the pocket. 'Or drinking.' She brandished in her other hand a book with a blue and pink striped cover, its title, *Preparing for Baby*, stamped on in letters of gold. 'Mark' (she had already decided on the name and sex) 'is to be the perfect child.' She reached up and put her arms round a bull neck. 'With a big strong father like you, how could he fail?'

George glowed. As the begetter of her child, he knew himself to be her hero. He dropped the newspaper on to the carpet, and the fall and rise of monarchs was forgotten. He swept her slim form to him. 'With such a pretty and devoted mother, how could he fail?' He kissed the tip of her nose.

'Don't treat me like a child! Kiss me on the mouth.'

Though startled, he obliged.

'I was in Morgan Brothers' yesterday, and they had a marvellous yellow cot for ten pounds —'

'Ten pounds! We can't afford that, love.'

'This is the biggest moment of my life.' Her fluttered her eyelashes. 'Isn't our son worth ten pounds?'

'Of course, but . . . My income isn't —'

'We'll live on potatoes.' (Once again, the potatoes soon failed to dominate the menu.) 'We'll get a lodger. Bed and Breakfast. We'd easily get four pounds for the room alone. Then a bit more for his food, whatever it costs, plus something for the cooking. I'll put an advertisement in the *Tunbridge Wells Chronicle*.'

Mr Tremble, when he arrived, was a retired man recently widowed, and therefore perpetually on the edge of tears. He played trombone in the local brass band. Thursday was practice day.

The first morning he slowly descended the staircase, his thin body hanging over a half filled chamber-pot which he carried in a trembling hand. 'I'm going to empty this into the outside u-r- rinal.' His r's were very strong.

'Mr Tremble, do leave it upstairs,' said Judy. 'I can deal with it when I do your room.'

The next morning he rattled his way down, the cup in which Judy had brought him his early tea dancing in its saucer. She was unable to persuade him to leave this in his room also, and the slow moving rattle descended every day.

'That man gets me down,' George burst out finally.

Judy sprang to protect her financial investment. To the yellow cot in the 'perfect' nursery had been added a matching yellow chest of drawers for holding toys, nappies and the like. 'He's an *old* man. He *can't* change his ways.'

On the first morning after his arrival, she had served the three of them with a breakfast cereal, then brought in the toast. Mr Tremble sat unmoving.

'Help yourself, Mr Tremble.'

His sunken blue eyes gazed at her in astonishment. 'Where's The Fry? Isn't there going to be a Fry?'

She hastened to cook him bacon and eggs.

'I'm going out now,' he said in a reverent tone, 'to put flowers on The Grave.' A moment later he was back again. 'I forgot The Hat.' He covered his cropped grey hair with a bruised looking headpiece, and stooped his way down the lane towards The Grave.

Next morning, and thereafter, Judy was careful not to omit The Fry.

'The Wife,' observed Mr Tremble, his eyes watering, 'always served The Fry. Always.'

George, leaving the rugby field one afternoon (he always continued with his rugby until the end of the Easter term, that is, the end of March or beginning of April), was surprised to be greeted by a sexy smile. Betty Coombes was displaying her legs, well shaped but over slender for her full blown figure, in fish- net stockings. Cradled in the crook of her right arm was her ginger tomcat, grown to an enormous size since he had been 'doctored'. He looked like a good-natured cushion.

She lifted up Emperor and gazed into his golden eyes. 'Jeepers, creepers,' she sang, 'where did you get those peepers? Jeepers, creepers, where did you get those eyes?' She kissed him on the nose.

'Are you out for a walk?' enquired George.

She passed a beringed hand over her raven hair, set off with two Spanish combs. 'Judy said you were playing rugby. I came to watch those muscles of yours in action.' She billowed her ripe charms at him.

George's surprise moved up a notch into astonishment. What had brought all this on? 'I must be getting home to my tea.'

'Emperor and I have to be getting back too. Don't we, Emperor? It's time for our saucer of milk. We'll walk along with you.' At his gate she paused. 'Look us up at the Rainbow some time.' She fluttered her long false eyelashes. 'We've some nice girls there who would like to meet you.'

George's astonishment moved up a further notch into alarm. 'I've a nice girl at home,' he said a little stiffly.

Betty showed two pearly rows of teeth, lifted up one of Emperor's velvet forepaws, waved it at George in farewell, and flaunted her way down the lane.

As he strode along the path to his front door, he became conscious of Judy's blue eyes on him through the window.

In the kitchen cum dining-room cum sitting-room, she pointed to the smaller table which she had set by the window with the best view of the garden. 'Your tea's ready.'

He noted her knitting disposed with careful carelessness on the arm of a chair, the exercise books which he had been correcting left in orderly disorder on a window seat. A home, she was wont to say, should look lived in. Things should be left lying around just where they would naturally be (though nature would sometimes be assisted with a touch here and a push there).

He bisected a crumpet dripping with butter. 'What's with Betty? I didn't know she was a rugby fan.'

'I'm proud of your strength. I said she ought to see you playing.'

He watched her jigging up and down on her heels and smiling at him. Was there an element of playacting? 'I don't think you ought to encourage her.'

'Why? What has she done?'

'Er — nothing.' Betty Coombes had, after all, made Judy's wedding clothes. She was Judy's best friend. He must tread warily.

'She admires you.'

'Judy, what is all this about? I know you're interested in people and like to — to help them arrange their lives. I know that Betty is, so to speak, between marriages. But you're surely not . . . Are you tired of me already?'

'No. Of course not.' She picked up the book with the blue and pink striped cover. Standing on one leg, she curved the small foot of the other round her calf. 'I'm over a month pregnant. There's always a risk of a miscarriage.'

'It says so in *Preparing for Baby*?'

'I think we ought to give up intercourse for the time being.'

He put down his knife and stared in front of him. 'Of course. Yes, of course. The baby comes first. The baby comes absolutely first.'

'The book says some people disagree about there being a risk —'

'Oh, never mind that. Never mind that. I wouldn't be ready to take so much as a half per cent risk. I know how much the baby means to you.'

'And to you?'

'Of course. But you come first.'

He picked up his knife and began to bisect a second crumpet. 'I'll manage.' He dropped the knife and it clattered on to the plate. 'You haven't been discussing me with Betty Coombes?'

She put down the elevated foot and took a step back. 'You'll have to do something. I was only trying —'

'I'm not an animal. The baby's just as important to me as he is to you. If you can go without, I can go without. Discussing me with Betty Coombes!'

Her eyes were round. It was the first time that she had seen the stolid George so roused. 'You're — you're a virile man.'

'Precisely. Not a virile animal.'

'But you've got to do *something*.'

George cast a harrassed look about the room. 'Well, then, couldn't we manage something between us. A hand, perhaps.'

'I think that's disgusting.'

'Then why not leave me alone? I haven't pressed for anything. Just leave me alone to manage my disgusting body as best I may. Leave me my privacies.' He rose from the table, trembling.

'You haven't finished your tea!'

'I must get back to the school. I have to take over from Charlie.'
He marched to the door and closed it behind him.

'George! George!' She ran to the window.

He shut the gate and was gone.

His great stride along the lane brought back a measure of calm. Judy, jealous of female shadows on a cinema screen, arranging a liaison between Betty Coombes and himself! That her love of managing people should proceed as far as this! Betty Coombes, her best friend, desired Judy's husband, and Judy considered that she had it in her gift to bestow him upon her! Temporarily, of course. Doubtless that was understood. So the matchmaker in Judy could suppress the jealous woman! Perhaps he had over-reacted. Perhaps she had feared that his physical necessities might lead him into foreign fields where she couldn't hope to remain in control, and she was merely seeking to keep him nearer home.

He had reached the wayside shrine. The Madonna bent her tender gaze upon her Baby. Ahead, the grey-plastered pile of Worcester Hall Preparatory School reared its bogus castellations to the thin haze of the now early April sky.

It being Saturday, he turned right towards the playing fields and the sound of boys' voices. On Wednesdays and Saturdays there were no afternoon lessons. In the finer weather of spring, summer and early autumn, the boys were taken into the fields.

The Head Boy Juniper Major, his face shining with Clean Living, was batting in the nets with an impeccably straight bat. The bowling was provided by his younger brother Juniper Minor the pianist (still striving to perfect *Soldiers of Christ, Arise*). Juniper Minimus, waving a small Irish Republican flag, was making an anti-British speech to two of his classmates who, engrossed in a game of French cricket, were paying not the smallest attention. Huntington and Godfrey-Travers were engaged in a bicycle race clockwise round the perimeter of the playing area, which comprised all three cricket cum rugby pitches. Slygrin, as usual being thoroughly silly, was riding his bicycle round in an anticlockwise direction, strictly forbidden in order to eliminate head-on collisions. Tunney the Fat Boy, a lad alas with an unhealthy mind in an unhealthy body, had intimidated some of the smallest boys into kicking a soccer ball at him to give him practice in keeping goal, the goal being indicated by two rolled up sweaters placed on the grass. The diminutive Carruthers was attempting to punt a rugby ball almost half as big as himself.

George caught sight of a grey head illuminated by hazy sunshine. Charlie, burdened with his weight of learning, drooped as he strolled over the grass. His hand was suddenly raised dramatically. Was he enacting to himself some Shakespearean role? No, it was to arrest Slygrin upon his sinful path. A notebook was elegantly extracted from the side pocket of a frock coat. Plainly Slygrin was being given a Bad Mark. Details of this, and of the imposition set, would later be transferred to the Conduct Book kept in the staff room. The Conduct Book was surveyed at the end of each week by Mr Featherstonhaugh. Three bad marks within the same week exposed the culprit to the risk of The Slipper.

'Hello, Charlie! I'm ready to take over.'

'You look upset. Anything wrong?'

'No. No. All is well.'

'Just had to throw the Old Vic at that sly customer. Can't stop playing the silly ass for one moment.' Unconvinced, he was still surveying his friend's rugged countenance. 'Got a favour to ask. Don't hesitate to refuse. It will land you in being on duty all day tomorrow, Sunday, and one does need a respite from the little blighters. Neither Commander Robinson nor Snipe is free.'

'You want me to take on your evening duty?'

'Then I'll do yours the next day, so you'll have that day totally free. At least of duties. When are we ever free of classes?'

'Of course, Charlie. Hope it doesn't mean that Mrs Hare is poorly.'

'Mrs Hare is always delicate. But this time it's the vicar of St Andrew's. Unwell, and can't take the Sunday services. He's an extraordinary man. Very Low Church. Intensely dislikes bishops. Because of their robes, calls them peacocks. He dislikes the younger generation too, unless they're members of his choir. In fact you could almost say that he likes everybody except mankind.'

George managed a grin. Charlie always had the effect of cheering him up. 'He can't be very popular.'

'He's half emptied his church. At the rate he's going, he'll finish up with a congregation of three: God the Father playing the organ,

God the Son taking up the collection, and the Holy Ghost cleaning up afterwards.'

George put back his curly head and his mighty shoulders shook. His roar of mirth caused Juniper Major to take his eye off the ball, make an appalling stroke, and have his stumps uprooted; Juniper Minimus to drop his Republican flag and lose the thread of his harangue; Huntington and Godfrey-Travers to get their front wheels interlocked and so bite the dust; Slygrin to stick in the boundary hedge through which he had been trying to force his way to visit without permission the sweet shop along the road; the Fat Boy to concede a goal; and Carruthers, attempting a mighty punt to touch, clean to miss the ball and fall flat on his back.

'You're an outrageous fellow, Charlie. I've a good mind to recommend you to the Archbishop of Canterbury for excommunication — or perhaps for a bishopric. You'd certainly liven things up.'

'Well, it's a deal then. I take over from you on Monday. I'd never let you down, except in a crisis.'

A titter arose. Unnoticed, Mr Snipe was at that moment passing behind them, his sharp nose pointing in the direction of the small wooden pavilion. Under his arm he carried a load of freshly whitened cricket pads. These he would deposit on their shelf in preparation for the coming summer term.

When George opened his gate that evening, the kitchen-dining-room appeared to be in darkness. On entering, he found Judy, astonishingly wearing her long unseen little blue cape, finishing off her cooking on the coal fired iron range. The sole light was provided by four candles in saucers on a shelf and two in tall candlesticks on the main table. Candles always indicated a special supper.

She noted his eye on the splendid chocolate mousse, his favourite sweet, between the table candles. 'Chicken curry not too hot, just the way you like it, coming up.' Though her lipsticked smile was bright, her blue eyes regarded him anxiously.

He kissed her. 'Sorry for the huff this morning, darling. You were only trying to do your best for me.'

'George, are you sure —'

He laid his finger across her lips. 'Don't, love! Remember, I've been a bachelor of many years' experience.'

'But George —'

'Don't love, *please*. I can manage. No trouble at all. Now where's that curry I've been hearing so much about?'

As they ate it he said, 'I've done a duty swap with Charlie. Means I'll be up at the school virtually all day tomorrow.'

She looked up sharply. 'You'll be away all day?'

'It — it isn't the first time I've had to . . . It's a Sunday service he has to take. Isn't that all right?'

'Perfectly all right. But I'll miss you.'

'I could come down briefly —'

'No, no. There's absolutely no need. No need at all.'

His brown eyes regarded her. Had there been a touch of urgency?

When he returned in the evening, she beckoned him with her crooked finger. 'Come up into the nursery.'

There, to join company with the yellow cot and chest of drawers, and now also a play-pen, were a pair of saffron curtains, pelmetted, extending, to give an appearance of height to the room, from ceiling to floor. She must have spent most of the day putting them up!

But his admiration was marred by shock. 'Why didn't you tell me?'

'I wanted it to be a surprise. Don't worry about the cost. My rent will take care of that.'

He regarded the curtains dubiously. Was the modest sum received weekly from Mr Tremble really able to cover it all? But, because of the initiative she had shown in managing their home and conducting her pregnancy, he still had faith in her. Many a time he had admirred the energy with which she, such a little thing, had slapped the distemper on to the wall with the big brush.

Next morning she abruptly left the breakfast table. He heard her vomiting into the sink. He followed her to the scullery.

She rinsed out the dishcloth and wiped her mouth. 'Morning sickness.'

'Is there anything one can take for it?'

'Glucose is supposed to be good.'

When he returned in the evening, he pushed into her hands a brown paper bag filled with sticks of barley sugar. 'Got it from the school tuck shop.'

She threw her arms round his neck and kissed him.

Chapter Seven

Towards the end of the summer term, in late July, Judy engaged the services of Rose.

'I'm six months pregnant, George.'

'Five, isn't it?'

'Well, five. I need domestic help. She's only coming part time. She still has her job at the school.'

'Yes. Yes, of course.'

'You look worried. Is it the money? That distended vein in my leg . . . The doctor said I should take things more easily. My blood pressure is a bit high.'

'No, no. That's all right. I'll take on additional coaching.'

'Yes, that's the solution.'

When Rose appeared a day or two later, George, stripped to the waist, was washing himself in cold water at the sink. He had been sunbathing in a nook outside the back door. There, he had been marking the papers of the Senior and Junior General Knowledge Tests; two marks for a correct answer, one for a wrong one with traces of rightness in it, nought for an out and out mistake or no answer. The tests, for the whole school, took place each summer term. One of the questions in the Junior test had been, 'What do we call a ship that goes under the water?' Carruthers' answer had been firm. 'Waterlogged.' George's red-ink filled pen, reserved for correcting exercises, had descended and written down a 'one'. Then, with a grin, he changed it to 'two'. Damn it, the fellow hadn't been wrong!

At the sound of the knock on the door, he half turned and called over his shoulder, 'Come in.'

She entered diffidently, a country rose now in the twentieth year.

'Don't mind me.' He poured a mug of water over his thick curls. The water streamed down his sweating neck and shoulders. 'Shan't be a minute. Just cooling myself. Did Mrs Brown tell you what to do? She's down in the town visiting friends.'

'I was to tidy and clean the house.'

'You carry on.'

Her soft work-strong hands moved about their task. Her gentle eyes were on his wide brown shoulders and the supple undulations of the muscles of his back as he vigorously towelled himself.

He turned. 'Nice to have you with us, Rose.'

'Thank you.' Was he noticing her frock? It was her Sunday best. No. He looked at her, but he had no eyes for her. She went to the wall cupboard and extracted a dustpan and brush.

Next morning Judy lingered in bed and George descended to get her a cup of tea. He found a letter lying in the wire basket of the letter-box. It was addressed to himself. A typed envelope it was, with the firm's name and address printed in the upper left hand corner.

Mystified, he opened it. 'Dear Sir, We respectfully draw your attention to the enclosed account for goods purchased by Mrs Brown. Payment on this account is now much overdue. All our previous requests to Mrs Brown for a payment have gone unanswered. Doubtless this is due to an oversight on her part . . .' He glanced at the attached invoice. His eye caught the words 'infant's cot', 'chest of drawers', 'play-pen', 'curtains'. There were also dresses and other items.

Stunned, the tea unfetched, he strode upstairs. 'Judy, what is this?' He brandished the letter under her eyes.

She sat up in bed. 'Oh,' she said perkily, 'they make a fuss. A small payment will satisfy them.'

'You said you were taking care of the nursery bills out of your rent from Mr Tremble.'

'You don't do the shopping. You don't know how much prices have gone up. You don't give me much.'

'You said you were taking care of the nursery out of your rent payments.'

'I didn't mean it *literally*.'

'Judy, you must mean it literally. We can't afford anything like this, even with my coaching. You must know that very well. How could a good manager like you do such a thing?'

'A small payment —'

'Judy, love, they won't stand for a small payment. They'll expect a very substantial payment. Have you been pledging my credit anywhere else?'

'No. No, this is the only one.'

He was watching her small features closely. There hadn't been much conviction . . . 'These things get around in a small town like this. If I'm taken to court, for how long d'you think I'd hold my job?'

'I'll pay them the whole of my next rent.'

'Judy, your rent is only four pounds a week, plus a little for meals. They'll expect at least ten. I'm sorry, love, but this has come as a great shock. You must see that.'

'You've got an Oxford MA. Surely you could ask for more money.'

'I wouldn't get more. Schoolmasters are poorly paid. I'm sorry, love, but I must ask you to give me the whole of Tremble's rent every week until we've caught up.'

'Oh, very well.'

'You'll still make something out of cooking his breakfasts. We can't afford to spend any more on the nursery for a while. I'll have to write to these people telling them to close the account. I'll promise to clear it at the rate of five pounds a week — if they'll accept that. It's certainly all that I'll be able to scrape together week after week. We're already living up to the last penny of our income. I'll get your tea now.'

'I don't want it.'

'Do have your tea, sweetheart.'

'I've changed my mind.'

'Judy, I'm sorry —'

She turned her back on him and put her nose into the pillow. 'I want to rest.' He had plenty of money. Plenty. Of course he had. His family had plenty of money. Why didn't they help?

He glanced uncertainly at her. Then, with heavy heart, he left the room. It was their first real quarrel.

Thereafter she lost interest in Mr Tremble. One morning she even forgot The Fry. More in sorrow than in anger he rose from the table, put on The Hat, collected some flowers from the garden and, his eyes watering, made his way heavily towards The Grave.

A few days later, gripping the bannister with his trombone-playing earthernware hand, he called down, 'Mrs B-r-rown, I want me biscuits.'

'I'm busy at the moment.'

It was George's turn to hasten to protect what had now become *his* investment. 'I'll bring them up to you, Mr Tremble.'

'I can't stand that man,' she hissed. 'It turns my stomach, emptying his chamberpot every morning.'

'Let Rose do it, love.'

It was only a few days later when Mr Tremble again addressed Judy from over the bannisters. 'Mrs B-r-rown, there isn't any paper in the urinal to wipe me a-r-rse.'

With a stifled cry Judy, snatching up her knitting bag, stormed out, slamming the front door behind her.

'One moment, please, Mr Tremble!' The harrassed George sprinted after her. He saw her maternity gowned form moving towards the town, doubtless to the Rainbow Inn and Betty Coombes. 'Judy! Judy! What is it, love?'

'Either that man goes, or I go.'

'Love, what about your — our — account with the shop? Then there's Rose's wages.'

'Let your family help, since you *say* you haven't the money. It's *their* grandchild. They *want* a grandchild, don't they?'

'We can't ask them. My father's only his pension.'

'I should have stayed with Captain Archie Simpson. There's a bit of money around down there. This day after day penny-pinching! You'll have to choose between Mr Tremble and me. I'm not going to stay another day in the house with that disgusting man.'

'All right, Judy. But I can't put him out on the roadside just like that. The law wouldn't allow it, for one thing. I'll give him a fortnight.'

'You only have to give him a week's notice. He pays weekly.'

'Be reasonable, sweetheart! As you said yourself, he's an old man. It still isn't easy to find accommodation after all the houses that were bombed in the war. Of course, if he can find a place in a week . . .'

'What about Mrs Finch?'

'With all those children! What room would she have?'

'When I was working at the school with her and Rose, they said they had a garden shed where they could put the boys. That would leave them a room. They need the money. Sergeant Finch is never out of the pub.'

George sighed. 'Very well. I'll speak to Tremble.' He put his great arm round her shoulders. 'Come home, love.'

'No. I arranged to spend the afternoon with Betty. She's helping me with my knitting for the baby. As I've come this far, I might as well go down a bit early. Archie'll stand me lunch.'

George, his shoulders uncharacteristically slumped, returned to his house. Captain Archie Simpson! That bounder! He searched in a cupboard and found a roll of toilet paper. Ascending the stairs, he extracted the cardboard centre of the exhausted roll from the wire wall-holder and inserted the replacement.

He descended to the sitting-room. From the table he picked up a pile of exercise books. Carrying them and a chair past Rose in the scullery, he took up his place in his usual nook outside the back door. He pulled off his shirt. The warmth of the sunshine, bathing his face and hairy chest, momentarily soothed his worry. For a time his pen moved over pages making red corrections. But his mind hadn't escaped from its turmoil. Dimly he was aware, through the wide open back door, of Rose peeling potatoes at the sink.

He was aroused to his surroundings by the strong smell of cheap scent. She had emerged to deposit the potato peelings into the bin just behind him. As she bent forward to do so, she put her head exaggeratedly close to him. The scent was from her hair! She must have scented it specially! His pulse quickened. He returned to his correcting and she to the washing of china. But he couldn't forget her bid to make him aware of her.

Half an hour later she was at the door again. 'I've finished in the house. Mrs Brown said I was to pick blackberries for supper. Will I take the milk pail or the basket?'

'The milk pail might be better. Hold the juice.' He turned about in his chair. Her light brown hair was gathered simply in a bun on her neck. Her skirt was shabby and unfashionable, but scrupulously cleaned and pressed. Her white laundered blouse fell softly over her breasts. Her cardigan was neatly darned at the shoulder. He stood up. On an impulse he said, 'I'll come and help you.' He pulled on his shirt.

They moved slowly along the hedgerows in the direction of the school, she taking the right hand side, he the left. When they reached the shrine, they turned right towards the playing fields. Each time his hands became filled with blackberries, he crossed over to empty them into the milk pail. Their fingers became purple stained. Once, the back of his hand touched hers as she held the handle of the pail. Neither spoke.

They passed the playing fields, at the moment silent and deserted. He glanced behind him. They were out of sight of the school buildings. He crossed the lane and stood beside her, picking from the same bush. Still neither spoke. Even when the pail was full, they strolled on. She changed the pail over to her further hand. From time to time the backs of their nearer hands touched.

He took her hand, so much larger than Judy's but soft and feminine for all that. He led her into a field. They descended the slope towards the bank of the river. In that golden afternoon, the smell of the long grass filling their nostrils, they sat down out of sight of the passing punts.

She sank back on to her elbows. A ladybird landed on her. Bright in its metallic coat of red dotted with black spots, the ladybird made its way across her lap to reach the grass on the other side. Just as it had succeeded in doing so, George, now reclining on one elbow, reached across, picked it up carefully, turned it round, and set it down again on her skirt.

The ladybird obediently set off on the return journey that had been dictated to it by the giant hand that had descended from the sky. On reaching the grass once more, it found the same gentle but masterful hand descending upon it and redirecting it back. The ladybird was not quite so compliant this time. Though it returned in the general direction, it began to assert its individuality by doing so only on a diagonal that took it ever upwards towards Rose's blouse. Once more it reached the grasslands. But this time it was Rose who picked it up and directed its progress back across her blouse.

From here on George assumed command of operations, turning and returning the ladybird across the snowy expanse of the blouse. In doing so, his fingers several times touched (inadvertently) Rose's breasts. She sank off her elbows and lay back with her legs stretched out together and her eyes staring straight up at the sky. The ladybird was forgotten. It succeeded in reaching a blade of grass, where it perched. George rolled off his elbow until he was lying on top of Rose. So they remained, motionless, under the late July sun. In that silent concourse of their still bodies, nothing was declared and nothing was denied and everything was evaded: the difference in their ages, the difference in their education, the fact that he had a wife. Debts, exercise books, sexual privation, melted away and floated down the river with the punts.

At length they stirred and walked back hand in hand. When they reached the Madonna, their hands parted. At his gate he took the pail of blackberries from her. They looked at one another. Then she turned and made her way down the lane to her home. In all that afternoon, the sun a fiery wheel rolling across the sky, the punts dropping down the river under the willow trees and vanishing like dreams — in all that afternoon they had exchanged not a single word.

As for the ladybird, a little fatigued by her long walk, and pondering on the strange ways of mankind, she too went home — and *she* wasn't saying anything either.

Chapter Eight

On parting from Rose Finch, George set down on the garden path the milk can brimming with blackberries. Some of them were touched with red; it was early in their season. With a greater feeling of peace than he had known for some time, he stripped off his jacket and rolled up his shirt sleeves, displaying hairy muscular forearms. A rose scented movement of air began to dry the patch of perspiration on the back of his shirt. The sound of a mowing machine drifted in from the distance. A young bird, perched on top of the fence, took off with its wings frantically fanning the air and landed again on the fence a few yards further on. After a rest, it repeated the exercise. On the path a fledgling picked up a hairpen, doubtless one of Judy's, decided it wasn't edible, dropped it, and hopped on its way in search of something tastier. 'More, more,' piped another fledgling. A parent, appearing apparently from no where, hopped up silently, rammed a small worm into the ever open beak, and departed.

He deposited his fourteen stone on a wood and canvas garden chair, turned his face to the evening sun, and closed his eyes. What did he think of Rose? In a way, nothing. He knew no more of her now than he knew before. She hadn't altered the general course of his life in any way. The episode had been nothing more than a spontaneous and distinctly surprising expedition up a side turning. She had been femininity, an island of peace in the restless toss of the waves, a brief holiday from the difficult tasks of being a schoolmaster and a husband to Judy. She had been a nice girl who had fulfilled the need of the moment. He must never allow it to happen again, of course. Still . . . The way she had thrust her scented hair towards him . . . It had been rather flattering from a girl of her age — what, twenty perhaps? — to an old buffer of thirty-six. Not that Judy herself was all that much older. Twenty-six when they had first met.

Still only twenty-seven. Hm . . . There was the ghost of a smile. Perhaps he was overdoing the 'old buffer' bit!

So, when he opened his eyes at the squeak of the gate and saw Judy, the quick clip-clop of her high heeled court shoes sobered now to a more matronly progression in brogues, he had no feeling of guilt but rather one of resuming once more the course of normal living. And, since they had parted on bad terms, that meant apprehension.

To his relief, he saw that her vividly lipsticked mouth was half open in a smile, revealing her small white teeth. The ear-rings at her dainty ears, matching the blue of her eyes, caught the level shafts of the sun and shot blue points of fire at him. Her light brown hair was permed as perkily as ever. Her intensely youthful prettiness contrasted with her matronly six months pregnant body, the loose hanging maternity dress, the slightly dilated vein on one of her otherwise immaculate legs, a vein that the doctor had assured her would return to normal when the pressure was taken off it after the birth. She had relented and, for a time, they had made love short of penetration; the baby's domain was on no account to be approached. But these occasions had grown ever more seldom as she had increasingly diminished the role of wife in favour of that of mother-to-be. George understood. In this at least they were as one.

'Sunbathing as usual!' She fluttered her long lashes at him, but the glance behind them probed, gauging his mood. 'Look what I've done!' She fished about in the large cloth bag she was carrying and extracted a tiny woollen cardigan — blue, of course. Was it not to be a boy, and his name Mark, after her father? She had been so emphatic about the strength of the presentiment she had received, standing before the Madonna, as to its being a son, that he had not had the heart to urge her to keep an open mind. 'All done with practically no help from Betty. Say I'm a clever girl!'

He smiled. 'You are indeed a clever girl.'

'Encouraged, she put away the little garment and resumed her approach. Conscious of her increased weight, she lowered herself gingerly on to his lap. Her gaze travelled about the rose bushes. 'I love this cottage; every part of it fills me with joy. And our twilight teas when you are off duty. I look out of the window to see if you are coming, and there you always are right on time with some little sweetmeat bought in the school tuck shop.'

He knew that this was her way of apologising. She could never bring herself to say sorry. He smiled again. 'What about a song?'

'You first.'

He rendered *Lullaby of Broadway* in an out of tune voice that always made her laugh. 'And now you.'

'Which?'

'My favourite, of course.'

It was no longer possible to wear the little blue cape. Neither was it possible to curl herself up like a kitten in his lap, but she went as near to it as she could. She put her mouth close to his ear, and her voice was soft. 'Tiptoe, to the window, by the window, that's where I'll be — Come tiptoe, through the tulips, with me . . . ' She placed her arm round his neck. 'I don't know why I bother to go down to that Rainbow Inn. You're worth more than the whole lot of them put together.'

'Oh, I'm a rather dull sort of a chap.'

'No. You have breeding. You have dignity. They all know it.'

He kissed her on the lips. 'Well, thank you, darling.'

She drew in her breath sharply, moved restlessly on his lap, then drew it in again. 'Junior's getting obstreperous.' She had first become aware of the movements of the baby a month back. She drew in her breath again and rose from his lap. 'Cut it out, Mark! What d'you think you're playing at?' Her eyes fell on the milkpail of blackberries standing just behind his chair. 'So Rose didn't forget! What a pile, so early in the year! They'll have to be cooked; they're only half ripe. It must have taken her hours.'

'I helped her.'

'You helped Rose pick blackberries!'

'I was just browned off correcting exercise books, exercise books, exercise books. After our — tiff — I couldn't concentrate.'

'I ought to feel jealous.'

He stood up, lifted the can with one hand, put the other round her shoulders, guided her towards the front door, and said, 'On the day that you start being seriously jealous of anyone, darling, on that day you'll really be wasting your time.'

'There are lots of pretty girls.'

'But only one Judy.'

She carried the blackberries into the scullery and returned. He made his way to the pile of exercise books on the table, where the blue and pink striped *Preparing for Baby* always lay ready for instant consultation. This never ending accumulation of exercise books had grown more and more merciless as he had increased his coaching of outside pupils, to add to the already heavy load of the work of the school itself.

He heard an exclamation from Judy. She stood at the foot of the staircase. Her plucked and pencilled eyebrows were raised in alarm. 'I almost tripped.'

'I don't think you need be too scared of that. I've noticed you adjusting all the time. As the baby grows, you lean back more and more.'

'Do I? Oh, well. Not to worry.' She went up slowly, holding the bannister.

He sat down. The roses out in the garden nodded their heads at him through the window pane. With a sigh he peeled open the cover of the top book. He turned to the breast pocket of his jacket, hung on the back of his chair. From the battery of pens and pencils he selected his correcting pen, primed with red ink.

He had hardly underlined the first mistake, when the urgent cry descended the stairs. 'George! George!'

Throwing down the pen, he leapt up the steps two at a time.

She was standing at the basin in the toilet tugging at one of her fingers, her face pale with panic. 'My hand's swollen. I can't get my rings off.'

'Take it easy, love. There's no problem, no problem at all. I'll get them off with soap and water.'

He succeeded at once. She stood trembling, beads of moisture on her small brow. The previous week, on a crowded afternoon bus from Kingsbridge to Tunbridge Wells, she had developed the same panic. With her increased bulk, she had felt hemmed in and unable to escape. George and she had been obliged to move up to the seat by the exit. It had been the beginning of her claustrophobia.

On arrival, they had gone to their dentist. One of her teeth was to be extracted. Again the panic as the mask was pressed down over her face prior to the administration of gas. In its place a local anaesthetic had had to be injected.

As she had come out of the surgery she had said to George, 'I asked the dentist for calcium tablets to prevent the loss of any more teeth. He said they were no use. The body couldn't absorb them. He said that the only hope was to have calcium injections, and that they weren't much good either.'

George's forehead, beneath its thatch of thick curly hair, had furrowed. 'I don't believe it. I don't believe a word of it. If the baby's developing skeleton is drawing away calcium, how can the body not desire it and be able to use it if it's accompanied by the right vitamins? Let's go to a chemist.'

Thereafter he had daily fed osteo-calcium tablets to her, gradually increasing the dose as her pregnancy progressed. In the event, she lost no more teeth. She also reported that an edginess in her muscles had become a thing of the past.

A few days later she really came a tumble. Hearing the bump, he charged upstairs and found her sitting on the floor in wild distress.

He sat down beside her and gathered her to his great woollen-sweatered chest, rocking her to and fro. 'There's no danger of a miscarriage, sweetheart. None at all. None at all. It's quite common for women to have the odd fall.'

Her sobbing ceased. 'How d'you know?'

'I can read too.'

'*Preparing for Baby* said so?'

'*Preparing for Baby* said so.'

'Oh. And it doesn't bring on a miscarriage?'

'Extremely rarely.'

'I don't know what I'd do, George, if I lost Mark. He's the moon and the stars to me.'

'I know, love. I know.'

'I dream of the time when he'll be born, and I wheel him round the Christmas shops, and hold him up to look at Santa Claus.'

Thereafter she moved with even greater caution. George, noting this, left each morning for the school without anxiety. Rose was always quietly helpful when she could be present; so much he learnt from Judy. Yes, Rose was indeed a nice girl.

But he had little room for her in his thoughts. Her presence was crowded out by his heavy burden of work. It was crowded out by Judy's approaching confinement and her vivid reactions to every smallest adventure or misadventure, poured out in a cascade of words that left small space for any of his own. The memories of the episode by the grassy bank ever further and further slipped away; slipped away like the slender punts into the haze sucked up from the evening river by a huge orange sun. As for the ladybird, she had long ago dismissed the entire affair from her mind.

And Rose, who had to see George on and off not only in his home, but also at the school when she was setting the tables or serving at the hatch? Ah, Rose . . .

The tension between Judy and Mr Tremble refused to go away.

'Before I — we — give Tremble notice to quit, we must first have found somewhere for him to go.' George's brow was crinkled under his thatch of red curls; however was he going to make up the lost revenue? 'You're close to Rose. Have her sound out her mother about this room you say she has.'

Judy's eyes sparkled. She hooked her arm through his. 'Let's both go now! It's after their tea time. They'll be in.'

They proceeded down the lane at her matronly pace. The slated roof came into view, thrusting up above the roadside blackberry bushes. And there was the wooden gate, its bottom hinge adrift, spelling out in white metal letters, 'The Brambles.'

George's large fingers struggled with the knot of the string securing the gate, before he succeeded in opening it. Above them Rose stood in the small vegetable garden. Her back was turned to them as she hung her laundry on the line, including the frumpish bloomers favoured by her mother and herself

'Hello, Rose! Let me help you.' Judy's hands, still small and elegant despite the slight swelling of pregnancy, busied themselves alongside the large work-strong hands of the younger girl.

'There's no cause for you to be doing this, Mrs Brown. You should be saving your strength. Did you want to see my mother?'

'My husband and I are interested in that room for Mr Tremble.'

'Mother'll be glad of the money.' For a moment Rose allowed her eyes to rest on the rugged George.

She led the way into the house. George's eyes too found a moment to linger on the dark brown hair gathered so simply in a bun on the nape of the neck, the skirt shabby but scrupulously clean and pressed, the cardigan neatly darned at the shoulder. He felt once again the sensation of peace steal over him.

As they entered the kitchen-sitting-room (*The Brambles* was not unlike George's cottage, if less well built and on a smaller scale), shouts arose. Three boys, whose ages George reckoned at approximately ten, eight and six, lay locked in a wrestling match on the threadbare carpet. A fourth boy, age about four, sat beside his mother at the table drinking a large mug of cocoa, part of which stained his chin, mouth, and some way up his cheeks. Evidently Sergeant Finch, at present up at the school, was resolved to ensure the continuation of his name.

As Judy entered behind Rose, Mrs Finch examined her visitor doubtfully. A girl who announced that she wasn't 'anything really'! Mrs Finch unknotted her grey head-scarf, then knotted it more firmly into place.

But the next moment her spare figure rose to its feet. Her eyes, the same grey as her scarf, scanned respectfully the three golden crowns on the pocket of the magnificent brand new dark blue blazer. 'Good afternoon, sir.'

George stooped in through the doorway. 'Please sit down, Mrs Finch. Don't let us disturb you.' He pulled back a chair from the table for his wife. 'You've a fine bunch of lads there! I've got my eye on them as future recruits to the town rugby team!'

Mrs Finch clapped her hands. 'Off you go, the three of you, or the gentleman and I won't be able to make ourselves heard. Go on! Into the garden!'

They trooped out cheerfully.

'Is this the whole of your family?'

'No, sir. The eldest be five girls, Rose here, and the other four in service.'

'My heavens! That's a great family for these days!' He took a chair beside Judy.

Mrs Finch laughed as she resumed her seat. 'You can credit his nibs with that. When he's had a glass or two, I'm not even there. I'm just the football field on which a furious battle is fought between him and his genes. If there hasn't been a satisfactory outcome, then extra time is played. Blows are struck, cries for help are heard, and on one occasion even a bottle flew — the baby's.'

During this astonishing Rabelaisian outburst from the Plymouth Brother, or rather Sister, Rose's eyes had been fixed on George in ever growing consternation. At that moment the kettle on the range began to boil. She hastened to make the tea.

George, equally dumbfounded, pointed the conversation in a safer direction. 'Sometimes babies look like their sex, but usually you can't tell.'

'Oh, with my eldest son you could tell. Rose here as a baby was pretty, but he wasn't pretty at all. He was ugly. He had a long nose and a scowl. I was proud of him.'

George's expression of astonishment was equalled only by Judy's. 'Well,' he said, 'that's certainly one way of looking at it!'

Rose had interposed her buxom person between her mother and George as, leaning elaborately from his left side across the table, she placed a cup of tea on his right. 'I don't think you take sugar, Mr Brown.'

'Quite right, Rose. Must keep in training.'

'I'll fetch you a cup too, Mrs Brown.'

Judy raised her plucked and pencilled eyebrows archly. 'Ladies should be served first!'

Rose, blushing, hastened back to the teapot.

'Come on, laddie,' said Mrs Finch to her youngest, 'and say your prayers. Excuse me, Mrs Brown. I heard you telling Rose that you'd come about the room, but the little lad is tired out. He won't be a minute. Come on, Tommy, show the lady and gentleman how well you say your prayers.'

Tommy, after wiping some of the cocoa off his face with the back of his plump fist, began to rattle off his petitions. 'God bless Daddy Mummy brothers sisters grandpas grannies uncles aunties friends our father which art in heaven hallowed be thy name thy kingdom come on earth as it is in —'

'Tommy, Tommy, I won't tell you again! Thy kingdom come, they will be done . . .'

'Thy kingdom come thy will be done on earth as it is in heaven give us this day our daily trespasses —'

'Bread! Bread!'

'Give us this day our daily bread and deliver it from evil —'

'Tommy! Tommy!' She rumpled his mop of hair, rubbed the remaining cocoa off his face with a damp cloth, and kissed him with rough affection. 'Yer going to be an old heathen like your dad, ain't yer?' More kisses. 'Ain't yer?' She prodded him in the ribs until he squirmed and giggled. 'Off with you to bed.'

The tired little fellow rushed off to a small bed in the corner and scrambled in. His mother followed, pulled the blankets over him, kissed him on the forehead — and he was asleep.

'Well, Mrs Finch,' said George, 'if you're able to make a room available for our tenant Mr Tremble . . . He's a reliable payer.'

'I'd be glad of the money, sir. The older boys can go outside in the big shed. It can be made comfortable, even for the winter. And they're young! As I told Mrs Brown, I want to set up a Christian Guest House with what little I've saved these years. The more so now as I'm afeared my husband might lose his job at the school. I is afeared, sir, that he's fallen into the clutches of the Demon Drink. You won't tell at the school that I said that, sir? We need the money.'

'I wouldn't do anything to lose a man his job, Mrs Finch. I wouldn't like to lose my own. But he may lose it for himself. No school can afford — '

At that moment unsteady steps approached down the lane, accompanied by an unsteady voice raised in song. Both ascended the path up through the garden. A brown leathery face appeared at the window. A broken nose, red and pinched, was pressed against the pane. The song ceased. 'Hi, 'i, wot 'ave we 'ere? Hold — hold on till I see wot we 'ave 'ere.' He entered, bumping his head against the lintel of the doorway.

George decided, if trouble was to be avoided, that he had better make sure that he was recognised at once by the unfocused gaze. He stood up. 'Hello, Sergeant Finch! We've come to see if your good lady can make a room available for our Mr Tremble. You remember Mr Tremble?'

Sergeant Finch, though disposed to be friendly to the point of familiarity, on the other hand showed no desire to be out and out disrespectful to a member of the school teaching staff. Nor had he understood a word of what had been said to him.

Swaying gently, he caught hold of one of the lapels of the dark blue blazer. Rose's brown eyes once again became wide with concern and she took half a step forward.

'Cold for July, ain't it, boy? July! We ought to be sweating. Get out of this ruddy climate. Get away to Ors-trile-yer, boy.' Sergeant Finch spoke in a kind of good humoured fury. 'This country's done for. A proper mess they've got us into. Get away to Ors-trile-yer, boy. The minister for this and the minister for that, and them lords, all they know is Oxford and Cambridge and how to get drunk. Fiddle-faddle, fiddle-faddle, that's all they do. Why can't they leave us in peace? There's always a war here, or a war there. Life's funny, life's mysterious. I don't understand it. Don't do any work, boy, it'll only poison your mind. They've got themselves into such a mess now, they won't be able to get out of it. There's millions of men and women going to die. There's no escaping it now, boy, you know that?'

George, feeling it to be appropriate, nodded gravely. He half turned away his face to escape the alcoholic breath.

'All the cards,' resumed Segeant Finch, lurching dangerously, letting go George's lapel, and catching hold of the back of a chair, 'all the cards are down on the table. That's why they can't escape. Fiddle-faddle. Don't do any work, boy, it only turns men's 'atred against their own country. They come down 'ere, these bishops and lords, fiddle-faddling us. They must think we're daft. We're done for. It's one thing or the other now, boy, you know that, don't you?'

Again George, now escaping most of the fumes as Sergeant Finch clung to the chair, nodded gravely.

A note of dispair entered Sergeant Finch's voice. 'Life's funny, life's mysterious. I don't understand it.' He turned and pointed out of the window at the crooked chimneys of the oast-houses rising against the blue Kentish sky. 'I 'ate the country. I like town life. I'd like to live in London. There's not much fog there now. They was worse in the old days when the traffic was horse drawn. What 'appens when an 'orse gets frightened? Why, he steams. And that adds to the fog. D'you understand me, boy?'

Judy smiled. 'Why d'you live down here, then?'

'It's me old mother, m'am, in Tunbridge Wells. She's been hanging on for years. Eighty. But she's just gorne. Yes, just gorne. She's been 'anging on for years — fiddle-faddling.' Clutching at things, he moved towards an inner room. At the door he paused. 'Get away to Ors-trile-yer, boy.' He sniggered. 'The women in Ors-trile-yer is very hot.'

Mrs Finch's voice was sharp. 'Mind your manners to Mr Brown.'

Her husband winked at George. 'No disrespect. It's her fault. If ever I do anything a bit wrong, I do the decent thing and blame it on the wife. Always do the decent thing, boy, and blame it on the wife.' He swayed towards Judy, now leaning forward with her elbows on the table, so that her thighs might partly take the weight of her distended abdomen. 'No disrespect, m'am.' A bloodshot eye swivelled back to George. 'So long, boy, and good luck!' But, from its expression, it was clear that its owner didn't give very much for George's chances.

He vanished into the inner room. His voice arose in a fresh dispair. 'Life's funny. Life's mysterious. I don't understand it.' There was the crunch of bedsprings. Almost immediately afterwards snores arose.

Mrs Finch crossed to the door, glanced in, then closed it. 'Sir, please excuse —'

George held up his hand. 'That's all right, Mrs Finch. That's all right. But I can see why you're anxious about his job. If it's any comfort to you, mostly he keeps himself under a much better control at the school. Now, we've imposed on you long enough. Mrs Brown and I must be getting home. I'll have a word with Mr Tremble.'

He helped Judy to her feet. She linked her arm through his. Rose, of the gentle face and wholesome country prettiness, was at the front door in a flash to open it for them. As they passed through, George was conscious for a moment of a white freshly laundered blouse, under the unbuttoned cardigan, falling softly over breasts as soft.

Mrs Finch joined her daughter, who stood watching them slowly descending to the gate.

'You shouldn't be looking at a married man like that.'

'I can't help it, Mother. When he's near me, I just go into a jelly.'

The elder woman put an affectionate hand on her daughter's shoulder. 'What's the use of it, love? You can't show it to him. You can't speak of it to him.'

'Then I must love him in silence.'

Mrs Finch sighed. 'Well, you may have your chance yet, for that wife of his will come to no good.'

'Mother! You mustn't talk about her like that! She really loves her child. I seen it for myself.'

'Aye, she loves her coming bairn right enough. That's her great good. That's her great good. But I still see in her evil and destruction.'

'Mother! What are your reasons? Give me your reasons.'

But Mrs Finch's thin lips merely compressed themselves into a hard line.

As George and Judy walked into their kitchen, Mr Tremble was in the act of drooping his way down the staircase, his now empty afternoon teacup dancing in its saucer, his thick earthernware right hand gripping the bannister.

'Mrs B-r-r-own, I didn't have me biscuits.'

Judy, her blue eyes still asparkle, found the charity to reply, 'I'm so sorry, Mr Tremble. I quite forgot to put them out.' But tact was never her forte. 'We were at the Finch's, finding you another room.'

George's startled brown eyes were on her. 'Judy!'

Her expression of happiness faded, to be replaced by that of the old hostility towards their tenant. 'He had to be told some time.'

'Love, there's such a thing as the right way, at the right moment!'

Mr Tremble had halted three steps from the bottom. His cup and saucer ceased to rattle. 'What's this then?'

George drew a deep breath. 'Mr Tremble, things aren't working out here. We didn't like to say anything until at least we could offer you another lodging at the same rent. You may prefer to go somewhere else, of course. But Mrs Finch is conveniently close, and she will look after you exceedingly well.'

'You're putting me out of the house!'

Judy, perhaps regretting her former abruptness, shook her earrings. 'There's no hurry, Mr Tremble. Take — take a week.'

'What did I do wrong? Was it because of The Fry?'

'George's eyes were filled with concern. 'No, no, Mr Tremble, of course not.'

'Was it because I took flowers from the garden for The Grave?'

'Mr Tremble, you were most welcome to the few flowers you took.'

'Is it because I asked for toilet paper to wipe me a-r-r-se?'

Judy shuddered.

George's eyes lost a little of their kindness. 'No, no, Mr Tremble, though I think my wife would have preferred that you ask for it in — in less picturesque language.'

'So she thinks I'm common; not good enough for her?'

George's expression hardened further at the implied attack on his wife. 'Frankly, I myself would prefer that you use other words.'

His lodger banged down his cup and saucer on the table, crossed to the hat-stand, took from it his bruised looking headpiece, and planted it on his cropped grey hair. 'I'm not satisfied. I'm not at all satisfied.' He picked up the case containing his trombone. 'I may decide to see a solicitor.'

He was gone.

Judy's small forehead crinkled. 'Filthy old man. Arse! Urinal! Can't he call it the WC, the toilet, the lavatory — anything else?' A touch of anxiety entered her voice. '*Can* his solicitor do anything?'

'Oh, that's just talk. I'll give him a week's formal notice this evening. After all, he's got somewhere else to go.'

She nuzzled up to his broad shoulder. 'Thanks for standing up for me. I know you're worried about the loss of his rent. We'll think of something.'

'Yes. Yes, of couse.' His tone was doubtful.

Meanwhile Mr Tremble was transferring his thin form to the brass band rehearsal in the Church Hall. During this, he kept viciously thusting out the tubing of his trombone while playing Berlioz's *Hungarian March*, to the detriment both of the music and the back of the euphonium player performing immediately in front of him.

That evening while George, on Late Duty, was sitting in the staff room, the door opened suddenly. His bushy red eyebrows rose. There, framed in the doorway, was a thin droop! Tears teetered on its eyelashes.

Mr Tremble spoke. 'Your wife said you were here. I've just come up from The Grave.'

The Reverend Charles Hare, at that moment engaged in altering slightly a sermon on the Resurrection which he had already twice delivered, screwed a startled monocle into his eye.

'I'm prepared,' said Mr Tremble, 'to accept the arrangements that you have made for me.'

'Good! That's great!' In his huge relief, George rose to his feet.

'Try not to think too badly of us. Mrs Finch is a most conscientious woman, and I know she'll take every trouble in doing for you. "Doing for you!" Sounds ominous!'

'Is that a joke?' His voice was plaintive. 'I never can see jokes, especially since The Wife Passed Over.'

Charlie also rose, crossed to his locker, and produced his silver teapot. 'Come and join us in a cup of tea, Mr Tremble. Come and join us in a cup of tea.'

Chapter Nine

As Judy, after George had departed for the school, daily perched on the side of the bed massaging her abdomen with olive oil to prevent stretch marks, and brushing her nipples with a toothbrush to harden them against the development of abscesses when the baby began to suckle, she dreamed of Mark. He would be everything that she could not be; and that George, she sometimes began to think now, could not be either. He would be a famous author in a plum coloured smoking-jacket. He would sit at a table, herself at his side, at some great international gathering, autographing with a gold fountain-pen the copies of his books held out to him by his adoring readers. He would be an eminent barrister, extracting, kindly but firmly, for his mother some of the money bags that George and his family were undoubtdly sitting on. He would be an ambassador in a black frockcoat with white ruffs at his wrists. The blue sash of some distinguished order would sweep across and down his white starched waistcoat from his right shoulder. He would whirl her away into the beau monde of Paris. She read the French names on the bottles of scent and other toiletries that she had got George to buy her on their honeymoon, and in a kind of trance whispered them to herself. Mark would take her with him on his travels and show her fabled places: supercilious camels munching in the shade of date trees, and minarets seen at evening across crimson desert sands.

She bought a cookery book. One day she set down before George a culinary confection not easily distinguishable from ordinary Irish stew. '*That*,' she exclaimed, 'is cordon bleu cooking. That would cost you two pounds in any London restaurant.' In the days that followed, he suffered almost in silence a number of her 'cooking is an art' meals. The cookery book was brandished in her left hand as she stood at the iron range stirring pots with her right, while he sat at the table waiting. After the twenty minute lecture, the Indian curry ended up on his plate as a small black mess. (But, on more normal occasions, she was a perfectly good cook.) He endured, because he sensed her need to fill in her humble social origins with something; to play a role; to make herself count. But even for him there came the sticking point.

One day, on his return from the school, she greeted him at the door by holding out the back of her hand for him to kiss. Her eyes were heavily made up with 'eye shadow', her finger-nails brightly enamelled. He obliged.

'You have just kissed the hand of a Frenchwoman.'

He laughed. 'OK. Bon soir, ma chère femme.'

'I'm not joking. From now on, I'm telling everyone that I'm a Frenchwoman. I've already told Rose. I want you to tell everyone the same.'

He stared at her. 'Are you serious?'

'Of course.'

'But — but you can't even speak French!'

'My teacher at school told me that, for someone who couldn't speak French, I had a very good French accent.' Gesticulating, she spoke some English sentences like a foreigner.

'Judy, this is absurd! I can't do that. I'd feel a fool.'

'Oh, you're such a stick in the mud! Facts, facts, facts. Always so precise. Can't you ever take off into your imagination?'

'Judy, this isn't imagination. This is a simple lie. You can't expect me to go round the school lying to my colleagues on the staff. It isn't even a good lie. You may get away with it with Rose, but in English speaking countries French is just about the most widely taught of all foreign languages. All the staff, all the boys' parents, have been to expensive schools and are very highly educated. Many of the boys themselves, for their years, are very brilliant. They're all doing French. You couldn't get away with it for a minute.'

'It's *not* a lie.' But she had been shaken. 'It's just, I suppose, that I like to make up stories. I'd like to pass my whole life drunk, just seeing the world through a haze.'

'What!'

'I didn't mean it *literally*.'

'Well, love, if you tell people you're French or, better perhaps, of French extraction, I'll just keep my mouth shut. I'll not deny it.'

'People have often said to me that my whole manner and temperament is French.' Her face brightened. 'Perhaps I *am* of French extraction.'

He smiled and kissed her. 'Perhaps so, sweetheart.'

But next day Judy was down to earth again, almost literally, complaining of some rising damp in the future nursery which involved a part of the wall near to the cot. Sensing her rapidly building alarm for the future health of the baby, he stepped in quickly to remove it by wheeling the cot across to the opposite corner. She was calmed — for the moment.

Pregnant or not, her body, all five feet of it, was very nearly as energetic as ever. She was up early with her paintbrush, tin of paint, bottle of white spirits, and oily rag. In the kitchen cum dining-room cum sitting-room, she pointed to an old chest of drawers that Betty Coombes had bought for her at an auction.

'I'm going to make it' — a vigorous sweep of her hand — 'a work of art.'

'Well, I'll move out of your way then.'

He set off for the school a quarter of an hour ahead of time. A thrush was having a tug-of-war with a worm. Finally succeeding in pulling it out of the ground, it wound it round its beak and flew off. Rooks, cawing silhouettes, flew across the misty outline of a hill, behind it the lurking sun. After glancing at his wristwatch, he turned away from the school towards the playing fields and the river beyond. He passed a wild garden of willowherb, its emerald and mauve spires pointing at the sky.

He paused, and looked down the hill. The sun, rapidly gaining strength, was already sucking up vapour from the river. This vapour, blown by a light air, rose up and over the high banks as out of a witch's cauldron. Some cattle were moving through the mist like horned wraiths. A stork unexpectedly came pacing round a bend in the shallows. For a moment George's eyes rested on the long grass of the bank.

He turned back. As he walked up the school drive, butterflies danced over the beds, flying flowers. Through the line of windows of the dining-hall, he noticed a figure moving to and fro. It was Rose, clearing the tables after the boys' breakfast. A sudden curiosity made him pause just out of her sight by a corner of one of the windows. He watched her, seeking to rediscover what it was that had caused him to walk with her that day. She moved with a sturdy placid grace from table to table, collecting the used knives into a metal container that would later be lowered into the washing machine. She wore a sleeveless snow white blouse, and her arms were soft and rounded. Her buttocks, broad and firm, moved beneath her blue serge skirt. Her tanned stockingless legs were soft and rounded too. Her hair was dressed in a bun, and he caught a glimpse, when she turned her head a little, of a soft cheek. She was womanhood, placidity, softness — peace.

There was a sudden clatter. She had dropped a knife on to a plate. He started. He strode with averted face to the staff room.

As he dumped on to the communal table his rugby kitbag, which he used also for transporting his school books and papers, he became aware of the stocky figure and jutting jaw of Commander Robinson, fifty years of age and ex-Royal Navy. George, the tough rugby forward, respected him; respected his iron but scrupulously fair discipline.

'We'll miss you, Commander. Hope there are wall bars in the gymnasium of your new school!'

The other smiled faintly. He knew that George was referring to his seldom used practice of slippering culprits made to bend over holding the lowest bar. 'There are excellent wall bars thank you, Brown. They descend even lower towards the floor. Well, I'm to be accorded the honour, it seems, of sitting beside the Head. Seems I'm to make a speech. I'd better get into Assembly early. I'll — I'll miss the old school after all these years.'

He hastened to the door, but George had time to note the tear in the corner of the Commander's eye.

'I'm really sorry that old Robinson is going. Of course, before he retires, he needs this higher salary. He's a real — gentleman.'

The Reverend Charles Hare, who had been sitting drooping interestingly in his seat, a scholarly man in pensive mood, came to life. His teeth gleamed over his spotted bow-tie. 'A gentleman is a man who, on hearing a lady singing in her bath, puts his *ear* to the keyhole.'

From somewhere in the room the machinery of Mr Snipe's titter started up, reached a well ordered climax, and died away.

'The Common Entrance results should be out, shortly after the beginning of the holidays,' said George.

'Yes, and from the vault of heaven doubtless will issue a vibrant Voice crying, "Well done, thou good and faithful servant! Thou hast passed thy Common Entrance with over sixty per cent. Enter thou into the joy of thy Eternal Headmaster." Hm. Better bestir myself. Got to take that dratted Three A this morning. Chatter, chatter, chatter. Ah, well . . . To the toilet! The wise man goeth when he can; the fool goeth when he must.' He twinkled through his monocle.

George's eyes followed the grey hair, cut in a bob on the neck, until the staff door had closed behind its owner. 'Come on, Snipe, we'd better be leaving too. Assembly beckons.'

After Juniper Minor had accompanied the school in the singing of *Glory Be to Jesus* (he had still to complete his studies of *Soldiers of Christ, Arise*), the Headmaster addressed the boys from behind the tall desk on the dais. Commander Robinson, brought forward from the rest of the staff, was seated beside him.

Mr Featherstonhaugh, in his usual effort to boost his medium height, stood on the outside edges of his shoes with his ankles turned inwards so that the inside edges propped up against one another. There followed a eulogy of Commander Robinson, in the course of which the school motto, *Mens sana in corpore sano*, was given a passing reference (the Head Boy Juniper Major being required to shoot up from his seat like a Jack in the Box to furnish a translation); the question of stepping back to square leg was touched on lightly ('A Funk, sir,' was Juniper Major's summing up of the matter); while the related topic of Clean Living was not entirely neglected.

'What can we learn from the example of Commander Robinson?' cried Mr Featherstonhaugh. 'We learn that we must never let our parents down, our House down, our school down. Above all, we must never let *ourselves* down.'

By the time that the Commander, jutting out his jaw even more aggressively than usual in a successful fight to stem the tears, had concluded his reply, moisture was seen to be trembling on more than one schoolboy cheek, while Carruthers was openly weeping. Only Juniper Minimus, surreptiously fingering a small paper Union Jack which he proposed during the Milk Break to burn publicly in the playground, remained unmoved.

Thereafter, on turning to everyday school matters, Mr Featherstonhaugh turned also to his usual suave gentlemanly voice. Stroking his neatly clipped moustache, and with a half smile on his lips, he brought up the matter of the boys who had so over eaten when out on a Sunday to the home and birthday party of a classmate, that they had become too ill to return to school. His youthful and easily swayed audience, perceiving the half smile, turned at once from grave to gay and tittered.

'But seriously, it's a rather shocking thing that, after two days, Hawkins and Bonsall are still not feeling well.'

From one of the desks a hand flew up. 'Please sir,' cried the host triumphantly, 'Hawkins fainted.'

Mr Featherstonhaugh regarded his interrupter, but his expression remained bland. His eyes travelled along the rows of desks. 'Shillington, your father and mother are worried by your low marks in French. Why, Shillington, are your marks in French low?'

'I don't know, sir.'

'Shillington, a boy is either able and lazy, and needs The Slipper; or backward, and needs coaching. Which d'you need, Shillington, coaching, or The Slipper?'

'Coaching, sir,' said Shillington firmly.

The ghost of a smile illuminated Mr Featherstonhaugh's face. 'Hm. We shall have to see what can be arranged.'

Every boy knew that the Headmaster's slipper was not an object to be trifled with. From time to time he had sent to him by George Brown, as Games Master, a list of those who persistently made a nuisance of themselves on the field of sport. On one occasion he was sent a list of boys who had volunteered to repair and paint the wooden cricket pavilion. Glancing at the list hurriedly (he was anxious to get away to bowl at the nets to Dorset-Chumleigh, a fearless batsman who cared nothing for the safety of his legs or, come to that, his head either in which, truth to tell, there was remarkably little); glancing at the list hurriedly, he had sent for them all and slippered the lot. When George pointed out his error, he had remarked mildly that it would do them no harm, and that they would find plenty of paint in the carpentry shed.

* * *

Assembly over, George, like the rest of the staff, repaired to the class of which he was Form Master.

'Atkinson.'

'Present, sir.'

Atkinson's name was duly ticked in the Register of Attendance.

'Brownbody Major.'

No answer.

'Brownbody Minor, where's your brother? This is the third time he has been absent.'

They were twins, Brownbody Major having gained his seniority by entering the world only one hour sooner.

'Sir, he's with Matron. He had his chilblain pills this morning. Then he often gets hot and goes red in the face.'

'Chilblains in July!'

Brownbody's freckled nose quivered with pride. 'Sir, if it gets cold and he has his hands outside the bedclothes, he can get chilblains at any time.'

'Well, tell him to wear gloves or the Headmaster may get annoyed and start wielding his slipper. Then your brother may go red somewhere else.'

'Please sir,' cried Brownbody Minor gleefully, 'he puts exercise books down his trousers.'

George manufactured a severe expression. 'Exercise books, eh! Well, tell him not to use his geography book. I refuse to correct a battered geography book.'

'Yes, sir. I mean, no sir.'

'Dorman Minimus.'

'Present, sir,' said Dorman Minimus, his ears sticking out.

'Dorman Minimus, do stop picking your nose. You really are the most disgusting little boy.'

'Yes sir,' said Dorman Minimus, desisting, but starting to nibble his nails instead. Suddenly he broke wind. The boys nearest him began to giggle and hold their noses.

George, whose inflexible rule it was to ignore a fart if humanly possible, continued stony faced to the end of the Register.

That Saturday evening he strode up to the cottage, six foot one and fourteen stone of exuberance, full of his news and with no presentiments of disaster. Judy, as usual never very far from the window when he was expected, glanced appreciatively at his vast tweed jacketed shoulders, the row of pens and pencils clipped along the edge of his breast pocket. He had never changed from the prevailing dress of his Oxford days, grey flannel trousers and tweed jacket or blazer.

'In spite of Commander Robinson's very strict regime,' he said, 'there wasn't a dry eye by the time he'd finished his farewell speech. Boys like discipline; to know where they stand.'

He noticed that her eyes were fixed on him with an expression of intense interest. Usually she was more given to talking than listening.

'He's in Charlie's house, isn't he?'

'Yes. In the flat above Miss Lewis. Why d'you ask?'

'No particular reason. Just interested.' But a moment later, at the range stirring the soup, she said casually over her shoulder, 'Has the flat been re-let?'

'Not to my knowledge.'

It wasn't until the next day, at the late Sunday breakfast (he didn't have to go to the school), that she remarked as she poured out the tea, 'That damp corner in the nursery, if it's damp in the summer, what's it going to be like in the winter? It looks to me like rising damp.'

'Not upstairs, love! Damp from the ground can rise only about four feet or so. Besides, the baby — er — Mark will be right across at the other side.'

'But the atmosphere will be damp. It could be dangerous for the baby. Why is it damp in that corner?'

'It could be some tiny fissure in the wall, or the roof. Or the plaster just there might need replacing.'

'Why not have it done, then?'

'We must concentrate on clearing your — our — debt to Morgan Brothers. It's still only July. We have, you might say, two more months of summer. Even October isn't too bad. Mark doesn't arrive until November. We can get in a man before that to coat with bitumen that part of the roof, and re-point or re-plaster the wall where necessary.'

She pressed herself up from the table and crossed to a shelf. She raised the mother-of-pearl lid of the little music box, and the tinkling strains of *The Bluebells of Scotland* arose. 'We must have it done straight away. If you *say* we can't afford it, then Angus must go.'

George's rugged features were suffused with concern. 'Darling, you can't sell your mother's present to you; all that you have of her now! Just think what it would bring between us! The memory might grow into a resentment that could even wreck our marriage.'

'It's not just the damp. This cottage is *killing* to clean.' The vivid blue eyes under the plucked and pencilled eyebrows became flirtatious. When she next spoke, the words arrived in a rush as though she had first taken a deep breath. 'Why don't *we* take Commander Robinson's flat? It's modern. I'm sure it'll be dry and smaller and easier to clean. We could sell the cottage and be clear of our debts.'

George put the piece of toast, into which he was about to bite, back on to his plate. But his mouth remained open. 'You're asking me to sell my parents' gift to me! That they found the money for at great sacrifice, so that I should have a secure roof over my head!'

'I didn't mean it *literally*.'

As he picked up his toast once more his hand trembled. 'Judy, all this is really too bad! It's no time at all that you were telling me that you loved this cottage. You said that every part of it filled you with joy.'

'People can change their minds.'

'But not one thing on Monday and another thing on Tuesday! In an important thing like this, people look back over a reasonable period of time and make a summing up of their feelings. But with you, the emotion of the moment is all.'

The blue eyes looking at him had ceased to be flirtatious and become resentful. 'You seem to think that you know me better than I know myself.'

He rose from the table. 'Judy, sweetheart, I really think I'm beginning to. Honestly, love, you sometimes don't seem to know yourself at all.' He reached into the side pocket of his shabby Oxford dark blue blazer (the brand new one hung, as most of the time, in the wardrobe). 'Don't you see that a sale of the cottage would really amount, like the account at Morgan's, to a renewed attempt to live above our means. We'd in fact be living on capital.'

Extracting his secateurs from his pocket, he walked heavily towards the door.

'Aren't you going to finish your toast?'

'My appetite's gone.'

He moved among the rose bushes, taking off any flowers that were dead or any leaves that he thought were diseased. But a few moments later he was back in the room.

Putting down the secateurs and the clippings on the table, he called out to Judy, now in the scullery, 'I'm going for a walk. Back soon.'

His mind was in tumult. His beloved cottage had for long now constituted the very centre of his existence, even if he had treated it as little more than a shelter. From this hub had radiated out the four spokes of his life: his roses, the school, the rugby field, and the parents, even though far away down in Cornwall, who had given him his home, and whose devoted eyes ever watched his progress. As for Judy's 'I didn't mean it literally', he had come to recognise it as but a favourite formula of retreat prior to renewing the attack at a later time.

He felt the need to walk and walk and walk. He turned right along the lane, past the Finches' house *The Brambles*, and so on down towards Kingsbridge. A few torn clouds rested on the hill tops, but otherwise the black wings of rooks sailed in sunshine over green-gold fields of wheat, and the oast-houses pointed their crooked spires at a blue sky.

Presently he entred the outskirts of Kingsbridge, with its half timbered houses. Ahead, the garish pile of the Rainbow Inn seared his eye, but he veered away hard left to the town's small Riverside Park. Two little girls were playing at 'Father and Mother'. The first little girl, who was doubling both as Father and the shrieks of the baby, let out a series of piercing cries. The other slapped the doll in her arms and ordered it to be quiet. The shrieks ceased. She addressed her playmate. 'Daddy, the baby's been very naughty today.' At the far side of the park two small boys flayed the air as they aimed murderous blows at one another, all of which fortunately missed their target. A slightly larger fat boy down on a small beach by the river, surrounded and assisted by a bevy of little girls, was collecting coloured pebbles. He kept stretching open the top of the front of his bathing trunks and ordering them, in a nasal tone, to 'dump 'em in there.' A large stout lady was calling to her tiny dog, 'Come here, else Mummy spank. D'you want me to whip you? D'you want Mummy to whip you?' As George passed the beach shelter, a medium sized black mongrel with bristling whiskers stood at its entrance. On catching his scent, its pug nose wriggled in an expression of alarm, then settled into one of suspicion, and finally relaxed into one of contempt.

George threw himself down on the grass, cupped the back of his head in his great palms, the fingers interlaced, and allowed the sunshine to play on his face. The image of Judy filled his mind. Such a little thing, only five feet tall . . . Her matronly figure so contrasting with her littleness and her intense prettiness . . . He found deeply moving her total involvement in making a safe nest for her coming chick. But he could not, he just could not, sell his parents' gift.

He tried to escape for a spell out of the conflict by dozing. Usually, tired as he was with overwork, he had to fight off sleep, but now that it would have been welcome it would not come. In any case he was roused by a violent blow. Opening startled eyes, he saw a dragon hovering over him. There it was, fiery mouth open, long scaly tail, floating in the blue sky. His gaze followed down the line attached to it. It focused on a small grubby hand. The hand was attached to a boy lying on his back and bawling his head off. Plainly he had been flying his kite walking backwards and had fallen over the recumbent figure.

His mother appeared. She began to scold her son, demanding, even as he clutched his damaged knee, that he apologise to 'the gentleman'.

George rose to a squatting position. 'Hurt your knee, old chap? Here, let me give it a rub. That will make it well.'

He began the massage. The boy, seeing the kind brown eyes looking at him, ceased his bawling.

'No harm done to either of us.' George smiled at the woman's concerned face. 'I myself as a boy always used to walk backwards when I flew my kite.'

But the jolt of the boy's tumbling over him had also jolted his mind into a decision. He retraced his steps, passed his cottage, and strode towards the school.

Chapter Ten

George Brown paused on approaching the gate with the large board beside it bearing, in Gothic lettering, the legend, 'Worcester Hall Preparatory School — Headmaster: Richard Featherstonhaugh, M.A. (Oxon)'. He glanced to his right, his ear caught by the sharp impact of ball on racquet. Passing through the gate, he saw that the tennis court, running along part of the grey-plastered castellated front of the main school building and the end of the pre-fab Art Block, was occupied by a foursome. The Reverend Charles Hare and Mr Snipe had formed themselves into a doubles combination to confront the combined might of Junipers Major and Minor who, despite their tender years, were a formidable pair. They represented the school in the number one doubles position. Indeed Juniper Major was not only captain of tennis, but also of rugby and cricket.

Mr Snipe got in his fast first serve (fortunately, for his opponents, his second was a lamentably weak affair). Charles Hare stood upright at the net. His right elbow rested on his hip. Palm uppermost, he held out his racquet before him like a frying-pan ready to receive a pancake. He flicked, to the far outside line, Juniper Major's good return of the ball, thus placing it too wide for either brother to reach. As George watched fascinated, Charlie took further points. He did so even when handicapped by Snipe's weak second serve, which allowed the opposition to advance up the court and slam back angled returns. If Charlie's bad sandle shod feet would not allow him to go to the ball, so good was his anticipation that he seemed, like some Muhammad in reverse, to cause the ball to come to him.

The match narrowly taken, two sets to one, by the seniors, both boys and masters repaired to the staff room. The boys of course were not permitted to enter that holy place. They hovered by the door, awaiting promised biscuits. These delivered, they were dispatched to their changing room.

'Useful pair,' said Charlie, crunching. 'Juniper Major, in particular. That boy could win the Wimbledon Junior Championship in a few years' time.'

'You're pretty useful yourself.' George laughed. 'I've never seen a more unorthodox style in all my born days! But you just seem to mesmerise that ball on to your racquet.'

Charlie, now filling the staff room kettle at a tap, spoke over his shoulder. 'Anticipation. My daughter too has very good anticipation. The bough doesn't fall far from the tree. Daren't run about too much. My heart, you know — I may be wrong.' He transferred the kettle to the gas ring. 'It isn't just my heart. I have to think of my breathing too. I'm an asthmatic, you know.'

'Quite. This church service you're taking —'

'Not a service. I'm in charge of a parish fund-raising effort. Stalls selling God knows what, and donkey rides for the children.' He groaned. 'You might say: a fête worse than death.'

Mr Snipe, pulling at his heavy crop of pimples, dutifully tittered.

The kettle started to sing. Charlie produced from his locker his large silver teapot. He poured in a little water to warm it. Screwing his monocle into his eye, he examined it. 'I date this eighteen hundred and five, or perhaps ten.' He emptied it at the sink, placed some tea in it, took it to the kettle, and filled it. 'Have some tea, Mr Snipe. Made properly, the pot taken to the kettle so that the water remains on the boil, not the kettle to the pot. Then allowed to stand for six minutes.' He shone his teeth. 'If I have one criticism to make of you young people nowadays, it is that you will not take the pot to the kettle.'

Mr Snipe's mouth opened in anxious moral concern. Thrusting his long sharp nose towards the cup, duly delivered to him after the six minutes, he took a sip. 'Yes, I see what you mean, Mr Hare.'

Suddenly George spoke. 'Charlie, I'm very worried.' He laid out his dilemma before his friend.

'Don't trouble yourself, old fellow. Letting the flat's out of the question. I promised Miss Lewis that I'd let the upstairs flat only to someone of whom she approved. I don't like the woman. But with all her infirmities she has difficulty in sleeping at night, and I had to consider that. I gather that both you and your good lady are at the moment in bad odour with her.'

George's face brightened. 'You might certainly say that!' He lifted his cup and began to enjoy his tea.

'I tell you what. I'm in good time. I'll drive you down and have a word with Mrs Brown, if you like. I have to change. Won't be long. Both, help yourselves to biscuits.' Taking his cup of tea with him, he departed to the staff bathroom.

Ten minutes later, transformed into The Venerable Dean, he drooped back arrayed in his canonicals. 'Did you hear, there's to be an election for a new Pope?'

George set down his cup with a clatter. 'What! Has the Pope died?'

'Worse than that! He's joined the Methodists.'

George, now in high good humour and mock rage, swung a ham of a fist that missed the Reverend Charles Hare's chin by a foot. 'Don't think that wearing your collar back to front will save you.'

Bidding Mr Snipe (he was on Sunday duty) goodbye, they inserted themselves into Charlie's small black car.

George, to break the ice, advanced first up the path to the stone built cottage, while Charlie hung a little way behind.

Judy had evidently heard the sound of the engine, for she was already at the door. Her scarlet lips smiled ingratiatingly; plainly she had been made highly uneasy by his long absence after their quarrel. 'Just in time for tea! Made you your favourite chocolate cake!'

'Oh, lovely!' But his pleasure was assumed. Face to face with her, it became borne in on him that *his* goood news was *her* bad.

She rushed on, not noticing, behind the large form of her husband, the approach of Charlie. 'There's no need to sell the cottage. We could let it. That way we wouldn't be living on capital. As it's a complete house, it would bring in more money than the flat would cost. That would pay our rent, make up for the loss of Mr Tremble, and settle our debts.'

'Judy — Judy, love, there are problems. Charlie's been kind enough to stop off on his way to a church appointment to explain.'

She started as she caught sight, over George's shoulder, of an advancing grey bob of hair. The grey bob, accompanied by the rest of its owner, rounded George like a ship rounding a promontory.

'That sounds like a very good scheme of yours, Mrs Brown.

Unfortunately, the power to let the flat doesn't lie with me. All along, Miss Lewis has had the right of veto over who lives above her. I understand that you two are not very popular with her at the moment. I don't myself particularly care for the good lady, but — there you are!'

Judy fluttered her lashes at him. 'Oh, I could soon settle that. I often quarrel with people and then make it up. People like me because I like people.'

Charlie shone his teeth, uncertainly. 'I'm sure that's true, Mrs Brown —'

'Call me Judy.'

'— Judy, but a baby as a tenant is a huge hostage to fortune. George and I are old friends. It would be embarrassing if ever I had to ask you to leave.'

'Darling,' said George, 'you know Miss Lewis. She may be sweet today, but she can as easily turn sour tomorrow.'

'Not if I let her know that she's welcome to help with the baby when he's born. She wants to be a mother. Nearly every woman does. Apart from being Matron to the boys, this is the nearest she can get. Just think what it would mean to her to hold a baby!'

George's eyes dwelt a moment on the light brown curls, the plucked and pencilled eyebrows, the vivid blue eyes so eager, the ear-rings twinkling at her dainty ears. His girl! His little girl! How could he deny her? Besides, there was much good sense in what she had said earlier about the cottage's paying their rent with something to spare. And Miss Lewis and the baby — that had been quite shrewd!

'Well . . .' he said.

Judy pressed her advantage. 'If things go wrong, Charlie, we'd leave at once. No fuss, no arguments.'

'Hm. I'll have to consult my good lady wife. Well, off to meet my fête!'

The joke hung sadly over the rose bushes, lonely for the titter of Mr Snipe. Was Charlie, as he hastened back to the little black car parked outside the gate, thinking perhaps that here was a young woman that would slip out any promises that would see her over the moment? That George, though becoming wiser, was still too loving to see with eyes undimmed?

The next day, possibly the greatest crisis day in the history of the school since that other Black Monday when Mr Featherstonhaugh, demonstrating a cricket stroke in the nets, had been struck in the genital organs by a leg break bowled by the cricket captain; and had had to have an ice pack, pending the arrival of the doctor, applied by Miss Lewis, her eyes averted — the next day an unexpected staff meeting was called for after lunch. This concerned itself with nothing less than the celebrated Affair of the Missing Peppermint Creams, whose overtones were destined to reverberate along the corridors of Worcester Hall Preparatory School long after the mystery had been resolved. The papers in which the peppermint creams had been wrapped were discovered by Ferrett Minor and Grubb Minimus in the rubbish basket of the form room of Two A at approximately (no, let us, in so important a matter, be as precise as possible) between the hours of three and five on Monday the twenty-first of July, 1952. George, patrolling the corridor as Master on Duty, had, one great hand on the doorway, regarded the scene. What he saw had caused him to propel his six foot one and fourteen stone fully into the room.

The rubbish basket, a waist high structure, lay on its side, with most of its contents spilt on to the floor. Messrs Ferrett and Grubb were engaged in that celebrated investigation which was destined in no small measure to isolate the culprit from a handful of suspects. George, feeling his own pulses quicken, had ruminated at the time on that cruel primitive love of the chase. Yet somewhere in the school was a small frightened boy watching the hounds pressing in upon him ever more closely. But the Master on Duty was there to fulfil a function. George, a slight expression of distaste on his rugged features, had, after tapping on the door of Mr Featherstonhaugh's study, laid the facts upon the table of the Most High.

Now, surrounded by his staff, the headmaster in his turn laid the facts before *them*. 'I think it a near certainty that the gentleman concerned is — Fanfani- Gonzales.'

Miss Lewis metallically changed her position.

Mr Featherstonhaugh added significantly, 'He's a lad of Mixed Foreign Extraction; British only by naturalisation. I had occasion more than once during the term to quarrel with him in the nets for stepping back to square leg.'

'A funk.' The word could scarcely be heard as it breathed through Miss Lewis's parted lips.

'Y-e-s. And very probably' (Mr Featherstonhaugh divided out the words so that their import fell like a hammer on every heart) 'a — peppermint — cream — eating — funk.'

Miss Lewis's metal shudder amply illustrated the chill that had descended upon the company.

Mr Featherstonhaugh shook his head gravely. 'I can't see Harrow's accepting him in a few years' time, even assuming that he proves capable of passing his Common Entrance with his stomach *crammed* with *sweetmeats*.'

'Like Carruthers, a very greedy little boy.'

George looked up sharply. 'I really must protest, Matron! I would point out that Carruthers is now seated at *my* table. He is no different from any of the other boys. He shows no signs of anything other than a normal healthy appetite.' Out of the corner of his eye, he observed Mr Featherstonhaugh noting this attack on his Head Matron and Head Housekeeper. But justice was justice. 'I really must protest at a helpless little boy being saddled with a reputation. A reputation earned by a single act on that fraught first day of his arrival at the school.'

Miss Lewis clattered to her feet, her lips compressed. 'If you will excuse me, Headmaster, I must see to the bed linen.'

Mr Featherstonhaugh rose. He held the door open for her as she motored out of the room. George watched the Head's back. Doubtless, when he turned round, it would be to reveal a face of thunder. There would not, of course, be an explosion in the presence of the staff. But, at the end of the meeting, there would be a murmured summons to the study.

On the contrary, a diplomatic little smile had been arranged under the neatly clipped moustache. Carruthers had been appointed, in his very first term, as captain of the Pink Dormitory on the head of his more than usually gentlemanly accent. As to a straight bat, that could be inculcated later in the nets. There, it was to be hoped that no tendency to step back to square leg would reveal itself. Such a tendency had, in fact, *not* revealed itself. And the more than usually gentlemanly voice had remained. Hence, doubtless, his present captaincy of the Brown Dormitory.

'Miss Lewis has not been very well lately. I don't think we need read too much into her chance remark about Carruthers.' He glanced at George, and the smile was still there. 'A rather promising young man. And now to a less promising young man. I've already offered Fanfani-Gonzales the alternatives of owning up before the end of the day and being given the slipper, or maintaining his silence and, on his inevitable exposure —'

Mr Snipe was leaning forward in his seat, white lipped.

'— writing out one hundred times, in his best script, I MUST NOT BE SILLY.'

The staff, who knew Fanfani-Gonzales to be no funk, waited to see whether his Italian pride inherited from his mother, and Spanish courage got from his father, would break down. In the event, they held firm until the junior boys left prep at (let us be exact) five minutes after seven o'clock post meridiem for cocoa and bed. At twenty past seven post meridiem by Miss Lewis's Swiss watch, guaranteed not to gain or lose more than two minutes in the course of an entire year, and presented to her by her father, a retired stockbroker living in Penge — at twenty past seven precisely Fanfani-Gonzales was discovered in a corner, contrite, and weeping copiously into his cocoa.

Judy did not wait for Charlie to consult his wife. The day after the above events saw the little matron, carrying in her womb her six months conceived baby, making her way in her low heeled brogues towards the brick building. Through the window of the sitting-room ahead she saw the single armchair, and the knitting and bottles of medicine on the small table beside it. The bookcase contained only a few volumes on hospital nursing and, on its top shelf, a bottle of temporarily pain relieving sherry and a solitary wineglass. The few draperies seemed starched; the few ornaments frozen.

She pressed the white electric button on the doorpost. She heard the bell ring, but there was no response. Impatient as always, she at once pressed again. Still no movement. The occupant should be at home at this hour!

Leaning back and walking carefully (no more falls!), she made her way round the house. There, on the rectangle of lawn bordered by flower-beds backed by a hedge, stood a metal garden chair. The woman seated on it wore a flower patterned muslin dress. A floppy straw hat protected her from the July sun. Music arose from the small radio she held on her lap. She tapped with one foot and her free hand to the lively tune. Perhaps, escaping for the moment from her crippled body, she saw herself as a slim young girl at a country dance.

'Miss Lewis! It's Judy Brown.'

The radio was abruptly switched off. A face, the forehead crinkled, the mouth pursed up, was turned to regard the newcomer. 'What is it, Mrs Brown?'

Small white teeth and cherry lips produced a smile. Brogues jiggled on their heels. 'I've come to visit you.' She advanced quickly. 'May I lower myself on to your lovely lawn? Bobik is getting such a weight. Ah, that's better.' She leaned back to extend her abdomen, her arms stretched out behind her.

'Bobik?'

'George and I sometimes call the baby Bobik, just for fun. After the child in Chekhov's *The Three Sisters*, you know. We saw the play at the Arts Theatre.'

Miss Lewis's lips pursed even further. 'I haven't heard any too well about that lot down there. The Headmaster thinks that the town would be the better without them.'

'Oh, d'you really think so? I feel that the theatre ought to be encouraged. Are you a theatre goer?'

'I shall have to be leaving, Mrs Brown. I've the school blankets to see to.'

'I'd like to help you, if I may.'

'I should have thought that you ought to avoid all unnecessary standing.'

'I could sit and write down the items as you dictated them.'

'Mrs Brown, our previous association on the domestic side of the school work was not a very happy one.' She pushed herself to her feet and stumped her way towards the nearby wheelchair.

'That was my fault entirely.' Judy too got herself to her feet. 'I don't want a job. Just to help.' The next words came in a rush, and the smile was produced again. 'Perhaps you could sometimes help me with the baby.'

'What's that!'

'You're a trained nurse. I should be so grateful for your advice.'

'Mrs Brown, I take it that you have a book on the subject. You'll find there everything that you need to know.' Miss Lewis settled herself into the wheelchair, disengaged her arms from their harness, and began to push round the wheels, manoeuvring herself off the lawn. 'Apart from that, relations between Mr Brown and myself are far from cordial.'

'But really practical help. Bath the baby, so that I could watch how you did it. As to my husband, he told me about the disagreement over Carruthers. I'm sure he regrets it.' (George had expressed no such regret.) 'In fact, we both regret it.'

'I can't go all the way down to your cottage.' The voice still retained its sharpness. Or — perhaps not quite.

'If we were in the flat above you. When Commander Robinson moves out at the beginning of August. I could bring the baby down.'

'Mrs Brown, I suffer a great deal of pain — '

'Under your guidance, the baby would be as quiet as a mouse at night. When he woke, I'd change and feed him immediately. Perhaps sometimes you wouldn't mind the pram beside you on your lawn.'

The eyes, a lighter blue than Judy's, filled with suspicion. Was this a ruse? But — a pram beside her on her lawn . . . The wheelchair began to be rolled towards the lane — not too fast.

Judy caught up and walked beside it. 'We've had a lot of expenses. Nursery furniture and so forth. We could let the cottage for more than the rent of the flat. That is, if you gave permission.'

'Ah! So you've approached Mr Hare?' The suspicion was back.

'Just a preliminary enquiry.'

'When d'you expect — Bobik?'

'End of November. His real name is to be Mark. Mark George.'

'Mark. Hm. And what if the baby is a girl?'

'I *know* he'll be a boy. I *know* it. And I'm *sure* he'll love you.'

'I'll have to think it over, Mrs Brown.'

'Please call me Judy.'

'I'll have to think it over — Judy.' She wheeled herself in through the school gateway. 'Exercise is good, but don't overdo it. Make your way home now. I'll let you know in a day or two.' The voice was still reserved but, just for a moment, was there a smile?

Judy, pacing her way along with her face tipped back to maintain her balance and collect sunshine from the blue above, broke into song. 'Tiptoe, to the window, by the window, that's where I'll be — Come tiptoe, through the tulips, with me . . .'

Back at the school George, the row of pens and pencils clipped to the breast pocket of his shabby Oxford blazer, sat at the staff room table, a pile of exercise books before him. The rhythmic tap of a pair of rubber-ended metal walking supports approached the door.

It opened. The head of Miss Lewis was thrust in. 'The daily task, the common round, Mr Brown!'

George's eyes were wide. She had positively cooed at him! He found his tongue. 'You might say that, Matron.'

'Had your tea? No, I don't suppose you've had a moment. I'll have it sent in to you.' She withdrew, and machined her way down the corridor to the dining-room.

George was staring at Charlie. 'Well, I'll be damned! And after the tiff over Carruthers!'

Charlie, bent over his newspaper like a reflective crane, raised his pale grey eyes. He tweaked at his white-spotted blue bow-tie. 'My, my! Who's suddenly become whose curly headed boy!'

'There's only one explanation. My irresistible wife has carried off her greatest coup!'

'You don't mean . . .'

'She's soft-talked the dragon into allowing us to share her den with her. No reflection on your excellent property!'

'My daughter's just the same. She could charm a snake without any need of a flute.' His teeth shone. 'Like myself, if I may say so. The bough doesn't fall far from the tree.'

'Well, I can't oppose Judy any longer. And the income from letting the cottage would be a godsend. But how do *you* feel about it?'

'Let's give it a whirl. It will relieve the monopoly.'

Mr Snipe had caught the play on 'monotony'. Sycophantic laughter arose from the corner where, on his knees, he was extracting a textbook from a floor level locker.

Charlie put away his newspaper and his humdrum reading glasses. Assuming his monocle, and bowed down under his weight of learning, he slippered his way in his round toed sandals towards the door. 'Well, to the toilet! The wise man goeth when he can; the fool goeth when he must.'

Mr Snipe's pimpled titter followed him out of the room.

When George gave Judy the news that evening, she hastened as fast as her condition would safely allow to *The Brambles*. High tea was about to commence. Mrs Finch filled a cup for her visitor. Judy had no sooner prepared to sip it, when she was caught, with her fingers on the handle, by her hostess's breaking out into a long grace. Judy kept her fingers there, under the pretence that she had merely been toying with it.

'Mrs Finch, I shall have to have Rose full time at the beginning of August. We're moving into Commander Robinson's flat and letting the cottage. I shan't be able to do any lifting.'

'We'd be glad of the money. Until I can set up my Christian Guest House with what little I've saved these years. When will the baby be born?'

'At the end of November. I hope it will be a boy.'

' 'Twill be a boy.' Mrs Finch nodded her head three times. ' 'Twill be a boy. Have no fear of that. I know.'

Judy sparkled her way home.

Chapter Eleven

As George advanced up the short path to the front door of his cottage, he heard Judy's voice announcing, 'If I don't do something exactly as he wants it, he beats me.'

He had just slipped away early from the school playing fields. It being the last week in July, the usual end of the school year speech and prize giving by Mr Featherstonhaugh had been in progress. Together, this speech and this prize giving constituted an extended and formidable ritual. There was even a prize for a boy who had never won a prize. But the fathers and mothers, sitting in rows in the sunshine on their canvas chairs, seemed content to endure.

He pushed open the door. He saw a pair of startled blue eyes, matched by the quiver of startled blue ear-rings.

With her usual dash and more than usual gesticulating of her small hands to cover embarrassment, she said, 'This is Mr and Mrs Gibbs. They're very keen to take the cottage.'

He regarded the young couple, apprehension in their faces. Smiling at them reassuringly, he gave them all the details that they required. He held open the door. Watching their retreating backs, it seemed to him that they were even keener to reach the gate. He recalled a previous occasion. Judy, ever gregarious, had got them both into conversation with some American tourists. As they stood on the pavement of Kingsbridge High Street, a plump girl with a homely but pleasant face, the inoffensive daughter of a local farmer, had passed them. She was barely out of earshot, when Judy turned to their new acquaintances and amazingly announced, 'She's a prostitute from Tunbridge Wells.'

He returned into the kitchen-sitting-room. 'Judy — Judy love — I know that you think our existence dull; that you want to invest it with drama.' She was not quite meeting his eye. 'But don't you see, it's one thing to make *yourself* a character in one of your dramas; to say that you're a Frenchwoman. But it's another to haul in other people without their permission. People, however imperfect, *care* about their reputations. I *care* that that young couple have gone away thinking that I'm a wife beater —'

'I sometimes wish you were.'

'I've become aware that this is something else that I've failed you in; another side of my dullness. But I just can't do it.'

'You're rough enough on the rugby field.'

'That's against people of my own size. Incidentally, your drama has just scared that young couple away. They could hardly get out of the place fast enough.'

She brightened. 'What about Mr Tremble?'

'I say, that's not at all a bad idea! No, no. We can't rob Mrs Finch of her tenant, or she'll never get that Christian Guest House of hers "with what little I've saved these years"!'

'We'll find her someone else. There are plenty of single men wanting a room.'

They met him, his eyes watering; The Hat, that bruised headpiece, compressed into place; his earthernware hand clutching his trombone; walking away from practice. 'I'm on my way to The Grave.'

Behind him a man, a cigarette hanging out of the corner of his mouth, stood between two kettledrums, their copper hemispheres gleaming in the sun. 'Give us a hand, Mr Tremble.' He began to walk over. He paused for an extended bout of coughing that shook the long ash onto the lawn. 'I've got to get my timps into the van. They are awkward devils to handle.'

'Timps?' queried George.

'Timpani, kettledrums,' quavered Mr Tremble. 'Same thing.'

When Mr Tremble announced that the rent of the cottage was too much for him, Kettledrums offered to move in and share. When Mr Tremble further announced that he couldn't forego The Fry, he must have The Fry, The Wife had *always* served The Fry, Kettledrums revealed that he was a master cook. 'Don't want to bang me own drum too hard,' he said, laughing at his joke, 'but I'm the best little fryer in Kent.' He also undertook to find a replacement tenant for Mrs Finch, one of the members of the band, a man formidable on the trumpet. The move was to take place, with Mrs Finch's agreement, at the end of a fortnight.

George and Judy celebrated the letting of the cottage with a game of her adored tennis on one of the courts in the town park. Six months pregnant, she was capable only of patball, conducted by each of them from half court on either side of the net.

When August and Rose together made their appearance, Judy was already at the flat to oversee the arrival of their possessions. George was at that moment in the bath. After knocking, Rose entered the kitchen. She stood listening to his voice threading its way uncertainly through, 'Come tiptoe through the tulips with me'. A moment later he emerged, draped in a towel fastened round his waist.

He noted her eyes on his broad hairy chest. 'Oh, Rose, shan't be a minute. Would you start by boxing up in these cardboard cartons all the small stuff you see around. It doesn't have to be packed carefully; just sufficiently well for us to ferry it up the lane. Of course all the furnishings, except the nursery furniture and curtains, stay here. The flat's got its own furniture anyway.' He disappeared up the staircase to the bedroom.

When he descended, tweed jacketted and grey flanel trousered, he stood a moment watching the movement of her hands as she packed. She glanced at him several times, he thought uneasily.

Finally she said, ''Tis terrible big hands I've got. A woman ought to have small hands.'

So that was it! 'They're very honest hands, Rose. Very womanly. How d'you keep them so soft?'

Her face was alight with happiness. 'I wear rubber gloves, mostly.'

He worked beside her. From time to time he glanced at her. She never lifted her eyes from her task. Did she share her mother's religious beliefs? She never showed any signs of it. Had she any system of beliefs? Or was it that her soft and yielding nature could not resist . . . Something in him did not care to pursue the thought.

Each of them burdened with a full carton, they walked side by side up the lane. The sight of the plump summer blackberries revived in him the all but buried memories of that other walk. Disturbed, he glanced at her. Was she remembering too?

On climbing the stairs to the flat, they found that Judy had ensconced herself in the very centre of the modern sitting-room, its large windows looking down on the lane. She sat perched on a tall stool from which she could command the proceedings.

'This is *my* flat. *I* got hold of it. I'm going to have things *my* way for once.'

George concealed a smile. He couldn't readily recall any occasion on which she had not had her own way in the arrangement of their home. But there was mingled tenderness and admiration in the brown gaze of his eyes; tenderness for the small figure carrying their child, admiration for a spirit as high as she was small. 'Where would you like these things to be put, sweetheart?'

She was in paradise in their new home — at first. Furniture was for ever being rearranged; ornaments regrouped. Finally the day came when Judy said, 'There's not a thing more that I can do.'

'You've got the flat looking marvellous. Tomorrow's Sunday and I'm not on duty, thank goodness. What d'you say to our both taking the day off? No exercise-book correcting, no furniture moving.'

With her love of her own neighbourhood, its buildings and countryside, she elected for a day of leisurely strolling. 'It'll help my confinement.'

'Good idea! But with plenty of rests.'

Her usual impatience was not to be contained, and they started early. Miss Lewis's daily delivered bottle of milk still stood on the doorstep. A plump little tit with a blue head was perched on it, pecking at the tinfoil of its top. Finally the little thief broke through to the cream below.

Judy watched, enchanted. 'Isn't it a beautiful bird!' she whispered.

But the blue tit heard, cocked a bright eye at her, and flew off.

As they made their way down the lane, she took her husband's arm. A row of tall poplars stood to attention along the fringe of a hill. Across a red sweep of fields, a cluster of blue-green trees basked in the early sun. The top of the slender church steeple pricked the sky like a thorn. In the distance, out of sight, stood Canterbury Cathedral, clothed in the frozen beauty of its stone. Now and then she would detach herself to secure, with her secateurs, some treasure from the hedgerows.

As the lane broadened out before joining the main street of Kingsbridge, she gripped his arm. 'What's that?'

A cow lay on the roadway. Four men in dark blue uniforms encircled it. Each directed a spurt of fire at the corpse from a flame-thrower.

'Keep well to the side of the road, mate,' called out the police sergeant in charge. 'She's died of anthrax.'

They passed, walking on the grass verge. Judy clung on to George's arm with both hands, her face turned away from the acrid odour. 'Ugh, I hated that. Poor creature!'

They sat down on a seat in the park. She took out a packed picnic breakfast from the haversack which he had been carrying over his shoulder At the scent of the food, a thin little dog crept out of a bush. Its black nose quivering, it stood looking at them with biscuit eyes.

'I think he must be a stray.' She threw a sandwich to him. It was gone in a snap, and the brown eyes burned for more.

George threw another. 'That's all, old chap, or you'll leave us nothing.'

Biscuit Eyes lingered, gave up hope, spotted two new arrivals, and trotted off in their direction.

Judy, every thought that crossed her mind needing to issue out upon her tongue, chatted away in the sunshine. George, his eyes closed, held up his face to the warmth. Except at night when he required his sleep, he was only too happy to supply the listening ear that was all that she seemed to want.

'Pregnancy,' she said, 'gives you immunity from infection. Never in my life have I felt so well. A sort of animal sluggishness and contentment. I wouldn't care if the roof fell in.'

He opened his eyes and laughed. 'I hope it doesn't do that!'

But he was delighted that she felt as she did. Increasingly he had found himself feeling with her nerves. He was uneasy about childbirth and its possible dangers. Nor did he fully appreciate how great was the urge that drove her on; not even after she had once said to him, 'Look at a woman's body. It's *made* for having children.' So her good health and confidence generated a measure of confidence in him too.

But later that evening, as they emerged from a small cafe where they had been having supper, during which she had been surprisingly quiet, she suddenly clung to him.

'What is it, sweetheart?'

'My confinement!' she said in a small voice.

A chill ran through him. 'You'll be all right, love.' He stroked her hair. 'We'll get the best doctor. No question of that.'

She cheered up at once. 'Yes. Yes, of course I will.'

Kingsbridge lay in moonlight, black walls and blue-green roofs. They were passing the station. The electric train from London, as it approached the platform, spat out sparks from its fiery feet.

They left the town behind and ascended the lane. The slender trunks of young trees on the brow of a hill were powdery etchings against an opal sky.

Just inside their gate, he caught her gently to him. 'What a lovely walk that was, sweetheart! What a lovely walk! I'll never forget it — no, not to the end of my days.'

She threw her small arms round his bull neck. 'And neither will I, George.'

'May I borrow Clifford please, Mr Brown?' After a tap on the door, Miss Lewis had thrust her head into George's classroom. It was the winter term. 'I want to run him down in the car to the doctor.' She lowered her voice.' He's got a little breaking out on his buttocks.' Her light blue eyes surveyed the class. 'Bulwer-Lytton and Thackeray are excused to go to the toilet after each class. All the rest are able to wait for the breaks. Tolstoy, you are strong enough now to be able to wait for the breaks.' She turned to George. 'Tolstoy wasn't strong enough last term, but he's strong enough this term.'

Later, she again thrust her head through a doorway. This time it was that of the staff room. 'I've left a pot under the bed, Mr Snipe. Some people like a pot and some people don't.'

Mr Snipe's pimples turned a deeper shade of pink.

'I don't know whether you like a pot or not.'

Mr Snipe mumbled that he did.

She addressed herself to George, correcting books at the table. Charlie was seated just beyond him. 'I wondered whether there was anything wrong, that neither Mr Hare nor you ate your bread and butter pudding at midday dinner.'

'No. No.'

'Because there's some tummy ache and diarrhoea at the moment going round the school. I wondered . . .'

'No, no. We're both quite all right.'

'Oh, I just wondered. We often have a wave of diarrhoea in — well, this is November — but in October or even the end of September.'

'Yes?'

'Yes.' Her voice fell to its confidential murmur. 'Two of the boys have diarrhoea at the moment. So I wondered . . .'

She withdrew.

'I believe,' said Charlie, 'that that woman *hoped* that we had diarrhoea.'

George put a warning finger to his lips as he caught the murmur, just outside the door, of Miss Lewis to her Assistant Matron. 'No result from the laxative? Stubborn! Stubborn! I think he ought to have another.' Still in close conference with her junior, she clanked away down the passage.

George removed the finger from his lips. '*Have* you got diarrhoea, Charlie? Or are you just too ashamed to admit it?'

'Her bread and butter pudding never gives me diarrhoea. It does, however, frequently involve me in constipation. With constipation, I find that I preach some of my very best sermons. With diarrhoea, one is a little apt, as it were, to hurry things. After a particularly stubborn and protracted bout of constipation, I preached a sermon on Passion Sunday that is still remembered throughout the parish. On the other hand, after an unusually sharp attack of diarrhoea, I spoke with such velocity on Palm Sunday, that I found myself having to follow on with the sermon that I had prepared for Good Friday, blitzed my way through the material for Easter, found myself storming on into Rogation and Ascension, and only just managed to pull myself up at Whit.'

'You're a liar, aren't you?'

'Sir, have some respect for my cloth.'

Mr Snipe, standing by his locker, had been gazing down his sharp nose at them with a bleak expression. Was a titter called for or not?

With a sigh of satisfaction, George closed the last of the exercise books and placed it on top of the pile. 'I must go down to the field and coach the Kingsbridge Rugby Union Football Club. They have first- and second-fifteen matches on Saturday.'

A quarter of an hour later he was surveying the thirty or so players grouped about him. 'Where's young Paddy O'Donovan?'

The captain of the first fifteen spoke.

'We thought it was better to leave him out for a spell. He's entering a seminary to study for the priesthood. He was sent off by the referee last Saturday for punching and kicking. He's to be a chaplain to the Sisters of Mercy.'

Chapter Twelve

At the end of November a pain, like a red hot poker, passed through Judy's body.

Charlie ran George and Judy down in his car to the private nursing home. George had a fixed idea in his mind that a private nursing home gave the best service, and only the best was good enough for his Judy. And this in spite of Miss Lewis's saying to him, quite kindly, 'If I were able to have a baby, I'd have it in hospital. You've got everything there, in case of an emergency.'

'I'll be thinking of you all the time, darling,' he whispered to Judy on the steps.

'I'll be all right, George. But remember to bring me flowers. A really big bouquet, bought in a shop.'

'Of course I will.'

He watched her, his heart in his eyes, disappear with the matron, a woman reputed to be in her nineties; disappear into what was for him a mysterious world of birth and pain and possible danger and experts in attendance. His religion didn't run very deep, was for him more a matter of public habit, but that night he prayed for his little Judy as he had not prayed since his childhood.

It was the following day when Miss Lewis next pushed her head into the staff room. 'Mr Brown, are you not going to visit your wife? I took the liberty of phoning through to the nursing home. She's looking forward to a visit from you.'

He glanced up sharply from his inevitable book correcting. 'Am I allowed to? I'd no idea. What time?'

'Any time that you're free. It's a private nursing home, you know!'
'What about five o'clock?'
'Five o'clock. Shall I phone them for you?'
'I'd be very grateful.'

With a smile of encouragement, she withdrew.

'I'd no idea, Charlie, that childbirth was an ongoing thing, with visits possible in the middle of it. I've always thought of it as a single event.'

'Oh no. My wife was three days in labour with our daughter.'

'Good Lord! Poor thing! My poor Judy!'

When he entered the room, his wife was half sitting up in bed. She greeted him with a cry of delight and then, when he had seated himself beside her on its edge, threw her arms round his neck and burst into tears.

'The pains have been coming ever since you left. Ever since. All night and all day.' But she at once cheered up and lay back. 'It hasn't been too bad, though. When they come, I just catch hold of the top of the bed and pull on it. Then, when they go, the contrast is such utter bliss that I even fall asleep for some minutes-until the next.'

Despite some further contractions that caused her to suck in her breath, their conversation was a happy one, and he left her in good spirits. 'I expect Bobik will be born tonight,' she said. 'Don't forget the flowers.'

Next day he phoned early from the school office.

'Mr Brown, things are going slowly.' It was the nursing home matron's voice. 'We are keeping Mrs Brown as comfortable as we can. The doctor expects the baby to be born this afternoon.'

A later phone call established that, right on the stroke of half past five from the church clock, Bobik, or rather Mark, had arrived. By half past six by George's watch, he stood on the door step.

'May I see her?'

The matron spread her professional smile across her ninety year old face, and gave her sixty-five years in service professional reply, 'Oh yes, we can't keep fathers away.' She led him to the door of the room. 'She's out of the anaesthetic. But you'll find her a bit woozy.'

She departed.

Judy, half raised, lay back on the pillows. She received George's kiss, and regarded the handsome bouquet of flowers with a smile that indeed was a little 'woozy'. 'When I came round I said, "Nurse, I had a lovely dream. I dreamt that the baby was born." "But he *is* born," she said.'

Placing the flowers on the bedside table, he kissed her gently again. 'Marvellous, darling! Marvellous!'

'Have a look at him.'

He crossed to the cot, standing some six feet away. 'Why isn't it beside you?'

'The Matron's old fashioned, I suppose.'

Within the cot, tightly wrapped up in a shawl, was a tiny form. The little nut brown head, covered by a few streaks of dark hair, bore two darker marks one on each side. For a moment they saddened George, seeming as they did to constitute an injury inflicted on this helpless mite. The gynaecologist's forceps, no doubt.

'Get my hand mirror from the dressing-table.'

Holding it over the cot, he watched her expression. There was no reaction.

'A bit higher. More to the left. Ah . . .' Her whole face lighted up. 'At first, after he was born, I felt nothing. But when you hear that cry from the cot, so feeble and helpless, from that moment you love it.'

Next day George visited again, only to be told by the nurse as she opened the front door, 'She's been crying her eyes out because she couldn't feed the baby. We told her that we could keep it alive for ten days on glucose and water.'

She showed him to the room. At once he noticed his flowers, now in a vase. She left husband and wife together.

Judy looked drawn, her small features red from her recent distress. She drew in her breath sharply as she shifted her position. 'It's the stitches. I can feel them now that the anaesthetic has worn off.' Her tone changed to indignation. 'The nurse tried to discourage me from breast-feeding the baby. She said that when she had a baby, she wouldn't feed it. The Matron supported her.'

'Well, I'll be damned! They're antediluvian in their ideas.'

'I insisted that the baby should be brought to me.'

'Good for you!'

'I couldn't give it a full feed, but they said that they could augment with a bottle. They dilute cow's milk and add sugar.' Distress returned to her. 'I hope that will be all right. If anything happened to Mark, I'd die.' But she as quickly cheered up. 'They said that my milk would get established.'

Before he left, the nurse appeared, tended to Mark in his cot, tightly ('so that he wouldn't miss the womb') rewrapped him in his shawl, and brought him over. Judy, painfully and determinedly, got herself up. The nurse departed. And so, for the first of many times, the erstwhile long term bachelor George beheld his son being suckled.

Presently Judy raised her hand and pressed a button set in the wall. The nurse bore Mark away for his supplementary feed. At a later time, at the first cry from the baby, milk was to spurt from Judy's breasts. As she put it to George, 'Mark needs me, and I need Mark. We depend on one another.'

When callers, other than a husband, were allowed, the honour of visiting first (after a brief visit up from Cornwall by George's parents) was accorded to Miss Lewis. She emerged from her specially adapted car. Rolling like a ship, she entered the lift. Each forearm clamped in its cage, altering into a metal crutch held by its T-top, she stumped into Judy's room. She sat down by the bed, shedding harness. George carried Mark over to her. She held the baby partly draped over her shoulder, where he lay like a little rag doll, his cheek against hers. She passed her hand in a soothing motion round and round his back, all her fears of future sleeplessness forgotten.

A day later Betty Combes, raven haired, voluptuous, made a muted (having regard for the baby) explosion into the room. From under her long dark lashes she flashed a glance at the burly George. Had he noted her elegant black dress trimmed with white lace? 'D'you like it?' She laughed. 'You like restraint, don't you?'

'Very nice. Very nice.'

She held up little Mark, her hands under his armpits. 'Jeepers, creepers, where did you get those peepers? Jeepers, creepers, where did you get those eyes?' She kissed him on the end of his button of a nose.

George regarded her. She wasn't bad for thirty. Or had Judy said that she was thirty-one?

The following day it was Charlie's turn. He drooped over the cot, bowed down with his weight of learning, his pale grey eye inspecting the baby through his monocle. 'He's going to be clever. He looks asthmatic.'

'He does *not*.' Judy's small countenance, now showing much less pain when she moved, was filled with protest.

Charlie shone his teeth. 'Asthmatics are clever. I myself am asthmatic. So is my daughter. Speaking as the plain man in the street (I may be wrong), I would say that we are two of the most asthmatic people in Kent.'

'Well, I hope he's clever without being asthmatic.' But she was somewhat mollified.

'I myself have only one child, my daughter. Didn't dare have another. My wife's Heart You Know. We may have been wrong.'

'They tried to stop me breast-feeding Mark.'

Charlie's eyeglass flashed. 'They tried the same thing on with my wife and myself. I threw the Old Vic at the nurse, I can tell you. I said, "We've paid for a private bed. This room has a very nice door. Please use it."' His teeth gleamed in sheer delight at himself. 'And she went!'

He made a stage departure to the lift, his magnificent upper parts sadly let down by the round-toed sandals with the strap across the instep.

George, happy with the improvement in Judy's condition, and resolutely breaking through his prejudices, called in on his half day at the Rainbow Inn. 'Is Mrs Betty Coombes available?'

There was no answer from the waitress.

He looked up to see her eyes fixed on the badge sewn to the breast pocket of his dark blue Oxford blazer (the new one). Perhaps she was fascinated by the glitter of gold from those three embroidered crowns. Perhaps she was trying to make sense of those three words spread across the two pages of the open book. He smiled. 'Dominus Illuminatio Mea; the Lord is my light.'

She started, and blushed. Her hard-leaded pencil wrote down his order. She tore off the page from her pad and placed it beside him. The piece of carbon paper underneath was lifted off, showing her copy of the order transferred on to the flimsy page below. The carbon paper was replaced, sandwiched between the next pair of pages. 'I'll see if Mrs Coombes is free, sir.'

There was an interval of time. Then George heard from behind him the sound of his tea's being brought. The tray was lowered on to the further edge of his table. The hands that placed the cup, saucer and plate; the teapot and hot water pot, and the shallow dish of buttered crumpets, before him, were immaculately washed and manicured. But — their backs were hairy!

His bushy eyebrows drawn together, he looked up sharply. His brow, under the hedge of red curls, crinkled further. A look of distaste spread over the rest of his rugged features.

'Betty's out. At her hairdresser's. Thought I'd bring over your tea myself. Time we got to know one another, eh? Seeing as we both are connected with Judy, as you might say.'

George's brown eyes surveyed the freshly pressed suit of loud checks, the firm unlined face and strong-growing sandy hair. Checks-Suit evidently expected to be invited to sit down on the chair opposite. George did not issue the invitation.

But neither did Captain Archie Simpson go away. 'I was in the Household Cavalry, you know. Blues and Royals. Joined the army at fifteen, was on active service at seventeen, and I've still only just turned forty. Retired on a pension after twenty-two years service. Put on my slippers, so to speak.'

'Yes?' George examined the trim medium height figure, the legs, clothed in narrow trousers and soft leather boots, planted firmly apart and jigging up and down on their heels. The man seemed no more than twenty-five!

'Yes.' The verbal floodgates were open and the words flowed through in a light rapid tone. 'I knew the famous comedian Jack Train, a close personal friend. I was in Paris with a general and two brigadiers. Talk of France! When I was back in London, I met a prostitute that I recognised as a girl I had come across during the war in the north of France.' A lecherous sideglance. 'Of course that started things up. She had had a little operation, and you could get there as often as you liked and nothing happened. If the police come up when I am talking to a French girl, I speak to her in French. That fools them!'

George, a storm cloud gathering on his craggy prop-forward brow, with as much clinking of pots and china as possible poured himself out a cup of tea, added milk, then replenished the teapot from the hot water jug.

But the light tenor voice was continuing. 'I know the London police well. If there's trouble outside a pub, they let it develop a bit, then they put in a couple of their biggest men who hammer everybody in sight. They let the pro's —'

'Pro's?' He was looking more closely at the face before him. Below the firm youthful skin were blemishes. The eyes were not quite bright, even a little sunken. A mix of army fitness and dissipation?

'Prostitutes. They let the pro's stay where they are if they'll let them slip into them once or twice. Hyde Park in London, that's the place for the pro's. The police don't know that they stand sixty yards back from the roadway, under the trees, four and five deep.'

George rose to his six feet one. 'I thought you said that the police made use of them. And now you tell me that they don't know where they are. Which is it, Captain Simpson? Which is it?'

'Eh? Well — well the new recruits don't.'

'I see, Captain Simpson. And now will you kindly let me pass. I've quite lost my appetite for your tea.'

'I say, there's no need to take that tone! Can't we be friends?'

'What do you think, Captain Simpson?' He continued to advance.

Archie surveyed George's fourteen stone and massive shoulders. He stood aside hastily.

At the exit, George found himself face to face with the two 'bouncers' he had noticed on his previous visit. They had just entered from the street. Despite the unpleasant feelings churning inside him, he found himself as before taking an interest in their large physiques. The stockier, wearing a bright yellow shirt with a red tie, was a six footer of about his own size and fourteen stone. The six foot five giant, in a black polo-neck pullover, with pock-marked features, must have been all of seventeen stone.

'Do you fellows play rugby? Could do with you packing down in my scrum.' He grinned.

There were no answering grins. The giant thrust his hardbitten features at him, half blocking his path. 'Were you having words with the boss?'

The smile left George's face. 'Words? Yes, I think you might say we were having words.'

And he brushed past him and made his way towards his cottage.

Back by the table, Archie raised his voice. 'Toffee-nosed schoolmaster! We've just lost a customer there that we can well do without.'

Chapter Thirteen

Judy, her arm linked through George's and leaning on him, slowly descended the front steps of the nursing home towards the Reverend Charles Hare's small black car. A flock of rooks, disturbed by this human activity, rose from a lawn, clamorous wings climbing the early December sky. They wheeled away towards the church steeple, rising in the distance above the tops of the trees like an immense thorn, and so vanished.

When Judy was safely into the back of the car, baby Mark, almost invisible in a huge shawl, but such of his face as showed closely inspected by Charlie's monocle, was passed into her by the starch-aproned nurse. Evidently the monocle was satisfied by what it had seen, for its owner uttered in an intellectual drawl, 'That young man will do very well, asthmatic or not.'

As the car pulled up at George and Judy's new home above Miss Lewis's ground floor flat, Rose advanced from the front door. George's eyes were on her dark brown hair gathered in a simple bun on her soft neck. He liked brunettes. Brown hair seemed to him to speak of sincerity, home making, quietness concealing deep waters. Judy had arranged for her to come in daily during the school winter holidays. Tenderly Rose received from George, seated beside his wife, the animated shawl. She gazed down at the tiny countenance. Was she seeing in it something of George himself? She bore little Mark indoors and up to the nursery. There she placed him in the crib which she had previously warmed with a hot-water bottle. George, carrying Judy's suitcase with one hand, and the other about her waist, slowly ascended the staircase. The sound of Charlie's car could be heard returning to his own home nearby.

It was a week later, as Judy sat up in bed at six in the morning giving Mark the first of his four four-hourly feeds, that she announced, 'Rose will have to go. I need the money for Christmas. It's already the fifteenth, and no Christmas shopping done.'

George, in bed also, stared at her. 'Love, you took on Rose for a month! You can't let people down like that. She'll have been counting on the money.'

Judy moved Mark over from one breast to the other. His rosebud mouth enfolded the dark brown nipple. 'I thought you'd be glad. You're always saying that money is short.'

'Yes, but . . . Love, a contract is a contract. People have the right to be treated decently. What about yourself? You had a hard time.'

'I'm feeling miles better. I promised myself that I'd take Mark round the shops and show him Father Christmas. I thought of nothing else in the nursing home. Father Christmas might give him a rattle.'

'But why then did you take on Rose for the whole of the holidays? Why not just for a week?'

'She mightn't have come for just a week. There are plenty of holiday jobs in the town.'

'Judy dear, this is awful!'

A querulous note entered her voice. 'I can't stand this arguing. My milk is only just getting established. You could drive it away if you upset me.'

He looked at her pale washed out face. 'All right, sweetheart. I'll speak to Rose.'

He did so next morning as she swept the sitting-room. 'I'm so very sorry. She's always changing her mind, I know.'

Rose stood holding the long handle of the brush, her dark eyes fixed on the little pile of the sweepings. ''Tis all right.'

'She had a long confinement. It's left her very emotional. Here's your wages for the week.'

Uneasily he contemplated the deep gloom in the gentle face as she received the cash. She needed the money! His hand plunged into the inner pocket of the shabby blazer. Extracting his wallet, he drew a note from it, caught hold of her hand, and forced the money into her palm. 'That'll tide you over until you can find another job. You're due for a week's notice.'

She pushed the note with equal vigour back into his hands. 'I can get a job tomorrow.'

To his astonishment, he saw a tear on her cheek. He could hardly be expected to know that she was seeing a tiny countenance that was a replica of his own; seeing a month of caring for George's baby now lying in ruins about her feet.

She turned her back on him, put her face into her large work strong hands, and her buxom form trembled. She made for the door.

He caught up with her in the porch. He put his palms on her soft shoulders. His brown eyes, filled with concern, peered round at her half concealed face. 'Rose, dear, you're *due* for a week's notice. You've a *right* to the money.'

She shook her head vigorously, and once more he caught the scent that, it seemed, she always wore when he was present. 'I don't want no money. I can get a job tomorrow.'

As she hastened away, he called after her lamely, 'Well, I'll see you next term.'

'What was all that about?' were Judy's first words as he entered the bedroom. Mark was having his ten o'clock feed.

'She refused to take an extra week's pay in lieu of notice. Said she could get a job tomorrow.' He deemed it expedient not to mention Rose's distress. It would seem like a reproach to his wife.

Judy was triumphant. 'There, I told you so!'

He also deemed it expedient not to point out to her that she had told him nothing of the sort. But his mind was burdened. A little later he was knocking on Charlie's door.

The Reverend Charles Hare eyeglassed the rugged form. 'Come in! Come in!'

'Is your daughter at home? I heard that she'd arrived.'

Was his daughter at home? Charlie stood reflecting a moment, his shoulders bowed in his eminent barrister pose. He wasn't sure. But he'd find out. He'd never let you down, except in a crisis. He wasn't prejudiced but, speaking as a plain man in the street (he might be wrong), he would say that she was exceptionally talented. He always said that the bough didn't fall far from the tree. As between her talent and his, it was, with all due respect, six of one and half a dozen of the other.

George smiled to himself as he followed the bowed figure heavy with its weight of learning. Charlie, triumphantly and outrageously, despite his frequent shrewdness about others, never told himself the truth about himself. But, then, he didn't know it.

The daughter, her extremely blonde hair doubtless inherited from her mother or her hairdresser; and her tall gaunt form undoubtedly inherited from her father, was introduced. She departed up the staircase, bowed over a tray of tea and sandwiches, to the bedroom of her mother, that perpetual invalid.

'Charlie, I'm worried! There's nothing that you can do about it. I'm quite shamelessly asking you to be a father confessor.'

'Sit down. Sit down. Tea is called for.'

The silver teapot was produced from a cupboard. A kettle was already simmering on the low turned ring beside the gas fire, its clays white hot.

George, conscious of his fourteen stone, lowered himself carefully on to one end of the elegant sofa. 'I thought that teapot never left your locker in the staff room!'

'Only in the holidays. Now, old boy, what's the trouble?'

'I don't like the way we've treated Rose.' He gave the story. 'But I can't argue with Judy. She's gone through quite an ordeal, with breast-feeding a further strain. Oh, I know that it's the natural and healthy thing to do in the long run, but it can be a strain in the immediate.'

The Reverend Charles Hare's features were unusually grave. With his back to George he said, 'You told me that your good lady wife used to smoke cheap scented cigarettes as a schoolgirl. Sometimes she had heart palpitations.'

George's brown eyes were wide. He stared at the figure kneeling beside the gas ring. 'What's this got to do . . .'

Charlie rose and walked across, a cup and saucer in either hand. 'Not too much milk in your tea, I hope? Er — you said, jokingly I know, that whenever — er — Judy wanted something to which you were opposed, she always played the card that an argument brought on her palpitations.' He passed over George's cup and sat down at the other end of the small sofa. 'Forgive me for bringing it up. I do know how deeply fond you are of her, and I do want to stress —'

'No, no, Charlie. I *did* tell you that. And I *did* come to you for council. But . . . I'm puzzled. She's been pretty well off smoking since we married. She never mentions her heart nowadays.'

Charlie leaned his thin form towards the burly George and fixed him with his monocle. 'Perhaps she doesn't need to — now.'

'Now?'

'She's a very determined lady about — er — feeding the baby herself, and I admire her for it. I don't see her dropping the first of the four feeds for even as much as five months. Five months during which you, allegedly, might drive away her milk.'

'Judy's not a bit like that!' George's bull neck was beginning to redden.

'Forgive me, old man, but *nine* months probably before the last feed is given up and the baby is fully weaned. That's the way it was with my good wife. Are you sure —'

George set down his untasted tea on a nearby octagonal Indian table, inset with little pieces of ivory suggesting a pattern of leaves. 'Honestly, Charlie, you've got her all wrong. She may wheedle, but she doesn't go in for that kind of moral blackmail.' He rose. 'Besides, her milk will get more and more established as time goes on. Well, I'd better be on my way home. She'll be wondering where I am. Sorry about the tea.'

At the door, Charlie shone his teeth. 'I'm afraid I offended you.'

George put his hand for a moment on his old friend's arm. 'Certainly not. Oh, in all this discussion about breast feeding, we've quite forgotten poor Rose.'

'But she told you that she could get a job tomorrow!'

'Yes . . . That's what's puzzling me. Why was she so desperately upset? Perhaps she felt that she was being treated in an extremely offhand manner, which she was. I can think of no other explanation. Well, I shouldn't have messed up your — your arrangements like this.'

Charlie shook his head. 'No mess. Come any time.'

As he returned to the sofa and his tea, his daughter was drooping her way towards the kitchen with the now empty tray. He removed his monocle and substituted his spectacles. 'Don't they say that love is blind? In the case of our George, very blind. I'm afraid that young lady is going to lead his kind heart into trouble, money trouble most like. Push him to live beyond his means. And that's something that a master at a school like this can't afford to do. He has to remain respectable. Or he's out.'

He picked up *The Times*, and buried himself in the columns of that most respectable of journals.

Judy, in her determination that Mark should visit Father Christmas, and against George's pleas that she should give herself longer to recover her strength, not to mention that the baby would be too young to focus his eyes on Santa Claus, set out down the lane a week before Christmas. George wheeled the pram, and his wife hooked her arm into his. But they hadn't even reached the bend towards the town, when he felt her weight on him growing ever greater, and her movements ever slower.

'I can't go on, George. I think I've got a dropped womb. It happened to a girl at the Rainbow Inn.' She burst into tears.

He let go of the pram handle and enfolded her shaking body in his arms. 'Of course you haven't, darling. A long labour like yours is bound to have taken a great deal out of you. It's that same old impatience of yours driving you on. You'll slow up your recovery if you can't contain it.'

'I've just dreamed and dreamed of wheeling Mark round the shops.'

'And so you shall. Leave it for three days, stay up a little longer each day, and we'll try again.'

Later he bore Mark to his cot. He stood a moment regarding his son's little crumpled face buttoned up in sleep.

The second expedition was successful. Mark was pushed down the large toy shop to the grotto at the end, and lifted on to Father Christmas's lap. His tiny fingers were gently prised open by Judy, a small rattle was thrust by Father Christmas into his chubby palm, and his fingers instantly closed about it. Judy, tired but satisfied, elected to return home at once.

Two days later she issued out on her own, wheeling the pram. Mark must be exhibited to all at the Rainbow Inn. As she passed *The Brambles*, Rose was hanging out washing on the line.

Judy met the situation with her customary dash. 'I'm sorry, Rose, that I called our arrangement off. But you know how it is.'

''Tis all right. I have another job now.' Her voice was restrained. Her eyes never left the baby in the pram.

'I knew you'd find something.'

Judy resumed her progress. She addressed Mark, buttoned up in his little blue woollen jacket, on his head a blue woollen cap crowned by a white bobble. 'I once swore that I would never sink to Rose's life; to a life of launderng and darning and hanging out washing on a line. And here I am, washing Your Lordship's nappies!' She leaned forward and gave him a playful tap on his button of a nose. 'You think I'm your slave, don't you? Don't you? Well, you're quite right. I am. And shall I tell you why I am? Because you're my future, my hope, my everything. You're *me*.'

When Judy was not back at five, George began to worry. Oh, she should be safe enough with Betty Coombes and her cushion of a cat. Even that Archie Simpson (a look of distaste suffused his craggy features) would see that she was all right. But it was just about the shortest day of the year, and dusk with its accompanying chill was already closing in.

He rose from his armchair and made his way down to the cottage. The latter had been let to Mr Tremble and Kettledrums with the proviso that George should remain in control of the garden. Threading his way among the pruned back rose-bushes, he reached the pigeon box. This was mounted on the top of a five foot post to put it beyond the reach of cats. Half of the long shaped box had had its solid sides and end removed, to be replaced by wire mesh. In this half, the pigeon spent most of its day regarding the world about it, with an occasional peck at its bowl of bird seed, or a drink from its bowl of water. He found that it had already retreated into the greater shelter of the other half.

'You'll have to come out of there in a moment, you know. If I don't give your bedroom a clean, you'll get one of your bird diseases. Besides, it's time you had a fly around. And look out for cats.'

The pigeon turned his head sideways, regarded him with one eye which it blinked, but made no other comment.

'I'll start with your living-room . . .'

He opened the wire meshed door, Pulling out the droppings-fouled straw, he tossed it on to a nearby compost heap. He returned with a small bundle of fresh straw in his left hand and the nozzle end of the garden hose in his right. After sluicing down the area, he spread out the straw.

'Now, out you come!'

He stretched his left arm down the length of the box, but the pigeon escaped his clutch by retreating to the very back of the compartment. He fetched out a pinch of seed from a bag in his left pocket and sprinkled it on the clean straw. The pigeon turned its other profile, examined the bait with its other eye, blinked — and remained where it was.

'Very well. Pigeons are said to like water. So let's wash out your bedroom with you in it. That will drive you out.'

The jet of water was directed at the fouled straw. The pigeon turned its head downwards, regarded the water swilling about its feet — and didn't budge.

'Oh, come out, you silly creature!'

He increased the force of the jet by turning the nozzle. Judy and the pram had still not passed the gate, homeward bound. He couldn't spend much longer over this stupid bird; he must walk down and find out what was happening, Archie Simpson and his 'bouncers' notwithstanding. The pigeon was getting wetter and wetter, the dusk was deepening, the temperature was falling. Should he close off the jet? Or should he increase his efforts to drive out the bird, so that he could dry it with a cloth? His growing anxiety over Judy and Mark, and over the pigeon, combined to induce in the usually steady George something approaching panic. He opened the nozzle to its full. But this merely pressed the pigeon into a corner, its face pushed up against the wall, its body quivering under the liquid bombardment drenching its back.

He closed off the nozzle and threw the hose down on to the ground. 'You must take your chances,' he almost shouted.

A light came on in a lower room, and he had a glimpse of Mr Tremble's nose pressed against the window. Kettledrum's chalk white face, the inevitable cigarette hanging out of the corner of his mouth, also appeared. The sound of a prolonged bout of coughing, muted by the intervening pane, reached George's ears. He'll kill himself, was his passing thought. Shouldn't wonder if he hasn't got anaemia!

Shutting the cage door, he strode out of the gate. But he had only reached the turn towards the town, when he saw Judy hastily pushing the pram up the slope.

She stopped, panting. 'Thank goodness you've come. I'm exhausted. I let the time slip by. Mark must have his six o'clock feed.'

He took the pram from her. 'Love, you're still trying to do far too much! Couldn't Betty Coombes have pushed the pram at least part of the way?'

'She had to go on duty. Let's hurry. Mark's hungry, and my breasts are bursting.'

But as soon as the baby was suckling, George's thoughts turned uneasily to the pigeon. He told her the story. 'It's getting cold. I may have to bring it in for a spell, droppings or no droppings.'

Changing into his old blazer, he slipped a torch into his pocket. As he strode along, the breeze nipped his ears.

In the ring of light from the torch, the pigeon sat a sodden spiritless bundle, its soaked feathers, robbed of trapped air, unable to keep it warm. He reached to the length of his left arm. As he grasped it, it made no resistance. Cradling it in the crook of his right arm, and lighting his way with his left, he tramped back up the lane.

He looked down at the bird. 'If it wasn't for those infernal droppings of yours, you'd make a very nice house pet. D'you know that? There's nothing I'd like better than to have you strutting about the house.'

In the dusk, the soaked feathers offered no comment.

As he entered the sitting-room, Mark, drowsy and sated, looking not unlike a miniature drunk, was being borne towards his nursery and his cot. George switched on the black and white television and tuned in the picture.

Sitting down in his chair, large to match his proportions, he manoeuvred the pigeon on to his left shoulder. 'Now watch, and try to absorb some culture.' Soon he, and perhaps the pigeon, were deep in a monochrome drama. Judy joined them.

Half an hour later, George felt a movement from the silent bundle. Ten minutes later, there was a slight flutter of wings. A moment after, right into his ear, there came a sound soft as velvet.

'Did you hear it coo!' said Judy.

George rubbed his cheek against the bird's downy head. 'You seem to have found your tongue! Dried out, have we, in the warmth of the room? And made an awful mess of my shoulder, I'll be bound.'

He crossed and knelt down in front of Judy, the pigeon still on its perch.

She surveyed his blazer. 'Not a spot!'

He stood up, took the pigeon into his hands, and stroked it. 'Not a spot, eh! You've surpassed yourself.'

He stretched out his great palm and stood the pigeon on it, facing towards him. He reached out his lips towards it, pursing them up in a kiss. The pigeon responded at once, poking forward its own head and touching his lips with its peak.

'Just look at that!' said Judy. 'He really seems to love you.'

Down at the box, he placed the bird on the roof of its bedroom. 'I suppose one of these days you'll desert me; fly off to join the others in Sergeant Finch's pigeon loft. If I don't want that to happen, I must get you a mate, mustn't I?'

The pigeon made no reply. If it were entertaining any plans for its matrimonial future, it was playing its cards close to its feathers and keeping tight-beaked about them.

He replaced the wet bedding in the inner part of the box with a generous handful of dry straw. The pigeon snuggled into it. George departed.

Once more the yellow ragwort clothed the corners of the fields. Once more the rooks were cawing silhouettes flapping into the April sun. Once more George found himself involved in a crisis staff meeting called at the request of Miss Fetlock. Both Art Mistress and Riding Instructress, Miss Fetlock possessed horse-like teeth which suggested that at any moment she might break into a well-bred whinny. By a gallant army major out of a clergyman's daughter, her breeding could not be faulted. A stayer rather than a sprinter, she could be counted on when the going was heavy, and had been on the staff for fifteen years. She was, however, not without speed, and had applied herself so assiduously to the previous curate that he had fled the parish. His successor also had more than once on a Sunday been observed dodging about among the gravestones when he spied her approach. At night, she stabled herself in lodgings down in the town.

Slygrin, it emerged, that very morning in Art Class had been caught out once again, this time by Miss Fetlock, being — well — just being thoroughly silly. There was a deep significant silence, as always when the English upper classes find themselves in the near presence of obscenity. One was forced to ask oneself: was there *nothing* that this boy could not accomplish with plasticine?

Mr Featherstonhaugh, presiding from the head of the table, shook his head. 'I've had to beat him, of course. Pity. After being very *piano*' (Mr Featherstonhaugh, who had spent the previous holidays on a package tour to Florence, assumed his most Italianate accent) 'very pee-ah-no for me in class, he had just begun to move.'

Mr Snipe's eager nose, which had never been to Italy, stabbed into the conversation. 'He's been very piano' (his pronunciation was barely Italianate) 'for me too.'

The Headmaster suppressed a shudder.

But his disciple had now locked on to the word. 'Yeldham Minor has also been very piano.' This time it was unblushingly English. 'However, he's begun to move.'

Mr Featherstonhaugh hastily glanced at his watch. 'I think we must get back to our classrooms. The boys have been waiting some time. We can't ask too much of the form captains.'

George at once found himself in combat with young Chesterton-Galsworthy.

'Chesterton-Galsworthy, quite apart from your statement that the Amazon flows through Egypt, this is once again a wretchedly poor essay. Poor, not just as a piece of Geography, but as a piece of writing.'

'No, sir. I mean, yes sir.'

'Chesterton-Galsworthy, you don't appear to possess one ounce of literary instinct.'

'Yes, sir. I mean, no sir.'

That evening, Chesterton-Galsworthy was again in trouble, this time with Mr Snipe. It was in the building complex at the end of the playground which comprised the two senior dormitories, Mr Snipe's sitting-room and bedroom, and the gymnasium.

'I was passing along the path by the bathroom wall, when I heard you saying to Campbell-Lammerton' — Mr Snipe's lips began to twitch — 'not to beat about the bush' — Mr Snipe's lips entered into a full state of agitation — 'to come straight out with it' — Mr Snipe's lips were now in outright agony — 'I've pissed in the bath. Is that true?'

'No, sir. It was only a joke, sir, as it was Campbell-Lammerton's turn in get into the bath after me.'

'You may regard it as just a rather harmless joke now, Chesterton-Galsworthy, but in a few years' time' (he stared at the boy fidgeting before him in his striped pyjamas; he must be all of thirteen) 'it could be much more serious.'

'No, sir. I mean, yes sir.'

'In any case it is not the sort of language one expects to find in the mouth of a little gentleman. Now pull yourself together and go to your dormitory.'

'Yes, sir. I mean, no sir.'

As Chesterton-Galsworthy pyjama-ed his way out of the room, the full enormity of what had taken place sank ever deeper into Mr Snipe's consciousness. His lips writhing in torture, he cried out after the small retreating back in a kind of strangled thunder, 'A LITTLE GENTLEMAN DOES NOT PISS IN THE BATH.'

Meanwhile George, his spell of dormitory duty over, was making his way down the lane when he perceived Judy hastening towards him.

'I thought you would never come!' Her small face was pale. 'Mark is ill.'

'What!'

'He's just had a green motion. I had a cigarette and a drink down at Betty's, and it's made my milk upset him. Never again! Never again!'

They hastened towards the flat.

'Look, he's four months old now, you've just dropped his two o'clock feed, and for the first time in his life he's had solid food. Couldn't it be that?'

'The vegetable puree was very fluid and there were no lumps in it. I made sure of that. No, it was the nicotine and alcohol in my milk. I was a fool.'

'Well, you'll have to watch that in future of course, but he'll be all right, love. He's a sturdy little fellow.' He looked at her drawn features.

She halted. They were beside the little wayside shrine. He saw that her eyes were fixed on the painted Mother cradling in her arms her painted Baby.

'The birth and the feeding have been a great strain on you, darling. I suppose you felt the need of the lift from the drink and the cigarette. Don't you think that Mark ought to go on to the bottle? You've given him four months?'

She was shaking her head vigorously. 'I'd give my life for Mark. I'd give my life for him. I'd defend him against anyone who offered him harm, no matter what the consequences. I feel — I feel there's something in me of the Madonna.'

Chapter Fourteen

Judy stood with her hand on the handle of the pram, gazing at a row of houses buried in gardens fiery with the colours of June. Everywhere was laburnum, its yellow flowers hanging in scores of parallel festoons, vivid chrome against the dark green leaves and looking like lanterns in a Japanese night; some of the branches taking the shape of flaming pagodas. Among them was the copper-crimson jet of a copperbeech. Two trees stood white with may blossom. Nearby stretched away fields white with daisies, rifts of summer snow; or carpeted with buttercups.

She moved forward again. Presently she was into the High Street of Kingsbridge. Pausing before the window of a tobacconist, she gazed at the packets of cigarettes. Her eyes fastened on one of them. Framed within the circle of the lifebelt illustrated on it, were the head and shoulders of a handsome bearded sailor with a curly moustache, a nautical cap on his head. In the harbour behind him were moored two square-rigged vessels, spreading out their spars against a blue sky.

'Every nice girl loves a sailor,' she sang softly, gazing down at the six months old Mark. 'Well, this nice girl mustn't love that sailor too much, must she?'

She prodded him playfully. His toothless mouth spread open.

'What a *lovely* smile, darling! Last time I smoked a cigarette, I upset you, didn't I?' She held out her left hand and smacked the back of it with her right. '*Naughty* Mummy!'

Mark gurgled.

'But oh, how I long to have one! And a drink! Just one little drink!' She sighed. 'But you're worth it all. You're only asking for two breast feeds a day now, aren't you?' She sighed again. 'But three more months to go!'

She went round to the side of the pram. Lifting him a little with one hand, she puffed out his pillow with the other. 'We must give you the very best possible start in life, mustn't we?' For a moment she put her cheek against his warm plump little face. 'You're worth it, you're worth it, you're worth it.'

Suddenly Mark sneezed, a tiny little sound. But it shadowed Judy's face. 'Miss Lewis hasn't given you her cold, has she? I asked her to be careful.'

She resumed their progress. At the show window of the Rainbow Inn, she perused the photograph on its stand of the six hostesses in their neglige, their bosoms half spilling out of their bodices. As far as bosoms were concerned she could, at least in her temporary development while feeding Mark, approach a little nearer to holding her own. Through the window she caught sight of a lush figure. An abundance of dark hair fell about its cheeks as it leaned over the bar, a vast ginger cat at its buxom elbow. Betty Coombes was exactly the woman she needed to confide in at that moment. If, in so doing, she of necessity approached the bar, it was simply because she wanted someone to talk to. That was all. Someone to talk to.

She wheeled the pram towards the doorway. A customer was emerging. She caught the sweet smell of alcohol on his breath. She cast an almost frightened glance at the bottles within. Abruptly she turned the pram and continued along the street.

Making her way up the lane, she passed the cottage. Mr Tremble, a drip at the end of his nose and the battered hat on his head, was in the garden among George's roses. Seated on a wood and canvas folding chair, he was smoking The Pipe, doubtless having just returned from a visit to The Grave. Kettledrum stood beside him, the usual cigarette hanging from the corner of his mouth. The long ash at its end fell on to the grass, dislodged by the bout of coughing that shook his bowed form.

'You'll have to do the same as me,' Judy called out with a smile. 'Give them up. And I know how hard *that* is.'

'Ah, it's too late for me now, Missis.' His voice was a croak. 'Both me lungs is gone. They'll have to put me in a box soon.'

'Oh, don't say that!'

'I don't know what he' (he jerked his thumb at Mr Tremble) 'will do for his fry then.'

Even on reaching her present home, she still continued onwards. Only the little wayside shrine brought her to a halt.

She gathered up Mark into her arms. 'Look at the baby, sweetheart, with his golden halo!'

Mark's eyes, large in his small face, dutifully inspected the Child, but he offered no comment beyond blowing a bubble.

'And look at his Mummy! She has a halo too, hasn't she?'

Mark blew another bubble.

'*She* would never let her baby down, would she? Of course she wouldn't. Never, never, never.'

Meanwhile George, now thirty-seven years of age but his six foot one and fourteen stone body as athletic as ever, strolled across the playground of Worcester Hall Preparatory School maintaining the law. It was his turn to be on Late (afternoon and evening) Duty.

He heard a sound coming from the Art Block, that smart modern prefab with its pinewood walls fitted with rows of windows, and its flat felt lined roof. He opened the door quietly and peered in. Miss Fetlock, the Riding and Art mistress, her back to him, had apparently kept in her senior class as a punishment for unsatisfactory work. From time to time she was given to setting little examinations to her oldest pupils on the history of art. Now, while they continued with their drawing, painting or modelling projects, she was marking their papers. 'Oh!' Her thick blue pencil angrily crossed out something. 'Fool!' Whose paper was it? Judging from the expressions on the faces ranged before him, some of which he noticed had become aware of his presence, everyone was on edge. 'Idiot!' She lifted the lid of a silver box on her high desk, at which she sat on a stool of corresponding height. She took from the box a eucalyptus lozenge which she popped into her mouth. The blue pencil slashed at the paper. 'Ass!' George signalled to the boys to take no notice of him. Before his fascinated gaze, the little pile of corrected papers rose. The little pile of lozenges in the silver box diminished. The point of the blue pencil snapped. The Art Block filled with the scent of eucalyptus.

'Excuse me, Miss Fetlock —'

She started round, shying away from him.

'I didn't want to disturb you. But the boys are now assembled in their classrooms, waiting for tea. I need a prefect in each classroom to keep an eye on things. I wonder could you spare just the prefects?'

Miss Fetlock gave a well bred whinny. 'Of course, Mr Brown. I didn't notice how the time had run on. I must get home myself. Boys, clear your tables and put away in the cupboards. Prefects, leave your work as it is and go at once. We'll tidy up in the morning.'

Ten minutes later she was to be seen, in her tweeds and heavy brogues, striding away down the lane looking as if, at any moment, she was about to break into a canter.

George returned to the main building. There he patrolled the long corridor, off which opened most of the classrooms.

Presently the voice of Carruthers, now nine years of age, piped up at his elbow. 'Please, sir, a prefect has sent me to report myself because my tin of marbles was making a horrible noise as I was running along.'

George struggled to control his features. The innocence of the explanations as they always reached him! Much more likely that the once homesick Carruthers, now no longer 'pee-ah-no', or even 'piano', had been shaking the tin vigorously as the leader in a centre of din. Indeed, one could have reported of him that he had begun to move quite forceably.

George extracted one of the pens clipped inside his breast pocket, their tops emerging in a line above its edge. From the side pocket of his blazer he produced a piece of paper. This he held flattened against the corridor wall.

'Now, Carruthers, I'm writing down your name just as a warning. If you're not sent to me again, the paper is thrown away and that's the end of the matter. But if you *are* sent to me again, then I underline your name, it goes down later in the staff room Conduct Book, and you get an imposition. Is that understood?'

'Yes, sir.'

There was a loud clatter.

George's bushy eyebrows, startled, drew together. A shoehorn had just fallen out of Carruthers' right-hand trousers pocket on to the bare planks of the passage. He saw that the shoehorn was attached to the pocket by an immensely long piece of string. Also that Carruthers was engaged in blowing his nose. Evidently the action of pulling out the handkerchief had dislodged the shoehorn.

'Carruthers, what on earth do you want that for?'

'Please, sir, if I leave it in the dormitory, it gets taken.'

He gathered up the shoehorn and string and stuffed them, together with the handkerchief, back into the pocket, which consequently developed a bulge.

'But why the string?'

'So it won't get lost, sir.'

'But why such a long piece of string?'

'So it will reach to my shoes, sir.'

Carruthers sneezed, pulled out his handkerchief, and again there was the clatter.

'Does it fall out every time you blow your nose?'

'Usually always, sir.'

'Usually always, eh? Well, old chap, let's see if we can't organise something better. What's the other end of the string attached to?' He drew it out. He saw a small fisherman's lead weight. 'Now let's put this weight into your left pocket, so. There you are! Shoehorn and string in your left pocket, handkerchief in your right. How's that?'

'Yes, sir. Thank you, sir.' And Carruthers ran off happily.

At half past five the bell went for the tea of bread, butter and jam, and their own jams and cakes if they had any left. George moved from classroom to classroom, beginning with the youngest boys, releasing the forms one at a time to prevent a stampede. When he reached Carruthers' classroom it was to find him seated at a double desk, while another boy, at the other end of the seat, his elbow resting on the desk lid, was very slowly advancing the point of an open penknife towards one of Carruthers' eyes. The latter, his face contorted, the said eye watering, was tenaciously keeping it open and unmoving. George ordered the trial of courage to be discontinued, and not repeated.

Tea over at six, and prayers and *Glory Be to Jesus* concluded, the Headmaster and the rest of the staff left, and George presided from the Headmaster's desk over 'prep' in the Big Schoolroom. The boys had previously equipped themselves with the necessary text books and exercise books to cope with the preparation work set by their teachers. A shortened prep, however, was all that was required from the seven and eight year olds. At the half way point they left for the

Pink and Brown dormitories respectively. The nine and ten year olds were in their Blue and Red dormitories shortly after half past seven, and were expected to be in their beds as near to eight o'clock as might be, and there were allowed to read until Lights Out at eight thirty. The eleven, twelve and thirteen year olds, under the eye of the prefects, read in the library or continued their projects in the Model Room for an hour. Then they crossed the playground to the Green and Orange dormitories, elevens and some twelves in the first, remainder of the twelves and the thirteens in the second. There they came under the jurisdiction of Mr Snipe, whose quarters, together with the gymnasium, were included in the same two storey block.

As George began patrolling the dormitories in the main building, it was to hear in the distance the voice of Carruthers. He was now captain of a more senior dormitory, the Blue for nine year olds. 'Get into bed, Robinson, before I could to ten. One, two, three, four . . .' As George approached, the count had become, 'Eight, nine, nine and a quarter, nine and a half, nine and three quarters —'

George assumed sternness. 'Into bed, Robinson, when the dormitory captain tells you. What's this?' He removed an open diary from Robinson's hand. He read aloud, "Remember to bash Hill Minor up after Lights Out. Hill Minor's going to pay for it. Hill Minor is going to have his gob sloshed in." Gob sloshed in! What's Hill Minor done to merit so terrible a fate?'

'Please, sir, he's a sneak. He sneaked on me.'

'Sneaked on you! How? Where?'

'Please, sir, he told the Matron I hadn't used toothpaste when cleaning my teeth.'

'Hill Minor, that wasn't very nice of you! We don't like sneaks at this school. You know that.'

'Yes, sir.'

'Matron's quite capable of taking care of the dormitories unaided. And Robinson, remember, no gob sloshing after Lights Out. I'm taking Hill Minor for Geography tomorrow. I refuse to have him answering me through battered lips. I expect him to arrive in class tomorrow with his gob unsloshed. Is that clear?'

'Yes, Sir.'

George, controlling his craggy features with difficulty, switched out the light. He made his way into the playground. The school cat was sitting licking a paw, then passing it over her face again and again. Putting his head back, he filled the playground with a roar of laughter from his mighty chest.

The cat fled.

Next day after breakfast, George stacked up his kitbag with corrected exercise books prior to making his way to Worcester Hall. Suddenly Mark, sitting up in his pram at the window, gave his funny little sneeze. Judy was into the sitting-room from the kitchen like a flash.

'She *has* given him her cold!'

'Who?'

'That Miss Lewis! She promised she'd wear a face mask while looking after him. Boy babies are much more delicate than girl babies. And she's a matron! She's had some training as a nurse!'

'I'm sure he'll be all right. Look, it's a lovely day. We'll take him out into the sun. It's my easiest day of the week. I've a double free period before lunch and I'm right up to date with my marking. I'll cut lunch at the school. Then I start the afternoon with another free period.'

They took Mark to the zoo. The powerful tiger with his silken shoulders was an especial success, Mark waving his small hands about and blowing a number of bubbles. As they walked along the cages in the heated Bird House, George burst out laughing. He pointed to a metal label and read, 'Slaty-headed Scimitar Babbler.' A soft little unassuming bird sat at the back of its huge cage, seemingly not daring to look at the human beings staring in at it, silently (no babbling) and sadly gazing down its long curving beak, trying to live down the appalling name with which it had been saddled. Mark, becoming brown in the sunshine, sneezed no more, and Judy was comforted.

'Missed you at lunch,' were Charlie's first words as George appeared in the staff room.

'Wife was upset. Thought Matron had given our son a cold. So I took the family out to cheer her up. She's made her way to the Rainbow Inn to show off our offspring.'

'Speaking of the Rainbow Inn, would you rather have a loose woman in a tight dress, or a tight woman in a loose dress?'

Mr Snipe's titter had hardly been launched, before it died. Was this playing cricket with a straight bat? From a man of forty-four! A clergyman too! Surely here was more than a hint of stepping back to a moral square leg.

'Well,' said George, 'and speaking of the Rainbow Inn, I suppose whichever was the more likely to bring in the most customers.'

Charlie twinkled through his monocle. 'Either way, it's a case of throwing *girls* before swine.'

Mr Snipe, dumbfounded, thrust his head into his locker in a pretence of hunting for books.

Aside from the fact that Carruthers was repeatedly appointed a dormitory captain, Miss Lewis had not failed to notice Mr Featherstonhaugh's lack of support at that earlier staff meeting. In the interval, she had quietly been making certain enquiries. From these, she had learnt of the extremely straight bat that young Carruthers invariably presented in the nets to the bowling of the headmaster. Against a Straight Bat, she knew that she had no chance. Consequently she had silently withdrawn from that particular campaign. As to George's charge that she was saddling 'a helpless little boy' with an adverse reputation, initial anger had turned to hurt, then to self questioning. Was Mr Brown perhaps . . . Her enquiries had further revealed George's enormous popularity among the boys. A weak teacher who could not keep order was a menace to any school. He earned for himself contempt rather than liking from the very people making use of his weakness. Mr Brown, it appeared, was capable of maintaining a total control seemingly without raising a finger.

But, though George himself was ever more passing into Miss Lewis's good books, the Episode of the Cold had not been closed. Fortunately, when Judy's invasion of the dining-room took place the following day during the Milk Break, Mr Featherstonhaugh was not present. At that moment, immaculate in a dark grey suit, a dapper little smile under his dapper little moustache, he was seated in the sunshine at The Oval in London watching a test match. It was certainly to be hoped that one was about to see the ball being met with an impeccably straight bat (no question of any general stepping back to square leg). However, one permitted oneself to regard with an indulgent eye such senior batsmen, once they had played themselves in, hooking the ball to the leg side, and other similar liberties.

Miss Lewis, presiding behind the urn in her beflowered muslin dress, stared at the accusing finger pointing at her.

Sparks seemed to fly along it from vivid blue eyes backed by vivid little blue ear-rings. 'You knew you had a cold. Why didn't you wear a face mask? Why didn't you? Why didn't you?'

'Really, Mrs Brown —'

'Yesterday Mark was sneezing, and today he is coughing.' (Actually, he had given only one cough.) 'Baby boys are much more delicate than baby girls. You may have *killed* him.'

'Really, Mrs Brown, you're being ridiculous —'

George, who had been regarding his well nigh hysterical wife with a mixture of disbelief and horror from the moment the door had burst open, took a step forward.

'Ridiculous, am I? When you've put my son's life in danger? You're not a mother, that's easily seen.'

He saw Miss Lewis flinch. The barb had driven in deep.

Pressing on the table, and shaking with anger, she had lifted up her distorted frame from behind the urn. 'I shall report your behaviour, Mrs Brown, to the Headmaster on his return.' She glanced across at Charlie, whose monocle had just dropped out of his eye to the full length of its black ribbon. 'And I'm quite sure that Mr Hare, as Senior Master, won't expect me, after this gross invasion, to agree to your remaining any longer in the flat above me.' She sank down.

'So not content with infecting my baby, you're now going to put him out of his nursery —'

'That's enough, Judy!' George's arm was round his wife's shoulders and he was pressing her towards the door.

'Aren't you going to stand up for your son?'

'That's enough, Judy! That's enough!' He got her outside the door and closed it. 'You must be mad! You struggle to secure the flat, and then you throw it away like this! Well, you're not going in there again if I have to carry you home.'

But she made no further struggle. Indeed, under the iron grip of his great hand on her arm, she seemed to him to become not only submissive, but — to be almost smiling! He remembered then his protest, 'I *care* that that young couple have gone away thinking that I'm a wife beater;' and her reply, 'I sometimes wish you were.'

When they reached the flat, it was to find Mark uncovered in his cot, sleeping peacefully on his hands and knees, with his head turned sideways on the pillow and his little nappied bottom stuck up into the air.

The next day, on George's return from the school, Judy remarked, 'I don't think Miss Lewis meant what she said.'

'Oh yes, she did. Charlie has had to ask us to go. We'll be lucky if she doesn't mention what happened to the Headmaster. In fact, Charlie tells me that he actually requested her not to. If he hadn't given us notice, she would have done so like a shot. He's just trying to save my job.'

'After a few days, when she's calmed down —'

'No, Judy. Remember your own words? I do. "If things go wrong, Charlie, we'll leave at once. No fuss. No arguments."'

For a moment she was taken aback. But then, 'I didn't mean it *literally*.'

'This is one time you must mean it literally. Very literally. Charlie has been my closest friend going back a very long way. I cannot and will not let him down.'

She examined his face. She fell silent.

Two days later, returning from the school, he opened the front door to hear weeping from the flat above. He knew Miss Lewis to be at the school. He sprinted up the stairs. Judy was seated on the lid of the wooden chest which held a variety of teddybears and a large pink elephant, presented by friends and relatives for the future entertainment of Mark.

He went down on his knees and wrapped his arms about her small trembling form. 'What *is* it, sweetheart?'

She put her face against his. 'My nursery, George. I've poured so much work and so many dreams into it.'

'It's not being dismantled, love. We can move it into the cottage almost as it is, even to the curtains.'

Suddenly she shook herself free of him. She began to utter scream after scream.

He rose. 'Judy, what is it? You'll wake up Mark! You'll be heard all over the neighbourhood! We're not being put out on the street. We're being given time to make our arrangements.'

The screams ceased. 'You'll lose me my milk.'

George remembered Charlie's warning. He must stand his ground. 'Your milk is well established.' He added quickly, 'Love, you've done magnificently by Mark. By now you've given him six months. Why not call it a day?'

She shook her head. The ear-rings threw back at him their blue defiance. 'No, he's to have his nine months.'

There followed arguments in bed. Finally she turned her back on him and drew away to her own side. It was a weary George who rose next morning, got his own breakfast, and dragged his feet up the lane to work. Being a Wednesday, there were no classes after Games. On Changing-room Duty, he supervised the boys as they shed their cricket gear, took a shower, and dressed. He saw them down to the playing fields and left them in Charlie's care. Then, at four o'clock, and filled with apprehension, he made his way home.

He entered the flat to receive an immediate demand from Judy, her face drawn and her eyes red with weeping, that he should ask Charlie to press Miss Lewis to reconsider her decision.

'I can't do it to Charlie, love. I can't do it after all our undertakings to him. An agreement is an agreement. A contract is a contract.'

Suddenly the screaming started again, scream upon scream.

'Judy, you'll frighten Mark!'

'I hate you all, Miss Lewis, Charlie, you. You're all on the school staff, snooty upper class, ganging up against me. I'll commit suicide.'

'Judy, no one is ganging up against you. You're only being asked to transfer Mark's nursery, absolutely intact —'

But the screams drowned his voice. Aghast, he stood feeling helpless. Suddenly he knew, with an almost certainty, that if he turned his back on her and walked out of the room, the screams would cease. He began to move towards the door. Suicide! He glanced at the open window. He imagined the drop outside. She just might . . . He couldn't summon up the courage to walk on.

He swung round. 'All right, Judy! All right! I'll go back to the school and ask Charlie. He's on Late Duty.'

The screams at once died away. She stood looking at him in silence, her face drained.

Descending the staircase, he noticed that the door of Miss Lewis's sitting-room was ajar. But he knew that she would be up in the dormitories, sorting out the linen.

He opened the front door. He found himself confronted by a buxom form in a shabby skirt scrupulously cleaned and pressed. The cardigan was neatly darned at the shoulder. The white freshly laundered blouse fell softly over her breasts. Her dark hair was gathered in a simple bun on the nape of her neck. Her hands, large and strong from house and garden work, but soft and feminine for all that, were held folded in front of her, but clasping and unclasping. For all the agitation expressed in them, they yet brought some measure of calm into his distraction.

Her gentle eyes were wide. 'Is Mrs Brown all right? Mother and I could hear her terrible screaming right down at The Brambles.'

Almost with surprise he found himself holding one of her hands and pouring out the whole story. 'Please don't put it around, Rose. I suppose I shouldn't have told you. Tell your mother the minimum. If the dining-hall invasion gets to Featherstonhaugh's ears, it could cost me my job.'

She glanced quickly down at the powerful hand clasping hers in a painful grip. Despite the pain, her eyes were alight. 'I won't say nothing about that, not even to Mother.'

Somewhat calmed, he released her. They parted in the lane.

Down in the school playing fields, he caught the flash of Charlie's eyeglass in the sun. He told his tale, and made his supplication. 'I feel very ashamed, Charlie.'

'I heard the shrieking. I noticed some of the boys stopping to listen.'

'I wonder how long *my* job will last.'

'Don't let her bully you, George. One doesn't have to have big muscles to be a bully. There are other weapons.'

'I don't think she intends to bully, Charlie. It's just that in some ways she's never grown up. A child, or at least a small child, when it sees something it wants, wants it *now*. Judy wants what she wants, now. The rights or needs of others simply can't enter into the mind of a child. They can't enter into Judy's mind either, or at least not very easily. A child assumes that everyone in its immediate circle is there to serve it. Judy's a bit like that, except of course where Mark is concerned. She'd give her life for Mark. You can't reason with a small child. There isn't much reasoning to be done with Judy. A child, for some things, has a memory like a sieve. When Judy wanted to know where all my salary went, I wrote down the figures for her in simple form on a piece of paper. I included all the things she never thinks of: income tax, rates, insurance, repayment of debts. She said, 'It soon goes, doesn't it!' Thereafter she ceased to think that I was Croesus sitting on his money bags — for a few days. By then it was forgotten, and all the old resentments came creeping back. When a child can't get what it wants, it screams.'

'Try turning your back on her, old chap, and leaving the room. Deny her an audience.'

'Of course you're right, Charlie. In my heart of hearts I knew it at the time. But — there was a threat of suicide, and an open window . . .'

'I assure you it will work. My good lady wife also had a bout of hysteria. To be fair to her, the circumstances were different. She is perfectly capable of consideration. It was immediately after the birth. Post-natal depression. Baby Blues, you know.'

'Did you go to a psychiatrist?'

'A psychiatrist! Not on your nelly!' Charlie shone his teeth. 'A psychiatrist is a man who, for a large fee, tells a husband facts about his wife which the husband had discovered for himself, free of charge, twenty years before.'

'Judy is not totally without powers of consideration. Far from it. She is capable of sensitive feeling, even generosity. My father once wrote, "She is neither your intellectual nor social equal." Naturally I didn't tell her, but she knew that she wasn't approved of. Yet she always speaks to me most kindly about my parents. Moved a vase of dried grasses I had on the mantlepiece because it was partly obscuring a photograph of my mother, whom she pronounced "beautiful." But . . . She is full of dichotomies. Liking and disliking at the same time. Only it's more likely to be in extremes. Love and hate. We all do that to some extent. But most of us manage a certain — er — summing up. Before deciding about something, we survey a period of time. Say, the previous few months, or at least few weeks. Again, rather like a child, she reacts vividly on the spur of the moment to what is happening within that moment.

She doesn't look before and after. She lives within the moment.'

Charlie looked doubtful. 'Isn't there an element of playacting?'

From Charlie, the supreme playactor! 'Yes indeed. But she believes so utterly in her own playacting, that it's hard not to be mesmerised into believing it too. For her, small things are elephant-size. You remember those high winds a couple of winters back? She phoned the school to say that slates were being blown off the cottage roof. I spent the whole day in anxiety until I could get home. I searched around for the slates. Finally I managed to discover half a slate. Half a slate! A morning and an afternoon of anxiety for half a slate! There was a small damp patch in the room we were preparing as a nursery, so we had to leave the cottage and come to your flat. For Judy, that patch spelt possible death to her coming baby.'

'George, old man, I think this could be rather serious.'

'Serious?'

'It sounds to me like the first beginnings of neurasthenia. You know, anxiety reaction. Life is full of ordinary crises. Nobody enjoys them, but most of us can cope with them. For the neurasthenic, they appear to be ten times bigger, and they can't cope.'

'What happens?'

'Eventually they suffer a nervous breakdown. Why didn't you take your good lady out and show her the half slate?'

'She refused to go. Whether it's because she doesn't want to be proved wrong, or because she feels that it's something mechanical that she won't be able to understand, I don't know. She once told me that she never could do Maths at school. I think she's conscious that she has no great powers of reasoning. She — well — she just *isn't* very sagacious. At the same time she's driven by a desperate need to make herself felt. She wants to conquer a world that she can only half understand. And if she can't do it herself, then she must do it through a surrogate. I think she hoped that I would be that surrogate. But I've failed her.'

'Good heavens, old man, you're no failure!'

'Thanks, Charlie. But now I think she has another surrogate. He's too young to help her at the moment, but he lights up her future. His name is — Mark.'

'Hm.' Charlie produced a tissue from the pocket of his plum coloured frock-coat and began to polish his monocle. 'Go home now, George. I'll seize my chance this evening to beard the dragon in its den — that is, if dragons do have beards. But I think the lady will be hard to shift.'

'Once again, thanks Charlie. I still feel ashamed to have asked you.'

'Not at all. Not at all.'

When, later, the dragon did emerge from its lair, that is, the linen-room attached to the dormitories, and had listened to what the Reverend Charles Hare had to say, at least it breathed no fire. Poor young people! She, Miss Lewis, almost pitied them. For all their youth and mobility, they were for ever embroiled in emotional troubles. She was glad that she had never married. Yes, *glad*. The barb that Judy had fired at her, though it had sunk deep, had also served to remind her that, with the departure of the young couple and their baby, so also would depart her vicarious motherhood. No little warm bundle of scented wool in the crook of her arm, no wide eyes looking up at her, no small mouth opening as she spooned in the vegetable puree, no plump cheek against hers as she rubbed a tiny back, no longer, as she sat in the sun, a pram beside her! Besides, George's firm dealing with the situation in the dining-hall had further swung her sympathies towards him. He and she were both experienced fellow professionals who well understood the gross impropriety of the invasion.

And yet . . . And yet . . . She must not allow herself to sink into being a mere creature of impulse. She was the Head Matron and Head Housekeeper of an important preparatory school. Before, she had had such tranquillity as her distorted body would allow. None of the tension, ever more as the days passed, emanating from the flat above; a man's deep quiet voice interrupted by a sharp treble that sometimes took off into a sustained harangue. Sufficient it had been, before their arrival, to twist and turn at night, her radio playing quietly beside her for companionship, trying to discover some physical attitude that would give her a measure of rest. When the quest became impossible, a wine-glass of whisky from the bottle on the bedside table.

'I don't know, Mr Hare. I don't know at all. I must have time to sleep on it.'

Chapter Fifteen

Baby Mark had won the day. Miss Lewis proposed to convey her consent, during the boys' Milk Break, to his remaining in the flat — together with his parents.

Each boy as he, under the Head Matron's eye, filed past the Assistant Matron, received from the latter's hand the small bottle of State-supplied milk. Taking it with him, he made his way out into the playground. The bottles, when empty, were disposed of into a row of large baskets.

As soon as Miss Lewis was satisfied that all was proceeding smoothly, she clanked into the dining-hall. There she took up her accustomed position behind the shining dome of the urn. This had been carried in a few moments earlier on a wooden base by Mrs Finch and Rose, who had then melted back into their netherworld. The members of the teaching staff began to stream towards the dome as towards a temple, with all an Englishman's passion for hot tea and tepid conversation.

Miss Fetlock, taking the corner into the dining-hall close and lengthening her stride, reached the table first. She had been making notes on a pad regarding the brush work of Renoir, notes which she intended to continue. In order to free her hands, she pushed the pad into a small breast pocket in her tweed jacket, and her blue-leaded correcting pencil into her mouth. There she gripped it between her compressed lips like a bit. Reining herself to a halt, she possessed herself of a yellow cup and saucer from the long row of yellow cups and saucers. Moving along the table, she picked up the large yellow jug and poured a little milk into her cup. From the yellow sugar-basin beyond, she transferred some sugar with one of the teaspoons lying beside it, and retained the spoon. On reaching the end of her pilgrimage and arriving at the Dome itself, she committed her cup and saucer into the hand of Miss Lewis. Miss Lewis filled the former by reverently turning the tap at the base of the Dome. Room was left in the cup to weaken its strong contents with boiling water from a kettle. Strong or less strong, she knew, to a religious exactitude, the dedication of each member of the staff.

Behind Miss Fetlock loomed the great figure of George. Like the other male members, instead of leaving his jacket behind in the staff room, he carried it over his arm. This he did in order to ward off the Headmaster's possible disapproval. To do so conveyed the message: in *normal* conditions I should have been wearing it. Outside the windows, a July heatwave scorched the tarmac of the playground. Even the boys were content to stand quietly in the shade of the chestbut tree sipping their milk. George, his shirt sleeves rolled up to the elbow, passed his cup and saucer to the Head Matron with a hairy forearm and a restrained nod. He noted that she was studiously keeping her face expressionless. So it was out of the flat for them! What storms, when he later report it at home, would he have to endure? Well, at least Judy could not blame the decision on him. He also noted that the Matron's light blue eyes kept roving up and down the advancing queue. Was she seeking someone? Or just evading his glance? He would keep out of her way. Receiving back his cup, he retired into the staff room. At the window, he watched the perspiring circle of boys on Penal Drill. They were engaged in hopping round and round on one leg in the narrow offshoot of the playground between the main building and the Art Block. Even the shouted commands of Sergeant Finch carried a wilted note.

Miss Lewis was, in fact, looking for a tall bowed figure surmounted by a bob of grey hair and decorated with an eyeglass on the end of a length of black ribbon. She had decided that correct procedure, and her own dignity, required that it was to the Reverend Charles Hare she should communicate her decision. It would be up to him, then, to pass it on. But, as the queue tapered to its end, no such figure had made its appearance; no voice, supercilious and languorous with its weight of learning, had made itself heard.

Uneasiness in her eyes, she called out, 'Headmaster, is Mr Hare on Playground Duty? Should I have his tea sent out to him?'

A dapper black, edged with pink ribbon, Worcester College Oxford blazer, surmounted by a dapper little smile under a dapper little moustache, sauntered towards her. Had the school been situated in Equatorial Africa, and had it been at the very height of the drought season, Mr Featherstonhaugh would have worn his blazer.

'Ah, Matron, you should have been told. Mr Hare took the Sixth Form down to Kingsbridge to see some of the local industries.' His voice was filled with an urbane and gracious condescension upon Industry. Nevertheless it was devourly to be hoped that the bulk of the Little Gentlemen at Worcester Hall would proceed into the Church, the Armed Services, Politics, Law, Science, Medicine, Finance, Education, Publishing. And Industry? Well, a senior directorship perhaps . . . Art? It was a gentleman's duty to respect Art. But artists! There was hardly a straight bat to be seen among the lot. 'Of course they'll be back in time for lunch. They can have their milk then.'

'Certainly, Headmaster.'

But the light blue eyes were still uneasy. Miss Lewis was tenacious. When once she had decided on a course of action, she meant to see it through. And there was the baby . . . Well, nothing for it but to tell Mr Brown herself. But he wasn't about. He sometimes took his tea into the staff room. Yes, after she had served the second cups of tea, she would nail him there before the bell went for the next class.

In the staff room, George left the window, placed his empty cup on the table, and crossed to his locker. He had a Free Period next — free, that is, for the correction of exercise books. He lifted out a pile of them. Might as well make a start. In the evening he would have two sessions of private coaching. He sat down, took out the correcting pen from the breast pocket of the jacket (the older of his two Oxford blazers, actually) hanging on the back of his chair, and opened the book on the top of the heap. The schoolboy writing danced before his gaze. All he could see was Judy's drawn face, her eyes large and near to hysteria. He closed the exercise book. If, later, he would have to work on until after midnight, so be it. Catching up his blazer, but leaving the books where they were, he repossessed his cup and saucer. He peered into the dining-hall. Miss Lewis was, at that moment, bowed over the urn. He slipped in, and left cup and saucer on the further end of the table. He would spend the next forty-five minutes, despite the heat, walking about the town at the top of his speed. Improve his fitness. Restore his calm. Quickly he moved out of the room.

Miss Lewis had spotted the retreating white-shirted back. She struggled to her feet. 'Mr Brown! Mr Brown, just a moment!'

He had not reappeared. Hastily she slipped each forearm into its cage and gripped the T-tops of the metal crutches. Leaning slightly forward, her buttocks rolling, the rubber stubs covering the feet of the crutches tapping quietly on the polished parquet flooring, she made her way towards the door.

A suave voice raised itself. 'Can I fetch Mr Brown for you, Matron?'

'No thank you, Headmaster.' Mr Featherstonhaugh must not, of course, be privy to what she had to say. 'Mr Brown will be taking his tea in the staff room. We can talk there.'

She noted the deserted exercise books. Plainly he was visiting the toilet and would be back. She moved into the sunshine of the window. Her light short sleeved muslin dress allowed her to enjoy the heat; indeed, heat calmed her pains. Penal Drill had broken up. Outside the front gate, Sergeant Finch was proceeding somewhat unsteadily down the lane. That man would have to go! Her heart missed a beat. Striding past the boys standing in the shade of the chestnut-tree, and towards the same gate, was a burly form with a shock of red curls, carrying a blazer over its arm.

George had not heard Miss Lewis's belated call. Unfortunately for his intention of a swift non stop walk, Sergeant Finch, emboldened by beer, clutched his sleeve as he would have passed him. The neck of a bottle protruded from one of his pockets.

He put his brown leathery face close to George. 'Get away to Orstrile-yer, boy. This ruddy country's done for.' The sweet fumes of alcohol accompanied the advice. 'There's millions of men and women going to die. It's one thing or the other now boy; you know that, don't you? There's no escaping it now, boy. We're done for. They come down here, these bishops and lords, fiddle-faddling us. They must think we're daft. There's always a war here, or a war there. Fiddle-faddle, fiddle-faddle, that's all they do.'

George gently disengaged his sleeve.' Cheer up, Sergeant, things may not turn out as badly as you fear.'

He marched on.

The despair of Sergeant Finch pursued him. 'Life's funny, life's mysterious. I don't understand it. I don't understand it . . .'

Down in the High Street of Kingsbridge, a tall distinguished-looking grey haired man, wearing a regimental blazer, approached George. 'Hello, there!'

George stared at him. The hearty greeting had been addressed as to an old friend. He must know him. But who? Where? When?

The man glanced at the blazer over George's arm. 'What's the badge?'

Ah! He didn't know him! The man was either half-witted or a confidence trickster. 'Excuse me. I have to go now.' He dived into a nearby shop and bought a fruit cake. Along with his bad news, he would offer it to Judy for their 'twilight' tea.

When he emerged, the man approached him anew. 'Hello, there!' called out the hearty educated voice, as though its owner had only just seen him for the first time. 'Still in England, eh?'

Turning away, George heard a mechanical 'Ha, ha, ha,' following after him. He felt a little sorry for his brusqueness. The fellow was harmless. How lucky one was to receive a friendly greeting in an indifferent world even from a madman. He watched him making his way down the street until he disappeared from view, his long arm ceaselessly rising above his head and falling in greetings to the passers-by. No need to pity *him*! He dwelt in a world for ever peopled with old acquaintances.

After glancing at his watch, George lengthened his stride. Passing through the school gateway, he perceived Miss Lewis crossing the playground to the rhythmic tapping of a pair of rubber-ended metal walking supports. She called out something to him.

'Excuse me, Matron, but I must rush to take a class. See you at lunch time.' What could she want with him? She had made her decision about the flat plain enough. Did she just want to rub it in? Or offer excuses?

At lunch, bread and butter pudding was served. He looked down the length of the table at the row of faces. A number of them were pale, with strained eyes and bulging cheeks. He glanced across the room; Miss Lewis was making no attempt to approach him. He certainly had no wish to approach *her*. Yet there was no hostility in her expression . . .

Suddenly Shelley Minor's hand shot up.

'What is it, Shelley?'

'Please, sir, Keats is going to be sick on me.'

Which of the pale faces was Keats's? 'Keats, stand up. Are you going to be sick on Shelley?'

'No, sir.' Keats turned his face away from Shelley and at the same time struggled to his feet. The next moment his body was convulsed and he vomited upon his neighbour on the other side. Tennyson.

'Stay where you are, Mr Brown.' No hostility in her tone either! Indeed, almost friendliness! 'The Assistant Matron and I will deal with it.'

At the end of classes George, on Afternoon Duty, made his way down to the playing fields with the boys. Much had changed. Juniper Major had long departed to Eton. Juniper Minor had therefore become Juniper Major and, after a year as an ordinary prefect, Head Boy. Possessing no real instinct for music, but a dour perseverance, he could now offer not only *Glory Be to Jesus*, not only *Soldiers of Christ, Arise* but, in the true tradition of Mr Featherstonhaugh's Church Militant, was rapidly acquiring mastery over *Onward Christian Soldiers*. In Mr Featherstonhaugh's Christianity there was no possible room for stepping back to square leg.

The former Juniper Minimus, now become Juniper Minor and mellowing with age, had abandoned spending his pocket money on Union-Jacks-for-burning in favour of toffee. At this moment he was standing close to George practising his batting. Young MacDonald, a canny Scot, was seeking to demolish Juniper Minor's wicket, represented by a jersey bundled up on the ground, by bending down and trundling the ball towards it over the surface of the grass.

'MacDonald, if you do daisy-cutters, you'll get a bash. Please, sir, stop MacDonald doing daisy-cutters. They're foul.'

George considered. 'I think, MacDonald, perhaps you had better cut out the daisy-cutters for your own safety. I don't want to see Juniper Minor, his Irish temper inflamed beyond control, bashing you over the head. I don't think that that is the type of stroke envisaged by the Headmaster when he speaks of playing the game with a straight bat. Also, it won't help you to improve your bowling. One doesn't see many daisy-cutters bowled in Test cricket. Probably they won't be allowed when you go to your public school.'

'Sir, there are two things I like about my public school. There are flowers in the playground, and there's no capital punishment.'

'*Corporal* punishment is the word that I think you are searching for, MacDonald. Corporal punishment. In capital punishment, you sometimes lose your head. In corporal punishment, it's the other end that comes into danger.'

'Yes, sir.'

George looked round as his name was called. Charlie, who had duly returned with his squad of sixth formers in time for lunch, was drooping towards him.

'The Dragon has relented. You are to stay on in the flat.'

George drew in a deep breath, then slowly let it out. 'I think Baby Mark may have engineered that for us.'

'There's a proviso. I'd better give you the Dragon's words verbatim. "They may stay, provided that Mrs Brown behaves herself in future." '

'Hm. Well, thanks Charlie for all your efforts. It's up to Judy now. I think that even she will have learnt something this time.'

That evening George arrived home to find Mark, now eight months old, having abandoned crawling as too slow, shooting out his legs and bumping along backwards across the living-room on his small bottom.

After picking him up, kissing him, and setting him down again, he made his report to Judy. He omitted the proviso about behaving herself.

To his dismay, her face lighted up in triumph. 'She couldn't face losing Mark. I think I'll give her a piece of my mind.'

'Judy, this is no moment for attempting to regain your dignity.'

She brushed past him and made for the door. 'I've taken enough lying down. I've made a doormat of myself. Even a worm will turn. This worm is sick of being kicked in the teeth.'

If George's mind had boggled as it attempted to construct a picture of a worm on a mat, with raised head displaying two rows of teeth, he had no time to dwell on it. Striding after her, he caught her by the arm. 'Very well, now I'll give you Miss Lewis's decision in full, as reported to me by Charlie.' He paused a moment. Had there been a sound on the staircase? 'This is it, word for word. "They may stay, provided that Mrs Brown behaves herself in future." So much for your belief that it is now safe —' There was that sound again. 'Wait!'

He opened the door. Miss Lewis, her face showing the pain of the effort, had got herself half way up towards the flat.

She paused on seeing him. She clung to the banisters, panting. 'She doesn't give us much chance, does she, Mr Brown? I was on my way up to make my peace with her.' She turned round and began to descend. 'I'm sorry, but you'll have to go.' Down in the hallway she paused, her pale face, perspiration on the forehead, raised to him. 'As an experienced schoolmaster, you must know as well as I the unacceptable scandal of her invasion of the dining-room and of her hysterical shrieking. Indeed, your close friend Mr Hare must know it too. The only hope ever was that Mrs Brown would also come to know it. But she hasn't, and I don't believe she ever can. In one form or another it will happen again, and again. No preparatory school could survive that. It can't be kept from the Headmaster for ever. At least in your cottage you have a better chance. Its walls are thicker, it's more in its own grounds; it's a little further away from Worcester Hall.'

'All right, Miss Lewis. I'll make the necessary arrangements with our tenants. We'll move out just as soon as is possible.'

She stumped towards her room. At her door she turned, and there was a smile on her face. 'Mr Brown, your own very employment may depend on it. We haven't always seen eye to eye. But you know the workings of the school inside out. We'd — we'd miss you.'

Brown eyes wide, bushy eyebrows raised, mouth half open, George stared at her. 'Well, thank you, Miss Lewis.'

She turned into her room and closed her door.

George re-entered the flat, now strangely silent. Judy was standing on exactly the same spot as that she had occupied when he had left her.

'Love, you once told me that your father used to say that you would never learn from your mistakes. Was he wrong? We'll have to give a month's notice to Mr Tremble and Kettledrums. Miss Lewis is not going to change her mind again. And I can tell you why. She knows, baby or no baby, that she's right. And I know that she's right. And, when and if it gets to Mr Featherstonhaugh's ears, he will know that she's right. Ours is a very restricted and restrained world, love. Your bright and volatile spirit could never fly in that cage.'

'I can change.'

'For a week or two at the outside. No, sweetheart, our only chance is to live our private life in our thick stone walled cottage, wrapped about in our hedge and our roses and our love of Mark, I looking to the school for our bread and butter, and you looking to the town and the Rainbow Inn for jam, and for somewhere to fly. Some day, perhaps, you'll find out that I have no money-bags. When that day comes, you'll either rest content in our home — or leave me.'

Chapter Sixteen

George and Judy had no difficulty in vacating the flat and repossessing their cottage. Mr Tremble had himself come to report that the heavy smoking Kettledrums had died of a stroke. Being unable to afford the cottage on his own, Mr Tremble had arranged to return to Mrs Finch. George attended the burial service. The sexton cum grave digger, a jolly man given to chortling in the midst of the obsequies for no observable reason, seeing Mr Tremble weeping copiously, had tried to cheer him up by clapping him on the back. Underestimating the strength that resided in his arm from so much digging, he succeeded only in toppling him into the grave on top of the coffin. Anticipating the General Resurrection, Mr Tremble rose at once from the grave, was hoisted out, and was last seen bounding away among the gravestones with one hand holding together a rent which the seat of his trousers had sustained, crying out that his end was in sight.

Mark having now passed his first birthday and taken to a push-chair or, with his walking harness on, straining ahead of his mother with wobbling eagerness, Judy had sold his pram. She did not, she declared, want another child. She would devote her whole life to Mark. If there was little money, as George kept *saying*, it must all go on Mark.

George had caught the nuance. With a sudden gesture of exhaustion, he rose from the exercise books on the table. 'I should have thought that even you could see that I have no concealed money bags. If I had, why should I be flogging my guts out like this?'

Her tone became conciliatory. 'Couldn't you ask for a rise in salary? Just a small one.'

'Mr Featherstonhaugh already pays us an increment year by year.

Makes up for this inflation that the war seems to have accelerated. Or perhaps it's the trade unions that have.'

'What about our loss of rent from the cottage?'

'He'll want to know why we left Charlie's flat. I don't imagine that you'll be particularly keen to discuss that.' He caught Mark's brown eyes set on him. The one-and-a-quarter-year-old in his blue rompers, his bald head now growing an ever thickening crop of red curls, sat by the table in his high chair. Leaning on the little fixed feeding table of the chair, he had been scribbling with a pencil on bits of paper. 'All right, old chap, let's get on with correcting our exercise books.'

'Ex book,' said Mark, the words muffled by the thumb he had just thrust into his mouth.

George kissed the plump cheek and resumed his seat. And Mark, in would-be imitation of his father, resumed his scribbling.

Judy tried again. 'What wouldn't Miss Lewis give to have Mark playing beside her on her lawn in the summer!'

'Miss Fetlock has just moved into the upstairs flat.'

'What!'

'So we can forget *that*.'

'What about a State school? Archie says that they pay more.'

He looked up sharply from the book before him. 'You haven't been discussing me with Archie?'

'N-no. It just happened to come up in conversation.'

He examined her a moment. Still the very high heeled shoes to compensate for her petite figure, but the once shapely legs a little thinner. Still the small white teeth, the lipsticked mouth, but the suggestion of youth a little departed from her smile. Still the dainty features, but now a little tired. Still the elegant hands, but now the skin a mite roughened from housework and nappy washing. The plucked and pencilled eyebrows remained, but the vivid blue eyes weren't quite so vivid, the first beginnings of crow's-feet at their outer corners.

His annoyance melted. He didn't like to see his Judy ageing. *He* was born old, but she was meant for eternal youth. Of course she was nearly thirty now . . . Her drinking and smoking didn't help . . . 'I'm only two years off forty. It gets harder all the time, because they have to follow a scale and pay me according to my experience.

They prefer a twenty-two or twenty-three year old just out of university or teachers' training college. Much cheaper.'

'Offer to work for less.'

'The teachers' unions wouldn't wear that. Also, the school would expect a teaching diploma. My degree alone wouldn't be enough at a State school.'

'Well, I suppose I'll just have to sell Angus.' She opened the lid, and the strains of *The Bluebells of Scotland* tinkled out.

Angus! The final blackmail! Except that George had come to the conclusion that the mother-of-pearl music box would, in fact, never be sold.

She glanced at his unmoved face. 'Now, the supper!' She produced an Italian cookery book borrowed from he library.

George sighed. He felt himself to be in for one of her 'cooking is an art' meals.

She put the book down. 'But first I'm going to have a little glass of wine because I want to feed the dog.'

George suppressed a smile at the non sequitur. The dog was a male Yorkie. She had named the little Yorkshire terrier 'Bobik', transferring to it Mark's pet name before he had been born.

'Wine is civilised. My father taught me never to drink spirits.' She burst out laughing. 'Charlie once said to me, "You're always a perfect lady, even when you're drunk and disorderly." '

As soon as Bobik, sprigs of brown hair sticking up amusingly above his eyes, had his mouth and black nose buried in his bowl on the scullery floor, she re-entered the kitchen cum sitting- cum dining-room.

She picked up the cookery book. 'I'm famished. I haven't eaten all day.'

George, who nourished distinct memories of her having tucked into an exceptionally hearty breakfast, said nothing.

As she stood at the coal fired iron range, which served as both cooker and room heater, one hand stirring the pot with a wooden spoon, the other holding the book, her lecturer's voice never ceased to hold forth. But even this faltered, then died away, as she placed before him a straggle of spaghetti and vegetables now much reduced in volume through over cooking. George ate it without complaint. When she wasn't trying something new, her dishes were excellent.

'It's six months since I've done any Italian recipes.'

George refrained from pointing out that it was, in fact, three weeks only.

A few evenings later his book correcting was again disturbed. The front door trembled on its lock and the window rattled in its frame. The vibrations were descending from their front bedroom. He could imagine the scene. Judy, a glass of 'civilised' wine in her hand, would be gyrating to a dance record on their gramophone. He arose, rammed wads of paper into window and door frame at strategic points, and made a mental note to line their edges with adhesive foam-rubber strip.

When the gramophone at last ceased, it was to find George on his feet again. Judy had descended the staircase, her voice filled with panic. 'The photograph of Bobik has been stolen!'

He found the framed enlargement of the little Yorkshire terrier hung in the upstairs passage, she having forgotten that she had moved it.

Her artistic ambitions were not confined to enlarged photographs. Since she could not paint like her aunt, she must make a picture of her own person.

Her face flushed on returning from wheeling Mark around the streets, she exclaimed, 'All Kingsbridge is talking about my umbrella!' On the next occasion it was, 'The whole town is agog about my hat.' On a third occasion it seemed that the town had disappointingly failed to notice a dress that she had run up from bits and pieces.

After settling Mark down with his toys in his nursery, she descended into the kitchen. 'I'm so frustrated, George. I'm an artist without an art.' She began to storm about the room, finally picking up a cup and smashing it on the paved floor. 'A psychiatrist said that you should let your feelings out.'

'That's all very well for him! He charges for his advice, and doesn't have to pay for the replacements.'

Later he found, in the scullery rubbish bag, the pieces of the cup. It was an old cracked one that they both of them had condemned for disposal anyway. It seemed that Judy's dramatic and uncontrollable outburst had not been without a measure of control — and sense of theatre.

He returned from the school one day in the spring to find her awaiting him at the front door in wild alarm. 'The drains are blocked! The water won't drain out of the sink.'

He strode into the scullery, dumping his kitbag on the kitchen table as he passed it. Seizing up the rubber suction-cup by its wooden handle, and covering the top of the egress pipe with the cup, he worked the handle vigorously up and down. The block was almost immediately dispersed.

'Love, The Drains plural, as you so dramatically put it, were never blocked. This is just a short little length of pipe leading out through the thickness of the wall into a brief open gully. From that, the water empties via a grating into the far larger main pipe. There's no physical connection whatever between this short little bit of pipe and the big pipes of the main drainage system. Have a look for yourself. Just look out of the back door. It's obvious.'

She made no move from the sink.

'Do just look, love!'

She turned on the hot water tap and began to scrub clean the skins of some potatoes.

'Is it, love, that you think it's something mechanical that you wouldn't be able to understand? Because it's not like that at all. It's just common sense. Just one glance, and you'll see.'

She finished the last potato, and began on the carrots.

He turned away with a sigh of frustration. 'If the sink blocks, just clear it with the plunger.'

A week later, she again had him on the mat. 'You've been pruning that climbing rose which I planted. Last year it was a mass of roses. Now, there's nothing.'

'Love, it's too early for the flowers.'

'There aren't going to be any. Why did you prune it?'

His brow beneath its shock of red hair crinkled in anxiety, he marched out of he front door. He wended his way over the lawn between his rose bushes, and examined the plant on the trellis. 'It's a mass of buds everywhere. Come and see for yourself.'

But she merely silently left the porch and retired into the kitchen.

He followed her. 'Why wouldn't you look? There's nothing mechanical about this. A bud is a bud.'

Silence.

'Why are you so afraid of being wrong? If I make a mistake, I find it quite easy to admit it.' He kissed her on the cheek. The days of kissing her on the mouth seemed to have long vanished.

After a further moment of silence, she said, 'I can never win an argument against you.'

He put his great arm round her small shoulders. 'Love, arguments aren't a sort of battle! They're just a way of establishing what's best to be done. *I* don't want to win any arguments. If you're giving your opinion about somebody, or a house, or a garden, or a book, I'm only too happy just to listen. But if it's something that's going to result in action: expenditure of money, or unblocking a pipe, or establishing whether I've spoilt a plant by over pruning, I have to put in my tuppence-worth. It's not *I* that am winning. It's the facts that have to be allowed to win. If I had found that there were no buds on your climbing rose, or very few, I would have come straight to you and apologised. When I called out that there were masses of buds, it wasn't in triumph. It was in relief that I had done no harm, and to set your mind at rest.' He bent down and grinned into her face. 'You're trouble is, that you're too modest.'

'How d'you mean?' But a smile now hovered.

'You keep thinking of the times I knew something that you didn't, and forgetting all the times I learnt something from you. I learnt from you the value of good books. You've revolutionised my bookcase. Of good plays. Of keeping a pad on the scullery wall on which to jot down things as they need to be renewed. I've learned from you that the end of autumn isn't the end of table decorations from the countryside. That in the bleakest time of the year there are dried grasses and interesting twigs. How to feed Mark, to bath him, to put on his nappy. You forget all these things. But I don't. I remember them at all times — with gratitude.'

He gave her a peck on the cheek, and crossed to his books. She saw a tear in the corner of his eye. She brought him a cup of tea.

But drama on the stage was not enough for Judy. A woman friend's protracted labour was almost made to appear as though it were her own. She reported to George the grief of some neighbours over the death of their dog. Stricken, apparently, they were; almost prostrate. But when, shortly afterwards, George passed them standing outside their door, it was to overhear them perfectly composedly making plans for the disposal of the body. About a week later another neighbour was found to be suffering from a mysterious pain, the cause of which two doctors had been unable to establish. Judy, despite the twin handicaps of never having had any medical training, nor any opportunity of examining the patient, unhesitatingly pronounced the illness to be cancer.

She was for ever talking importantly of 'My Friends'. One evening George and his books were cleared away on to the small side table, while the main table was set for four persons, candles and all. 'I'm very worried.' Judy had turned on her tearful voice. 'Mary's been drinking, and is pissed. I must give her a little supper before she goes on duty. Some other of My Friends are coming to give her moral support.' Creamcracker biscuits, butter and cheese were produced. She went up an emotional notch, and switched on her full tragedy voice. 'She has to nurse three cancer patients tonight. Three!'

After ten minutes, nobody had appeared. George attempted to concentrate on his work. Judy disappeared out of the house, then returned fifteen minutes later. Still nobody after half an hour. Again Judy vanished, then re-emerged. It was now an hour. Finally Betty Coombes, obviously having been press-ganged, put in a token ten minutes appearance, sipped at a cup of tea, and returned to her duties at the Rainbow Inn.

As Judy cleared the table, she essayed one last half-hearted attempt at drama. 'I think that Mary is On The Needle.'

She ascended the stairs to inspect the sleeping Mark in his cot and to retire to bed. As, later, George laid aside the last corrected exercise book and clipped his red ink filled fountain- pen beside the rest of the array lining his breast pocket, his bushy eyebrows were drawn together in worry.

When he entered the school staff room the following morning, they were still drawn together.

Charlie appeared. 'Just been suppressing a minor riot. That slob Dorman was part of it, of course. Always picking his nose. I'm vain enough to want the light on my face so that they watch me. To bring them to order, I've only to raise one eyebrow, like that. 'Now misters,' I said, 'you get down to the Big Schoolroom for Assembly double quick. If you don't,' I said, 'your and my lines will run parallel until they meet — and I've got the stronger engine.' His large mobile features produced a flashing smile. 'And they went!'

George managed a grin.

Charlie examined the furrowed brow, half covered by red curls. 'You're worried, George.'

'Yes, Charlie, I am. We're sitting on a timebomb at home.'

'A timebomb!'

'Judy's smoking and drinking more than she used to. And that's beginning to affect my feelings towards her. To be blunt, there are times when I feel myself pulling away from the smell of alcohol. She kisses me, though only rarely these days, and her mouth is swimming with nicotine. But it's more than that. She wants to lead people, to direct their lives. And so she was largely able to do in the early days, when I had confidence in her. Indeed, I have learned a great deal from her. But now, for Mark's sake, for all our sakes, I must keep the home together. And that means opposing her when necessary, usually in money matters. The more she feels her influence over me slipping away, the more extravagant become her efforts to make herself count. That's something that's not going to go. Another thing. She feels our life to be humdrum. So she manufactures dramas. Well, I *am* a pretty dull sort of a chap —'

'Certainly not, George.'

'Oh yes, Charlie, I am. Once, a long time ago, she said to me, "I'd like to pass my whole life drunk, just seeing the world through a haze." I'm afraid, to escape from that dullness, she's going to slip away from reality into a realm of fantasy. Or into adventures that will bring no good. And that means that she will slip away from me, the symbol of dull reality. At present we are both controlling the situation. Just. But the thick stone walls of our home are eggshell thin. Our common love of Mark holds them together. One day soon the shell will break. Then she will hate me.'

Mr Snipe entered the room. He crossed to his floor level locker. The higher lockers he had thoughtfully left to his less mobile seniors. He knelt before it, extracting books.

Charlie, changing the subject, screwed his monocle into his eye. He assumed his intellectual voice. 'That Rainbow Inn has much to answer for. Especially at Christmas time, when all the children are being taken round the stores and introduced to Santa Claus. The trouble with the new television educated generation growing up, is that while every adult believes in Father Christmas, no child does.'

Mr Snipe turned. He directed his severe nose at the conversation, his mouth half open in anxious moral concern. 'Yes. And the police are having to move on youths giving wolf whistles at the girls going into work at the Inn.'

Charlie shone his teeth. 'A case of keeping the wolf from the whore.'

Mr Snipe, his usually pale cheeks rather pink, gave an embarrassed half titter. He moved nearer to his locker. To hide his embarrassment, he attempted to thrust his head into it. Partially missing the opening, he merely succeeded in striking his forehead against its upper edge.

It had not been a good beginning to the day for Mr Snipe. Earlier that morning, over in the more junior of the two senior dormitories, the Green Dormitory with the pixies all over its wallpaper, the one for the eleven to twelve year olds, he had to have young Keats on the mat.

'Shelley has complained that last evening, during Bath Night, he had to follow you after you had — well, not to beat about the bush — to come straight to the point' — Mr Snipe's lips had begun to writhe — 'pissed in the bath. Is this true?'

'Yes, sir. But it was only by accident, sir. I stopped almost at once, sir.'

'Keats, what would happen if everybody' — Mr Snipe's lips were almost out of control — 'er — pissed in the bath?'

Keats, a lad by no means unable to communicate (from time to time he had written some quite pleasing little verses), on this occasion could only stand staring at the wall opposite. All he could think of was, that if it were the *same* bath, it would eventually overflow.

The bell went for Assembly. It was to be Juniper Major's first public rendering on the pianoforte of *Onward, Christian Soldiers*. George, together with Charlie and Mr Snipe, rose. Glancing through the staff room window, he saw Miss Fetlock emerge from the Art Block. Slygrin, apparently having purloined some plasticine, was flying in terror across the playground. Miss Fetlock, pointing her blue leaded correcting pencil accusingly at his back, cantered in pursuit. On reaching the further end of the playground, she reined herself back almost on to her haunches. Triumphantly repossessing the plasticine, she boxed him on the head. Slygrin let out a howl. Then, seeing herself in danger of being late for Assembly, Miss Fetlock turned herself towards the school buildings and broke into a gallop.

It being a Wednesday in November six months later, a half-teaching day and George not on duty down in the playing fields, he sat at the small side table in the kitchen, the merciless pile of exercise books before him.

The gate outside squeaked as it was opened, then closed. A rapid clip-clop advanced up the path, and Judy entered. '*Must* you have that radio on?'

A large hand stretched out and switched off the set. He scrutinised her. Was her aggressiveness due to drink? Or was it just defensive? She had gone out to Kingsbridge, leaving the now nearly two year old Mark with Rose, to shop, a matter of an hour at the most. Yet here she was returning three hours later. She would know that *he* would know that the missing two hours would have been spent in gossiping with cronies, accompanied by smokes and drinks, at the Rainbow Inn.

She went into the scullery, but the next moment was out again. 'Where are Bobik's bones?' The little brown Yorkshire terrier was bouncing about and yapping in delight at her return. He had also spied a tin of dog food in her net shopping bag. 'Bobik's bones were left where he could find them. Why did you move Bobik's bones? Where are Bobik's bones?'

In the effort to improve their relationship, he had tried appeasement, the pleasant reply. Plainly it wasn't achieving its end. Something a little more thrusting, perhaps, was called for.

'Judy, *I* don't mind your looking in at the Rainbow Inn to meet your friends.'

A jolt passed through her small person. Startled blue eyes stared at him. 'I've been shopping.'

'After you've finished your half an hour or an hour's shopping, I don't mind your spending a couple of hours with your cronies.'

She recovered. 'Well, as I never have any of your company, I might as well.'

'If you took a job, then I could do less coaching and we should have more time together.'

Now she was really startled. 'I've got to be here to look after Mark.'

'Mark is beginning to take up less of your time, what with his playing beside me or being over with Rose at The Brambles.'

'What job could I get as a schoolmaster's wife? I can't go back to the Rainbow Inn. I could sell Bobik, I suppose.'

So Bobik had taken over from Angus the music box in the blackmail stakes! 'That's a good idea!' George was enjoying being on the attack for once.

Judy backtracked hurriedly. 'It would save only about a pound a week.'

'Two at least. Perhaps three.' As he watched her gathering consternation, he relented and left the subject. 'Bobik's bones were all over the scullery floor. I stepped on them and nearly came a cropper. Couldn't he just have one at a time? I've put them together in a neat pile by the side of the sink.'

Next afternoon Judy took out Mark herself. In the bakery cum confectionery, she lifted him out of his push-chair. Clutching in his chubby palm the handle of the shopping basket, a miniature copy of his mother's, he stumped up beside her to the counter.

'Have you got a round sponge cake with a cream filling suitable for icing? I want to ice it myself.' Smiling, she looked down on the tiny figure. 'It's for his birthday.'

Without a moment's hesitation or exchanging a single word, as though galvanised by an electric current, the three women, serving behind the twin counters set at a rightangle to one another, moved off in three different directions to the wall shelving behind them. From here and there they picked out little cakes, emerged, and in a thrice Mark's basket was filled to the brim.

One of the women bent down and gently held his free hand. 'What age are you, love?'

'He'll be two tomorrow,' said Judy.

'Two! My oh my! You *are* getting a big boy, aren't you?'

And, a month later, at two years and one month, it was as an even bigger boy that he toddled about the nursery after Judy, 'helping' his mother in the fixing up of streamers, the inflating of balloons, and the parcelling up of Christmas presents. Later she wheeled him down to Kingsbridge for a matinee performance. The magician announced a 'laughing' competition for children under five, to be accompanied up on to the stage by a parent if necessary. Mark, despite his limited vocabulary, had understood and was not to be gainsaid. Judy, smiling, made her way up the aisle with him. The synthetic laughs of the other children were restrained by shyness, but not so that of Mark's, whose piercing tones filled the auditorium and carried off the prize, a white china pig in whose entrails pennies could be saved. When he got home he was allowed, lifted up by Judy and his hand guided, to transfer the lighted match to the tall red Christmas candle set up in the window.

'Everybody will see it, darling, as they pass up and down the lane.'

She kissed him, then lowered him into the confines of his playpen, brought downstairs for the occasion. She had set it close to the range for warmth, but not so close that a chubby hand, stretched out through the bars, might touch it.

She retreated into the middle of the kitchen where George stood watching. No exercise books, no coaching; it was the Christmas holidays. She looped her arm into his. He responded at once to the affectionate gesture; Judy was always at her very best at Christmas time.

'Father Christmas,' he said to Mark, 'will come down that chimney tonight and fill your stocking.'

Mark, clutching the top of the railing, bent down sideways to gaze up the great hood of the chimney hovering over the range. In tones as piercing as those that had won him the china pig, he cried out, 'Father Chris! Father Chris!'

His parents, exchanging glances of delight, for that moment were as one again. Next morning they were awoken early by his shouts as he discovered that Father Christmas had indeed come down that chimney and had indeed filled his stocking. Later, to the strains of *Jingle Bells* played by a record on the gramophone, and in the light from miniature candles in little holders clipped on to the branches of the Christmas tree, they entered the kitchen to open the parcels on the breakfast table.

Judy, who throughout had master-minded all these rituals, was determined that not one of them should be omitted. Perhaps her childhood sojourn in the orphanage, with its second-hand toys, was the source of her passion for a full family Christmas in a home of her own. Even on the day after, Boxing Day, she had arranged for Rose to take Mark to The Brambles so that George and she might have a Christmas-tide drink and a session of carol singing at a pub. Considerate of his feelings, she had avoided The Rainbow Inn and taken him to the Kingsbridge Arms. Sergeant Finch was at his accustomed post, leaning over the bar; and at his accustomed activity, attempting to catch the eye of the buxom barmaid with the pendant watch pinned to her blouse. George, seeing the look of bliss on Judy's face, endured the smell of drink and the swirls of tobacco smoke.

As they emerged, she took his arm again. 'Thank you, George, for sitting with me in there. I know that you would much rather that we had been out walking in this sunshine, or having a cup of tea in a restaurant.'

'No no, love. Christmas time is Christmas time and the carols were fun — even if I can't sing in tune! Besides, it was nice being *really* together again.'

Back in the Kingsbridge Arms, Sergeant Finch had at last caught the barmaid's notice. Eyeing her well filled blouse he said, 'Lucky watch!'

Chapter Seventeen

'I'm a failure!' Judy's blue eyes gazed at her husband. It was a year later and the third time recently that she had so spoken. The idea seemed to perch like a demon on her shoulder. 'My aunt paints pictures. *And* sells them. I'm an artist without an art.'

He intervened quickly. 'No, you're not. Or at least, if you're without an art, you're certainly not without a craft. Just look at the bedroom chest of drawers which Betty Coombs got for you at that auction! You said at the time that you'd make it into a work of art, and you just about did. You painted it. You enamelled it with flower patterns. It's beautiful. Why don't you do the same with smaller pieces? Sell them in the local shops. Besides which, you've had a beautiful child after a long and painful labour, breast fed over an extended period at some strain to yourself and a lot of self denial, and perfectly brought up ever since.'

She cheered up at once. 'But I need working capital. Fit out a studio. Equipment.' The list grew longer and longer.

He laughed. 'Judy, dear, you always want to start at the top! In just about everything in life, one has to start at the bottom and work one's way up. The idea is to make money, not spend it. Start with the minimum, and devote part of your takings to expanding.'

Her small features were already becoming resentful. 'You *must* have working capital. My father told me so when I was a child. You must spend money to make money.'

He was caught. How to marry his need to encourage her, with his inner knowledge that she was more than likely to throw in her hand at the first setback, with any money put into the venture down the drain?

'Love, I'm already paying off a number of debts. I just can't manage another. Of course it's a bit slower starting at the bottom, but it can be done. Lots of people have had to, and lots have succeeded. Your father had a proven ability as an agent and an existing office that he wanted to expand.'

But her interest was gone.

One day she got caught in a heavy downpour. Taking off her blouse and skirt, she hung them to dry on a towel-horse before the range. Wearing only her bra and panties, she sat warming herself with her back presented to him. It was a small shapely back, but suddenly seemed less engaging after Rose's more ample proportions. A little later she resumed her outer garments.

She looked at him. 'I thought I had a rather nice back.'

So that was it! She had been hoping to arouse him. 'A very nice back indeed!'

Suddenly she was aflame. 'Is it any good our going on?'

'Judy, dear, what do you mean?' He said it only to gain time, and because he didn't know what else to day. He simply could not pretend to feelings he did not have.

'You look at me as though I were a piece of furniture.'

He saw that the matter could no longer be evaded.

'Judy, marriage is a permanent thing. Or supposed to be. If you're not going to accept loyalty, affection, understanding as love, what chance has marriage got? How can you found anything permanent on eroticism, which is near to being uncontrollable? Comes and goes, like a kettle, on and off the boil. "I see a tall dark *stranger*," says the gypsy fortune teller. "*Stranger* on the shore," writes the poet. "*Strangers* in the night," sings the songster. "Stranger", always "stranger". In other words, novelty. Is lack of novelty to be allowed to break up children's homes?'

She was dumbfounded. She went into the scullery. But a moment later she was back. '*I* don't believe in breaking up children's homes. I wouldn't want Mark's home to be broken up. Why don't you give yourself a bit of a break? Have a day in London. Take Mark with you. He's always watching the trains, but he's never travelled on one. It wouldn't cost any more. He's only three; he certainly wouldn't need a ticket.

Little Mark was entranced also by the London Underground, its trains shooting like snakes into tubular metal burrows. As he knelt up on the carriage seat, his father's protective arm around him, and pressed his snub nose against the window, his astonished brown eyes watched the side of the tunnel passing at an unbelievable speed, his ears filled with the clatter of the wheels over the rails.

Still in the Underground system, but up on the much less deeply buried District Line, here and there even open to the sky, a pigeon at one station hopped in through the open double doors and began to peck at invisible fodder on the floor.

To Mark's consternation, a moment later the doors closed together with a bang as the train set off again. 'Look, Dada, the pigeon can't get out. He'll be lost.'

'I think he'll be all right, old chap. He's lived all his life in London. He knows what's what.'

And, sure enough, when the train next halted and the doors slid open, the pigeon dismounted as unconcernedly as the most practised of commuters.

'How does he get back to his nest, Dada? There's no sky here.'

'I honestly don't know, old fellow. Unless he takes a train back again, I can only suppose that he makes his way up the staircase. We're not very deep here. Town pigeons are so used to people that they are very bold.'

But if the District Line wasn't deep, the Tube leading to Piccadilly Circus certainly was. There, would be found the longest series of escalators for the entertainment of Mark. 'Moving stairs,' he cried in awed excitement. He grasped two of his father's fingers tightly in his chubby palm as he stepped on to the first of them. 'More moving stairs, Dada!' Finally they transferred on to the last and longest of the escalators, steeply trundling its way up to the lights of Piccadilly Circus — lights flashing on and off, and running up and down the sides of buildings.

After viewing them for ten minutes, even Mark's sturdy little legs were tired out and it was time to go home. As George queued for his Underground ticket, Mark stood aside with his arm round his favourite teddybear, the floppy one, for companionship; but his eyes, in this strange vast subterranean world, with its stream of people ceaselessly hurrying past in apparently some sort of race, never left his father for one instant. To reassure him, George gave him a triple nod, and Mark gave him three nods back. As Mark did so, George noticed that a woman behind him in the queue was watching with a smile the tiny form clutching its teddy.

Later, down on the platform, George felt some uncertainty. A uniformed figure was walking away from him. 'Quick, Mark, sit here.' He lifted him on to a seat. 'Now don't move, sweetheart. I just want to ask that railway guard which train we take.'

He sprinted after the official. He had gone only three quarters of the way, when he became aware of the rapid patter of small feet following behind. Mark's nerve had failed him. The only person in this strange and awesome world, capable of getting him safely home, was ever further distancing himself. George caught up with the guard, got his information, then turned to meet his son. There were no tears. Mark was just happy to be holding his father's hand again.

When they reached home, a note from Judy informed them that she was at a party at the Rainbow Inn. George 'pottied' his son, gave him supper, heard his prayers, the ones that he himself had been taught in his childhood; and read him a story. Then he lit his nightlight, a squat candle encased in fire proof foil and guaranteed to burn for eight hours; and fulfilled his promise to leave the landing light on and the nursery door open a chink. But the tousle of red curls had hardly touched the pillow, when the tired little fellow was asleep.

Judy's inner nature had not, could not, be silenced. When, on an occasion that they were walking side by side, he attempted to take her arm, she shook off his hand. If they left the house together, she would walk off rapidly into the lane without waiting for him to close the door, leaving him to catch up with her. When he tried to kiss her, she turned away her face. She just would not accept fondness; that fondness which she saw as the enemy of passion. And certainly not George's brown eyes looking at her with understanding, a better mind than her own, a mind perhaps ready to drift into paternalism.

The cumulative effect of the snubs took toll of George's feelings too. Sometimes the kettle seemed to be irrevocably off the boil.

One afternoon, entering the bedroom to fetch his blazer, he found that the two side by side divans, so long their marriage bed and made up as one, had been parted by a foot and made up separately. He stood still, stricken by this new token of their drift apart.

There was the sound of clambering up the staircase, followed by an attempt to turn the doorknob. More sedate steps followed, and the knob was turned by a grownup's hand. Three year old Mark burst into the room, followed by Rose.

'Hello, Dada. We went for a big big walk.' The little boy flung himself into his father's arms.

'Oh, Mr Brown, I'm so sorry. I should have knocked. Mark had me all of a fluster to get in.'

'That's all right, Rose.' He noted her gentle eyes regarding the divans. He set down Mark a little hurriedly. 'Now as soon as Rose has put you to bed in the nursery, I'll come up and read to you.'

'You won't forget my nightlight, Dada?'

'I won't forget, darling.'

'And to leave my door open?'

'Or to leave your door open.'

Avoiding Rose's eye, he left the room and, after fulfilling his commitments to Mark, the house. At the gate he passed Judy, arriving punctually as ever where Mark was concerned. Neither of them spoke nor looked at the other.

'Charlie,' he said, as he took over duty from him at the school, 'I'm not a deeply reflective chap where philosophical matters are concerned. My religion, I'm beginning to suspect, is largely habit, respectability, what is gentlemanly, good form. Easy to maintain in my bachelorhood. But Judy is ever more turning into a tornado tearing my safe and settled existence apart, calling into question all my moralities until I don't know what to think. Well . . . You've your wife's supper to get, and I have to see the Day Boys off.'

As Charlie left, he touched George's shoulder. 'We'll talk about it tomorrow.'

A few minutes later George was once more finding tranquillity, as he always did, among the boys and in the school routine. Here at least was an ordered universe. God was in his heaven and all, fundamentally, was right with the world (provided, of course, that one kept a straight bat, didn't step back to square leg, didn't misuse plasticine, avoided being silly, didn't piss in the bath, and passed one's Common Entrance Examination).

Leaving prefects in charge of the classrooms where the boarders, the majority, awaited the tea bell at half past five, George made his way to the school gate. There the dayboys, satchels over their shoulders, awaited transport home either in their parents' cars or on a town bus.

'Sir,' cried a voice, 'there's a boy in the garden next door and he wants to kill me. He shoots arrows straight at my eye, and throws darts and spears at me. But he can't hit me.'

George grinned. 'He sounds a delightful neighbour!'

'And then, sir,' continued the voice in a mixture of indignation and high glee, 'he dresses up in a sheet and says he's a ghost and tries to frighten me to death.'

Other voices took over. 'Sir, I believe they launch ships by throwing bottles at them.' 'Our dog, sir, is going to lay some puppies.' 'Sir, Robinson says he wants to go to Australia so that he can write back naughty postcards saying what he thinks of the school.'

George looked round and identified a face all freckles, surmounted by a hedge of hair standing up on end. 'Oh Robinson, are we really as bad as all that?'

'Sir, he's only saying it because he was very disappointed yesterday.'

'Good heavens! What happened?'

'Sir, when he gets on the bus, he sits at the very back. Then he chooses a girl in front of him. Every time somebody gets out, he takes their seat if it gets him nearer to her.'

George fought off a desire to put his head back and roar with laughter. 'What's the nearest he's got to her?'

'Please, sir, two seats behind her, and then she got off.'

Another voice intervened. 'No, sir, yesterday he got to the seat behind her. And then *he* had to get off.'

'Oh, Robinson, that's really too bad! Why don't you start from further up the bus, old chap? Then you won't have to write that postcard.'

At that moment the bus appeared. It stopped with a squeaking of brakes.

As the eleven year old mounted, George tapped him on the top of the head. He spoke in his ear. 'There's a very pretty girl! And the seat beside her is empty.'

With another squeak the bus gathered speed, and George was unable to see the outcome.

As he returned through the gate, Sergeant Finch passed him, relatively sober. But, as the gallant sergeant was directing his steps towards the town in general, and the Kingsbridge Arms in particular, that would soon be put right.

At home, Judy's attempts to make herself count became more feverish.

She started his supper going on the range, then announced that she was dodging out briefly to take up the offer from a friend of a glass of champagne. When she returned, she said that they were offering their guests thirty different cheeses. *Thirty* cheeses, she emphasised.

George looked up briefly from his work, but made no comment. She went out again for a further alleged glass of champagne, and doubtless a further taste of those thirty cheeses. Rising from the small side table to fetch a book from the bookcase, he saw a half empty flagon of cider, together with a tumbler, partly concealed behind her armchair. Was *this* the 'champagne' from which she had been taking nips when he hadn't been looking?

A few days later, believing that it would give her pleasure, he presented her with a bottle of white wine for her birthday. Filling herself a glass, she stood sipping it leaning against the front doorpost, and looking out through the porch.

'Are you trying to get me drunk?' she enquired. He noticed something unnatural about her voice. What was it? Yes, it was raised a little above normal. 'Why are you trying to get me drunk?'

'After I've given you a bottle of wine for your birthday? What a miserable thing to say!'

'Oh!' Her face fell. She moved quickly away from the doorpost and back into the room.

With a fed up expression on his rugged features, he crossed the kitchen to fetch a book of maps. In doing so, he glimpsed two women making their way slowly down the lane. So it was for their ears that Judy had mounted her charade of amorous intrigue, only to have her performance dashed! He made a note not again to win that genuine smile of gratitude, which a bottle could be counted on to elicit. Always, as she drank its contents, did it only engender a scene, and so make a rod for his own back. In future, he would present her with made-up flowers from a florist.

Two days later she was at it again.

'I can't have those dogs there,' she called out as she stood in the porch, Bobik the Yorkshire terrier at her side.

Determined to nip the forthcoming drama in the bud before it could flower into its full misery, George advanced quickly and stood beside her. Bobik, his tousle of brown hair arching over his eyes, sat between them. The lane was empty.

'They've just gone round the corner,' she said.

He spoke quietly. 'No, Judy, they were never there. Why d'you do it? Why d'you *do* it?'

'I suppose I'm bored with Kingsbridge. I think I'll have a glass of cider. I suppose I can have a glass of cider without being told that I'm drunk?'

'Certainly.' he returned into the kitchen. Speaking over his shoulder he said, 'I can't recall ever telling you that you were drunk when you had had only one glass of cider. Nor, indeed, when you had had more than one.'

Producing a bottle, she did indeed have more than one. He knew he was in for further trouble. Doubtless because of her small size and unbalanced nature, drink had a disproportionate effect on her.

'Get me another flagon.' She had reached her aggressive stage.

'Judy, you've had enough, and we can't afford it.'

'If you don't get it for me, I'll go out myself and get it with the housekeeping money.'

Despite his six foot one and fourteen stone, in fact, because of them, he felt helpless before her five foot nothing and six stone twelve.

When he returned with the bottle, she settled herself before him on the flagged floor, drinking glass after glass. Then she began to splash the cider over her clothes. He watched her, brow furrowed under red curls. Presently he realised that he was only making things worse by providing her with an audience. He also realised that it was an old and washable skirt that, apart from the floor, was receiving most of the splashings. Indeed, her brand new cardigan was escaping completely. He remembered her smashing of the already cracked and discarded cup.

He rose from his chair. 'Well, I'm doing no good here.' He picked up his kitbag. 'I've my usual quota of work to do, so I must do it at the school.'

Before she could react, he had already closed the door and was walking up the lane. Little Mark was alseep in his bed. He had been promoted from his cot with its bars, but still liked to have his bed against a wall, with the backs of two or three chairs partially fencing him in on the other side. He would be perfectly safe. Was he not Judy's treasure, her future, indeed, her life?

George did not go immediately to the school.

'Charlie,' he said, as he sat on the elegant sofa, 'a sober-sides is at a terrible disadvantage in the presence of a drunk, because he is *responsible*, whereas the drunk, at least partially, isn't.'

'Quite.' Charlie, wearing his glasses, had been reading *The Times*. On George's appearance, he had hastily substituted his monocle.

'I'm walking a tightrope every day. She is still quite capable of erupting into the school a second time and losing us our livelihood. Oh, she's a bit more responsible when drinking than she lets on to be. But . . . Quite simply, she can't fully comprehend what's going on. At any moment, if too much pressure is put on her, I feel, as you yourself suggested, that she'll have some sort of mental breakdown. There's pressure on me too. I fear to lose my cottage, in effect, if I have to look for work elsewhere. There's the endless having to stand up to her on money matters if we're not to become involved in a spiral of debt; a spiral that would end in a local scandal that itself would lose me my job. The fear of the breakup of Mark's home. Indeed, the fear of losing Mark himself if she walks out on me, taking him with her.'

Charlie, who had already put the kettle on the lighted gas ring, produced the silver teapot out of a cupboard. He had begun bringing it home with him every night. 'She couldn't do that, George. You're his guardian.'

'Oh, in theory, perhaps. I'd be given "custody". What does that amount to?' He gave a hollow laugh. 'The right to decide whether he goes to Eton or Harrow. Some choice, on my income! My life with Mark is walks together in the woods. Having him sitting at my elbow imitating what I am doing. Reading a bit of the Bible and a story to him at bedtime. Comforting him when he comes a tumble. I'd get the custody, but Judy'd get the "care". A mother's position is very strong. And rightly so. She has carried the burdon of birth, though the court would be saying that it is doing whatever is best for the child. But in any case I could never consider for one moment taking Mark from Judy. He is her everything.'

He paused as Charlie placed a cup of tea on the little octagonal Indian table with its ivory insets.

'I could never demand of a wife that she should have a baby, nor deny her one. I'm never able to take the part of those moralists, with their rarefied abstract principles, who would deny her an abortion if that's what she wanted. *She* is carrying the burden, not they. Let them by all means apply them to their own lives, but not bulldoze them into the lives of others. I would never weigh as equal in the balance the foetus with its undeveloped intellect, against its highly sensate mother. Suffering is awareness.'

Charlie, holding his own cup, lowered himself on to the other end of the sofa. 'Drink up your tea, old fellow. Drink up your tea. It's getting cold.'

Suddenly George was grinning. 'You and your cups of tea in a crisis! What magic they weave! What calm they bring! Charlie, you're one in a hundred. No, in a million. One of these days I'll steal that magic teapot of yours.'

Judy regarded Rose as she left the cottage after delivering back Mark from his walk. George was finishing his afternoon tea of buttered toast before departing for Late Duty at the school.

As soon as the young girl, still only twenty-three, was out of earshot, Judy said, 'I wish I had her complexion! I did have once.'

'You're still only thirty,' he put in quickly.

Evidently she wasn't fishing for a compliment, for she continued immediately, 'Do you think that Rose is beautiful?'

George considered. Judy, like anyone with an enormous need to talk, also required an enormous amount of material to talk about. Since her interests were personal rather than intellectual, that meant people and news about people, in short, gossip. Almost everything that came into her head had to issue out upon her tongue, with little forethought to monitor the flow. If he said that he didn't think that Rose was beautiful, to forestall possible jealousy, he knew that Judy was perfectly capable of passing on his words to Rose. That, he was determined not to allow to happen. Indeed, since Judy had elected to ask him a direct question, he would in any case have given her a direct answer.

'Oh yes, Rose is undoubtedly beautiful in a wholesome country way. Why d'you ask?'

'No special reason.'

But she had grown very quiet. Pouring herself out a glass of cider, she departed upstairs. Now what misery was she preparing for him? Judging from the sounds descending through the ceiling, she was not in their bedroom, but in another next to it with its own entrance, which she had taken over as her dressing-room. Bedroom and dressing-room occupied a space upstairs, at the front of the cottage, which exactly matched the area of the kitchen-sitting room. At the back of the cottage, the area of Mark's nursery upstairs matched that of the bathroom downstairs, while the toilet upstairs stood over the ceiling of the scullery. He encouraged himself with the reminder that Judy had always made abundantly clear her liking for Rose, entrusting to her Mark's afternoon walks, and thus leaving herself free to visit the Rainbow Inn. He suspected that she was picking up pin-money by waiting on table; and he was glad of it. It was most unlikely that any of the school parents would visit the place, and it took some of the financial pressure off him.

There was a clopping of high heels down the staircase. On the bottom step, Judy struck a pose. She had got herself up in a voluminous blouse, a sweeping dress, and a hat concocted out of bits and pieces. Her face was grotesquely over made up with rouge and lipstick. '*Now* who's beautiful!'

'Oh Judy, Judy, what *do* you expect me to say?'

'Oh, you're a stick in the mud!'

She helped herself to a second glass of cider. Switching on the black-and-white television, she tuned herself into the programme of her own choosing. She had placed her chair in front of, but a little to one side of, him, so that she presented her back without obscuring his view of the screen. As their relations had worsened, so had George found that watching television with Judy had presented an ever greater hasard. Just as on that first occasion when he had taken her to the theatre to see the dramatised version of Jane Austen's *Pride and Prejudice*, so did she always sink herself into the story with a greater intensity than anyone he had ever met before. Objectivity was a concept largely unknown to Judy.

Sipping from the glass of cider, often replenished, in her left hand, she ever more frequently began to thud with the palm of her right hand on the padded arm of her chair. This was by way of applauding every sentiment in the dialogue with which she agreed; an agreement pointed, he knew, at himself. A character the worse for drink appeared on the screen. 'Oh, he's drunk, the naughty man. The naughty man is drunk. Oh look, the naughty man is drunk.' Ad nauseam. Judy's was not a subtle soul.

He endured for a time. Then he quietly picked up his kitbag. At the door he said, 'The row you're making is giving me a headache. I wanted us to have a nice evening together, but you never can watch a programme just for its own sake. They all have to be pressed into the domestic battle. I'm off to the school. Judging by the weight of the exercise books in this bag, I'll be there till midnight.'

He closed the gate behind him. All had fallen silent in the cottage.

When he returned and made his way up to the bedroom, it was to find it occupied only by a single divan. Judy had removed herself and her bed into the dressing-room next door.

Chapter Eighteen

George woke up and stared about him. Even after a week, the bedroom seemed strangely empty with no Judy in it; his bed strangely narrow-seeming with no matching divan, albeit separated by a foot, beside it.

Desolation? Or relief?

Certainly contact with Judy in any situation was becoming increasingly hazardous. Ever more frequently, after her almost daily shopping cum Rainbow Inn visiting expeditions, she would arrive back at her front door supported by one or two of her women friends. Swaying perilously as she negotiated the kitchen on her way to her new bedroom and bed, her speech slurred, she would reassure the company. 'I know what I'm doing. I know what I'm doing.'

The friend or friends would depart.

She had developed a fresh device for preventing his 'winning arguments'. This consisted of making her accusations in a continuous flow that left no space for reply. Having delivered her speech, she would instantly sweep away to the sanctuary of her bedroom. She would also, in the evening, switch on the television, ask him which programme he wanted, then take exception to his choice. On his replying that, in that case, he would like any programme *she* liked, she would answer: not so, but he must have the one he had chosen. She would wait for some item in it, whether of picture or speech, that would give her the excuse, then make a grand theatrical exit from the kitchen. Upstairs, she would bury herself in one or other of her books from the library, having read all those she had bought for the house. Finding himself alone, he would switch off the set and turn to his school work.

In general, his best escape from unpleasantness lay in keeping silent. When action could not be evaded, he wrote on a slip of paper his plans and his reasons. This he slipped in under her door. A note could not be shouted down, and her irresistible curiosity would ensure that it was read. Doubtless because of a toxic liver, on two or three occasions her voice took on a low ugly note that he had not heard in the past, and her vocabulary a descent into the gutter. Once, when he could not produce some money she wanted, she growled out, 'You parsimonious shit!'

She announced that 'Mabel', some married woman friend of whom he had not heard before, was in hospital with cancer. It was a cold winter evening, but the front door of the cottage was left dramatically wide open, allegedly so that Mabel's husband could walk straight in with the latest news. As George, exercise-book correcting at his small side table, had suspected would be the case, no husband ever appeared.

'Judy,' he called up the stairs (she was snugly in her room), 'an hour has gone by. May I close the door? It's freezing down here.'

She descended, pulling on her overcoat. 'You just don't care that Mabel's in hospital dying of cancer. Selfish bastard! Now I've got to walk down to find out.'

'Judy, if her husband arrives, all he has to do is to —'

The door banged behind her. The garden gate creaked open, then creaked shut.

An hour and a half later she swept in, smelling of drink. 'She has died under the knife.'

'That's dreadful! I'm so —'

But she was up the stairs. Her door crashed.

He sighed, and returned to his books.

Some time later he became conscious of humming from the scullery. A little later again, having as usual forgotten her fib, she broke off from preparing Mark's food to call out, 'I'm just going over to visit Mabel at the hospital. Back in an hour.'

'What! So this Mabel, whoever she is, hasn't died after all! You'd make even one of your friends into material for sensation!'

'She's very ill. She has an opening in her throat. They have to clean it out with a feather.'

In his anger, he had risen from his seat. He now sat down again and resumed his work. 'Judy, you have disgraced yourself.'

She went upstairs, then returned with her coat. 'You're a hard man to live up to, George. Your utter honesty!'

Parsimonious shit! Hard man to live up to! There might have been two Georges!

'*I'm* no saint, Judy. Not by a hundred miles.' He refrained from adding that his standards of truth telling were merely those of the majority; that it was hers that were — capricious.

'No. You're like your father. That time we stayed with your parents, he was very kind. I brought down an armful of Mark's washed nappies to hang up on a towel-horse at the corner of the fireplace. But he moved his chair to one side and insisted that the towel-horse should be placed immediately in front of the fire.'

'Throughout all our troubles, Judy, you've always spoken kindly of my parents. It's much appreciated.'

She smiled, and was gone.

But then came the trials by jury.

Since Judy had never had the smallest difficulty in believing that whatever she wanted to be the case, was indeed the case, it followed that she was totally confident that all these 'juries' would take her part, her part being the insufficiency of the cash received from her husband.

The first jury was Rose herself, occasionally engaged by Judy.

'I despise you!' Judy had raised her voice as she stood in the porch drawing on her gloves against the November chill. 'You don't love Mark. You only love yourself. He doesn't love you. He only loves me.'

She departed to fetch the now four year old Mark from his play school down in the town.

George glanced towards the scullery where Rose was washing some clothes in the sink. He was not too disturbed as to what she would have made of it all. He couldn't imagine that Judy would succeed in getting very far in that direction.

The second 'trial' was a much more serious and unpleasant affair. Among her host of acquaintances was one whom George thought of as 'One-lung' (she had lost the other to smoking-induced cancer). This he did not do out of unkindness. He did it out of a sheer inability to keep track of such a multitude of first names. One- lung at all times stank heavily of alcohol. According to Judy, her house was filthy, but that was only because of the number of dogs that she kept. Not only was she a magnificent judge of dogs, but also a superb cook and gardener. (George, knowing Judy's inability to deal other than in linguistic extremes, in his own mind modified these adjectives.)

One-lung, so attractive had she been to men, had been married four times, and four times she had been abandoned. This, on each and every occasion, was due to the extreme unpleasantness of the husband concerned. When George had ventured to hint that one abandonment, or even two, might be ascribed to the men; but when it came to *four*, wasn't it just possible . . ., Judy had rejected the innuendo.

To find the money necessary to nourish so many dogs, One-lung augmented her Disability and other state allowances by putting in a Claim for a heavy and therefore expensive winter overcoat. She then used the minimum part of the money to buy the cheapest coat she could lay her hands on at a jumble sale. This coat was a protection against a possible check up by a representative of the Inspector. Other similar claims would be made from time to time, despite the growing suspicions of this Inspector, himself, she averred, a man only marginally less unpleasant than the husbands.

George returned from the school one evening to find Judy sitting at the kitchen table drinking tea with no less than three of her cronies, including One-lung. None of the four looked at him as he passed. Rather did they seem to concentrate the more studiously on sipping their tea. Since he had school work to do, it was obvious that he must ascend to his bedroom. As he made his way up the stairs, an idea flickered in his mind. Were they a panel assembled by Judy to observe him; to sit in judgement on his actions?

He had hardly reached his room, set down his kitbag, and begun to close his door, when he found the four women crowded round it resisting its closure. Indeed One-lung, breathing alcoholic fumes, was pushing her way into the room. He was saved at least from this invasion by the efforts of another of the women, whom he identified later to himself as 'Breasts'. Breasts flung herself across the path of the advancing One-lung and elbowed her back.

Speaking to Judy, and motioning with her eyes towards One-lung, she said, 'You can't let *her* in.'

Both Judy and, surprisingly, One-lung seemed to accept this, for the pressure on the door ceased. George, glad to be saved from the One-lung incursion, allowed Breasts to enter the bedroom and close the door.

He pulled up the bedclothes on the unmade divan, then surveyed the dusty and spotted floor. 'I'm sorry about the mess. Woke up late this morning and had to rush to the school. Normally I make the bed and run the vacuum cleaner over the carpet.'

He sat down on the divan. Breasts sat down beside him. She was of about Judy's age, looked a pleasant enough woman, and emitted no fumes. He found himself running on and on excusing himself, never doubting that he was under judgement. It had been tacitly agreed, nothing put into words between Judy and himself, that his bedroom was his sanctum, even to cleaning it.

Finally he came to an end. He awaited Breasts' cross-examination, but she remained silent. Finally she opened her bag and extracted some photographs. She presented them to him. There were six, all of herself, two in bathing costume. These last established that she had attractive legs and firm well developed breasts. So she had not come into the room to grill him on Judy's behalf! She had come into it to make a bid to supplant her! Filled as he was with relief that there was one person in his house, and doubtless from the Rainbow Inn, not hostile to him; he yet was conscious of a strange indignation that his wife was being betrayed by one of her friends. However, he returned the photographs with a pleasant remark or two. Breasts departed. Downstairs, she must have spun some satisfactory yarn, for he heard them all leave.

Next day, walking down to the playing fields, he passed her lingering at the side of the lane. To make contact with him? The contempt he felt must have been reflected in his face, for she turned away, humiliated. A little later, during a brief shopping expedition into the town, he met someone whom it was quite impossible to abash. She came along the pavement towards him, raven haired, red lips parted in a sexy smile, ample hips swinging, well shaped legs, if too slender for her full body, in fishnet stockings.

'What,' exclaimed George, 'no Emperor to wave a paw at me?'

Betty Coombes's smile vanished. A tear trembled on one of her long false eyelashes. 'My lovely Emperor has gone. Seems I pampered him and he got too fat. They had to put him down. I miss looking into those golden eyes.'

'I'm so very sorry.' He changed the subject quickly. 'I take it my name is mud in the Rainbow Inn!'

He described the visitation from the jury of four, omitting the contretemps with Breasts.

Betty laughed. 'They're some of a bunch that sit together drinking at their own table. We call them the Unmarried Married. Most of them have been deserted by their husbands, and that's all that they ever talk about. But don't worry. Oh, there's the occasional complaint. But woe betide anyone who joins Judy in it! She turns on them like a tigress. Complaints are a privilege she reserves to herself. Any attack on you, and you become a saint.'

George grinned. 'That sounds like Judy all right. She never does things by halves. At home, I'm the Devil Incarnate. But you've cheered me up no end. You generally do.' He lent forward and kissed her on her rouged cheek.

'Well! I never expected that! I'm a dangerous woman to kiss, you know. I've always had my eye on you.'

'Oh, you're too occupied with your marriages. Did you ever manage to marry your seven foot sergeant?'

'I was nearly there. And then he was drafted overseas.'

'Too bad! And about Emperor also. I'll miss him myself. He was an institution.'

One-lung wasn't finished yet. George returned from the school and made his way up to his room, only to find himself having to pass by her, and Judy, in the upstairs corridor. When he emerged again from his room to descend for his tea, it was to find One-lung advancing upon him shouting out accusations, with Judy just behind her threatening him with the lighted end of her cigarette held forward over One-lung's right shoulder. As ever, he was involved in the balancing act of considering what was best for avoiding a scandal that might lose him his job; what would give little Mark the best chance of a pleasant home; and what was due to his own dignity. To have this woman threatening him in his own home was intolerable. The sight of a policeman's uniform might most safely solve the triple situation. It could shake both women into the reality of just what they were doing, without the risk of a court case or a newspaper report.

There was little room in the narrow passage. He had no option but to shoulder both of them aside. 'I'm going for the police.'

He was down the stairs and out of the house before either of them could find a word.

He sat at a table in the office, the sergeant at the other side. 'There isn't much we can do between husband and wife. Yesterday we received a telephone call from a lady. When my officer went over, the first thing he saw was husband and wife strolling down the street hand in hand.'

'What about this woman, this slcoholic? I don't know her full name, but I've heard my wife calling her "Sue".'

'Is she well known as an alcoholic?'

'Oh yes, I think so.'

The sergeant wrote down the name on a pad. 'We'll make some enquiries. Is there nothing you can do yourself?'

'I'm six foot one and fourteen and a half stone. My wife is five feet and six stone twelve, or was. She seems to be getting thinner these days.' Through his worry, he found a brief smile. 'Like yourself, I'm in a job where I have to be respectable. Schoolmaster. I have a little boy who must have as peaceful a home as possible. Well, I won't detain you. If I have to use force, I'll make it the absolute minimum.'

'That's right.'

By the time he got home, he found that he had lost his appetite for tea. He went upstairs. One-lung and Judy, each with a paintbrush in hand and a chastened air, were making a show of distempering the walls of the corridor.

His wife had, on a number of occasions, mentioned to him in admiration her aunt's jutting jaw and dominating manner. And Judy was never the one for being slow to adopt a role. Was she not of the same blood? A couple of evenings later she descended from her room into the kitchen where he sat at his school work. One-lung was with her. Each held a glass of wine in her hand.

'This is Sue.' Before he had a chance to respond in any way, Judy rapped out, 'Stand up!'

He did just that — and marched out of the house. He had no intention of going again to the police station, but he had every intention of letting them suppose that he had.

After a short delay, he returned home. One-lung was already vacating, for he met her coming down the lane. He turned upon her a face of iron. She looked apprehensively at him. He saw her no more.

But Judy was not quite finished yet. Shortly afterwards she walked into the kitchen accompanied by a nice looking middle-aged couple. Obviously knowing that she would have to be quick if he was not to walk out on her, she almost immediately began to make a scene.

At once he rose. 'I'm sorry,' he said to the couple, 'but this has happened before.'

The husband nodded. 'I understand.'

Up in his room, George heard howl after howl of weeping ascending to him, and the voices of the couple trying to calm his wife. He felt sorry for them. It seemed unlikely that Judy would ever again succeed in co-opting them as a jury.

Prayers and *Onward Christian Soldiers* being concluded, Mr Featherstonhaugh rose to announce, 'I have something rather unpleasant to say to the school. I would ask the ladies of the staff if they would be so kind as to withdraw.'

As they rose to do so, Miss Fetlock gave a little whinny of disappointment. There was nothing she liked better than earthy things; things of the earth. She was never happier than when mucking out a horse-box or a stall. The last to leave the Big Schoolroom, she closed the door reluctantly behind her.

'Now I'm going to be perfectly frank about it,' said Mr Featherstonhaugh. 'I'm saying it to you, and I'm saying it in front of the masters. I'm not going to beat about the bush. I believe in coming right out with these things. There was an absolutely disgusting smell in the Third Form room — Three A — when I walked in during the fourth period.'

Miss Fetlock, lingering a little behind the departing ladies and with one ear turned towards the door, gave a little shiver of delight.

Then, seeing the others looking back at her, regretfully she hastened to catch up.

'Food going bad inside you,' continued Mr Featherstonhaugh. 'Whichever boy was responsible, I want him to see to it that he goes to Matron for an opening medicine. Disgusting habits! Now pull yourselves together. Organise yourselves.'

Later, as the masters filed into the staff room, George, who had missed Assembly to make out a list of the first rugby fifteen for an inter-school match, looked up from his writing. 'What was all that about?'

'Oh,' said Charlie in his most bored intellectual drawl, 'some boy farted, and he's kept in the whole of Three A. Of some men it's said, "He's a man of many parts." Of this boy it will probably be said in later life, "He's a man of many farts." Anyway, it's the best laugh I've had since my mother-in-law's funeral.'

George glanced at Mr Snipe. From the latter's mouth, open as ever in anxious moral concern, there emerged a doubtful titter. Was not such language a bit extreme from the Senior Master, a man of a dignified now forty-five years of age, a clergyman?

Charlie picked up off the table the piece of paper on which George had written out the team. 'I see you have Dostoevsky playing at scrum half. I hope he's better at rugby than his young brother is at Scripture. I asked him who he thought the Devil was. And the answer? "Sir, he lives under the ground and says naughty things." What rubbish some mothers do fill their heads with!'

George rose, stretched out his hand to receive back the team list, and went over to the green baize board to drawing-pin it up. 'Or do they? I had given my all, during half a period, to explain to Two B what cavemen were. And when I asked Figid Minor to describe them, it came out as, "Sir, they crawled about on all fours and had funny faces." '

'You're right. I had told a class in Religious Knowledge, as we're supposed to call it now, how Jacob had passed himself off to his blind father Isaac as being his elder brother Esau, and so got the blessing that was his brother's birthright. And it came out as, "Sir, he stole his brother's birthday." '

George laughed. 'Who said that?'

'Shelley. That boy's a perfect atheist!'

Chapter Nineteen

The trees, clothed once more in their foliage, stood at their noblest. At their feet, khaki coloured grass was flushed here and there with mauve drifts of willow-herb. The big faces of dahlias peered over a stone wall.

Winter and spring had passed, and summer had come, with no more juries. But things were not less strained in the cottage. Yet, down at the Rainbow Inn with her multitude of acquaintances, and after two schooners of sherry and half a dozen cigarettes, there were always times of happiness for Judy. Above all, were there such times with her beloved little four year old boy.

At the moment he was still in bed in his nursery. A cousin of his own age, Pamela, was spending a week with them. She had been bedded down in Judy's room, to prevent the two children talking at night and so keeping one another awake.

Judy, below in the scullery doing her early morning chores, heard Pamela's voice. 'Mark, when you come out, can you put my blue ribbon on like my Mummy does?'

'Yes, I think I can.'

Judy, a smile on her face, ceased washing the china to listen.

'I'm very pretty this morning. And can you do my buttons up?'

'Yes. But I'm still in bed. Mummy says I can get up.'

'I'm glad she said that.'

Judy heard Mark's small feet pattering across the ceiling on his way to accomplishing his tasks.

'Will the world ever end?' It was Pamela's voice.

'Yes, everything will die, even the swans.'

'And giants.'

'And the houses will fall down and the chairs break.'

The new apocalypse ended as, doubtless, Mark's fingers busied themselves with the ribbon.

'Goodbye, Mark! Pamela!' It was George, leaving for the school.

'Goodbye, Dada. Goodbye.'

Later, Judy took the two children down the lane, across the town, and to the park. A June sun blazed down on the small beach by the wash of the river. Mark let go her hand to rush about the meadow. Pamela followed after him.

Returning, he took his mother's hand again. 'Mummy, I feel awfully chargey.'

'And so do I,' said Pamela, joining now. 'We must have our picnic lunch.'

'And can me and Pamela bathe then?'

'Daddy says you mustn't bathe until an hour after a meal, or you might get cramp.'

'Mummy, you let me paddle after a meal, but you won't let me bathe. You're mysterious. You're nice but mysterious. Mummy, the swans are allowed to bathe, but I'm not. I don't really call that fair.'

'I told the swans that they were not to bathe if they had just had a meal. They said that they had had their lunch long ago.'

'Mummy, what a dreary life you have!'

She bent down, took his chubby hand, and kissed him on the cheek. 'Do I, darling?'

He put his other arm round her neck. 'I play, and build castles, and have my dinner. That's best of all.' He let go of her to pick up the inflated rubber ring with which he encircled himself when learning to swim. Throwing it down beside her he said, 'Would you guard my wubber wing and my bucket, in case a wobber springs up out of the sand and steals them.'

He joined Pamela, already paddling.

Judy, her blue eyes for the moment clear of their ever more frequent expression of strain, never left his plump little arms and legs and his shock of red curls. Lunch was postponed.

Presently, however, her attention was caught, as was that of everybody on the beach, by the arrival of a Yorkshire terrier puppy; a miniature of her own Bobik left, to his annoyance, chained to his kennel by the back door. The puppy at once began to yap at the swans. They took not the smallest notice of him as they glided majestically by. He responded by raising his tiny yap to a crescendo which shook his entire body. Everybody began to laugh. One of the swans changed course and moved towards him. He retreated, his barking raised to the point of hysteria. Finally he rolled backwards over his fat little bottom and ridiculous stub of a tail. The resulting shout of laughter drove the swan away.

The puppy turned his attention to the human beings lying on the beach. He scurried up to first one, then the other, his stump wagging furiously, his snub nose snuffling at them. A short distance from Judy a young girl in a bikini lay on her back sunbathing. Suddenly the puppy ran straight up her body. She wriggled and squeaked with delight. When he reached her face, his little pink tongue appeared and he began to lick her all over. Her squeals increased. For a moment Judy shared in the general mirth. She looked at the soft lithe body of the girl, her milky skin. She studied the backs of her own hands, and her arms. The brief happiness left her small features. Once, it seemed so long ago now, she too used to show off her figure on a beach. These days she had to manage with make-up and feminine fabrics. What was she? Thirty-two. She should have lasted better. Her smokes and drinks, perhaps . . . Well . . . There was Mark. There was always Mark.

'I've been asked by friends to a dance at the Riverside Rowing Club.' It was a week later and little Pamela had left. 'Why don't you go too, just for once?'

'Judy, you know my lack of a ear for music. Not to mention my clumsiness. And the expense.'

'They're giving me a meal. And paying my entrance. There'd only be yourself.'

'What would I do with myself there?'

'You could dance with anyone. You could ask me for a dance or two.'

'Couldn't we just go together? I'd raise the money somehow.'

'No. I want to go with these people.' Her face had hardened.

At the 'Riverside', he found himself getting on quite well. The girls and women he asked seemed more than willing, and more than helpful showing him the steps.

Suddenly, in the middle of a dance, he noticed all heads turning in the same direction. He followed the eyes. A man was leaning back over a piano in a corner of the room, his hands spread out behind him on the top of the instrument. Judy stood before him, passing her hands over him caressingly. Apparently he was doing so to escape her attentions.

George, continuing to dance, considered what to do. If he crossed the room and carried her out, it would increase the scandal. There might well be some parents of his school present. If he attempted to dance with her, in her resentment at his interference she was capable of anything. The party of people, with whom he had seen her arrive, seemed to be nearby. Her host and hostess were seated sipping their drinks. Doubtless the man trapped between Judy and the piano was one of their number. Better to leave it to them to sort things out. When the band stopped, he excused himself to his partner and left the club.

Rose, baby-sitting, stood up as he entered the kitchen.

'I'll take over now. Things aren't going well at the dance.' He shook his head. There was a small break in his voice. 'Things aren't going at all well.'

'I'm sorry, Mr Brown.' Her eyes were anxious. 'Can I fetch you a cup of tea?'

'No, you get home now, Rose. You'll need your rest before the school tomorrow.'

Suddenly he followed and caught up with her in the porch. He took her hands into his. 'You bring me peace, Rose, just by being near me. Just by being near me, you bring me peace.' He stooped and kissed her cheek.

Her eyes alight, she made her way home.

The following day, on his return from the school, Judy herself broached the subject. 'My hostess said to me, "Judy, you disgraced yourself." I said to her, "Why did you let me *do* it?" '

'Judy, dear, you'll have to make up your mind whether you're an independent being or an automaton. When it suits you, you claim a fierce independence. And equally when it suits you, you claim to be a puppet with other people pulling the strings.'

'But if you're drunk —'

'Judy, if you're drunk, you've *chosen* to get drunk. So you're still responsible for everything you do thereafter. If you can't behave when you're drunk, then don't drink.'

'Other people drink.'

'But they can hold their drink. You, it seems, can't.'

She became thoughtful. 'Sometimes I'm frightened by life. Drink puts up a wall between me and life. I can only face life through a haze. In the orphanage we used to have second-hand clothes, second-hand toys. A Charitable Outside Public gave them to us, we were told. We were never allowed to forget that Charitable Outside Public. As we grew older the time, when we would have to leave the shelter of the orphanage, always came closer. What was going to become of us then? Another second-hand existence among first-hand people? I was pretty. I depended on my prettiness to see me through. Men stood me drinks and cigarettes and meals and parties because I was pretty. Often they paid my debts. Or they gave me money and called it a loan. I got used to borrowing and not paying back. For me it became normal. *You* married me because I was pretty. Women depend on their looks far more than do men. Men's jobs, if good, give them a standing. They become more attractive as they grow older because their more senior posts give them more power and prestige. Women in the main do not. My prettiness is fading . . .'

George had been listening with respect in his brown eyes. Judy had always been able to express herself well; it was not for nothing that she was a vast reader of fiction and biography.

'No, Judy, it is *not*. Good heavens, you're only thirty- two!'

She spared him a brief smile. But she was out neither for compliments nor to act a part. This was Judy sober; Judy facing life.

'Yes, George, it is. My mirror tells me it is. My only source of power is waning, and the trap is closing on me. I tried once to be Mrs M A, but I couldn't. I was a second-hand person trying to live with first-hand people. I must be myself. I must be with people who don't look disapprovingly at me when I have a drink or a cigarette —'

'*I* never look at you with disapproval. I sometimes feel anxious lest you injure your health. Mark and you are all I've got.' He smiled. 'I want you to live for ever.'

There was no answering smile. There was only a vigorous shake of the head with its still smartly permed light brown hair, its twinkling blue ear-rings. 'No, I don't want to live to be old. Once my independence goes, and once I've seen Mark safely set in life, I want out.'

He felt a chill at his total exclusion. 'I'd find a world that hadn't Judy in it very empty. You may at times be a pain in the neck, but nobody could say that you were ever a bore. Compared with you, the rest of us are only half alive.'

She looked at him more kindly. 'Without me, you'd be rid of a load of worry.'

It was his turn to shake his head vigorously. 'Worries are part of live. I'd find life empty without you. Young or old, Mark will always want his Mum.' There was a tear in the corner of his eye. He sat down. His great paw on the kitchen table gripped into a fist.

Now she put out her own hand, still immaculately manicured but grown thin, and closed it over his. 'You're a good man, George. Whatever happens to me, Mark will always have a good father.'

But Judy, always one thing on a Monday and another on a Tuesday, was quickly back in the old groove: drinks, smokes, crude attempts to arouse his jealousy. He was once more responding with a prideful determination to let these attempts fall as flat as possible. Littleness begat littleness, and the larger moment was forgotten.

There was her, 'If you can't afford to stand me drinks and cigarettes, then I must go out with those that can.' There was her suggestion, on returning from a party at the Rainbow Inn, of love making. 'How could I help it, when everyone else was doing it?' There was an account of her being driven back from a dance. 'He said, "Let's get out of the car and walk down to the river bank." I said no. He said, "I don't want intercourse." I said, "Then why do you want to go down to the river bank?" So he drove me home.'

Next morning, as George prepared to go to the town on school business, she asked him to send a telegram for her to this man. He promptly agreed. Accepting her written message, and without reading it, he had it sent off. But a day later she did a right-about face, or appeared to. 'This man has sent me flowers by "Inter-flora", but I've thrown them out.' And, sure enough, when he set off for the school, there they were in a neat bunch in their shop cellophane wrap, ostentatiously laid out in the porch. Of course it *was*, George reflected, the best way of bringing them to his notice!

But a graver matter was on its way. Coming early, being bored by the film, out of the Kingsbridge cinema to which Judy had prompted him to go, he heard someone mention his name. He looked round to see his wife hanging on to the arm of a man in a naval officer's uniform. The latter was tottering along as though drunk, and holding a bottle by its neck in the other hand. Or, having been alerted by Judy to her husband's presence, was he feigning drunkenness? Judy would never leave Mark, sleeping in his nursery, alone for long. Suddenly George knew, with all the force of a certainty, that they were on their way to the cottage. Judy was about to have a party there. He strode past them, with never a glance, for home.

On the kitchen table were assembled a large number of bottles of drink of various sizes and sorts. Evidently it was to be a 'bottle' party, each guest supplying at least one. People must have been leaving them in earlier in the evening. But where were they now? He went upstairs. Mark was asleep. He heard voices approaching up the lane. He descended again and stood in the porch, feet planted apart, a Titan ready to do battle.

In the dusk, he made out a group of about a dozen approaching up the garden path. They halted. A voice said, 'May we come in?'

'No.'

There was an embarrassed titter.

'Let us at least come in and discuss it.' This time it was Judy's voice.

'No.'

George's great shoulders were hunched, as they were when he took part in a rugby forward charge. Nobody seemed anxious to attempt to pass him.

He began to make out some of the faces. He recognised the perfectly friendly couple co-opted by Judy as a 'jury', who had had to deal with her on that previous occasion. And then he picked out the grey bobbed hair of Charlie!

'Everybody is welcome to come in, except one man. Him, I will not have in the house.' Listening to tales of love making at the Rainbow Inn, yes. Sending telegrams, yes. But arranging a party in his cottage without troubling to consult him, almost as if he didn't exist! And bringing one of her men friends into Mark's and his home!

There was a consultation. A voice said, 'We can go to the Riverside Rowing Club.' The husband of the pleasant couple advanced. 'May we collect our drinks?'

'Certainly.' George stood aside, then retired into the kitchen.

The pleasant couple and Charlie entered, holding paper bags.

As the bottles were transferred into them, Charlie, his pale grey eyes filled with concern, said, 'George, I had no idea at all that this party was being held without your knowledge. All we were told was that you were at the cinema, and would be joining us later.'

'You weren't to know, Charlie. But . . . A home isn't just four walls. It has an aura. This is Mark's and my home too.'

'Yes indeed.'

They departed. Later in the evening there was someone in the porch. Judy? George jumped up from his school work. It was the tall slightly bowed figure of Charlie, a black felt hat covering his grey hair.

'Left early. Wife not feeling too well. Er — by the way, I had a word with a certain party. Told him that Judy was a married woman, living here with her husband and child. I don't think you should have any future trouble in that quarter.'

'Charlie, what a man of courage you are! Shall I ever be out of your debt?'

'Not at all. Not at all.'

He drooped his way up the lane. George, emotionally drained, went to bed.

Later in the night he was wakened by Judy's crying hysterically down in the kitchen, and the voices of the same couple trying to calm her. Evidently Charlie's intervention had been successful. Tired out, he drifted off to sleep again. When he next woke, it was to hear her sobbing in her bedroom. This was plainly something much bigger than before. Had she regarded this man as her chance to escape from himself into a more congenial companionship? He remembered her words, 'The trap is closing on me.' In her eyes, perhaps, the last chance?

As he was dressing for the school in the morning, there was a light knock on his door. It was pushed open, and a small head covered with red curls peered round its edge. Seeing his father, little Mark pattered into the room in his bare feet.

'Daddy, I've been awake all night. It was a nasty night. Mummy was crying. I wonder why? I tried to help Mummy. I got out of bed and opened her door a little. I thought she was afraid of the dark.'

George went down on his knees and gathered his son to him. 'I think you were quite right, old chap. I think that was just it. I think she was afraid of the dark.'

Chapter Twenty

It was mid September and the beginning of the Winter Term at Worcester Hall Preparatory School. The harvest gathered in, the reddish fields now stretched away in stubble to the dark blue-green trees standing at their further fringe. The big faces of the dehilas still peeped over the stone wall.

'I must get away for a holiday, George. I *must*. I want to stay with my aunt in Stroud. She's the only family I've got.'

He looked at the strained features, her eyes large with misery. Judy could hardly bring herself to speak to him these days. If he ventured the smallest disagreement, however gently couched, she burst into tears. She seemed to him to be very near to a total breakdown. Somehow the money must be found.

When it was, there was not the least let up in her hostility. A loving farewell at the station to Mark, was followed by a scornful peck of a kiss on his own cheek.

'Daddy,' said Mark, as they made their way towards the Junior School down in the town, 'is Queen Mary pretence?'

'No, old chap, she's real, but she's dead now.'

'What has she got on top of her, gravel or sand or earth?'

'Earth.'

'Does she mind being dead, Dada?'

'When you're dead, you feel nothing.'

'I wish I was Father Christmas.'

'Why, old chap?'

'Because he never dies. I wouldn't like to have my birthday on Christmas Day. It's too much niceness on one day. Daddy, would a lion eat a man?'

'Oh yes, he would.'

'Would he eat you?'

'I'm afraid so.'
'Would he eat me?'
'Yes.'
'But he wouldn't eat a little dog, would he?'
'Oh yes, he would.'
'Heavens, Daddy, lions aren't fussy, are they!'
'Not a bit.'
'Would he eat a man if he had measles?'
'He would, measles and all.'
'Daddy, if a lion ate a man who had measles, would the lion get measles too?'
'I don't think so. I've never heard of a lion having measles.'
'Daddy, I saw a Scotsman this morning wearing a quilt.'

They had reached the tarmac expanse of the Junior School playground. In the right hand corner stood a prefab classroom raised up on small brick pillars to make it level and also damp proof. This, a private school for which George had had to pay fees, had been Mark's Play School. Now, only two months short of his fifth birthday, he had been allowed to join the State Junior School standing at the top of the slight slope of the playground. It would be another two years before he would be eligible for Worcester Hall Preparatory School. There, as a child of a member of the staff, he would receive his education free.

The Junior School was a long one storey building consisting, from right to left as they looked at it, of a changing-room and toilets, a classroom for the seven to eights, one for the six to sevens, and a third for the five to sixes. Mark identified the peg on which to hang his mackintosh not only by his Christian name on a label above it, but also by a small picture of an elephant. The other pegs had other animals. His satchel slung over his shoulder, he accompanied his father along the verandah to his class. George kissed him goodbye. Late by special dispensation, he hurried to work. On future mornings, Rose would deliver Mark to his school before making her way to Worcester Hall. She would also collect him at half past three and take him to The Brambles until his father got home.

Assembly being over, George went straight to the staff room. Charlie, flapping one hand round and waving his monocle about in the other, was holding forth. It appeared that the new French master was having a set-to in Mr Featherstonhaugh's study because one of his pupils, a dayboy, was having coaching down in the town. 'Some teachers, if anyone else takes their precious pupils, howl to the moon like wolves deprived of their pocket money.'

George assumed a thoughtful expression. 'I never before realised that wolves receive pocket money.'

'Probably not. Probably not. They're a much maligned species. Well, you can't have everything, as the actress said as she snatched back her knickers from the bishop.'

A strangled cry was heard. George looked behind him to see that Mr Snipe's head had clean disappeared into his locker. The Reverend Charles Hare's Bat, this time, had clearly *not* been Straight. The disciple of Mr Featherstonhaugh had consequently not been amused. But was his head stuck? George took an anxious step towards him. The next moment Mr Snipe had pulled it out unaided, and was hurrying from the staff room.

George watched him, bushy eyebrows raised. 'Where's he going?'

'In that hurry! Plainly to the toilet.' The Reverend Charles Hare shook his grey head gravely. 'He is *not* a wise man. Did you get the wife away safely?'

'Oh yes. It was hard to raise the money, but she had to have a change.' He sighed. 'Let's hope it does some good.'

'You'll have to write a popular song. They seem these days to make fortunes.'

'As a matter of fact, I have. What d'you think of this? "I'll be your faithful hound, if you'll throw me a biscuit of love."'

Charlie twinkled through his monocle, now replaced in his eye. 'Not bad! Not bad at all! What's the second line?'

'There isn't one.'

'That's the whole of the lyric? Just one line?'

'Yes. And it's taken me six months to compose it. D'you think it should do well?'

Charlie stroked his chin. He produced a judicious expression. 'It's certainly unusual. There can't be many songs consisting of one line.'

'We used to sing such a song when we were young,' George protested. 'It went: "We're here because we're here because we're here because we're here — We're here because we're here because we're here because we're here."'

'But that's *two* lines. Pass me that book beside you, silver plate.'
('Silver plate' was Charlie's tongue-in-cheek pronunciation of the French *s'il vous plaît* — please.)

George obliged.

'Well, I must go and take that dratted Three A. Olive oil!' (Charlie's even more tongue-in-cheek pronunciation of the French *au revoir*.)

'Olive oil!'

Letters, from time to time, began to arrive from Judy, no address given, but carelessness about addresses and dates was not uncharacteristic. The letters were extremely pleasant — and extremely empty. There was just almost nothing of Judy in them; Judy, whose every thought exploded out upon her pen, as it did upon her tongue. And no mention of her aunt. Finally there came a letter, still pleasant, still uncharacteristic, but this time with an address, if only care of a London post office. Little Mark wrote to her at once. 'I am missing you, and I am sure you are missing me. Your darling Mark. Daddy is helping me with the spellings.'

One day George took him out, and also Bobik the dog. Mark in front of him seated on a cushion tied round the bar, George pedalled his bicycle slowly along. The Yorkshire terrier scampered beside them. They came to a wood. The bicycle was laid down on its side, the front wheel was fastened with a lock and chain to its own front forks, and the machine was concealed under a bush. Mark pressed his way forward, ahead of his father, along a much overgrown path. The undergrowth pushed into his face and scratched his bare legs.

'I'd cry, Daddy, if this gets any worser.'

George lifted him on to his shoulders. When the path became more open, they played hide-and-seek, Mark hiding and his father seeking. But when the roles were reversed, things did not go well. His father out of sight, and even Bobik rustling away after adventure elsewhere, the five year old found himself alone in a world of bushes twice his height and trees soaring into an empty sky.

'Daddy! Daddy!'

George, hearing the terror in his cry, rose from his hiding place and ran to him. He went down on to his knees and swept the small figure into his arms. 'That was a silly game, old chap. We won't play it any more. Let's go home.'

But, as they cycled along, Bobik pattering after them, Mark declared, 'I like hide-and-seek, Dadda, when *I'm* hiding.'

Later, as George was leaving him at bedtime after reading to him a passage from the Bible, and a story, Mark said, 'Daddy, I'm very happy tonight, because I've got my teddybear, and my ball is found, and my door is open. Dada, I wish I was Bobik, because then I could stay up as long as I liked.'

A letter from Judy, care of another London post office, spoke of her imminent return. George's spirits rose. He wanted his Judy back and his little family together again. Two days later came another letter, also affectionate, but postponing the return by three days. George's small feeling of disappointment enlarged into frustration when a third letter put off the date by a further week. He wrote, 'Mark and I are asking ourselves, "When is Mummy ever going to come back to us?"' He enclosed a postal order for ten pounds.

Then came the letter which explained the emptiness of those previous, and the present postponements. 'This is to give you the most horrible of news. Go away somewhere and read it by yourself. I must stay with this man until the baby is born.' So she had met up with her naval officer again! Never been to her aunt! 'Then I'll get it adopted. Another pregnancy, after such a difficult one, would be hard enough to bear in the best of circumstances. He has offered to marry me. I found a letter in his flat from his wife, who left him. There was a passage in it which read, "You are a drunken bad tempered little tick of a man." You are the very best of men, George. No woman ever had a kinder or more considerate husband. Oh George, what was wrong with me? A scornful peck on the cheek at the station when you said goodbye. "*Must* you have the radio on" when I returned to the cottage after shopping. On being turned out from my nursery, I woke up to find myself in a land of enemies. When you worked late at the school, I used to leave out a snack on a tray. Then I stopped. Then I did it again on one occasion and you said, "How charming of you!" That was a terrible night for me; everything nearly came all right. I was sick in mind. I am not all bad, though neither am I much good. I dreamt, when it was all over, that I came back expecting you to meet me, and when I got out at the station you were not there.'

Well, here certainly was some of Judy back again. But was it the whole of Judy? *Mark* was the centre of her being, and there was no mention of him. Were her expressed feelings for himself genuine, after so much hatred? Perhaps they were . . .

Hard on the heels of this letter came a scribbled note, the writing wild. 'All I can think of now is Mark. He was so little trouble, really. Running across his playpen and looking up the chimney, crying out hysterically, "Father Chris! Father Chris!" *That* was happiness. My heart is broken. I will never acknowledge any other baby except Mark as mine. Where he is concerned, there is something in me of the Madonna. It is my only good thing.'

Ah, here at last was Judy, the whole Judy, the heart and centre of Judy!

The postal avalanche continued. The address this time was in Derby. 'I have a job here.' So she had left her naval officer! 'This is a horrible little attic room, with the smell of gas always around. Down below, and just opposite, is the place where they make the Rolls Royces. One by one they roll through the gates. When the hooter goes in the evening, commonplace little men stream out, and it's hard to realise that it is they who have made these beautiful machines. I was definitely unbalanced. If a psychiatrist advised an abortion, I could have it legally.'

'Abortion'. George's brown eyes stared at the word. He ran big fingers through tight red curls. At the first opportunity, he hastened to the public library. He found the word in an encyclopaedia. And, in the article which followed, two others. 'Haemorrhage' and 'sepsis'. Haemorrhage! That meant bleeding! Sepsis! That meant infection! His Judy, in her gas permeated attic room, going to some quack (no psychiatrist was going to say that she must have an abortion) and dying there! As he re-entered his cottage to take over from Rose, back with Mark from his afternoon walk, beads of sweat stood on his brow.

The kitchen was empty! They should have been back half an hour ago! He went to the foot of the staircase. 'Rose, Mark, are you there?' Silence. He rushed up. Each room was empty. A traffic injury? He went out into the porch. But which way to go?

He heard a sound behind him. He turned. The doors of a wardrobe in the corner were pushed open from within and little Mark appeared, grinning with delight. 'We were hiding, Dada.'

Rose emerged.

The usually self contained George, already stretched nearly to the limit, now went over that limit. 'What did you think you were doing, Rose?' he roared. 'I thought that you both had had an accident.'

Her soft hand flew to her mouth, and her gentle eyes were wide. 'Mark has been talking of nothing else except the game of hide-and-seek that he had with yourself in the wood. He wanted to play it again. I hadn't the heart to deny him. I meant no ha-r-rm.'

Mark was staring in terror at his father, almost as though he didn't recognise him. Suddenly he turned and scampered up the staircase as fast as his small feet could carry him. George heard his footsteps entering his nursery.

He turned and looked at Rose's fresh young face. She must be twenty-five now, but she hardly seemed to have altered from the nineteen year old English rose of his imagination. Strange that she had never married. Nor even shown any signs of having a boyfriend. Heaven knows, the trick she had played on him was modest and innocent enough! Did he expect her to have *no* spirit? Just to be an almost silent soothing presence?

He went to her. She drew away in hurt pride. He broke down her resistance and swept her into his arms. 'Of course you didn't mean any harm, sweetheart. Of course you didn't. I've had a very upsetting letter from Judy. I love my wife, she's the mother of my son, but it's been a great strain at times. You've helped me keep my sanity.'

He began to rain down kisses on her brow, her cheeks, her lips. Eyes closed, she held up her face to receive them. Sexually starved, he beat her broad buttocks with his great hand. She pressed her hips against him as she felt his orgasm. She cried out as her own body went into paroxysm. Breathing heavily, they clung together for a spell.

At last he kissed her cheek gently and said, 'I must go up to the nursery and make my apologies to Mark.'

'I will get him his tea.'

* * *

Morning prayers over, Mr Featherstonhaugh, standing behind the tall desk on the outer edges of his shoes, drew himself up to his full five foot six. Gone was the dapper smile. George, seated behind him on the dais with the rest of the staff, had never heard him more angry.

'Shakespeare Minor, you have been reported to me by the prefects for punching Marlowe Minimus. This is a cultural school, Shakespeare Minor, where music art and drama are encouraged. If you are going to kick and hit boys, you don't belong in a prep school. You don't fit in. Parents send their boys here in the feeling that they won't be kicked and hit around. If you want to bully, then go to a state school, where the boys will *hit*' (he thumped on the desk) 'you, and *kick*' (thump) 'you, and very nearly *kill*' (two thumps) 'you. Judging from the grin on your face, young man, you seem to think that I am making much ado about nothing. To correct that misapprehension, I may have to resort to The Slipper.'

Shakespeare Minor's face abruptly lost its smirk. This smirk in any case had been engendered by nervousness rather than defiance.

'Whether this is to be or not to be,' continued Mr Featherstonhaugh, 'depends very much on yourself. Your father tells me that you have ambitions to go on the stage. From the way you are progressing at the moment, Shakespeare, frankly I doubt whether you will ever so much as see the inside of a theatre.'

The Headmaster paused to pass a finger over his dapper little moustache. He straightened his Worcester College Oxford silk tie, with its pink and black stripes.

'And now to two other matters that have been causing me concern. There are certain boys down in the town who, on coming out of school, spend the time loitering in the neighbourhood of the big stores. These stores have reported to the police a rise in the number of thefts they have suffered recently. As a result, five boys will be appearing in court tomorrow. I have been told that two or three of our dayboys have been seen among the loiterers. I have no reason to doubt their honesty but' (Mr Featherstonhaugh's voice lifted a pitch) 'I will not countenance loitering. A boy who loiters lets his form down, his House down, his school down, his parents down. Above all, he lets *himself* down.' His voice rose yet a pitch higher, until it became the cry of the Evangelist proclaiming his certainties to the people. 'A LITTLE GENTLEMAN DOES NOT LOITER.'

He eased the cuffs of his black blazer, with the Worcester 'bird' badge on its pocket, and its pink tape trimmings.

'Some of the staff have reported to me an increase of romping in the school. I will not have this romping. I am going to stamp out this spirit of disorder that is invading the classrooms. I'm going to stamp out this — r-r-omping. Now pull yourselves together. Get yourselves sorted out.'

As Assembly was dismissed for the boys to make their way to their various classrooms for the calling over of the respective registers, Juniper (both his elder brothers had now departed the school) was observed to be wearing a frown. He would *not* bend the knee to the English tyrant. It was every Irishman's right to romp.

George wired a further ten pounds to Judy, and the words, 'Do nothing. Writing.'

He wrote, 'Keep away from quacks, whatever you do. You may have been in a highly emotional state, but essentially you knew what you were doing. No psychiatrist is going to say that you must have an abortion to preserve the balance of your mind. You will have to have the baby.' He held his pen poised over the paper. Come back home. Come back home. The cry echoed and re-echoed round his head. But he could not bring down his hand to put the nib on to the paper. 'You are a drunken bad tempered little tick of a man.' He shrank from taking the alien child, and of such a father, into Mark's nursery. Sufficient for the moment to let Judy know that he had not abandoned her; sufficient to save her from the hands of the quacks. He must bide his time and see how things developed.

In answer to his wire, there came another tumble of words from Judy, this time back in London. 'Thank you, George, for money that you could ill spare out of an income of only fifteen hundred pounds, which I now realise is all that you've got for us all and for everything; and for wanting to help. If we should never meet again, I shall always remember *that*, with gratitude and love. This man has given me a hundred and fifty pounds to go to a doctor he knows about. Later he doubled it to three hundred. The doctor does it by curettage, scraping the womb, in his private nursing home, and he records them as appendectomies. I had to walk across an absolutely palatial consulting room. At the other end, behind a huge ornate table, sat a polished, well groomed, smooth talking man. He said his fee was five hundred pounds. He must have read the expression on my face, for he continued straight on in his suave voice, "I can give you the address of a doctor who will do it for three hundred. He has a nursing home, so he can give you that all important after care." I found him in a big house in Chelsea. His drawing-room, dimly lighted by little red lamps, was filled with huge pieces of dark mahogany furniture. He was a small man, and his white face kept twitching. He does it by inserting rubber bougies, which stimulate the womb into expelling its contents. He has an ordinary public dispensary in the suburbs, and he does it under cover of that. When things start up, you go to him and he runs you out in his car to his nursing home. In Derby I was selling cosmetics from a stand in a trade fair, and I was only paid a commission on what I sold. When I came to London, I had to live on some of the three hundred. I asked him if he would do it for two hundred, but he said he was often paid four hundred. He gave me the address of a doctor who would do it for a hundred and fifty. He uses a German paste. He gives no after care. You just take a room and wait until it happens. Then you phone a doctor and report it as an ordinary miscarriage. This doctor was living in a small house in the suburbs. He was a greasy looking man. He kept taking my hand in his soapy fingers and calling me "my dear". The idea of waiting alone in a strange room for it to happen, and then phoning and hoping that some doctor would come in time, terrified me. I left him. I must get another job and raise the money to go to Twitch- face.'

This was more than George could stand. No matter what the consequences, no longer could he leave his little Judy floundering, apparently alone (the naval officer seemed to have dropped completely out of the picture), in this furtive sub world of hard faced men. He wrote a letter pouring out his love for her, urging her to refrain from an abortion, and to come back home. He inserted a money order for fifty pounds.

But Judy, having noted the previous lack of an invitation to return, and having received fifty pounds from Betty Coombes, had already contacted Twitch-face. She had felt doubly pressed to rid herself of the unwanted baby, if she was to make an all out bid to return to Mark and George. When George's money arrived, she added it to her resources.

The bougies having been inserted, in due course Twitch-face drove her to his nursing home. This was a tall red brick building in a line of similar buildings. The nurse in charge turned out to be a mixture of jitters and a light hearted sense of humour. Perhaps the latter was to give relief from the former. When she wasn't engaged in looking out of a window to assure herself that no police were around, she was entertaining Judy, and doubtless the other inmates whom Judy never met, with anecdotes accompanied by peals of laughter.

There was the famous London musical comedy actress who had been there five times. On the first of these occasions she was found to be infected with syphilis. It was war time, and the lately discovered penicillin was being reserved for treating the Allied war wounded. So Twitch-face had to treat her with the forty-year-long well tried injections of arsenic into a vein, and bismuth into a muscle. There were the two Eastend working class girls who forced Twitch-face to return them their money on pain of their reporting him to the police. There was the occasion when the police found a girl with the bougies in her, and Twitch-face had to bribe the sergeant with eight hundred pounds to forget the matter. There was the time when Soapy-fingers almost killed a girl with his German paste, and not only he, but Twitch-face and the suave doctor in the Westend had fled to the Continent for a fortnight as a precaution. There was the disclosure that Twitch- face was pressurised by his wife and daughter to live his dangerous life, in order to afford to keep them in the forefront of West End society.

Finally Judy, in her bed-sitting-room with bathroom-toilet unit, experienced a mini-labour and was delivered of the foetus and afterbirth. She stood by the nurse looking down at the foetus in the pan of the toilet. A boy, the nurse pronounced. Judy's relief was punctuated by an unexpected stab of mental pain. There it lay, a cockle-shell, a tiny coil of life, containing within it all the mechanisms to construct a six foot man, an engineer perhaps, an artist, a statesman. There it swirled and disappeared as the nurse pulled the chain, treated like a bit of flotsam, its only sepulchre a sewer. Sometimes the sadness came back to Judy in later years, but her greater feeling was relief. The way back to her home was now clear. Had not George urged her to return, even when pregnant?

He found her, three days later, standing in the porch regarding him, uncertainty in blue eyes. With a cry of delight he threw his arms about her. But there was a question in his gaze.

She nodded. 'I had it done.'

'Mummy home again,' said Mark, as she tucked him into his bed. She smiled. 'Mummy home again.'

Later, she came into George's room and into his single bed. In her passionate desire to make up to him for all her former snubs, she fairly threw herself into his arms. At first he responded. But, because of her over-reversal of the roles, her drowning him in her caresses, to his horror he found desire slipping away. He fought to retain it. What a home-coming to extend to her! Finally, helpless, he lay supine, awaiting the terrible moment.

It was not long in arriving. She turned her back on him and, in a bitter silence, drew to her side of the bed.

Nevertheless her deep sense of gratitude, and her consciousness of the wrong she had done him, in the months ahead made some sort of a marriage possible. An unspoken pact caused him not to ask her for the name of the man, nor she to give it. But Judy could not change herself. Her drinking and her smoking once more increased. Soon things were worse than ever.

Chapter Twenty-one

Betty Coombes burst her way up the lane between the blackberry bushes, now in November barren of their berries, with something of the impact of a frigate under full sail sweeping up a tidal estury. At first glance she appeared not to have a care in the world. A closer scrutiny of her voluptuous person would have traced a certain rigidity, the absence of the sexy smile, an anxious expression in the dark eyes half veiled by the long false lashes.

As she passed The Brambles on her right, twenty-five year old Rose, the rolled up sleeves of her cardigan displaying dimpled elbows, glanced up from her task of digging a bed prior to planting daffodil bulbs. Next, on her left, she passed George's stone built Rose Cottage, its bushes cut back hard; but Judy's rose, climbing up its trellis, was eccentrically producing a second crop of blooms. A little beyond, also on the left, were Charlie's two red brick houses, the first empty at the moment of both its tenants, Miss Lewis the Matron, and Miss Fetlock the Riding and Art Mistress, attending to their duties at Worcester Hall Preparatory School. Charlie too was away from his home, doubtless struggling with the chattering of the latest dratted Three A.

However, at the moment of her arrival he was seated, as Senior Master, at the roll-top desk of the All High, Mr Featherstonhaugh being in Oxford to watch a rugby match between his own Worcester College and the powerful Brazennose. On her being shown into the pine panelled study, Charlie turned himself round in the swivel chair. Despite his weight of learning, he got himself languorously to his feet and held out a limp hand.

'Miss Betty Coombes, isn't it?' He drew up a chair. 'How can I help?'

'I mustn't sit down, Mr Hare —'

'Charlie.'

'Charlie. Judy suddenly became ill at The Rainbow. Shouting, crying. The ambulance men gave her a sedative. They think it's a nervous breakdown. They've taken her to the Annex of the Mental Hospital. Mark is happy enough playing in our Children's Room, but it's getting near our busy time . . .'

'Of course. Of course. George is on Evening Duty down on the playing fields. I'll ask Mr Snipe to take over.' He screwed his monocle into his eye. 'Perhaps, as you're passing that way . . .'

'Thank you. I'll collect him.'

She flaunted her way down the lane accompanied by Mr Snipe, both of them following his sharp nose. From force of habit, when in the company of a man, she made a number of 'passes' at him. These served only to cause his mouth to open in alarm.

George's bushy eyebrows drew together as he observed the unlikely combination advancing over the grass. He received her news with startled brown eyes. It was all she could do to keep up with his stride down the lane. The tall poplars stood like sentinels along the edge of the field. A new plantation of evergreens on the brow of a hill had their hair powdered with a light fall of snow.

Seeing her difficulty, he slackened his pace. 'This is the first chance I've had to thank you for the fifty pounds you sent to Judy before — er — before the — the termination of her pregnancy. I must reimburse you, of course.'

'Certainly not, George. Judy's my closest friend. You had expenses enough.'

'Why should you pay? What about that naval officer?'

A quiver passed through her ample person. Her slender legs in their fishnet stockings missed a pace as she stood for a moment looking at him.

She resumed walking. 'Did you think . . . Didn't you know . . .' She drew a deep breath. 'He wasn't around to do — to do any paying. He had rejoined his ship.'

'Oh? Oh. But Judy wrote that he had given her three hundred pounds.'

'Ah . . . Perhaps — perhaps that was before he went.'

He looked at her. She seemed rather to have rushed it out.

They parted at the entrance to the Rainbow Inn. On seeing George, the stockier of the two 'bouncers', wearing his bright yellow shirt with the red tie, the six footer of about George's size and weight, approached. He was quickly joined by the six foot five giant in his black polo-necked pullover, a scowl on his hardbitten pock-marked features, at which even George glanced with a touch of apprehension. On catching sight of Betty Coombes, they retreated again.

Ten minutes later, George sat in the consulting-room. The psychiatrist scrutinised him across his large table. He had a smooth clean-shaven face, a completely bald head, and made George think of an egg.

'I'm afraid you won't be able to see your wife, Mr Brown. She's in deep sedation. We've diagnosed neuresthenia, anxiety reaction. Mrs Brown's treatment begins with a period of prolonged sleep, she being allowed to wake up just for meals.'

'I see.'

'She can't sleep properly because she's nervously exhausted, and she can't recharge her nerve batteries because she can't sleep. We have to break that sequence.'

'I understand.'

'She's expected to be in for three months.'

'Three *months*!'

'It can be quite a long business I'm afraid, Mr Brown.' The Egg arose and accompanied him to the door. 'We shall take great care of Mrs Brown. We get good results here.'

George's shoulders were slumped as he returned to the Rainbow Inn to collect Mark. Was he really not to see his Judy again for three months!

'Daddy, where's Mummy?'

As they walked home, he looked down on the curly red hair, the chubby little hand of the five year old enfolded in his. 'Mummy's not well, because she's very tired. She's gone to hospital to have a long rest. So we'll both have to look after each other. And Rose and Mrs Finch will help.'

'We'll correct exercise books together, won't we?'

'Of course.'

'Daddy, an aeroplane was flying over my head this morning. It was only about — about *four inches* under the sky.'

But November the Fifth was upon them, Guy Fawkes Day was

Guy Fawkes Day, and Mark must be considered. George, in a Free Period, slipped down to the town and bought two pounds worth of small fireworks. As he, on his return, manoeuvred aside the piece of string securing the gate of The Brambles, Mark rushed down the steep garden path, and came a cropper. Evidently he was not too badly injured, for his lusty roar quickly subsided to a whimper, maintained with difficulty to exhibit at the fount of sympathy. Even the whimper departed at the sight of the fireworks, let off that evening among the stubbly rose bushes.

A week later, came a typed letter from The Egg's secretary, stating that Mrs Brown might receive a short visit. The letter emphasised that the meeting could take place only after he had first seen the doctor. George set off in November morning sunshine, a note in his pocket from Mark to his mother written, with his father's help, in a large wobbly hand.

The front door of the nursing home or 'Annex', a pleasant creepered redbrick building with the forbidding stone Victorian Mental Hospital looming behind it, stood wide open. He pressed the white button of the doorbell. He entered the hall, looking about for signs of someone on duty. No one appeared.

Tentatively, he stepped into the corridor — and saw Judy! A thin little figure in a flimsy flowered dressing-gown, she seemed to be wandering at random. In the same moment, she saw him also. She rushed into his arms. Her lips fluttered as the words poured out in an almost incoherent passion of affection and tearful relief. Immediately afterwards they were replaced by an equally incoherent rush of recriminations; that very hostility, it seemed to him, that was eating out her mind and causing her illness.

The flow of words ceased. She glanced nervously up and down the corridor. 'The Matron mustn't see us. I'm not supposed to meet you until you have first seen the doctor.'

He studied her. The erstwhile so aggressive and independent Judy, now so thin and distraught, in fear of a Matron! He began to divine how helpless, her mind broken, she must feel to manage her own life; how totally she must feel herself to be in the hands of those ministering to her.

Slipping Mark's letter to her, he said, 'Which way to the consulting-room? I've been there only once.'

She pointed, the letter clutched in her palm. With another frightened look up and down the corridor, she vanished into a room.

Once more George faced The Egg, dressed in its white coat, across the wide table. The Egg, possessed of the knowledge, via Judy, that she and her husband no longer had sexual intercourse, was engaged in absorbing the thick curly red hair, the crinkled brow, the forceful bushy eyebrows, the steady brown eyes, the craggy jaw, the wide shoulders clothed in the new dark blue Oxford blazer, the great hands folded on the lap. Here was no lack of vitality. In fact, here was what Betty Coombes had once referred to as a 'good-looking hunk of man'.

'The basis of your wife's condition is emotional strain. She will recover only if, on the one hand, emotional conditions improve or, on the other, she becomes indifferent to you.'

'I am a kettle, doctor, which has been put off the boil so often by snubs, that it becomes difficult to boil again, if only in defence against the next snub.'

'Sexual relations are important.'

'My wife takes the kettle off the hob not kindly, but abruptly. Then, when it suits her, she picks up the kettle and demands that it boil immediately.'

'What about your both taking tranquillisers?'

George shook his head. 'No, doctor. It's natural for you to think along those lines. You live in a world of pills and medical drugs.'

The Egg looked at him sharply.

George put in quickly, 'No reflection on you. You have to, dealing with patients in the condition in which they come to you. But I've lived in a world of no smokes or drinks to speak of, of fresh air and hard exercise, of careful diet. The idea of manoeuvring my body with pills and drugs is very repugnant to me. Very. I long for my wife to recover, but . . . I've a right to health too.'

The Egg reflected. 'There must be a lot of incompatibility.'

'At first she tried to live my life. But the differences have come out more and more. If I tried to go into hers . . .' He smiled. 'I should end up as your next patient.'

The Egg rose. 'Well, Mr Brown, we'll do our best. There's been a little improvement already. If you'll come out through these French windows and turn to your right. Take a seat in the garden. Mrs Brown will come out to you presently.'

Autumn had managed to extend itself into November, and there was pleasant sunshine. The rectangular garden was sheltered and given privacy on all sides by a thick hedge. The centre was a lawn. There were seats round the periphery, some of them occupied by patients talking with their visitors.

When Judy, wearing her overcoat, joined him on the seat, she was altogether more collected. 'Most of the women here are in for husband or boyfriend troubles. Most of the men are in for business worries.' She had, for George, the unexpected and generous candour to add, 'Whenever one of us women claims that husband or boyfriend was responsible for our being here, the Matron always replies, "Oh, you all say that!"' But the next moment she had turned sour again, complaining that some woman patient had given her a present of fruit, and that she had nothing with which to repay her. As he left, he pressed two pound notes into her hand.

He was back at Worcester Hall in time to preside over his House at midday dinner. He took his seat at the foot of the polished table running along the left hand wall of the dining-room, with Mr Featherstonhaugh presiding at its head over *his* House. Across the room, at the table along the right hand wall, the Reverend Charles Hare, as Senior Master, presided at its head. Commander Robinson having departed the school, his seat at its foot was now taken by a new master, Mr Grock.

The betting in the staff room was that Mr Grock, despite unusually excellent paper qualifications in science, would not last another term. Two at the most. He was not — well — he just did not *fit*. Pot-bellied himself, he kept an unclipped curly haired poodle which he constantly overfed. As a result, the dog frequently vomited. Mr Grock woke a murky shirt and collar, a brown bow-tie generally crooked, and chain-smoked small cheroots. His hobby was taking photographs of any girl, or group of girls, that he came across. He would seat her, or them, on the brow of a bank, or top of a wall, with the admonition, 'Let's see plenty of stocking tops.' The girl, or girls, by no means averse, would oblige him with his stocking tops. How did Mr Featherstonhaugh ever come to take on such a man? The consensus opinion in the staff room was that, cheroot-less and poodle-less, he had appeared at the interview in his Sunday suit.

In the centre of the dining-hall, at right-angles to the two long tables seating the seniors, were the three shorter tables for the younger boys. Miss Lewis, as Senior Matron, was presiding as usual over that for the first year boys; the Assistant Matron over that for the second year, and Mr Snipe over that for the third year, though some of the more advanced in work or games helped to fill the long tables. At the moment Mr Snipe was bending low over his plate inspecting it for bones. He seemed about to dart down at any moment and impale the fish on the end of his nose.

All this George was observing with a smile, happy to be back in the familiar give and take of the school after the depression of the nursing-home. Despite everything, he loved his Judy, but she always, except for moments ever more rare, brought strain with her.

Later, in the staff room, Charlie tried a joke. 'He's the sporting type, and never gives girls a second thought. The first thought covers everything.'

From habit, George glanced across at Mr Snipe. For once, the latter was not squatting down at his locker. He was looking out of the window at Sergeant Finch, his commands a little slurred as he conducted a later than usual Penal Drill. From the window there emerged only a great silence. Mr Snipe turned. No open mouth. Just lips buttoned up.

Charlie tried again. 'She was kissed savagely by a Primitive Methodist.'

Nothing. The Reverend Charles Hare had lost his disciple or, rather, Mr Featherstonhaugh's disciple.

To recover his dignity, he screwed his monocle into his eye. His drawl a little exaggerated, he turned to George. 'Pass me those exercise books by your right elbow, s'il vous plaît.'

'Charlie! You shock me! What abominable French! S'il vous plaît, indeed! *Silver plate.*'

Charlie accepted the books. 'Of course. Silver plate. Got to take that dratted Three A. I won't say goodbye, as it's possible that I might survive. So just let's make it, au revoir.'

'Charlie! Charlie! Can't you talk French as good as what I learned you? Not, au revoir. *Olive oil.*'

'A second apology. Olive oil, of course.' He drawled out of the room.

Near the end of November, Judy was allowed home for a few days for Mark's sixth birthday, on the condition that she took a daily afternoon rest in bed.

'My treatment consists of plenty of rest and sleep, plenty of food, quietness, the removal of all pressures. The nursing-home supports us by keeping its gate and front door wide open at all times. They tell us that if things get too much for us outside, we can walk back in through that door any time of the day or night.'

'Right, love. You stay put. Mark and I will do the birthday shopping.'

'And Mummy, I want it to be a picnic sitting on the floor beside your bed.'

She managed a smile. 'Do you, darling? And what are you going to buy? As if I couldn't guess!'

Cakes, cake candles, biscuits, a bottle of lemonade and a box of crackers were purchased, followed by a short walk outside the town.

'Look, Daddy!' Mark's six year old finger pointed skywards.

Also pointing skywards were the black fingers of factory chimneys. Under heavy clouds, in the early gathering November dusk, a hundred sharp points of light, illuminating the factory complex, winked in and out through the moving branches of the trees. A tongue of flame leapt like a torch from the summit of the tallest of the stacks.

The picnic on the floor by Judy's bedside was marred for George by Judy's snide remark, as she observed the large form of her husband seated cross-legged beside little Mark, 'You're like an overgrown schoolboy!' He gazed at her, his mouth open to protest that he was doing it for Mark's sake. He closed it again. Judy's mental state was far too fragile to sustain any come-backs, however mildly couched.

Next afternoon, Rose baby-sitting, he took Judy at a quiet time of the day to the Riverside Club. It was strange to observe his erstwhile gregarious wife's fear of meeting anyone she knew. There they played her beloved table tennis, ranked second only to tennis itself. Just before shop closing time, Betty Coombes appeared in her car to drive her friend back to the hospital annex. On the way, Judy stopped off to buy thirty shillings' worth of wool to knit George a scarf for Christmas.

He received from her a letter very pleasantly thanking him for the weekend, and hoping that he would visit soon as she was feeling lonely. He replied by sending her a pound, then telephoning her. She was unpleasant, and hung up on him. When he tried again next day, the pleasantness had returned. He walked to the Annex. She awaited him at the gate ahead of time. He handed her the bag of shopping she had commissioned him to do for her. After sitting talking to her on a grassy bank, he took her to a little cafe.

As she poured out the tea from the large cream-coloured pot, she said abruptly, 'My hair's coming out.'

He looked at her across the small round table by the bow-window. Her features, tired, all perkiness gone, yet still retained their daintiness, the eyebrows plucked and pencilled. The blue eyes were no longer vivid, even a little sunken. The vivid lipstick had given way, in consort with her greater maturity, to a more sober salve. There were some grey strands in her light brown hair.

He chose his words carefully. Throughout, she had been on the edge of hostility. 'It's only a temporary thing, love. It will thicken up again as your health improves.'

'As your health improves' — should he have said that? Allow her to come back with: it will never improve while we're together ...

She shook her head. 'No. Women's hair thin as they get older.'

He didn't venture a reply. At the gate, at five o'clock, they said goodbye, and he pressed another pound note into her hand.

As the world of the school closed about him again, it brought with it its usual power to restore his spirit: the boys along the touch-line chanting, in support of the school rugby team, 'Two, four, six, eight — whom do we appreciate — S-C-H-O-O-L; or, more sycophanticly when the staff, their numbers augmented by boys from the second team, were taking on the school, 'Whom do we appreciate — S-T-A-F-F; Carruthers, a younger brother of the former Carruthers now departed to his public school, 'There was a terrible landslide, sir. It was supersonic and heckish.'; or Hawkins, after telling an anecdote illustrated with violent gestures, 'That wasn't a very good story, was it?', and Brenchley's crushing reply, 'No. I wasn't listening anyway.'; or Sully Minor's, 'Sir, may Hemingway and I have a friendly fight?'; two boys each heatedly claiming that he was the uglier; the suspected 'dorm' feast of crumbly biscuits passed round from bed to bed after Lights Out; the equally suspected reading of a 'comic' under the bedclothes by the light of a pocket torch; the shout of, 'Hey, chaps, Four A, when they saw it was raining and we'd have to stay in our class-room, have thrown in a stink bomb and ruined our Break. There's a full scale war on.'

Judy was allowed home again for Christmas. She was always at her best at Christmas. Her exhaustion apparently a thing of the past, and having hurled herself into decorating Mark's room, she was already, while her son was still out of the way at school, shopping down in the town for toys for his stocking. No sooner were they hidden and he returned from school, than she had drafted him, a willing recruit, into clipping little candles in holders on to the lower branches of the Christmas tree, while she did the higher. The candles would not be lighted until Christmas Day.

When the school Christmas terms were over, George and Judy together always took Mark into the stores of Kingsbridge to visit Santa Claus. On the previous Christmas, George had explained that Santa Claus had the magic power to move from shop to shop. Glancing at the bright little face of his now six year old son, he felt that this would no longer do. Moving faster on his feet than he had ever been obliged to do on the rugby field, he pointed out that the fat jolly man in one store was the real Father Christmas, whereas the thin rather lugubrious person in another was merely a man dressed up as Father Christmas. Saint Nicholas would doubtless have approved.

At a hideously early hour on Christmas morning, the quiet of the cottage was shattered by the shouts of Mark informing the household that Santa Claus had indeed descended the chimney and filled his stocking. Mark was invited into his mother's room and bed to empty the stocking under their joint eyes. George, by arrangement, moved in with a tray of tea, and milk for Mark. He sat by the small table watching them with a smile.

In the afternoon they went for a walk just outside the town by the factory chimneys. Once again, her fear was that they might meet someone she knew. 'What are people saying about me?' She flicked an anxious glance at him. 'Are they — are they saying that I'm — mad?'

'Of *course* not, darling. What an idea! You're not in the Mental Hospital. You're only in the Annex. A nervous breakdown is a perfectly usual occurence. People just associate it with strain, mental exhaustion. Like going down with flu.'

'Oh.' She managed a smile.

A moment later a young married couple approached. Judy half dodged behind George. But her friends had seen her, and waved. The naturalness with which they had greeted her was reassuring, and she was soon chatting to them. Meanwhile George, who didn't know them, played football with Mark, the 'football' being an old tin can by the side of the road.

The husband approached George. 'Mr Brown, we've managed to persuade your wife to come with us to the Rainbow. Just to meet all her friends. They've been asking after her. Just over a coffee. She's told us that drinks and smokes are out.'

'Of course. Nothing could be better. Mark and I will expect her later at home.'

But, instead, one of the 'hostesses' appeared with a note from Betty Coombes. Judy had become ill. Betty had run her back to the nursing-home in her car. Leaving Mark in Rose's hands, George strode down the lane. Judy, already under sedation, could not be seen. He left in a note expressing his concern and love, and gratitude for the wonderful Christmas she had made for Mark and himself.

Chapter Twenty-two

Not long after Judy's return to the annex of the Mental Hospital, there arrived a typed letter from The Egg. 'After receiving Electric Convulsive Therapy, Mrs Brown has shown a marked improvement. We are planning on two more E C T treatments. We have sessions every Monday and Friday. After that, it will be perfectly in order to visit her.'

Despite the grim sounding words 'electric convulsive', George, focusing his attention on 'marked improvement', walked to the school with his heart singing. Even Mr Featherstonhaugh and his mannerisms filled him with the sort of pleasure that it is possible to find in the familiar: Mr Featherstonhaugh crossing the playing fields and demanding to know, 'Who are those little boys over there?' — when he knew each one of them perfectly well, his parents, his father's profession and financial standing; 'Young man, if I have any more of this, I'll beat you'; his midday tot of whisky, which he tried to disguise by keeping his closed hand in front of his mouth as he spoke; watching a 'six' being struck by a member of the cricket team against a visiting school, 'That was a magnificent blow!'; in his most urbane voice to a new member of the staff reporting difficulties with an unruly pupil, 'If you have occasion to quarrel with anyone . . .'; staff meetings which generally took the form of his standing up at the head of the table with his hands in his trouser pockets, making little fidgeting movements as though he wanted to be 'excused', and dictating the course of future policy rather than consulting his colleagues; shaking his head with a smile (he taught Latin and Greek) and saying of one of his pupils, 'He's *not* a Classic.'

Much else had happened besides. Juniper Major, his face still shining with soap and still employing the straightest of bats, was now at twenty-one a cricket 'Blue' at Oxford. Juniper Minor at nineteen, just about to enter the same university, had abandoned the playing of hymns (even *Glory Be to Jesus*), and become a percussionist in an amateur jazz band. Juniper Minimus at sixteen had ceased the burning of paper Union Jacks and joined the officer corps at Eton, intent on following in the footsteps of his father, the retired colonel. At eighteen years of age Huntington and Godfrey-Travers, no longer interested in inspecting one another's private parts, had become interested in the parts, both private and public, of the teen-age daughters of a clergyman with long blonde hair (not the clergyman, the daughters; the clergyman was as bald as a coot). At about the same age, Chesterton-Galsworthy, Keats, Shelley and Tennyson were intent on becoming stockbrokers in the City. Tunney, once champion of the Brown Dormitory; and the elder Carruthers who had bloodied his nose in defence of the Blue, at seventeen and sixteen respectively were the closest of friends at the same public school and had a joint collection of spiders. Ferrett Minor and Grubb Minimus, together with Fanfani-Gonzales on whom they had so ably pinned the abominable crime of the Missing Peppermint Creams, now at fifteen, in the public school holidays and the best of friendship, had formed themselves into a detective agency. Much of their time was spent in wandering up and down the High Street of Kingsbridge looking for clues. (So far they have made no arrests, though the finger of suspicion has more than once pointed at the sixteen year old Slygrin.)

George met Judy at the gate. They sat down on their bank, the first daffodils of early February already beginning to thrust their green spears above the grass.

'The electroplexy is terrible.' She was near to tears. 'All I could do was look at that oxygen cylinder beside the chair in case of emergency. That's all I could think of — that oxygen cylinder. I thought: well, if I go, I go. They put a cushion to your back in case you break your spine. They shove a gag into your mouth as well. Then your body receives a hideous jolt, and you're out. You come to sobbing and sick, and with an aching skull.' Her face brightened. 'But I feel greatly relaxed.'

After two more E C T sessions at the Annex, George received

another letter from The Egg. 'She appears to have made a good recovery, and should now be able to return home.'

At that home, life soon returned into its old groove; an armed peace, a wary manoeuvring.

One day Judy, on returning from her 'shopping' (one third shopping; and two thirds gossiping, drinks and smokes at the Rainbow), she spied ahead of her up the lane, through none too well focused eyes, a spare figure, a grey scarf about its hair. The usual expression of suspicion in Mrs Finch's grey eyes had been replaced by one of anxiety. On Judy's closer approach, the large work strong hands began to unfasten the piece of string securing the gate, 'The Brambles' spelt out upon it in white metal letters. Without the support of its string, the gate at once drooped, its bottom hinge adrift.

Mrs. Finch emerged through it. 'May I have a word with you, Mrs Brown. What I've always afeared has happened. Sergeant Finch has lost his job at the school. He was drunk in front of the boys. Maybe Rose and I will now lose our jobs too. Except what I get from Mr Tremble, all I have is what little I've saved these years.'

Judy's ready sympathies were at once engaged, as they always were with anyone who had, as she invariably put it, 'a drink problem'. On one occasion George had come across her, in Kingsbridge High Street, standing on guard over a man. It was Old Ben, sprawled in an open space near the public pavement. Like a tigress defending her young, she was snarling at any passers-by who stopped to view him. Some of them were laughing at her. The rest hurried on. When the taxi she had phoned for appeared, she opened her purse and paid for his transport home.

'Oh, so your husband was drunk, was he! The naughty man was drunk, was he! What a terrible thing! You leave it to me, Mrs Finch. I'll get my husband to see about this. He's a House Master, you know.'

Despite her one time speech to George of being a second-hand person, half of Judy still liked to think of herself as Mrs M A, co-opted by marriage into the first-hand world of her husband and son. So Mrs Finch's supposition that she, Judy, could influence events, had its power to flatter. Also the power to drive her without thought into a thicket of thorns.

'Judy, I'll be lucky to hold on to my *own* job!' George's brow, under its hedge of curls, was crinkled in consternation. 'I can't walk up to the Headmaster and demand that he retain the services of a sergeant who fell down flat on his face in front of a platoon of boys!'

'Perhaps he tripped up.'

'Judy, he was reeling about as he approached the boys. They all saw him. Through the dayboys, it will be back to their parents by this evening.'

'He'll have learnt his lesson.' It was the turn of Judy to experience consternation, as she contemplated the appalling loss of face with Mrs Fitch that threatened. 'It won't happen again. I'll see to that. I'll have a word with him.'

'Judy, no word from you is going to make him change direction on a road down which he's been travelling for years. Even assuming that he were able to take in what you were saying.'

Desperation drove her into anger. 'What am I to say to Mrs Finch? Tell her that you wouldn't lift a finger to help her?'

'It's your own fault, Judy, for taking me for granted. Don't you think I might have been consulted first? No school could afford to keep a drunkard on its staff; not unless it wished to close itself down.'

'Oh, you're *hopeless*, as usual. If *you* won't do anything, *I* will.' And the next moment, still none too steady on her feet, she had exploded out of the kitchen, banged the garden gate behind her, and was marching up the lane.

George had been seated, having an afternoon Free Period, book correcting at the main kitchen table. This was in order to provide space for Mark also. The six year old, back from his Junior School at just before four o'clock, was playing at 'schoolmaster' and needed room for his papers.

His father jumped to his feet. 'Back in a minute, old chap. I must see what Mummy's up to. I'll ask Rose to come over.'

He sprinted across to The Brambles. Mrs Finch, knotting the scarf more securely about her black hair streaked with grey, came to the door.

'Mrs Finch, my wife has just set off for Worcester Hall to save your husband's job. No way, no way, will she succeed. This time Sergeant Finch has gone right over the top. What she *will* succeed in doing, unless there's a miracle, is to lose me mine.' There was a movement in the kitchen. 'Rose, sorry when you've only just brought Mark back from school, but would you look after him? I must get to Worcester Hall as fast as I can.'

She hastened forward, drying her hands on her apron. Her gentle eyes were large. 'I will surely.'

'Thank you.' He touched her shoulder.

A moment after, he was charging up the lane, and then between the flower-beds leading to the grey-plastered castellated building. At the top of the steps to the open front door, the blood surged back on his heart as he heard a shrill voice raised in what appeared to be a non-stop harangue.

The staff room door was open. It being the end of classes, almost the whole of the staff had gathered to receive some instructions from the Headmaster. Even the Matron was present.

Judy was white faced as she pointed a trembling bony finger straight at Mr Featherstonhaugh. Her features were contorted and her voice had now risen to a shriek.

George, maddened by the sight of his position at the school, built up by him over so many years at the cost of so much unremitting work, being lost in front of his eyes; his beloved cottage in effect gone, for, sold or let, he would have to move out; his little boy's chance of a prep school education at Worcester Hall being shattered; caring nothing for what the assembled company might think, picked up his wife, tucked her under his right arm as he was wont to tuck a rugby ball when leading a forward charge, and swept with her out of the room.

They were quit of the school and a third of the way along the lane before he set her down. Silent, her face flushed, she tried to rush past him, only to bump into his massive form.

'If you don't return home, Judy, I'll carry you down to the police station. It won't take them long to detect that you're stinking like a brewery. You've lost me my livelihood, your livelihood, most unforgivably, Mark his livelihood and his chance of a first class education at a fine school.'

Judy had been sobered. Perhaps also there had been a touch of pleasure at his violence. At any rate her voice was quiet as she said, 'I can earn Mark's living and mine at the Raimbow. Cooking, waiting on table, flower arranging, free meals.'

'Well, go home and do that, then. You've finished *me* off. Not that I suppose that will worry you. I must return to the school to apologise to the Headmaster. And doubtless to get my notice of dismissal.'

He turned on his heel and was striding away from her. She stood a moment watching his broad back. Much of her talk of work at the Rainbow Inn had been bravado. She walked home.

Rose, seated beside Mark at the kitchen table, got to her feet. 'Thank you, Mrs Brown, for trying to help my Dad. But 'twas of no use, was it?'

'No, Rose. I'm afraid not.'

Mr Featherstonhaugh, sitting in his swivel chair in the pine panelled study, while giving George his term's 'notice', also revealed that he knew of Judy's previous incursion. He endeavoured to maintain his suave demeanour. Was there apprehension in his eyes?

'I doubt if you have the power to dismiss me.' The word 'Headmaster' was pointedly omitted. 'It is right that wrongful dismissal should be impeded by the law. Otherwise employers become little tin gods, and employees doormats. In other words, both finish up less than men.'

He became aware that the apprehension on Mr Featherstonhaugh's face had enlivened into an expression of outright alarm. George found that he had marched forward to within two feet of his employer. His six foot one and fourteen and a half stone were almost poised over the swivel chair. This wouldn't do at all! Without turning, he took three long strides backwards. He was further cooled when the Headmaster appealed to George's own school experience. 'A school like this can't survive such scenes.'

But when the Headmaster was so unwise as to enlarge on Judy's shortcomings, George's bull neck began to redden. 'She has gallantry. She has spirit. She has been through a very hard experience in hospital. D'you expect everybody to play life all the time with one of your precious straight bats in your smug little domain?'

Mr Featherstonhaugh rose to his five foot six. No standing on the outer edges of his shoes in an effort to increase his height. He was looking straight up into his Games Master's eyes. 'I think the time has come, and more than come, Mr Brown, for you and me to part.

You are no longer the *gentleman* who joined my staff so many years ago.'

'I can hardly wait to shake the dust of your pat ready made judgements off my shoes.'

'The pat ready made judgements, as you call them, of the prep-public-school system still produce most of the leaders in our society. They are the steel in Britain's spine.'

George stared at Mr Featherstonhaugh. Then he strode to the door. Just before he made his exit he said, with a suggestion of respect, 'So you *do* have an insight and a faith!'

He closed the door behind him. Then he opened it again. 'I wish to apologise, Headmaster. After serving the school for so long a time, I should have known you better. I should have known that that was no way to speak to you. Finding my whole life suddenly falling about my ears, I was an animal in a quagmire just threshing around.'

Mr Featherstonhaugh, still shaken, had sat himself down. He looked up in surprise. Then his dapper little moustache moved. 'That's all right, Brown. That's perfectly all right. Now you take your time about finding another post. You can count on a first class reference, of course.' He paused, and ran a thoughtful finger along the pink tape edging of his black blazer. 'We must hope you won't encounter a recurrence of the same — difficulties.' Seeing George's brows gathering together at this possible fresh attack on his wife, he put in hurriedly, 'No offence intended.'

George's craggy features slowly cleared. 'And none taken, Headmaster. You have, of course, merely put your finger on the spot. That's going to be the trouble, isn't it? Even if I go to Timbuctoo. Well, I don't think you need to fear a repetition in any immediate future. I think that my wife will have learned that these invasions achieve nothing whatsoever; indeed, bring disaster. I'll ask for her absolute undertaking that she keep right away from the school. Otherwise I'll seek a court injunction.'

Mr Featherstonhaugh's swivel chair creaked as he leant forward in alarm. 'D'you think, Brown, that it's advisable —'

George raised a large hand. 'Have no fear, Headmaster. I'm perfectly aware, after Sergeant Finch and now this, the school can't stand having its name brought into the local court. The threat in itself will suffice.'

* * *

March brought with it once more the yellow ragwort in the fields, the drifting mists from the river — and a fresh crisis for George. Knowing Judy to be out, he opened her bedroom door and threw on to the bed a packet of biscuits she had commissioned him to get from the school tuck shop. As the parcel bounced on to the coverlet, it caused a piece of paper to flutter on to the bedside rug.

George strode forward to pick it up. The blood seemed to run back on his heart. It was a printed receipt headed, 'National Assistance Board'. He ran his eye down the document. She was paying out of the housekeeping money a weekly sum of twelve shillings and seven pence towards Legal Aid. Was it on account of assault; his carrying her out of the school? He would say nothing and await developments. Who but Judy would be so careless as to leave such a document lying about! He replaced the piece of paper on the beflowered coverlet, removed the packet, closed the door behind him, and left the biscuits down in the scullery.

The developments were not long in coming. An ominous letter from the Assistance Board informed him that Mrs Brown was seeking Legal Aid in regard to Divorce Proceedings. With it was enclosed a typed copy of a letter from Judy stating her income. The Assistance Board asked him for his comments on it, and a statement of his own. He scrutinised her figures. Again and again Judy, never the best of mathematicians, had under represented what she received. A payment that he had made to her of four pounds and eighteen shillings, that is, all but five pounds, was recorded as four pounds. Mark's lunches at the Junior School, paid for by George's parents, were left out of the reckoning. By the time he had finished his additions, her true housekeeping allowance, in cash and kind, was recorded as one third larger. His own available income, he stated with the utmost exactitude. He cycled down to Kingsbridge and slipped the letter into the post-box of the Assistance Board.

Shock followed shock. A letter arrived from his parents in Cornwall. It enclosed an account, sent to them by Judy, from a Kingsbridge grocer, threatening legal action unless twenty-two pounds were paid in settlement. Again, at the first opportunity, George returned to the town, this time to the public library. From the reference shelves he pulled out a large volume, *Everyman's Own*

Lawyer. What were a wife's powers to pledge her husband's credit? It was a complete defence for the husband if he could show that, relative to his income, he made his wife a sufficient allowance for necessities; and that he had not made previous settlements on her behalf with the tradesman concerned. He returned the invoice to the grocer, quoting the law. There was no come-back. He informed his anxious parents accordingly.

Feeling lonely and vulnerable, George consulted Charlie, drooping in a corner over a cup of tea.

'I should let your wife know that you're aware of the Proceedings, old man. Find out her intentions. If necessary, you'll have to engage a solicitor.'

'Can't afford it, Charlie.'

'You'll get Assistance. Especially as you would be defending. I believe there's a list in the post office of solicitors prepared to act under Legal Aid.'

Back at the cottage, Judy's eyes opened wide with the vehemence of her reassurance to George. 'I just wanted to get Counsel's Opinion. That's the beginning and end of the matter.'

Ah! So it seemed that she had been advised that she had no grounds for divorce! She always spoke as though she had the courts in her pocket where the housekeeping money was concerned. Indeed, latterly she had begun to treat her adultery as though it had been his fault. So intensely was she able to believe that anything that she wanted to be the case, was indeed the case; she nearly had power to mesmerise him into believing it too. He found himself almost shaking his head as he thought: but surely adultery is a *fault* in law! Surely one doesn't have to produce more money at the expense of going into debt! One can be *sued* for debt! As to the physical assault, doubtless her own conduct on the occasion had left her too vulnerable to proceed. So her reassurance acted also as a reassurance of the correctness of his own views. Feeling easier than he had for weeks (a whole month had slipped by since that printed docket had fluttered off the bedspread), he went upstairs. After knocking, he entered Mark's room. The six year old immediately charged his father's knees in a rugby tackle. George duly obliged by falling headlong to the floor.

* * *

Once more the suburban gardens of Kingsbridge were drowned in the golden cascades of the laburnums, the vivid streaks of the copper beeches, the falling spray of may blossom. Once more the fields were awash with daisies. Once more the blood seemed to run back on George's heart as he stood in the kitchen gazing at the document that he had just extracted from its envelope. Judy was out. She had elected, after seeing Mark into his Junior School, to go shopping. Had she done so on purpose, knowing what was to be? George was to learn that when such a case came into court, lasting two days, the first for the plaintiff, the second for the respondent, that those two days were but the tip of the iceberg. By far the greater part occurred out of sight, over months and months, in a thrust and parry, in an attack and defence, of solicitors' letters; of Counsels' Advice and settling the Plea and settling the Answer.

He pushed the document into the pocket of his tweed jacket, and picked up his kitbag. As he strode along between the bushes, at the beginning of July thick with red unripened berries, the harsh accusations struck at, and re-struck at, his mind. 'Mental cruelty.' 'Failure to maintain.' Feeling very helpless (Judy had a solicitor behind her, while he had nobody), he set down his bag on the staff room table. He hardly noticed Charlie's shining his teeth at him, Mr Snipe's open mouthed nod of greeting, Mr Grock the Science Master's curly-haired unkempt poodle swishing its tail in welcome, Miss Fetlock's well bred whinny. But he managed a smile, and a pat on the dog's head. Later, at the post office, he selected the solicitor nearest to the school.

The solicitor strode up and down his large office, reading the document. His young secretary, her blonde hair falling on to her shoulders, hung back watching the two men before retreating towards her reception desk.

The solicitor, a man in his thirties, halted before George. 'Don't you think it would be better not to defend, if you've been rough on the wife? I myself have been divorced and remarried, and I've been far, far happier.'

A head of red curls was shaken. 'Oh no, I couldn't do that.'

The solicitor considered for a moment the determined jaw. 'Very well.'

His secretary completed her withdrawal, closing the door behind her.

'Can I get Legal Aid?'

'I'll tell you what you do. Write to the Honorary Secretary of the Law Society. Give him my name and address, and say that I've agreed to act for you. They may, however, decide that they want to appoint a solicitor of their own. In the mean time, would you be able to write out your side of the matter? Let me have it back just as soon as possible?'

'Certainly. That must be done. I'll get straight home now. It has to be fitted in on top of a heavy schedule of school work and coaching.'

To ease his work load, without jeopardising his pupils' examination chances, George had long ago instituted a 'staggered' system. Each of his classes in the senior and middle school had two Geography 'preps' a week. In each case he made one a writing prep, and the other a learning one. The latter had to be tested on the next occasion, to ensure that it had been done. The essays took much the more time to correct. The tests merely consisted of ten questions, the answers to which could be quickly checked. So he made sure that, among his various classes, the essays didn't all come down on him at the same time. Even so, the writing out of his divorce defence, in his bedroom for privacy, kept him from his bed for an hour after midnight. The next evening, it kept him for two. From Judy, when they were obliged to meet, he caught the occasional wary glance. Neither of them mentioned the case.

The following day, after school, he sat in the solicitor's office while the latter read through the pages. He laid down the last sheet. 'I talked about your not defending. About your being rough on the wife.' He gave a sudden smile. 'You're a very kind man.'

George's rugged countenance was suffused with pleasure. He felt that his position was already beginning to strengthen. 'So we defend?'

A head of groomed brown hair was nodded. 'I only wish that all my clients had as strong a prima facie case. I don't think they'll go on with it. Have you a typewriter?'

'Yes.'

'I tell you what. Would you type this out and let me have it back tomorrow? It will save you expense.'

Over the next three late evenings, a rat-tatting came to Judy's ears. On the second day, after he had left for the school, she glanced into the room. There was nothing on his table except typing paper, carbon papers, and the small machine itself. Her brow crinkled, she went downstairs and lit a cigarette.

When George delivered his typed statement, and the completed Legal Aid form, to the solicitor, he said, 'Sorry. I just could not get it done before.'

The latter bowed his groomed head over the pages and read steadily. 'Excellent. Excellent. I'll send them off straight away.'

It was now ten days into July. George sent a carbon copy to his parents. A letter came back from his father. 'This whole affair is going to be very disagreeable for you, indeed very unpleasant for us all. Love and sympathy from us both.' This was followed closely by a postcard from his mother. 'I'm thinking of you and this problem all the time. We both think your typescript is excellent, answering all points clearly and briefly.'

In mid July came a letter from the National Assistance Board asking George for a date to come and see them in a neighbouring town. He bused to them on his weekly half day, after having obtained from Mr Featherstonhaugh a statement of his salary. He spent an hour and a half with the Board. Other papers were required. By the time that all was completed, it was nearing the end of the month.

In August, George received a letter from his solicitor enclosing a copy of one from Judy's. This demanded that he 'stay away' from home. In consternation, he went to the school office. Fortunately it was empty. He dialled. In reply to his expostulation over the phone that he couldn't possibly afford a second address, there came, 'Mr Brown, I shall certainly pass your representations over to Mrs Brown's solicitor. But I have to inform you that I am holding a paper in my hand in which your wife is seeking an injunction to restrain you from entering the family home. However, I'll do what I can.'

The very next day, George received a letter from Judy's solicitor forbidding him the house. He was to be allowed to see Mark daily. But he was to return his son each evening at not later than seven o'clock. Being ordered not to enter his own house, the gift of his parents to him! Instructed as to when he was to see his own son! Fire in his breast, he marched to the school telephone. By the time he had ceased speaking to his solicitor, he had realised that he must comply.

In the school library, he scanned the columns of the *Kingsbridge Chronicle* for the cheapest room. He booked it by phone at once, too bitter to trouble even to view it. That evening, he moved in with his luggage. He found it to be an attic room, reached by a small spiral staircase. The slope of the roof allowed his six foot one, headroom only along its centre. He returned home, but did not collect his son. He would leave that till the following day. The solicitor's letter had stipulated that he might, between seven and half past seven each evening, attend to the pigeon and the garden. But he must not make any attempt to approach his wife or the home. He opened the cage to clean it. Also to allow the pigeon its fly around. When he turned to entice it back with bird seed in its bowl, it had gone!

'To Sergeant Finch's loft to find a mate, I suppose. So you've left me too.'

He turned away, leaving the cage door open. Doubtless for a consideration of beer money, he could have reclaimed both pigeon and mate. But he had not the heart. Even the garden he left unattended. He wandered through the town. He had not eaten since lunch time, and almost nothing then. Ahead, light streamed from a sweet shop cum tobacconist still open. He bought a box of individually wrapped chocolates. Strolling round the park, he came upon a boy sleeping rough on the floor of a shed open at its nearer end. The boy was just about Mark's age. Under other circumstances, it might have been his own son lying there! Seeing a light tarpaulin at the back of the shed, he entered, and drew it gently over the small body. Bending down, he left half a dozen of the chocolates by the boy's mouth.

He returned to his attic home, and went to bed.

Chapter Twenty-three

On the tenth day of August, 1959, a letter arrived for George from the Legal Aid Society. It was handed to him by Judy at the front door of the cottage, as he returned Mark at the stipulated seven o'clock. The six year old had run straight up to his nursery to feed his hamster and clean out its cage. George had explained to his son that his mother was still suffering from strain, and needed a quiet house to herself. What explanation Judy had furnished, he neither knew nor cared to enquire.

As he tore open the envelope, he realised that he had forgotten to notify the Society of his change of address. That was something that must be put right at once. He felt his wife's watchful eye on him. The Legal Aid Society had undertaken his defence on a nil contribution! The phrase danced before his eyes: 'nil contribution'. And Judy had had to pay! Not much, but — she had had to pay. So she didn't have the courts in her pocket after all! He had a champion; he was no longer alone.

Even before this, some of his bitterness had evaporated as he had had time to think things out. The court had not taken sides against him when it had banned him from his home; after all, it had not yet heard his argument. It was merely, as near as might be, seeking to freeze the situation until the case could be brought before it. Judy had alleged mental cruelty; the judge could hardly leave them together. Furthermore, the court would chiefly be concerning itself with what was best for the child. On balance, a housewife might be expected to be more frequently on hand than a husband in a job that sometimes kept him late. Plainly it was easier for a father to vacate the home than a mother and child. As for his parents, at least they would have the consolation that their grandson was enjoying the benefit of the home which they had provided.

Once again he became conscious of Judy's scrutiny. The suspicion began to form that she might have steamed open and read the document. She certainly would have recognised the envelope with its printed heading, after having, doubtless, received a similar one herself in the past. Scruples about opening private mail would not have long held out against her abiding curiosity.

Suddenly she spoke. 'I feel like calling this whole divorce thing off.'

Ah! So she too was beginning to discover that the court was not in her pocket.

'Judy, I've spent hours upon hours, late into the night, drafting and re-drafting and typing out documents. In fact, I've well over half conduced my own defence so far. I just can't agree to have gone through all that for nothing. Especially now that my case has been taken up. I *must* find out how I stand. About money. About — everything. Otherwise it will all come down on me again.'

'I've no intention of taking Mark from you.'

He shook his head. 'Your mind is much too changeable. I must have everything, whatever it may turn out to be, down on paper, with the force of a court behind it.'

Her startled expression at once gave way to one of aggression, as she jumped to re-establish her stance of attack. 'I've a very strong case.'

'Well . . . We shall have to wait and see. I must go. I'm not supposed to linger here anyway. Except to do the pigeon and the garden. The pigeon has taken himself off. The garden I leave to you.'

Aggression gave way to alarm. 'I can't manage the garden on my own!'

'You're trying to get a divorce from me. Remember? If you succeed, you'll have to do without me entirely. Your days of having your cake *and* eating it will be over. Either care for the garden, or neglect it. If I'm to continue to work at Worcester Hall after these holidays are over, keep on with my private coaching, half run my own legal defence, and at the same time look round for another job, then I'll need all the time I can get.'

On reaching his garrett room, he closed and put away the Bible and brightly illustrated child's book lying on the writing-table. Some headroom had been created for its user by breaking out the slope of the roof with a dormer window. Further back, against the same wall and under the same slope, was a single bed. The ascent of the roof gave just enough elevation for him to make up the bed, and to enter it, from its outer side. Across the room was the door at the top of the spiral staircase.

Earlier, after hearing Mark his prayers, he had read a passage from the Bible, followed by a story from the children's book. Thus it had been at bedtime in his own childhood: prayers, Bible, story-book. George was not the one to break with the custom established by his revered parents.

It was early September, the school Winter Term just beginning, when he received in rapid succession two communications. The first was from his solicitor. It informed him that the Assistance Board had selected a solicitor of their own, and that he had sent on to him 'all the relevant papers'. It also wished him the best of luck, reiterated that he didn't think they would go forward with the case, and presented him with a bill for 'pre Legal Aid expenses', fifteen pounds and ten shillings.

Arriving at the school, George showed the letter to Charlie. 'Bit of a blow. I thought my Nil Certificate would cover everything.'

Charlie rose from his seat in the staff room, at the same time screwing his monocle into his eye. He bowed his long form over the document. 'Well, you chaps from Oxford can afford it. Talk of the City of Dreaming Spires! What with the small amount of work you do there, falling asleep or ogling the girls during lectures, it's more like the City of Dreaming Squires.'

George snatched back the letter in mock anger. 'Shame on you, Charlie! Only a Cambridge man could stoop so low.'

The following day came a typed communication from the new solicitor. It was grimly referenced Y/ZHF/87952/Brown, carried a London address, and said that 'this office' had been appointed to act for him. It concluded with a cold 'Yours faithfully'. George, in his various subsequent replies, tried to warm things up to a friendly 'Yours sincerely'. In vain. To the end of the case, he was met with the same unbending signing off.

One day, on his returning Mark, Judy begged him to stay to

supper. Their son had, as usual, run upstairs to attend to his pet hamster.

He stared at her. 'Judy, that's what they call "collusion"! You'll ruin your case.'

'I feel lonely, George.'

He studied the small figure standing before him in the porch. Her eyes were large in her strained face, and seemed near to tears. Her long thin fingers fiddled with the buttons of her cardigan. He had got the idea that those hideous E C T's had lifted her out of her breakdown. Had she suffered a relapse? He couldn't find it in his heart to refuse her. Nor to take advantage of her distress.

'All right. We'll have a gentleman's agreement I was never here.'

'Sit down. Make yourself confortable. Supper'll be ready in ten minutes.' She hurried away into the scullery.

As he passed the kitchen table, his eye caught a document lying on it. It also caught the printed heading, 'Further and Better Particulars'. Ah, so his London solicitor was already making demands and counter-attacking! It was Judy's turn now to be grilled. Pity gave way for a moment to triumph. He was, after all, fighting for his home and his reputation. He had been ordered out of the house that his own parents had given him. He had been told when he might and might not see his own son. He had had the most hurtful charges launched against him. Already loaded with work, he had been made to labour over legal documents into the small hours. It wasn't only Judy who was beginning to become weary.

A little later he pushed away his empty plate. 'That was nice. Very nice indeed. Well, I'll just see Mark up to his room. Pink Elephant will be lonely, Mark.' That vast toy stood in a corner of the nursery. 'He told me to tell you not to be long.'

'He'll be all right. I gave him a book to read.' The six year old, now almost seven, was always quick to enter into his father's nonsense and to cap it.

As George descended again after tucking the little fellow into bed, he heard the rattle of crockery being washed up. Judy hastened out of the scullery.

'George, do stay the night. I've kept your room clean and tidy, just as it was when you left.

'Judy —'

'Please, George. I feel afraid of being alone.'

'Judy, I have to be a bit careful myself. I was told that your solicitor had the papers prepared, to seek an injunction restraining me from visiting the house. He doesn't seem actually to have served them. But they're there, hanging over me.'

'Please, George, gentleman's agreement.'

Still he hesitated. Judy was not the one for holding to her word long. Always there was the ready formula for getting out of it. On the other hand, she would have her collusion on her mind.

'Well . . . I'll take my bed into Mark's room. Perhaps that will cover us both.'

Mark's brown eyes danced as he sat bolt upright in bed. 'Daddy, just you and me together!'

George grinned as he set up his bed some distance from, but parallel to, his son's. Soon both were sound asleep. Mark, at least. With George, anxious and over tired, slumber was shallow. And soon ceased, as he was disturbed by a sound. He opened his eyes to see that Judy had dragged in her mattress and arranged it on the floor between the two beds. She left, and returned with her bedclothes. Despite her tablets, she tossed and turned, and both of them were glad to see the dawn.

In mid September, George was again labouring over his papers, 'Addenda and Corrigenda', to cover all the new points that had arisen. Four evenings, finally finishing up in the early hours, it took to compose and type a document as long as his original deposition. He was driven on by the determination not to leave a stone unturned that might serve to restore his home and his reputation to him.

One day, emerging from the school, he found his solicitor's clerk seated in his car at the top of the lane. George joined him in the front seat and handed over the new papers. All points were discussed, even to the rival advantages of defending or not defending. Just before the clerk drove away he said, 'I don't think they'll go forward with your wife's case. It's the weakest I've ever seen.'

At the beginning of October, there appeared a demand from Judy's solicitor that Mark should in future be returned to 'the home' by six o'clock instead of seven. George felt no resentment at this; the evenings were closing in. The demand added, 'He may, however, be kept out late on two or three occasions for Christmas festivities.' Also there arrived for signing a lengthy statement from his own solicitor, based on the material that George had supplied in his 'Addenda'. It was accompanied by a letter. 'The papers in your case have now gone to Counsel for his Opinion and for him to settle the Answer.' A fortnight later another letter enclosed a copy of Counsel's Opinion. 'There is, in my view, a reasonable prospect that the Petitioner will not be successful in establishing her charges.'

Next day George was granted leave of absence by a very sympathetic Mr Featherstonhaugh. He took train for London, and found his way to an office block. As he climbed the staircase, he came to a door bearing a solicitor's brass plate. The name on it was not one that he knew. He continued up to the next floor. There, he found another brass plate. This time he knew the name. He pressed the bell button. The door opened, and there stood the clerk he had met in the car. Suddenly George felt an overwhelming conviction that the solicitor downstairs was Judy's; that his papers and hers were just travelling up and down between the offices. The State was bearing almost the whole cost of the case, and the State was doing it as economically as possible.

The clerk ushered him into an inner office. The solicitor, a middle-aged man wearing extremely thick glasses that made his eyes look very small, rose and shook George's hand with a friendly smile that belied the 'Yours faithfully' and the 'Y/ZHF/87952/Brown'. He motioned towards a seat.

George, after giving a few small tugs at his dark blue Oxford blazer (the best one) to make sure that it was 'sitting' properly, lowered his large form into the armchair. 'Nothing of course is certain in this world. But would you say that my wife has no real chance of success?'

The solicitor, watched not only by George but also his clerk, removed his glasses. Peering short-sightedly, he breathed on them before polishing them with a tissue. 'Oh no, I couldn't say that she has no chance. Her solicitor, after all, seems to be continuing. He may be relying on the psychiatrist's opinion that a divorce is necessary for her recovery. However, circuit judges don't allow psychiatrists to try their cases for them. I *can* say that your wife's case is very weak. If you defend, I wouldn't put her chances at higher than twenty-five per cent. Obviously she would have a very much better prospect if the case were undefended. Perhaps fifty-fifty.' He replaced his glasses.

'And if I cross-petitioned on her adultery? Would that improve her chances of a separation?'

The solicitor's weak eyes looked at him sharply. 'I thought you were determined to resist a divorce.'

'Most certainly, but . . . Now that I'm up in London, I ought to seize the chance to get your advice on all the possibilities.'

'Quite.' He put his fingers together, and tapped with the backs of his thumbs against his pouted lips. 'I don't think you have sufficient grounds on which to cross-petition. Adultery is no longer the be-all and end-all that it once was. In any case you can't sit on evidence. Put it into cold storage, to be taken out later when needed. You would have had to petition immediately. Otherwise you would be deemed to have forgiven her; in legal terms, to have condoned her misconduct. Unless you were proceeding on later new grounds. Then you could revive the previous misconduct in support. Divorce is not on demand. The decision lies entirely with the judge. And he will, first and foremost, he considering the interests of your son.'

George rose. 'Quite, quite. Points taken.'

The solicitor followed suit. He extended a cold hand, but accompanied by the warm smile. 'We've put you to a lot of trouble, Mr Brown. We've had more paper from you than in any other case we've handled.'

George took the politely expresses reproach. 'Sorry about that. But my child, my home, my reputation and the career that goes with it, are at stake. I've had to throw everything I have into the battle.'

But there was yet more paper to come. In mid November, just about the time of Mark's seventh birthday, celebrated separately with each parent, there arrived in his post a supplementary statement from his bank. This showed that Judy was issuing cheques on their joint account much in excess of her allowance. When he faced her with it in the cottage porch, tearfully she countered that she was writing cheques for the very least amounts possible. In evidence, she produced the cheque-book. It was in the wildest disarray. Although each cheque form had a government tax stamp on it which had to be paid for by the client, her large scrawling writing would mis-fill it, scribble it out, and write another. Although each cheque that was presented constituted a transaction charged for by the bank, it would be filled out for some trifling sum like fifteen shillings, so that the next day another had to be written, again made out for a trifling sum; sometimes involving a third visit to the bank. The book presented the appearance of a scribbling pad rather than a dossier of cheque forms.

He slipped it into his pocket. 'This can't go on, Judy. It's an impossible position. I shall have to see the bank. There's no way that they'll allow my overdraft to increase indefinitely.'

It was too late in the day for that, of course, so he marched back to his room. He wrote out a cancellation of his authority for her to draw on his account. Also a note to her saying that he would in future pay her allowance by postal order. Anticipating trouble with her solicitor, indeed with his own also, he made himself a cup of strong coffee, then set himself down to a five hour session of composing and typing. He set out his financial position in the greatest detail, supporting each assertion with proof. He attached her cheque-book and the statement from the bank. The whole lot were then enclosed in an envelope, and the envelope in his kitbag, there to await developments and always be on hand. By the time that he threw himself down on his bed without undressing, and drew an eiderdown over himself, it was three in the morning.

He had been right. Two days later he emerged, kitbag in hand, through the gate of Worcester Hall to find his solicitor's clerk once more waiting in his car. As George approached him, the clerk was regarding him with consternation. Judy, it appeared, had immediately written to her solicitor. 'You can't do this, you know. You'll have to restore the position.'

George, shaking his head, rounded the car and took his seat beside the clerk. 'I don't think you need worry. One thing this case is teaching me, is that no one is expected to do the impossible.' He passed over his statement, the proofs neatly clipped to their relevant pages. 'More paper for your unfortunate boss. But I'm confident that it's a checkmate to anything they can do.'

'Well, I hope so. It certainly looks complete enough. One thing.

Please don't write to your wife if you can possibly avoid it. Anything you write goes straight to her solicitor.'

Thereafter, George merely slipped the postal orders wordlessly into an envelope. He also learnt from Mark that his mother was waitressing at the Rainbow Inn.

'She earns nine pounds a week,' he exclaimed proudly.

George looked at the robust little curly headed boy perched on the chair. They had just finished the reading from the storybook. Seven years of age in November, Mr Featherstonhaugh had accepted him into the lowest form, where all the subjects were taken by a single mistress. The very prep school education that George had dreamed of for his son! But for how long? It was heartbreaking.

Later George was informed that his solicitor had felt able to say that his client was able to pay no more at present. There was no come-back from the other side. An amended Answer, drawn up by Counsel to take in all the latest developments, arrived at the end of the first week in December. George cycled into town and swore it before a Commissioner for Oaths.

Coming out from the Commissioner's office, he heard his name called from across the street. It was Judy! He went over quickly. She was trembling, and kept putting her thin hands up to her head.

'Take me to your place, George, and give me a cup of tea. My head's splitting. I've just come from an E C T.'

'I thought that was all over!'

'I go once a week. They take me in the ambulance.'

'A cup of tea? Of course.' As he took her arm to steer her across the street, it still trembled.

'I've had a miserable time with the E C T machine. It refused to work at the first try, and had to be adjusted. Sometimes I hope I don't come out of it.'

The higher they ascended the building, the more she stared about her. When they reached the spiral staircase, her small features registered amazement. On entering the tiny attic room, she stood dumbfounded.

'George, you can't go on living here. Mark said it was small, but . . .'

'I'm perfectly comfortable —'

'This is no place for a man like you. A six foot man, an Oxford M A! What if the school found out?'

'It's none of their concern. I've two homes to keep up now.' Remembering her condition, he pulled up the only chair for her. 'I'm perfectly comfortable, love.' He walked over to the miniature scullery. 'Now for that tea!'

'What would your parents think if they came up from Cornwall? Their son in an attic, while I sit in the four room, virtually a six room, house that they gave you.'

He smiled. 'Don't forget, their grandson is there.'

He brought over two mugs of tea. Handing her one, he perched on the bed. Her face was still flushed, her eyes wide and strained.

'I've got two rooms at the Rainbow. Enough for Mark and me.'

He jumped up, his tea slopping over. 'Mark is not to go to that place.'

'He'll be all right there, George. I wouldn't let anyone come within a mile of him. Except Betty.' Her small form shook in its vehemence. 'He'll be brought up exactly the way you would like. When he visits you, then he'll have his own room again. He'll make friends at Worcester Hall. If he brings any of them back immediately after school while he's with you, he'll have a decent home to bring them to.' Seeing him lowering himself on to the bed again, she drove home her advantage. 'There'd be only one home to keep up. You've had a lot of extra expense.'

'Well . . . Judy, if you were to get your divorce . . . This naval officer, where is he?'

A quiver passed over her — a quiver that had passed over Betty Coombes's more ample frame when he had raised much the same question, that time they had been making their way down the lane.

'He's with his ship, I suppose. I've never seen him since.'

'Who then? The baby . . .'

After hesitation, she said, 'Archie.'

'What!'

'He asked me to marry him.' She put out her hand quickly and touched him on the knee. 'He couldn't hold a candle to you, but . . . We're two of a kind. I need my cigs and my ciders. I can't lead your austere life.'

He gazed at her, feeling ever more keenly the void that had opened between them; feeling that she was indeed no longer his. That pain, that void, that was to be with him every day in the weeks ahead . . . 'The baby, won't it tell against you?'

'My solicitor says that we can ask the court to exercise its discretion in our favour.'

'But — an abortion?'

'I've only admitted to adultery.' Her wide eyes widened further in alarm. 'I've said nothing else. You wouldn't . . . ?

'Of course not. It's a criminal offence; certainly for the doctor who did it.' After thought, he added, 'Why didn't Archie help you more?'

'We had quarrelled.'

She was now more relaxed. Sipping the hot tea was helping too. Indeed the E C T's themselves, long term, brought relaxation.

'Judy — Judy, I'm not prepared to see you undergoing the misery of these E C T's. I happen to know that your psychiatrist thinks that only a parting will take the strain off you. I won't oppose the divorce. But your case is very weak.'

The old fire was back again. 'My case is extremely strong. Who told you it was weak?'

'My solicitor —'

'Oh, your solicitor! Your solicitor! Of course he'll tell you that.'

'No, Judy, of course he wouldn't. That's exactly what he wouldn't do —'

'How can you say that? He's on your side — '

'Judy!' He leant forward and pointed a large finger to within an inch of her face. 'Judy, you're not listening to me. *I'm* on your side. *I want to help you to get a divorce.*'

She started. Her blue eyes, no longer bright, even a little sunken, were staring at him.

'Now *listen* to me for once, and don't talk me down. Your solicitor, my solicitor, are *not* being paid to tell us what we want to hear. They are being paid to let us know, as accurately as they can, what they estimate our real chances are. I am able to listen quietly to my solicitor, so he's able to get through to me. In your present distraught condition, how much chance has your solicitor got to get through to you?'

'I've listened —'

He shook his head. 'No, Judy. He'd have seen you sitting there on the edge of bursting into tears. He must have had to handle you throughout with kid gloves. I repeat, I'm now on your side. Before, I was fighting with everything I'd got to keep my home together. Only a night or two ago I was up till three in the morning struggling over legal papers till I could hardly think straight. Now, seeing your misery, I've given up hope. But divorces aren't handed out on demand —'

'Surely, if we both say it's for the best —'

'No. You and I aren't the only people in the court room. There's another, even though he's invisible. And the judge will be looking chiefly at him. And that person is — Mark.'

Again she started. But George saw that he had now captured her full attention.

'The judge will be saying to himself: in all the circumstances, even after taking the difficulties of the parents on board, am I justified in speaking words that will give the sanction of the law to breaking up this little seven year old boy's home?'

'Ah!' There was a tear in her eye. 'Little Mark . . .' After a silence, she perked up again. 'There's no need for me to move to the Rainbow until after the case. The judge will see that Mark is in a comfortable house with me, and being taught at a fine school where you are on the staff. Mark will be seeing both his parents all the time. We'll never speak against one another in his presence.'

'Yes. Yes. Though the judge will want the most specific guarantees about the future. But first we must get the divorce. What are our chances? I'll just give you the facts, and leave it to you to make up your own mind. Before I got my Legal Aid solicitor, I had to have another. He thought your case so weak, that he didn't think it would be gone ahead with. My next solicitor's clerk said it was the weakest he'd ever seen, and he didn't think they'd proceed —'

She was beginning to get fired up again. 'But they *are* proceeding!'

'Yes indeed. My Legal Aid solicitor pointed that out. He said that he thought that yours was relying on your doctor's testimony. But he said that though you had a chance, he put it only at twenty-five to seventy-five.'

'I think that's ridiculous.'

'Judy, I'm on your side, remember? We must both of us look facts in the face. Even if I move over to your side, he still puts your —

our — chances at only fifty fifty. We're still just as likely to fail as to succeed. Of course no one can stop our separating. But if either of us wanted to marry again . . . Well, I'll let my solicitor know. Heaven knows what he'll think after all the work he's put in. Though we did discuss the possibility. I suppose they must be used to it. And for God's sake don't let them know about these — these meetings. Or your case is finished.'

'Of course not.'

'Judy, these "cigs and ciders", as you call it. Sherry schooners too, I think. You're killing yourself.'

'I don't want to live to be old. I haven't had a very happy life.'

He looked at her, so petite, now too so thin. Poor little thing! 'I haven't had a very happy life' — to have had to say that! But he dared not express his thoughts. Judy would *not* be condescended upon. Particularly in the form of pity.

Chapter Twenty-four

A very large form with thick curly red hair and brown eyes, and a very small form with thick curly red hair and brown eyes, emerged through the gateway and stood a moment surveying the scene. Behind them was the large board: Worcester Hall Preparatory School; Headmaster: Richard Featherstonhaugh, M.A. (Oxon). Once again the rooks, and their smaller cousins the jackdaws, were climbing the sky and, after sweeping their way over the crooked chimneys of the oast-houses, were setting course for the distant parish church, its thorn of a steeple piercing the air. Once again March mists rose from the witch's cauldron of the river. Once again the yellow ragwort decorated the corners of the fields.

'Well, Mark, cocoa, prayers, Bible, story, and then to Mummy's.'

They strolled down the lane between the brambles, and turned in at the small gate. The garden was barren but neat. The rose bushes had been cut back hard, and George had mown the already springing grass between them. The pigeon's cage had been removed.

As they entered the cottage, Rose emerged from the scullery wiping her hands on the drying up cloth. Even at twenty-eight, thanks to her simple hard working life, she had little changed from the nineteen year old who had first looked out at him from the school's serving hatch, wide hipped, buxom, gentle of eye. Still the white freshly laundered blouse fell softly over her breasts. But the shabby unfashionable skirt, and cardigan darned at the shoulder, had given way to a smart 'two-piece' — skirt and jacket light green to contrast with the darkness of her brown hair.

'His cocoa is ready.'

He smiled and nodded at her. 'Thank you, Rose.'

Later Mark and he walked to the Rainbow Inn. They made their way up the narrow alley to the right of the building and entered by the side door. After kissing his father, the seven year old ran up a back staircase to attend to his hamster.

On an impulse, George sat down as unobtrusively as might be at a corner table. Life had become much more peaceful since Judy had obtained her divorce, yet he had a sudden hankering to see her again. Wincing inwardly at the stucco horrors of the restaurant, he gazed about him. The two throwers-out, bouncers, were no where to be seen. Not that George, used in the combat of the rugby scrum to have to take on anything up to seventeen stone, sometimes more, had much fear of them.

As the waitress approached, he picked up the huge pink cardboard menu that stood, propped up and two paged, on the table. The single word, 'Archie's', was printed in sweeping green lettering across its front. Every other table in the restaurant had a similar menu similarly shouting out the name of the owner. George, though he, like Mark, had just had the school supper, ordered tea and toast from it. As the waitress retreated, he re-propped it up at the position that would afford him the most concealment.

Captain Archie Simpson himself, he of the dubious military title, appeared at the far end of the room. No less loudly did the bold checks of his suit shout out his presence. At this distance, his lack-lustre eyes and pasty complexion were not apparent. Thus the impression was one of youth, conveyed by his trim medium height figure and thick-growing cropped sandy hair. His feet planted apart, and jigging up and down on the heels of shoes with white panels let into their sides, he was giving instructions to another waitress, his eyelids lowered sexily. So that was Judy's new husband, or husband to be! With her own innate good taste, what did she make of the checks and the stucco?

As Captain Archie Simpson vanished into some nether region, so did Betty Coombes materialise out of the wall. That is, she pushed back those sliding wall panels to reveal her snowy elbows leaning on the wine bar. Two Spanish combs in her raven hair, two rows of pearly teeth thanks to her dental mechanic, dark eyes long lashed with some help from art, full breasted with some assistance from the same source, tight fitting dress low cut at the neck line due to her own scissors and needlework — all this was backgrounded by rows of bottles of various elegant shapes, mounted upside down so as to be ready to pour out their contents on the turning of a tap in their holders.

Suddenly, there was Judy descending the main staircase. Doubtless she had been seeing Mark into bed. Her eyes were fixed on a nearby table where four young men were laughing and joking. She paused just above them. George, knowing his Judy, as he still thought of her, saw that she had done so to show off her legs, once so shapely. To mask their thinness, she was wearing thick white woollen stockings. The young men became conscious of her. Then of her intention. They began to turn their badinage away from themselves and in her direction.

'Why are you so interested in us? Haven't you got a boyfriend?'

She fluttered her eyelashes. 'I've plenty of *men* friends.'

'Where are they, then? We can't see them.'

'They're — they're all at work.'

'You're fibbing, aren't you?'

As she became aware that they were not flirting with her, but mocking her, her anger blazed. 'I could have the lot of you thrown out. My husband owns this restaurant, you know.' She turned and began to ascend the stairs.

'Oh, so now you, a married woman, have a lot of men friends! Isn't that rather naughty?'

She disappeared from view, followed by a roar of laughter.

Underneath the fringe of his tablecloth, George's fists closed. He glared at the young mocking faces. In one minute flat he could be across the room and wipe the grins off them. He opened his hands. It would do no good. Indeed, it would only make matters worse. His Judy had, after all, rather laid herself open to it. He had his new job to think of; Geography and Games Master at a public school in a town not too far away, due to be taken up in six months' time. Mark would be nearly eight by then, but still of course too young to attend a secondary school. He was showing himself to be a bright pupil. Physically, he was very big for his age. They might stretch a point and let him in at ten, keeping him in the lowest class for two years, and then in the next class for two. But of course Judy had the right to have him in term time, and George only in the holidays . . . Perhaps, when Mark was ten, Judy might agree to reverse this . . . Ambition for her son filled her life; *was* her life. In the mean time, when his father left Worcester Hall, Mark would have to be moved to the state Junior School, a downgrading in Judy's scale of social values.

He paid the bill and rose quietly. So she was already re-married! The speed of it was not without its power to hurt. Nevertheless, as he made his way out through the side door, he felt satisfaction as he heard Betty Coombes's voice raised in wrath. 'You four at that table there, she *is* the wife of the owner. And if you don't cut out that noise, you *will* be thrown out. We've a couple of bouncers here who could do it in two minutes, without even noticing it.'

He walked home slowly, yet not noticing the beauty of the half-timbered houses. As he turned his back on the comparative bustle of the little town and made his way up the empty lane, the sense of isolation increased, and yet further when he entered the cottage. His cottage . . . His parents' present to him . . . In latter days, when Judy had been there on her own, even though with Mark, she had spoken of loneliness. Both of them had rid themselves of an impossible marriage, and yet . . . Even to have a bad tooth out left a gap. Doubtless that was why she had married so soon. To fill the gap. To dull the pain. His gaze travelled round the kitchen. There was the table at which little Mark had accompanied him in his 'book correcting'. There was the smaller side table at which, before Mark was born, Judy had prepared their 'twilight' teas, augmented with sweetmeats brought home by him from the school tuck-shop. There was the corner in which they always erected the Christmas tree. There, hovering over the old iron range, was the great hood up which baby Mark, his small plump fists grasping the top of his play-pen, had peeped, shouting out, 'Father Chris! Father Chris!'

A week later George was back again at his corner table, the large menu arranged to give him as much cover as might be, his tea and toast before him. Each school day, when delivering Mark to the side door, he had glanced up the back staircase in the hope of seeing Judy descending to receive their son. Each school day he had been disappointed. Now, Sunday, he would make a firmer bid at least to exchange a few words with her.

Ah! There she was, sitting at a table right out in the centre of the room. Not for his extrovert Judy to sit skulking in a corner behind a menu! Not for her the role of observer, sitting unobtrusively watching the world go by. For Judy, it was for the world to watch *her* go by. He half rose from his seat. At the same moment, she closed the catch of her handbag with a would-be angry snap. It had the desired effect. Heads in her vicinity turned. The drama had begun. George sat down again. He would not be welcome. Three times she rose and walked a quarter of the way across the room, peering out through the windows as though to see whether an expected friend had arrived. When that began to fail, she sat down, produced a paper tissue out of her bag, folded it several times, and held it compressed between her lips as though she was in some kind of pain. When that began to pall, she removed the tissue and instead put her hands over her eyes. But George, who knew his Judy, could detect even from his distance that she was noting the effect surreptitiously. When that had run its course, she dropped a saucer with a clatter on her table.

A man of about thirty, a commercial traveller perhaps with his smart suit and briefcase, entered and selected a table half way between Judy and George. He put down his briefcase on one side of the table to keep his place. Crossing to the tea, coffee and food buffet, he collected his meal on a tray. To George's astonishment, he saw that the briefcase had now been joined, though on the other side of the table, by a handbag. It was Judy's! But where was she? Her table was now empty. Ah, *she* was now at the buffet, being served with a cup of coffee and watching the man. Seeing the handbag, he removed his briefcase and himself to a neighbouring table. George again half rose from his seat. At the risk of a snub, should he join her to save her face? He sat down again. He would await events. Apparently unconcerned, she set down her cup of coffee and drew a pen and a small but thick pad from her handbag. Without once glancing at the man, she set herself to write for some five or ten minutes, tearing off each page as she completed it. Presently she began to read out what she had written, loud enough for the man to hear, but never showing by the smallest sign that she was aware of his presence. George listened anxiously as to what possibly incoherent nonsense might emerge. His brown eyes grew wider and wider at the excellence of what he was hearing. He remembered how she had selected his books and built his library. He remembered her decoration of the chest of drawers purchased for her by Betty Coombes. Judy might have been quite a good writer or craftswoman, except . . . Except that she lacked tenacity. Tenacity to learn her craft. Tenacity to pick herself up after failure and start again.

But what was he thinking of! This was his chance to meet her. He would be able to praise her writing with the utmost sincerity. That might well prove sufficient to turn aside any resentment at the interruption. He stood up. At that moment she suddenly gathered together her papers and, with a flicked glance of triumph at her target, was sweeping away out of the restaurant and up the central staircase.

If Judy had failed to notice George, someone else had not. She came sailing across the room, a full-rigged ship with all canvas set. George motioned her to the seat opposite him, and himself sat down. She would afford him the chamce of learning something more of Judy's and Mark's lives at the Raibow Inn. There were limits as to what could be gleaned from a seven year old.

Betty Coombes glanced at the crumbs of toast and the smear of butter on George's plate. 'Won't you have something more substantial? On the house.'

'No thanks, Betty. I'm fine.'

'At least more tea and toast.' She signalled to the waitress. 'The same again, Mavis. And a cup of tea for me.' She threw a glance at him from under her long lashes and puffed out her bosom. 'I have to watch my figure.' She laughed. 'Or nobody else will.' Again the glance.

George could like Betty Coombes. He could, indeed, like her very much. But he also liked naturalness, and could not find himself attracted by her florid artifices. He managed a smile. 'I think that plenty of people notice you.' He hurried on, 'Talking of noticing people, I couldn't help noticing how pale Judy is. Chalk white, in fact. In spite of the rouge over her cheekbones, which she never used before. Doesn't she ever go out?'

She laughed. 'Rouge! That's an old-fashioned word! We call it "blush" these days. No, Mark has his outings with the school and you, so he wants to stay up in his room with his hamster and his toys. She's even begun to pay one of the girls a few bob to do her shopping for her.'

George's face had grown graver and graver. 'Betty, this is serious. This cave existence. No exercise. No fresh air. Cigarettes and sherries. I know she went to' (a look of distaste flickered over his rugged features before he forced out the first-name) 'Archie for the schooners and cigarettes I couldn't afford. But she'll lose her looks, and then what? I can't visualise that gentleman as the faithful type.'

'He says he likes "that tired look". Besides, he isn't very tall. I'm taller. He doesn't like a woman who's taller than himself. They both enjoy the pub life. Living for the moment. But there's a strain developing.'

'A strain?'

'He grudges the time she spends with Mark. It's always Mark this, and Mark that. He doesn't have any feeling for children. He'd rather Mark wasn't there.'

A sharp look came into George's eyes. 'He doesn't mistreat him?'

'Good gracious, no. Judy'd tear his eyes out first. She doesn't allow him anywhere near him.'

George relaxed. The waitress appeared with the toast and tea.

As Betty Coombes poured out, a ring on every finger, her manicured nails an art in crimson varnish, she said, 'There's another source of friction.'

'Oh?' He bit into the slice of toast. 'This is delicious. Thank you very much. What friction?'

She smiled, and looked at him steadily. 'You.'

He put down the toast. 'Me!'

'You're a saint. You're a hero. You can do no wrong. Mark must be brought up exactly the way you would wish. Mark is having a *private* education. Mark is at a *prep* school. Mark is going to a *public* school. All of which does little for Mark's popularity either.'

'That sounds like our Judy. I was always either God or the Devil. Often both at the same time.'

It was a month later, April, and so the school holidays. Mark was in his room at the cottage when Betty Coombes called up in her car. Rose was first to the door, with George close behind her.

'George, can't stay. We're very busy.' Her dark eyes kept travelling from George to Rose, and back again. 'Judy had an accident a few days ago. Didn't want you to be told.'

'Oh, my God!'

'She'd had a drink too many. Quarrelled with a customer and followed him out into the street. Staggered off the pavement and got hit by a passing car. She's out of intensive care now and is asking to see you. Just shock and bruises. It's only a little out of my way. I can give you a lift to the hospital.'

'Yes, of course. I'm coming immediately.'

As he passed Rose, he caught the look of anxiety. Was she afraid that she was about to lose him?

When he reached the car, he paused. 'One minute, Betty.' He rushed back into the kitchen. Rose was walking disconsolately towards the scullery. He put his arms about her and kissed her. 'I can't abandon her, Rose. She's so little, so foolish, so gallant, so tortured. And she's the mother of my son. I love you, Rose, but what can I do?' He hurried back to the car.

Judy was propped up in bed, a small tray of tea things on her lap. She was examining herself in a mirror.

He kissed her. 'Don't worry. The bruises have nearly disappeared.'

He sat down on the bedside chair and gazed at her. She looked so tired, so tired. She kept turning away her face from him in a gesture of suffering.

'I comfort myself that this pain must pass away some time.'

She went on to speak to him, sometimes in an almost incoherent babble, of his superiority to Archie, and of Archie's being no father to Mark. Finally, she turned her sunken eyes fully towards him. 'Will you have me back?'

What could he say? She was in no condition to be denied.

At this moment, she herself rescued him from his paintul dilemma. Seeing his hesitation, she picked up her cup. The saucer fractionally stuck to it. Then it rolled off the tray and on to the floor. It had developed no more than a slight crack, but at once she became wildly hysterical.

He jumped up and put an arm about her shoulders. 'Judy, Judy, it's nothing. Nothing. Just a few pence. I'll pay them for it.'

It was as if she couldn't hear him. 'The Matron will be furious.'

The nurse hurried in. She motioned to him with her eyes that he should leave. As he passed her, she whispered, 'I'll give her a sedative. Try again tomorrow.'

He found her much calmer. 'Judy, I'm married to Rose. We both have a job to hold down. The world being the way it is, we felt we must keep it a secret. But yesterday told me that you at least must know.'

As he watched, the jolt seemed to pass right through her frail little body. But she recovered with her usual spirit. 'Oh. Oh yes. I see.'

His face was filled with sadness. 'Why couldn't you have accepted my limitations?'

When she next spoke, it was quietly. 'I bring most of my troubles on myself, don't I?'

He bowed forward and put his face in his hands. 'Yes, you do, sweetheart.'

He felt her touch his shoulder for a moment.

He left.

She returned to Archie, and they now hated one another.

Chapter Twenty-five

Although it was nine o'clock, George still sat in his canvas and tubular-metal folding garden chair. Rose was over at The Brambles helping her mother. Earlier, after returning Mark to Judy, he had strolled back, absorbing the beauty of the end of June evening scene: the khaki grass, burnt by a month of day after day Kentish sun, but still flushed here and there with mauve drifts of willow herb in the places that had been damp; the noble blue-green trees at the farther fringe of reddish fields, the rows and rows of ripening hops suspended on their trellises, the crooked chimneys of the oast-houses outlined against a cloudless sky hazed with heat.

Now, in the cool of the evening, he was thinking of his little sleeping boy's curly head on his pillow; his mother would have put him to bed promptly at eight o'clock. This in turn reminded him that only some three or four weeks of the summer term remained, and with it the end of Mark's private schooling for the time being. And *that* reminded him that only about the same period of time remained for himself in his beloved Rose Cottage. He had not been able to bring himself to sell his parents' gift. A furnished letting had been arranged from the beginning of August. Charlie had promised to keep an eye on things. Perhaps later, what with Judy married to the well-heeled Archie, and his own higher salary at the public school, he would be able to repossess it again as a holiday home. House-master at his new school, from August he had the married quarters that went with the post for Rose and himself. Room too for Mark, due to be with him in the holidays. If some of Rose's turns of speech, at her interview with the headmaster's wife, had once or twice caused a genteel eyebrow to be raised, her quiet goodness and domesticity had won the day. And of course there was George's long experience and Oxford degree.

As George rose, folded his chair, and leaned it in the porch, a thought came to him. Had Judy, down the years, been so wrong when she called him a stick in the mud? Had she been so wrong when she had urged him to seek a higher salary? Here he was, when the need had driven him, possessed of just that!

The rococo horrors of the restaurant at the Rainbow Inn were softened by the quieter lighting of the electric lamps suspended in clusters, one cluster to each table, and reduced to half their usual power by a 'dimmer'. The central sections of carpeting had been rolled up and removed earlier by the bouncers. There, clinging couples, including men with 'hostesses', gyrated to the strains of a five piece band. Judy perched on a high stool at the wine bar, a schooner of sherry at her elbow, chatting with Betty Coombes.

'Better check up on Mark. Hope this racket doesn't wake him.'

As Judy ascended the staircase, drippings of drink on the carpeting caught her eye. She quickened her step. On the landing, two or three stubbed out cigarette butts were added to the drips, and both led directly to Mark's room. The room was in darkness as she had left it, the door open a chink so that he should not be frightened if he woke. She pushed it back. The room was filled with cigarette smoke. Mark was still asleep. Lounging crosswise on her divan were two couples, glass of drink or cigarette in hand, in close embrace.

She stood a moment, fury building up inside her, surveying the drippings and the cigarette butts on the rug, her rug; the smoke, caught by the light from the open door, swirling about her innocent little boy in his bed. This desecration of his nursery! This invasion of their home! This insult offered to the most precious and intimate living space in her present life — this *temple*!

'Get out!' Her voice was a shriek. 'Get out. How dare you come into a private room. Bring all your filth into a room where a child is sleeping.'

Four pairs of eyes were turned on the small figure silhouetted in the doorway, every scrawny fibre trembling. One of the men surveyed her from head to foot, insolence in his features. 'Hello, hello! Look what the cat's brought in.'

Shrieking again, she advanced straight at him, fingers outstretched and her long manicured nails aimed directly at his face. He turned his head only just in time to save his eyes, but one of her nails caught his cheek and a smear of blood appeared.

He jerked to his feet. 'You bloody bitch. I'll get you for that.'

'Hold on, Sam.' The other man caught his arm. 'That's Archie's woman.'

At this moment Archie Simpson himself came running up the stairs, followed by his two henchmen. 'These people are my friends,' he shouted. 'Who are you to put them out?'

Judy turned on him. 'It takes scum to collect scum.' She slipped from him. 'I'm going for the police. Let them see the state of the room and a child sleeping in it. We'll see what a magistrate has to say.'

By now all four that had been on the divan were hastily, cigarette or drink in hand, making their way down the stairs, one of them holding a handkerchief to his cheek. As for Mark, with the incredible depth of slumber of a young child, he had done no more than stir at Judy's second shriek, then settled down to sleep again.

Archie turned to the six foot five giant in the black polo-neck pullover. 'Catch her, Tom. We can't have the police here.'

As Tom did so, Judy drew her nails down his face. Enraged with pain, he struck her on the brow, then on the chin. Blood welled out from the corner of her mouth. He caught her by the throat and forced her down on to the divan. Archie made no attempt to intervene.

The other bouncer, the six footer, he of the yellow shirt and red tie, dragged away the hands of his colleague. 'For God's sake, man. D'you want to face a murder rap?'

Judy dragged herself off the divan and fell on to the floor, face down. Her small frail back rose and fell as she fought painfully for breath, then ceased to do so. She lay still.

'Christ, she's dead.' It was Yellow-shirt who had spoken.

All three men stood a moment staring down at her. Then, without exchanging a word, they left the room and closed the door behind them.

As George propped up the folded garden chair at the side of the porch, he became aware of a scuffling sound at his gate. A dog? No. There was something on the top of the gate. He advanced, peering through the dusk. A pair of hands were gripping it! The next moment they vanished. He opened the gate. A small form was slumped on the ground. A child? He raised the child gently in his arms.

'My God, Judy! What has happened?'

Her reply was a mumble.

He carried her into the kitchen. There was a bruise over her left eye, and the right side of her lips were badly swollen. It looked to him as though someone had struck her first with one fist, then the other.

'Who hit you? Archie?'

She could hardly get the reply out. 'One of the bouncers. The bigger one.'

'Didn't Archie stop him?'

She shook her head feebly.

'Didn't stop him, eh! I think we shall have to look into this.'

He bore her up to her former bedroom and laid her down. After puffing out the pillows, he drew her up into a half sitting position. He descended to the bathroom and returned with a sponge and a bowl of water. By the time he had dabbed away the patch of congealed blood ('no teeth broken') the chill of the water had revived her enough for her to take the sponge.

'They thought I was dead.' He had to put his ear to her mouth to catch the words. 'Got away down the back staircase.'

'Hang on, I'll phone the doctor.'

She caught his hand. 'No doctor. No police. Rainbow goes, my home goes.'

'What about Mark?'

'Won't dare touch him. Betty there.'

He patted her hand and gently disengaged it from his. 'I'll get Rose to come over.'

At The Brambles, Mrs Finch was out, but the snores of Sergeant Finch could be heard emerging from the neighbouring bedroom. George gave Rose his news. 'See what you can do for Judy.' His jaw tightened. 'I've got to make a little visit to the Rainbow Inn.'

Her soft hand caught his, her eyes wide with alarm. 'There's two of them there. Three, including Captain Simpson. Maybe his friends.'

'Don't you worry, love. I've surprise on my side. I'll take the bouncers one by one. As to his friends, a man like Captain Archie

Simpson generally collects those of the fair-weather sort, hanging around for the free drinks. They won't be rushing to get involved.'

The pleading in the gentle eyes grew. 'Not the big one. He's huge.'

The line of his jaw became grimmer. 'Especially the big one. It was he that struck Judy. And even more Captain Archie Simpson, who employs him and did nothing to stop him.' He disengaged himself and kissed her. 'See to Judy. There's an angel! I'll be back in one piece.' And the next moment, despite his forty-four years, he was sprinting down the lane.

The myriad bulbs of the Rainbow Inn appeared before him, the showcase of the bosomy hostesses, and — a bright yellow shirt with a red tie. The six foot fourteen stoner stood just inside the door. George felt no particular animus against him; the man was but doing his job. But he had to reduce the odds against himself. Now, at the beginning of the nineteen sixties and in his middle forties, he was conscious of no loss of strength. But his rugby matches for the town had taught him that his stamina was not what it had been. The last ten or fifeen minutes of an eighty minute match left him fighting for breath and with legs feeling like rubber. What he had set himself to do, must be done quickly.

As he approached, Yellow Shirt stood with his back half turned to him as he kept an eye on the guests within.

George tapped him on the shoulder. 'Good evening.'

The bouncer swung round, his eyes alert. But the next moment they glazed as George's huge fist crashed into his jaw. Off balance and under his own weight, he burst through the doorway and fell on to his back, knocking over the nearest table. As cutlery and tablecloth went flying, the two girls sitting at it jumped up with a scream. Their escorts first looked furiously at Yellow Shirt and then, as he entered, at George. But he was past them like a whirlwind and making his way towards a towering figure in a black polo-neck pullover. Black Pullover, alerted by the screams, was also making his way towards George. After hesitating, the five piece orchestra, at a signal from Archie Simpson, doubled its volume of sound.

Pullover raised his fists to chin height, working them like a boxer. If he thought to intimidate George thereby, he could hardly have miscalculated more. To George, they were the fists that had cruelly smashed into the frail features of his little Judy. Flame seemed to flare in his chest and in his brain. He lowered his six foot one below them and struck upwards at six foot five. But it was not height that mattered so much, though Pullover's reach was thus the longer. It was weight that counted. Even one stone could make a difference. But here was only fourteen and a half stone hitting at seventeen and a half. The blow hardly moved his opponent. But it jarred George's own arm. Enraged, the black pullover rained down fists on him. One of them caught him on the chin. He staggered back and fell. His head struck the leg of a table. A darkness closed about him.

By now there was shouting and screaming from the nearby tables. The dancing had stopped as the music had become more and more chaotic, the musicians only half able to attend to their job. There was a movement among those nearest to the main door to escape into the street.

They found their way barred by Yellow Shirt, who had regained his senses and his feet. 'Nothing to worry about, gents. Everything under control. We don't want the police around, do we?'

George's head cleared a little. Was this to be the ignominious end to his attempt to avenge his Judy? He shook his head vigorously. The darkness drew back, but he was seeing two black pullovers, one overlapping the other, standing back with fists working. He felt that he had only one more attack left in him. Fisticuffs were useless; he was no boxer. But he *was* a rugby man. Many times had he led his pack, the ball tucked underneath his arm, in a charge, his massive shoulders hunched well up to take the weight of the coming impact. He shook his head again. There was now only one Polo-neck. He gathered his legs beneath and slightly behind him. Then, thrusting with all their strength, and targeting his opponent's midriff, with a roar he charged, dipping his right shoulder in a swerving rush that carried it below the flailing fists and into the huge body. There was a grunt. Polo-neck fell like a sack, not to rise again.

The next thing that George saw was Captain Archie Simpson, his mouth fallen open as he surveyed his fallen Goliath, now rolling in agony and clutching his solar plexus. But this particular David was not contented with his victory. 'So you hadn't even the guts, if you had the will, to protect your wife!' The fire was now blazing all over George's body. With his left hand he seized Archie by his thick cropped hair, and by his right hand grabbed his sex organs, and so raised him above his head as though he were, two handed, throwing in a rugby ball from the touch line to his forwards. He carried him, screaming with agony, to the counter and slammed him down on it, wine glasses bouncing about. Betty Coombes had skipped back out of the way. Archie rolled to the floor on the other side, face downwards and vomiting.

But, if he had not been a captain, he had certainly been a trooper in the Household Cavalry, and was a man of spirit and courage. Between bouts of sickness he called out, 'The bitch wasn't my wife, you bloody bastard.'

George's astonishment was broken by Betty Coombes's urgent gesturing with her forefinger. He was to make his way up the staircase. He did so. There was a door in front of him slightly ajar. Glancing in, he saw a divan and a bed. Everything was scrupulously neat and in a charming taste that reminded him of Judy. The same went for the glimpse into the sitting-room. The only object a little out of place was a vacuum-cleaner, that looked as if it had been recently used and was waiting to be put away. There was a small hump in the bed. He crossed. It was Mark, peacefully asleep! So this *was* Judy's abode!

He turned at the sound of Betty Coombes's whisper. 'We'll go out by the back staircase. Mark will be all right. No one will dare touch him. They've all had the fright of their lives. They're terrified of the police. Come to that, so am I. It's my living too.' She was hurrying him along a corridor. 'Have you seen Judy?'

'She's at the cottage.'

'Down this staircase.' She clutched the bannister, wobbling on her high heels. 'Poor love! How on earth did she make it?'

'Crawling part of the way, I suspect. At least along the lane.'

'Here's my car. I'll run you up, and bring her back. She won't rest easy until she's with Mark.'

He fitted his large form with difficulty into the front passenger seat of the little car. Betty took her place at the wheel, and they were moving away as quietly as might be. Indeed, a great silence had descended on the building, too, as though in an unspoken conspiracy between management, staff and clientele. The orchestra struck up, this time more composedly. Well, that suited him. To find himself headlined in the *Kingsbridge Chronicle* would scarcely have consolidated him in his new job.

'Rose is looking after Judy. Nothing worse than a very bad bruising and a cut mouth. Bad enough, but at first I feared all sorts of fractures.'

Betty swung the car left, and they were making their way up Bramble Lane. 'In times gone by, I did the first two years of the course for State Registered Nurse. Then I found that marriage suited me better.'

'To enormous men!'

'To enormous men. Come to that, you would suit me fine.' A glance of admiration from dark eyes. 'You were like a tiger down there.'

After a pause, he said quietly, 'I'm married.'

'To Rose? I thought so.'

'Talking of marriage, why did Archie say that Judy isn't his wife?'

'He wanted marriage, at least in the beginning, and she promised it. But she kept postponing.' Betty leant forward to pull on the hand break.

'Why?'

'My guess is, she wanted to have the same name as her son. And you. She was proud of you; you were her passport into a higher class.'

He laughed. 'You make me sound like royalty.'

'For her, you were.'

He opened the gate to Rose Cottage. 'Why — why did you say — you know, that time those young fellows were mocking her — why did you say that she was Archie's wife?'

Surprise lifted her shadowed eyelids. 'Were you there?'

'In that same corner. I left. It was either leave, or wade into them.'

'To hold her end up against those bums.'

Judy perched on her stool by the wine bar. 'Give me a schooner, Betty. I'm flogged. Mark's been playing up. Says he has a tummy ache. He seems to have had the usual school tea. I've given his tummy a rub, and at last he's settled down.'

After two more sherries, there emerged through the chink of

Mark's ever open door the sound of crying. Judy, drowsy, was now propping up her head on her hand.

Betty shook her arm. 'Mark needs attention. Another tummy rub.' She had to shake her arm again. 'Judy! Mark's crying.'

Judy looked at her heavily. 'Right. Give us another schooner, and I'll go up to him.'

'Hadn't you better go up to him first? It might be serious.'

'He'll be all right. I know what I'm doing.'

As Judy sipped the sherry, and Mark's crying continued intermittently, Betty, between serving customers, kept casting glances of ever increasing consternation at her friend. 'Judy, you *must* go up and see him. There's something wrong.'

'OK. OK. Give me a schooner and I'll take it up with me.' She swayed up the staircase, glass in hand. 'I know what I'm doing.' She slurred the words. 'Good night. I know what I'm doing.' She approached her son. 'Were you afraid of the dark, darling?' She switched on a low powered well shaded table lamp. She was a devotee of soft lighting. 'Mummy here now.' She kissed him, and he became quiet.

She closed the door. Lying down on her divan fully dressed, she sipped her sherry. Presently the still half filled glass slipped from her fingers and fell on to the bedside rug, spilling its contents. She was asleep.

But little Mark's appendicitis was not. The pain over his abdomen returned, woke him up, and increased. He began to cry again. But Mummy slept on. Why wouldn't she wake? The pain began to leave his tummy, and he snatched some sleep.

But not for long. The pain had now collected itself lower down, just above his right groin. 'Mummy! Mummy!' But Mummy slept on.

He must get out of bed and shake her. He felt hot all over. He got his feet and hands on to the carpet, but when he tried to stand up, the tenderness in his right side made him scream. 'Mummy! Mummy!' But Mummy slept on.

He began to crawl towards her. Suddenly he was sick. 'Mummy! Mummy!' He crawled some more. 'Mummy! Mummy! Mummy!' But his voice was weaker now. He vomited again, then lay in his vomit, insensible.

* * *

The last customer had left. Betty Coombes closed up her wine bar. There had been a particularly noisy party in her vicinity, and she had heard nothing from upstairs, Judy having shut the door. But her training as a nurse had left her feeling uneasy. That crying from Mark earlier . . . It just wasn't like his usual robust little self. Of Judy's utter devotion to him, there could be no question. But had she gone up in a state that would leave her capable of dealing with an emergency?

Betty's high heels clopped up the short staircase that led from the wine bar to the corridor. She tapped on the bedroom door, then pushed it open.

She turned. 'Archie! Archie! Quickly. I want a hand up here with Mark.'

He continued to move about the restaurant, collecting menus off the tables. 'Why should I have to deal with the brat? What's his precious mother doing?'

'His mother isn't in a state to do anything. And if you won't do anything either, then you'll have one child on your premises dead from peritonitis. And then you'll have the police in, and they'll want to have all the answers. And after that there'll be a post-mortem, and an inquest all over the pages of the *Kingsbridge Chronicle*. I think you had better help, don't you?'

Archie had turned white. 'OK. OK.'

'Bring up that stretcher. He must be kept flat. But first get the van round to the side door. And don't say anything to the staff.'

'They've all gone.'

At the hospital, the operation took place at once.

The surgeon came into the waiting-room. 'The tension inside the appendix was so great, and its wall had been so weakened by gangrene, that it ruptured even while we were moving it out. We were only minutes away from peritonitis. Couldn't your son have been got earlier to hospital?'

'We're not his parents.' Archie, in his relief, had risen to his feet. Smart in his narrow-cut grey check trousers and loose fitting leather jacket edged with fur, he jiggled up and down on the heels of his soft leather ankle boots. 'His parents are divorced. We're just friends of the mother.'

Betty put in quickly, 'She herself was too ill to cope.'

The surgeon removed his white cap. 'I see. Well, let her know that her boy is all right now. We'll take good care of him.'

They returned to find Judy sitting on the edge of her divan. With a look of stupefaction, she was regarding the spilt glass of sherry on the rug, the vomit on the carpet, her son's empty bed. 'What's happened? Where's Mark?' Her speech was still slurred.

Archie, his beating up at the hands of George not forgotten, was not to be robbed of his triumph. 'Some mother you are! Just look at you, still half seas over! If Betty and I hadn't rushed him to hospital, he would most likely have been dead now. "Only minutes away from peritonitis," the surgeon said.'

Judy was now suddenly sober. It was the moment for presenting herself as the automaton in the hands of others. She turned her sunken eyes on Betty. 'Why did you let me drink so much?'

Before Betty could answer, Archie jumped in. 'Oh, come off it! You're no longer fit to be in charge of a child. Why don't you leave him with your paragon of a schoolmaster?'

Judy sat shaken, and silent.

When she visited the hospital, Mark said, 'I was calling and calling you, Mummy. Why didn't you answer?'

She bent down and kissed him tenderly. 'Never again will I let you down, darling. Never again.'

Chapter Twenty-six

It was a few days from the end of the Summer Term at Worcester Hall Preparatory School, July 1961. George, at half past eight in the morning, after knocking, pushed open the side door of the Rainbow Inn. At once he heard Judy's voice calling to him from her rooms. He ascended the back staircase and entered, not by the first door which led into the bedroom, but by the second. He found the curtains drawn, and the room illuminated by a dozen candles. Judy was seated in an armchair at the furthest corner from the door. Four of the candles were grouped about her, two on each side. Each pair, in matching brass candlesticks, stood on its own small table. She was dressed in an ankle length brocade robe, its bronze patterns glowing in the soft light. Plainly, she had posed herself for his arrival.

His brown eyes widened further as he noted that Mark's breakfast things had been cleared away from the larger central table. Instead, his suitcase had been placed on it. Its lid had been left lying open. To reveal to him the meticulously packed and laundered clothes within? He wasn't due to have Mark until the school holidays!

He smiled. Signalling with his eyes towards the bedroom where he could hear their son completing his dressing, he said, 'You've packed him up early! There are still two days of the term left.'

She lowered her voice. 'Take him now. I've told him I'm unwell. And you're to keep him.'

He stared at her haggard face. Not even the soft light of the candles — that candle light whose romance she had always loved so well — could conceal its worn expression, as he knew was her hope. 'No, Judy, no. You're not to do this.'

She put her forefinger across her lips, and it was her turn to signal with her eyes towards the closed bedroom door. 'I nearly let him die. It could happen again.'

He was about to renew his protest, when the door burst open and the seven year old rushed into the room. 'I'm ready, Daddy.'

'Well, give Mummy a kiss, and we'll be off.'

She kissed him twice. 'Now hurry up, or you'll be late for Assembly. And take your hamster in his cage and leave him in at the cottage.

Her eyes, large, hollow, never left him for one moment as he followed his father, suitcase in hand, out of the room. George turned and shut the door softly.

Half way along the passage, he stopped. 'You go ahead, Mark, and wait for me at the bottom.' He set down the suitcase. 'Something I forgot to say to Mummy.'

He was back in half a dozen strides. He tapped at the door, pushing it open cautiously. She was just as he had left her, frozen in her candle lit pose and staring before her. He looked at the beautiful brocade robe, and he looked at her, and remembered her as she used to be. Suddenly it burst from him. 'You are the loveliest woman I know.'

A brief smile, a grimace rather than a smile, split the tense masklike features. But she said nothing. As he turned to leave, he said wistfully, 'Love me a little.'

Just as he closed the door, he heard her voice. 'George!' He opened it again. 'You're a good man, George. You'll be a good father to Mark.'

He called out in anguish, 'He is *your* Mark. He will be your Mark as long as I live. I'll bring him to see you.'

She shook her head vehemently. 'He is not to see me again. You must promise never to let him see me again.'

He looked at her sunken fever-bright eyes, at her raddled features, at her skin, seeming in the candle light parchment rather than skin — and understood.

'I promise, sweetheart. I promise. But I'll see that he writes to you, and I'll send photographs of him to you.'

She smiled at him then.

For a moment or two more, he lingered. What did she feel about another woman, Rose, caring for her child? She had never shown any hostility to Rose. And then it was that he understood something else. For Judy, there *was* no Rose, no Archie, no Betty. In that house, in that place, she was living in a capsule of time that contained only her little family: Mark, himself, herself.

He returned her smile. He closed the door quietly behind him.

Leaving the suitcase, and the hamster in its cage, at the cottage as they passed, Mark and he were just in time for Assembly. Rose was already at the school, working.

At the end of classes George, finding himself alone with Charlie in the staff room, poured out his heart. 'She couldn't be content with the possible. She would settle only for the moon and the stars. And so in the end she has lost everything: her son, her happiness, her health.'

'And you, old man. And you too.'

'Oh me! I'm hardly young Lochinvar riding out of the West on a white steed.'

Charlie lifted up his monocle, hanging on his chest by its black ribbon, and screwed it into his eye. 'You under-sell yourself, old boy. Sit down, and we'll have a cup of tea.'

Later, back at the cottage, George unpacked Mark's suitcase on the kitchen table. As he lifted the top shirt, the first thing he saw, snuggling in the shirt below it, was Angus, Judy's little mother-of-pearl music-box, all that had been left to her by her mother. Upstairs, Rose was putting Mark tenderly to bed. For the first time she kissed him, as though he were her own.

At the final Assembly of the term George, remembering the eulogy that Mr Featherstonhaugh had rained down on the head of Commander Robinson, leaving the school after long service, resolutely refused to allow himself to be manoeuvred into the same situation. He would *not* be held up as a paragon who had always maintained a healthy mind in a healthy body; who had always played Life with a Straight Bat. Reluctantly, the Headmaster had had to retreat before the firmness of his Geography and Games Master.

But George could not escape the farewells in the staff room. Miss Lewis, encased in her irons, stumped up to him in her most vividly beflowered dress. 'We'll miss you, Mr Brown. I know we haven't always seen eye to eye —' He lifted his hand sharply. 'When I look round this room, Matron, I see nothing but friends, old friends, good friends.' And he smiled at her his broadest smile. Miss Fetlock, removing her blue-leaded correcting pencil from between her teeth, with a nervous whinny presented him with a drawing of a horse. 'Done by your son, Mr Brown. A most promising artist.' Mr Snipe, now twenty-seven and his pimples long ago vanished, expressed his disappointment that he was to be denied the chance of teaching Mark when he became an eight year old. 'His Class Mistress was telling me that, after at first being rather piano, he was really beginning to move.' Mr Grubb, his bow-tie askew and his shirt collar awry, rose from his chair to shake George's hand. Then he sat down again to continue to feed biscuits to his unkempt poodle, which shortly afterwards was sick on the carpet.

Next morning a small black car, Charlie at the wheel, proceeded down the High Street of Kingsbridge. George had squeezed himself in beside the driver. Rose, making sure that Mark sat on the side that would be nearer the Rainbow Inn, occupied the back with him. Bobik, the little Yorkshire terrier, had been found another home. Now they were passing the Inn. Out of the corner of his eye, George noted that Rose, according to instructions, was directing Mark's attention down to his hamster, in its cage on his lap.

Up the side alley, well back from the street, lurked a small figure. Her chalk white face, so incongruous in the July sunshine, appeared all the whiter for the thickly applied red lipstick and her rouged cheeks.

Charlie nevertheless had spotted her. 'Look at that creature! She seems diseased to me. That place ought to have been closed down long ago. She's an absolute obscenity, out there near the public street with children passing.'

But George saw only permed light brown hair, a head sat perkily on a trim figure, and shapely legs jigging in their high heeled shoes. He saw only dainty features, vivid blue eyes raised to his, the twinkle of ear-rings as blue, a little blue cloak. 'No,' he said. 'She is the Madonna.'

Charlie stared at his friend before returning his eyes to the traffic. And all the way to the station he kept stealing glances at him. As they emerged from the car, he said quietly, 'Was that . . . ?'

George nodded.

'I'm terribly sorry, old man —'

George put his finger across his own lips and motioned with his eyes towards Mark. 'You weren't to know, Charlie. She was only forty.' His voice broke a little. 'Only *forty!*' Wisecracking seemed the safer course. 'For your sermons, d'you realise that you can make any old rubbish sound profound if you start with the words, "What is life but . . ." What is life but an ostrich, sucking at the nipple of a hippopotamus?'

'Yes. Yes, I see. What about: what is life but a custard pie, thrown into the face of the Almighty?'

'Excellent! You could get a bishopric out of that. Which one would you like?'

'Anything wrong with Canterbury?'

George assumed his most thoughtful expression. 'No, I haven't recently heard anything against Canterbury. By all means let it be Canterbury.'

But banter, that final refuge from sadness, failed at the last. For a moment they stood silent.

'Well,' said Charlie, 'let's get the stuff out of the boot. Goodbye, Rose. Goodbye, Mark. Goodbye, hamster.'

Rose took up two of the lighter pieces. 'Goodbye to yourself, Mr Hare.' To leave the old friends together, she drew Mark with his hamster after her.

Charlie, in his plum coloured frock-coat, extended an elegant arm. 'Goodbye, George.'

George felt the limp hand in his suddenly change to a grip. 'No, Charlie, it's not goodbye. Somehow we'll contrive to meet. It's only olive oil.'

'Olive oil, old man. Olive oil.'

As Charlie, despite the childish round toed sandals, made his best Old Vic exit towards his vehicle, he kept his back turned to his friend throughout. As he started up the engine and moved off, a plum coloured arm emerged from the window and waved.

George stood motionless. He watched the little black car traverse the whole length of the half-timbered houses of the High Street. Now it was passing that garish stucco palace of pleasure. Did the furtive figure still linger there? Now the little black car turned left and vanished; vanished towards Worcester Hall Preparatory School, that formidable factory for the manufacture of Little Gentlemen.

George took up the two big suitcases and joined Rose and Mark on the platform. But gradually, as he stood there, more and more he found himself failing to hear the excited chatter of the little fellow. Yet he was listening intently. Was it only a summer breeze finding its way among the rafters of the roof? Or was there borne on it a small soft voice singing close to his ear? 'Tiptoe, to the window, by the window, that's where I'll be — Come tiptoe, through the tulips . . .'

Abruptly, turning his back on the others, he strode into the nearby waiting-room, presently empty. He put his two big hands over his rugged features, and his great shoulders shook.

END

Brigid and the Mountain
Sean Dorman

On my right was the mighty and bare peak of Mount Shanhoun, in shape and proportion an almost perfect pyramid. Brigid stood by the door watching me. She wore a plaid kerchief over her head and tied under her chin.

Agnes's buxom body might have become more buxom, as her mother Brigid alleged, yet secretly I was attracted by it. She was so compact, so rounded, so sturdy and vigorous, so shapely, yes, even graceful, as she moved rhythmically, as I had seen her one day weeding a field of potatoes.

Under its first title of 'Valley of Graneen', before a revision, *Brigid and the Mountain* was Recommended by the Book Society. *The Times Literary Supplement*, after a long review, summed up the book in the phrase, 'beautiful restraint'. *The Scotsman* wrote, 'His sketches are vivid and sincere. The physical aspects of the valley are described with remarkable clarity, and Mr Dorman is equally successful in his portraits of the inhabitants.' *The Sydney Morning Herald* wrote, in the course of a review of over two hundred words, 'These sketches of Donegal are delightful.' *Irish Independent*: 'Of his days in the valley, his friendships, and his talks, (Sean Dorman) has moulded a book of much charm. There is writing of grace and high degree . . . Withal, it is a notable book.' *Irish Press*: 'Sean Dorman brought with him a receptive mind, an artists's observant eye, and some writing materials. The result is . . . a very pleasant book.'

ISBN 0 9518119 8 3   Price £4.99

The Raffeen Press

Red Roses for Jenny
Sean Dorman

Red Roses for Jenny . . . What did they mean to her? A father's affection? Or a lover's desire? If they meant either to her, or both to her, then why did she throw them away? Did her mother come to hear of them? Or the wife of the man who gave them to her? And Jim, what did he think? He must have seen them, and surely he must have been disturbed. Was Jenny carrying a child, or was she not? If she were, could Jim succeed on containing the scandal and so protect his mother's feelings? Canon Moss, for all his funny ways, was wise. Was his wisdom sufficient to save them all? And, at the end of the long day, why did Jenny restore the red roses to her office desk again?

After the great success of Sean Dorman's autobiographical first novel, *Brigid and the Mountain*, initially, until revised, entitled 'Valley of Graneen' and, under that title, a Book Society Recommendation; also praised by *The Times Literary Supplement*, *The Irish Press*, *The Scotsman*, Australia's *Sydney Morning Herald*, *Irish Independent*, and many others; Mr Dorman took time off to acquire the technique of the non-autobiographical novel. The result is *Red Roses for Jenny*, with its vivid characters and driving speed of narrative. If the mountain scapes of *Brigid and the Mountain* are fine, no less fine are the seascapes of *Red Roses for Jenny*, with storm scenes as background to a love between a man and a woman no less stormy.

ISBN 0 9518119 7 5   Price £4.99

The Raffeen Press

The Madonna
Sean Dorman

'A great twentieth-century novel.'

Judy Summers, arrested by the sound of men's voices, paused on her way to visit The Madonna. Her cheap gay cotton dress fluttered about her shapely legs. Judy Summers liked men. She liked them very much. Also, it had become imperative that she should acquire a husband . . .

They were beside the little wayside shrine. George saw that Judy's eyes were fixed on the painted Mother cradling in her arms her painted Baby. 'The birth and the feeding have been a great strain on you, darling. Don't you think that Mark ought to go on to the bottle?' Judy was shaking her head vigorously. 'I'd give my life for Mark. I feel — I feel there's something in me of The Madonna.'

George went to Rose. She drew away in hurt pride. He broke down her resistance and swept her into his arms. 'Of course you didn't mean any harm, sweetheart. I've had a very upsetting letter from Judy. I love my wife. She's the mother of my son, but it's been a great strain. You've helped me keep my sanity.' He began to rain down kisses on her brow, her cheeks, her lips. Eyes closed, she held up her face to receive them.

'*The Madonna* reads as inevitably as does Tolstoy and bears out Eliot's, "In my end is my beginning." If it reaches its proper audience, it will be read with a mixture of discovery and relief. The novel is still alive!'
George Sully

ISBN 0 9518119 6 7   Price £4.99

The Raffeen Press

Portrait of My Youth
Sean Dorman

Portrait of My Youth traces the earlier years of a remarkable Irish writer, Sean Dorman. The narrative, always lively, often extremely funny, sweeps the reader along on a bubbling current. There are fascinating glimpses of the British Raj in India as seen through a young child's eyes; of Algiers and Aden as seen through those of an older schoolboy; of student escapades at Oxford and in Paris in a more carefree era; of a visit to an extraordinary French family near Nice and Cannes: of sexual shenanigans in London's bohemian Chelsea; of difficulties with an alcoholic uncle famous as an Irish playwright; of meetings with literary and theatrical notables: E. M. Forster, Granville Barker, Sean O'Casey, John Betjeman, T. S. Eliot, Barry Fitzgerald, Dame Sybil Thorndike, W. B. Yeats, Laurence Olivier, Deborah Kerr.

'Delightful, humorous, full of marvellous observation.'
Colin Wilson

At the age of fourteen, in his first term at his public school, Sean Dorman was awarded a prize as the best prose writer in the school. He was the winner of an essay competition open to the public schools of Great Britain and Ireland. After graduating at Oxford, he worked as a freelance journalist in London, contributing articles to some twenty periodicals, and ghosting six non-fiction books for a publisher. For five and a half years he edited a theatrical and art magazine in Dublin, and for twenty-six years in England a magazine for writers. His three-volume hardback, *The Selected Works of Sean Dorman*, comprises autobiography, essays, novels, short stories and verse.

ISBN 0 9518119 9 1   1 Price £4.99

The Raffeen Press

Physicians, Priests & Physicists
Sean Dorman

The most potent reason for Sean Dorman's writing this book arose from the existence of his magazine *Commentary*. This monthly appeared in Dublin in the forties during five and a half years. At an average of two thousand copies a month, he felt it to be a certainly that copies still lurked in collections both public and private, even possibly in newspapers files, there to haunt him. In his youthful, pugnacity, had he somtimes overstated his ease and fallen into folly? If so, the only way out was to republish his essays or editorials, with inserted toning down remarks where such seemed needed.

The essays cover the subjects of: literary censorship; cancer, heart disease and arthritis-resisting diets and exercises, including exercises underwater in a hot bath (his wife suffered from arthritis of the hip, and died of smoking and alcohol-induced cancer); the existence or non-existence of God as found in the Bible; or in the discoveries about the universe as found in the work of scientists such as Aristotle, Ptolemy, Copernicus, Galileo, Kepler, Newton, Einstein (his Special Theory, and his General Theory, of Relativity, are explained in simple terms), and the somewhat later quantum mechanics, and the twistor and superstring theories. Other essays are entitled: 'How to Rear a Baby', 'The Adventures of Marriage', Jew and Gentiles'.

ISBN 0 9518119 1 6   Price £5.95

The Raffeen Press

The Strong Man
Sean Dorman

The Strong Man, a comedy in three acts, can lay no claims either to distinction or to having been performed on a stage. But it can claim to have been read by a considerable number of people who have reported that it caused them not only to smile but, on occasion, to laugh outright. Should something that has given rise to smiles, and even laughter, be left upon a shelf, or be entombed in a drawer? Of course not. It should be produced in a book. Also produced in this book are three theatre critiques. In days gone by, Ireland gave to literature great playwrights from that seeming hotbed of dramatic genius, Dublin University: William Congreve, George Farquhar, Oliver Goldsmith. Since then there have been: John Millington Synge, Samuel Beckett (both from the same university), William Butler Yeats, Oscar Wilde, Bernard Shaw, Sean O'Casey. Well known, but perhaps less well known than they ought to be, are Denis Johnston and Teresa Deevy. I have devoted a critique to each of them. Also to William Shakespeare, an Englishman, I'm told. The trouble with William Shakespeare, is that he has been allowed, unfortunately, to develop into a cult figure. Not only are his great plays produced, but his lesser pieces also are reverently laid out upon the stage, thus almost certainly denying many hours of theatre time to others with better work to offer. Such a lesser piece, here reviewed, is *Twelve Night*.

ISBN 0 9503455 6 3   Price £3.95

The Raffeen Press